T0375150

The Stones of Moya

Stone II
A Fate beyond Control

Marnie R. Mercier

iUniverse, Inc.
Bloomington

The Stones of Moya
Stone II—A Fate beyond Control

iUniverse books may be ordered through booksellers or by contacting:

iUniverse
1663 Liberty Drive
Bloomington, IN 47403
www.iuniverse.com
1-800-Authors (1-800-288-4677)

ISBN: 978-1-4620-1362-3 (pbk)
ISBN: 978-1-4620-1363-0 (cloth)
ISBN: 978-1-4620-1364-7 (ebk)

Printed in the United States of America

iUniverse rev. date: 4/21/2011

With special thanks to my mother and father and
to my beloved David. To all my supporters …
I could not have done this without you.

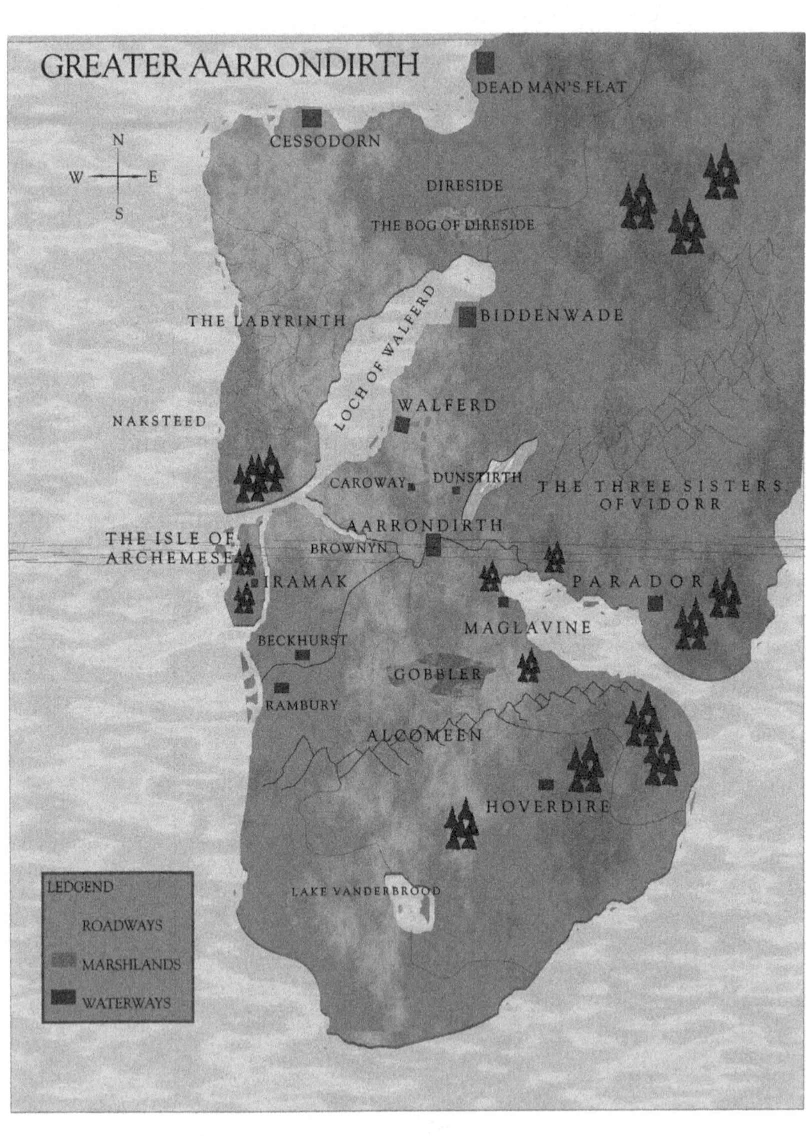
GREATER AARRONDIRTH
N
W
E
S
DEAD MAN'S FLAT
CESSODORN
DIRESIDE
THE BOG OF DIRESIDE
THE LABYRINTH
LOCH OF WALFERD
BIDDENWADE
WALFERD
NAKSTEED
CAROWAY
DUNSTIRTH
THE THREE SISTERS OF VIDORR
AARRONDIRTH
THE ISLE OF ARCHEMESE
BROWNYN
IRAMAK
PARADOR
MAGLAVINE
BECKHURST
GOBBLER
RAMBURY
ALCOMEEN
HOVERDIRE
LAKE VANDERBROOD
LEDGEND
ROADWAYS
MARSHLANDS
WATERWAYS

Will All be Lost?

Dusk was upon us. I took a heavy breath to quiet the pounding of my heart. My thoughts had not yet settled since our departure from Maglavine. Deep down, I knew our return to Aarrondirth would mark the beginning of the end.

As we descended through the forest, I looked at Darwynyen, who rode next to me on horseback, and I was flooded with memories of the evening we had shared before the gods, when we pledged our eternal love for one another. It was my misfortune that the precious moment would be forever overshadowed by the words of Darwynyen's mother Aldraveena, the elf queen. My thoughts turned to my father, and I wondered if he would find his way to Cessdorn before the next moon cycle and take over the Hynd, as Aldraveena had foreseen in her visions. If she was right, I would have to set aside my despair and come to terms with the outcome, for the odds would undoubtedly turn in his favor if the stones of Moya were once again reunited.

When we arrived at the old elvish lookout point, I was reminded of the night Shallendria, Darwynyen, and I had shared during our previous travels. I welcomed the familiarity of the place, and I thought of Shallendria, wondering if she had accomplished her objectives in Tayri and persuaded the elf council to join us.

"Hold here!" Sikes pulled the reins on his horse. "We will

keep in the shelter of the trees this eve and travel the open fields of Aarrondirth in the morning."

As I dismounted, I noticed a spiral of clouds building above the tree line.

"Are we in Aarrondirth?" Teshna appeared from one of my pockets, where she and Zenley had been resting.

"Of course not, silly!" Zenley appeared next, leaping into the air. "We have not even left the forest!"

"Oh." Teshna followed after him. "I was only asking."

"Come." Zenley fluttered his little wings. "Let us gather some food."

Teshna nodded, and they flew into the shrubbery.

"Have your fires!" Darwynyen shouted from atop a boulder. "They will go unnoticed here." As the elves in our company began to disperse, he met with Sikes and Falker. Rather than disturb them, I left Accolade with an elf that had begun to corral the horses and then made my way to the keep below the lookout point, the place where Darwynyen, Shallendria, and I had previously taken shelter.

As I descended through the bulky roots toward the door, I noticed the silhouette of an elf creeping along a branch in the distance, and I halted. At first, I assumed that it was a guard securing our perimeter. Still, the nature of his approach made me wonder, and I decided to investigate.

Twigs hit my face as I fought through the neighboring shrubbery. As I stepped into a clearing, I saw the silhouette jump from one branch to another as it made its descent. Suspicious, I knelt near a fallen tree. As the elf neared, I examined its features, realizing then that I had not stumbled upon an elf. Its back was bent, and the creature appeared to be struggling with its balance. Its bald head was larger than its body, its limbs lanky and frail, giving me the impression that it was malnourished. When it reached a lower branch, it leapt to the ground, pulling an arrow from the quiver on its back.

Unarmed, I had no choice but to return to the lookout point

and warn the others. As I tore through the shrubbery, I yelled. "There is a creature in the woods! He means to attack!"

"Arianna!" Darwynyen rushed to my side when I reached the encampment. "Are you sure it was not one of our scouts?"

"It was probably just a deer." Falker rolled his eyes as he approached.

"Falker is right," Sikes agreed as he reached Darwynyen's side. "No one would dare attack us here."

Darwynyen shook his head. "I see fear in her eyes."

Sikes stiffened, reaching for an arrow. "Arianna, tell us more."

"It was a creature of some kind," I replied anxiously.

"Stay here." Darwynyen eyed Sikes and Falker, removing his bow from over his shoulder.

"No." I stood to block his path. "I will take you to where I saw it."

Before he could respond, an arrow whistled past our heads. I crouched in fear. Darwynyen shielded me, scanning the trees. "Keep low, Arianna." He pulled an arrow from his quiver. "Find your way into the keep below the lookout point. Let us see to this intruder."

When they disappeared through the shrubbery, I followed.

Sikes met with Darwynyen near the clearing. "There is no one here. Whoever it was must have fled."

I was about to step out from the shadow of an adjacent tree when I saw the creature's eyes peering through a thatch of grass below a fallen tree. "There!" I pointed. "It is over there by the fallen tree!"

Darwynyen followed my finger, his bow ready. "Move and you will die!"

The creature slowly stood, throwing down its weapon.

Falker took me by the arm. "Stay back, Arianna."

"No." I broke from his hold. "I need to see it!"

"Stand back!" Darwynyen demanded; blocking my view as

Sikes secured the creature's wrists with a narrow strip of rope. "We will question him back at camp."

From over Darwynyen's shoulder, I could see the creature struggle for its freedom. Although it had elvish traits, its features were twisted and pronounced. Its eyes were large and dark, and it had long, pointy ears that extended upward along its balding head. Dressed in a tattered loin cloth, its skin was covered in filth, as though it dwelled in the wild.

"What is it … he?" I stepped back.

"Arianna, stay out of this." Darwynyen took hold of the creature's arm. "This matter is of no concern to you." He and Falker began to drag it along the ground in the direction of our encampment.

"Arianna." I heard Sikes from behind me. "Do not mind Darwynyen—he is right to be upset." When I turned, he brushed past me. "Let us follow them back to camp."

"Will no one tell me what this creature is?" I rushed to join him.

Sikes's pace slowed. "Have you heard of the Rinjeed before?"

"Yes." I blinked, remembering Darwynyen explaining how the creatures came into being as a result of the intertwining of our people's bloodlines, leaving me to again wonder about our children, should we choose to have them.

As we pushed through the last cluster of shrubs, I saw Darwynyen throw the Rinjeed into the light from the main fire. "Tell me now why I should not end your life!"

Terrified, the Rinjeed began to mutter and cry.

When Darwynyen pulled a blade, I rushed toward the fire. "Wait!" Pitying the creature, I knelt by it. How could I deny him if there was a possibility that my child could carry the same traits? "Can you speak?" I asked.

Darwynyen grabbed me by the arm. "You are wasting your time!"

I sharply pulled from his hold, returning my focus to the creature. "Why did you attack us?" I asked firmly.

"Arianna, do not …"

I silenced Darwynyen when the Rinjeed lifted his head to face me. "How can I not despise you?" His voice was gritty. "You created me and then you abandoned me …"

Confused by his response, I prepared to stand. I felt a searing pain in my temples. He was trying to make a connection. When I closed my eyes, he took me to a place I did not recognize. The land was barren. Massive caves opened from the surrounding cliffs. There were many of his kind there, chained to one another, forced to extract the value of the mines under the control of men who relentlessly battered them. Horrified, I tried to break from the connection.

As I fell to the ground, I saw Darwynyen kicking the creature in the stomach. "Release her!" he growled.

"Leave him!" My balance was unsteady. "He has shown me a glimpse into his past." A tear fell from my eye. "We must leave him to the forest. Now he must be shown mercy."

The men looked at me in disbelief.

"Have you gone mad?" Falker winced.

"No, I …" I looked at Darwynyen for support as elves from around the encampment began to gather.

He refused my stare.

"We must let him go," I insisted. "Now is not the time to make future enemies."

"Future enemies," Falker scoffed. "These creatures have yet to pay for their crimes of the past."

"Try to see things from our perspective," Sikes urged. "One of these creatures nearly killed Darwynyen when he was a child."

"I understand your concern," I replied boldly. "However, I feel compassion would be better served in this situation."

When Sikes and Falker looked at Darwynyen, he took me aside. "I love you, Arianna, but I cannot support you in this. I fear you have been easily fooled by his thoughts."

Angered by his remark, I spoke harshly. "I think it is you and your people who are ignorant in this matter. From what I have seen, your arrogance extends to anyone who does not share only your bloodline!"

Darwynyen stepped back with widened eyes.

Immediately regretting my words, I released a heavy breath. "Perhaps if you had witnessed the vision, you would have more compassion." I paused. "Can you not trust me this once?"

The Rinjeed knelt. "I see now my vengeance was in vain." There was desperation in his voice. "Leave me to the woods," he begged, clutching his stomach where Darwynyen had kicked him. "I give you my word that I will bother you no further."

"Please," I pleaded. "Let us not bicker, for he is only one and we are many. If we should disarm him, what threat would he hold then?"

Undecided, Sikes and Falker began to mumble to one another.

"Perhaps Arianna is right," Darwynyen conceded. "We should stay true to this journey. After all, we are not *barbarians*." His tone was filled with contempt. "Burn his weapons and set him free at once."

"What if he attacks us in our sleep?" Falker argued.

I turned to the creature. "Will you keep your word?" I assisted him to his feet. "Can we trust you?"

"Yes." He squared his shoulders, stretching out the hump on his back. "If you release me, I swear I will trouble you no further."

"I believe him." I looked at Darwynyen.

With a resigned nod, Darwynyen cut the Rinjeed's restraints. "Be gone!" he growled, tossing the creature's quiver and bow into the fire.

In response, the creature scurried off toward the forest. Before he was out of sight, he turned. Our connection was restored. *I do not understand why you defended me the way you did. I will think on it, I promise. But before I go, know that it was I who fired upon your companion when he was a child.*

My chest tightened as he disappeared into the shadows. Was

Darwynyen right? Had I been fooled by the creature's thoughts? No. The vision was real. It was the creature's confession that left me disconcerted. Had I just set free a potential murderer? If I had, there was little I could do about it now. At the very least, the Rinjeed had left unarmed, and by tomorrow, when we arrived at the fields of Aarrondirth, we would be safe from his reaches. It was only tonight I needed to worry about.

When I broke from my thoughts, I saw Darwynyen stomping off in the opposite direction. Remorseful for my previous actions, I followed after him. Sikes took my arm. "Leave him." He tightened his grasp. "Get some rest. If I know Darwynyen, as I do, he will need some time on his own."

I nodded. "Perhaps you are right."

He released me. "Where are your fairy companions?"

Surprised by his concern, I puckered my brow. "Why do you ask?"

"They have never been away from the sanctuary," he replied. "We must look after them."

"Oh." I bit my lip. "They left earlier in search of food."

"They know this area well," he remarked with a sigh. "If they return, I will send them to find you in the keep."

"Thank you." I glanced over the area and then turned. "If you see Darwynyen, will you send him my way also?"

"I will do what I can." Sikes pulled up his hood, glancing through the upper branches. "You should take shelter before it rains."

As he spoke, I felt a droplet of water strike my face. "If the weather is changing, will you not join me in the keep?"

"No." He turned and walked away.

Although the harshness of his response hurt, I had brought it upon myself, and took little heed as I made my way for shelter.

† † †

Dawn's light was breaking through the clouds when I emerged from the keep. Still exhausted, I stood at the crest of the stair and yawned. Rest had not come easily. In the absence of Darwynyen and the fairies, I had been left to spend the evening among strangers, where I was forced to ponder my previous actions. The quiet was my only comfort, and I was relieved, knowing that the Rinjeed had not made his return during the night.

Darwynyen stood next to the smoldering fire. From his appearance, it was plain to see that he had not rested. His eyes were cold, and when I stepped toward him, he turned, walking in the opposite direction. "Darwynyen, please," I called out to him. "We cannot leave things as they are." When he did not respond, I rushed to his side. "I apologize if I have wounded you."

With a heavy sigh, he turned to face me. "You should never have questioned me in front of my people; it is I to whom they look for leadership."

Realizing what I had inadvertently done, I felt further remorse. "Forgive me," I pleaded. "I was only doing what I thought to be right." I looked down for a moment. "Even so, I see now that some things cannot be so easily decided."

His eyes softened. "I understand that you perceive things differently. That is why I love you." He paused. "Regardless, you still have much to learn, and for the sake of the others you must set aside this presumptuous behavior and trust in my experience."

As I began to comprehend the complexity of the situation, I decided it was in both our interests not to argue. "Going forward, I give you my word that I will not question you in front of your people again, nor will I make my decisions single-handedly." I tried to read his face as I continued. "If you give me the opportunity to prove myself, in return I will ask for a little more compassion."

He sighed heavily. "What was it you saw in the Rinjeed that compelled you to stand by his side?"

Still guilt-ridden about the Rinjeed's confession, I evaded the question. "We should forget him and focus on the journey at hand."

"We will," he nodded. "But first you must tell me what you saw in his vision."

Although I wanted nothing more than to forget the Rinjeed, I could not deny Darwynyen, and I closed my eyes to recall the vision. "I saw a desolate place, under the command of the Man's Blood people, where many of his kind were forced to work the land for its value." When pain filled my heart, my eyes began to fill, though it was not for the creature. "What has become of my people? Have years under my father's command led them astray?"

"There will always be people who deny the path set out by Aarrondirth." His eyes lightened. "Arianna, if everyone saw things as you do, we would not be in this predicament to begin with."

Desperate to change the subject before Darwynyen could bring it back to the Rinjeed, I glanced over the area. "Speaking of those with a pure heart, I have not seen the fairies since yesterday."

"Do not fear." He pointed toward the keep below the lookout point. "They are with Sikes."

When I followed his gaze, I saw Sikes sitting on one of the larger roots, eating his morning mulch. On his shoulders were the fairies. "Why …!" I stomped off; my overreaction would ensure my escape from the conversation.

At my approach, Sikes stood, confused. He was about to speak. I raised my hand, looking at the fairies as they took flight. "Where have you been?" I glared. "I have feared the worst and gotten little sleep because of it!"

Startled, they looked at one another before Zenley flew forward to respond. "We took shelter in the trees, Arianna, as we always do."

When I realized that Darwynyen had not followed, I quieted. "I apologize, but you said you were only getting food." I continued before they could respond. "When the storm came, and then that creature, I feared the worst." Despite my antics, I was genuinely concerned.

Teshna flew to my face. "Not to be disrespectful, but we can take care of ourselves."

Zenley interjected. "What my sister is trying to say is that you have more important things to worry about than us."

I gave Sikes a fleeting look. "Regardless, in future, I will ask that you advise me of your intentions, especially when we arrive in Aarrondirth, for the people in my city might not be so welcoming." My tone deepened. "Remember, if it were not for me, you would not be here to begin with."

When they nodded, I left to find Accolade, knowing the sooner we were on our way, the sooner I could forget about the Rinjeed and his confession.

† † †

Heavy clouds kept the shadows in our favor as we made our passage across the fields of Aarrondirth. As I glanced back to the forest of Maglavine, I quickly forgot the Rinjeed. Instead, I thought of Aldraveena and the burden she had placed upon me. My despair quickly resurfaced. I could only hope that in time I would be better able to cope with the challenges and do right by my people, who, in the end, would suffer any repercussions from my failure.

As we passed through the old farmstead, the place where Darwynyen, Shallendria, and I had taken shelter in a hidden room below the barn, I glanced to the treed area. Although it had been days, the Gracken's attack was still fresh in my mind. Through the branches and shrubbery, I caught sight of the creature's horse chewing on a thatch of grass near the corpse of its master. Moments later the scent of decay reached me. Darwynyen also sensed it and kicked his horse forward.

When the farmstead was no longer visible, I returned my focus to the fields before us. Sunlight began to trickle through the clouds, forcing me to squint. As I put my hand to my brow, I noticed a dark mound in the distance. Curious, I directed my horse in that direction to investigate.

As I approached, the air once again became foul. To diminish its effect, I put my sleeve across my face. Accolade drew back, hesitating. As I steadied the reins, I realized it was another corpse, this time a dragon.

"Arianna!" Darwynyen called as he approached. "Stay back!"

"There is no need." Falker smelt the air as he rode up next to Darwynyen. "The creature is for certain dead."

Darwynyen slowly led his horse around the corpse. It seemed that I was not the only one taken aback by the creature's size. "It must have been in midair when it fell," he remarked, pointing to the indentations in the ground.

Sikes dismounted. "If an arrow dipped in Hellum's Dew struck it near the heart, death would have been swift." He pulled a blade from his waist belt and knelt next to the corpse.

"What are you going to do?" I frowned.

"I will take its talons," Sikes replied as he began to dig his blade into the rigid flesh around the creature's knuckles. "The inner marrow is a valuable resource in our people's magic."

"Oh," I uttered in dismay. Although the creature had long succumbed to its death I could not help but pity it, and when Darwynyen dismounted to join him, I turned Accolade and rode off.

† † †

The shadow of darkness was finally giving way to morning light when we reached the outskirts of Aarrondirth, the city of my birth. The sapphire skyline beyond the castle gave it a majestic glow, concealing the damage it had sustained from the dragon attack I had witnessed in Aldraveena's vision. Unlike the time of my father's rule, the outer walls were heavily guarded, assuring me of Madigan's survival.

At our approach, a horn sounded. "Who goes there?" a soldier shouted from the gate tower.

"It is I, Arianna!" I replied. "Open the portcullis!"

Moments later guardsmen appeared on the opposite side of the gate wall. As they began to crank the levers that forced the thick iron chains into motion, I swallowed deeply in anticipation.

When the opening below the portcullis was sufficient, I nudged Accolade through to the Royal Mile. Darwynyen followed, ushering in the elvish accompaniments.

Fragments of loose brick and sandstone were scattered along the cobblestone roadway. The rooflines on several of the taller structures had been decimated, and those that remained were scorched. Even so, the city's reconstruction was already underway, and as we made our way toward the castle, I nodded to the soldiers and men who shoveled the debris into an assortment of flatbed wagons. In acknowledgement, they bowed as we passed.

After a short delay at the castle barbican, we arrived at the main stable where Madigan awaited us. "Madigan!" I quickly dismounted from Accolade and rushed to embrace him. "I am so very pleased to …" Overcome with emotion, I choked on my words.

"You are safe, Arianna." He returned my embrace with vigor. "That is all that matters." After a moment's comfort he released me, looking to Darwynyen. "How was your journey?" he asked. "As you can see, much has happened since the time of your departure."

"The realm of Aarrondirth was not alone in these attacks." Darwynyen dismounted. "It seems the dragon's desire for revenge is far-reaching."

"How did Maglavine fare?" Madigan questioned.

"There was little damage," Darwynyen replied. "The beasts fled once they realized that our arrows had been dipped in Hellum's Dew."

"Then you are fortunate," Madigan remarked begrudgingly, and then he glanced over at the elves standing in formation behind us. "I have set aside some land for your people." He turned, signaling to a few of his men. "See to the elves. Take them to the west end of the courtyard." When the soldiers moved forward, he continued, extending his hand. "While they prepare their camps we can further this conversation in the study."

"Agreed." Darwynyen took me by the arm. "There are things we must discuss."

I tensed, knowing that Darwynyen was meaning to share my secret. "I would prefer to settle first." I contrived a yawn to conceal my anxiety. It was not the truth I feared; it was Madigan's reaction when he learned of the previous lies I had told to conceal my identity.

"Of course." Madigan nodded. "Besides, it will give me the opportunity to summon the others."

"We can settle later," Darwynyen spoke with insistence.

"I sense urgency." Madigan met Darwynyen's stare. "Has Aldraveena provided you with invaluable information?"

Darwynyen looked at me as he responded. "Invaluable, yes, but the words are for you alone."

"Very well," Madigan conceded. "Let us carry on as planned."

Darwynyen turned to Sikes and Falker. "I will meet up with you later." When they nodded, Darwynyen took me by the arm. "You know what you must do."

"Wait!" I turned back to Sikes. At this point in time, any cause for delay seemed warranted. "Do you have the …?"

"Teshna and Zenley are safe," he assured me, gently patting his pocket. "They know they are to stay hidden for now."

Madigan frowned. "Whom are you referring to?"

"We will explain later." Darwynyen pulled me up the stairs to the castle. Madigan followed.

When we entered the study, I became hesitant. Darwynyen nudged me forward. "Arianna has something to tell you."

I began to tremble, looking back at the door for an escape.

"What is it?" Madigan pulled out a chair.

I cleared my throat as I took a seat. Darwynyen squeezed my shoulder in support.

A worried look crossed Madigan's face. "What is it?"

Unable to find the words, I looked at Darwynyen. He began. "Arianna … She bears the blood of your line. Despite our suspicions, it seems Velderon was indeed Alameed's brother."

Madigan broke out in wry laughter. "Forgive me, but I thought I heard …"

"You heard correctly." I stood.

In response, Madigan's mouth fell open, as though he was waiting for one of us to concede a well-devised ruse.

I began to fidget from awkwardness.

"I do not believe you," Madigan huffed. "From the time Velderon arrived in Aarrondirth we knew …"

"No," Darwynyen countered. "Until now, we have only had our suspicions to sustain us."

"That man is not of my blood!" Madigan growled. "It sickens me to even …" His words broke and then he looked at me. "I meant no disrespect, Arianna. You will always have your place in Aarrondirth."

"My status is of little consequence." I held out my hands. "This revelation changes nothing. I still have no desire to serve. The throne will remain yours."

"It changes everything!" Madigan snapped. "How do you know that Aldraveena speaks the truth?" He continued before I could respond. "Even those with great power can make mistakes."

"Aldraveena was not the first to speak these words," I replied, ashamed. "In the end, she only confirmed the proclamation my father had originally made when I was his prisoner," I explained. "Be that as it may, his only proof was a medallion he carried that bore the royal seal of the Wyndam family."

"Then why did you speak nothing of this before?" He glared.

"Because I was not certain," I replied defensively. "You know as well as I that my father cannot be trusted!"

"Why now?" His eyes narrowed. "Why do you reveal this to me now?"

Unsure how to respond, I glanced back at Darwynyen.

"Do not resent the truth, my friend." Darwynyen spoke with assurance. "It has freed us from the doubt. I can assure you that your rule is not in jeopardy. Things will go on as they were." He paused. "Only now, Arianna will be able to stand at your side with honor."

Madigan moved to the southern window, which overlooked the courtyard. "Her place has and will always be at my side," he mumbled.

Darwynyen stepped back. "I will give you a few minutes on your own."

Before I could respond, he left the room.

"Madigan." I slowly stepped toward him. "You must be honest and tell me how you feel about this."

He kept silent.

"Can you forgive me?" I put my hand on his back. "The bond we share—I do not wish to sever it."

He turned to me with an intent look that startled me. "I could have loved you in many ways, Arianna." He paused as though he was feeling the risk in his next words. "I could have loved you as a man loves a woman." When I stumbled back, he continued, "Because your heart lay elsewhere, I let you go … but now everything seems different."

"It does not have to be," I pleaded. In many ways I felt his passion too. I shook the thought away. It was Darwynyen I loved. "Madigan, you are not alone in these emotions. I too have questioned the intensity of our bond, though through all the confusion, I believe that we are only smitten with one another." I avoided his stare. "And even if my feelings differed, a union between us would be impossible. Not only do we share the same blood, during my time in Maglavine, Darwynyen and I made a commitment to share our future as one."

His hand graced my cheek. "There is no need for you to explain yourself."

I turned to the window and glanced over the fields. "There is more." I paused, knowing my next words would be difficult for him to comprehend. "Aldraveena believes it is I who shall bring my father's evil reign to an end."

"You!" he scoffed.

"Yes." I nodded. "She believes me to be his only weakness."

"But …"

I interrupted. "My time in Aarrondirth will be short. Aldraveena has sent me on a quest that must be undertaken before the next moon cycle."

"For what purpose?" he asked.

"I will go in search of the great wizard Archemese."

"Archemese!" He scoffed again. "The wizard Archemese is dead!"

I shook my head. "He is alive and dwells on an island off the west coast."

"Even if your words are true," he countered, "why would you seek him out?"

"We will need him," I replied. "Time is not in our favor. Aldraveena fears my father is soon to take control over the Hynd. His powers grow by the day." I blinked heavily. "If he reaches Cessdorn before the next moon cycle, the skies will turn dark in the north. It will be a sign that the Stones of Moya have been reunited. Thereafter we will have only two moon cycles until he is able to obtain their full power."

"If it is her command, then so be it," Madigan conceded. "Who will accompany you on this quest? I do not believe it is wise for me to leave Aarrondirth at this point in time."

Although I did not want to go without him, he was right; the people of Aarrondirth needed his leadership. "I have yet to decide," I admitted. "I will make my decision after we have met with the others."

"Very well." Madigan released a heavy breath. "I will call a meeting in the defence area at midday."

"Is everything all right?" Darwynyen appeared at the door, startling us both.

"Yes." Madigan stepped from the window. "Everything is fine. You two should get some rest."

I yawned as I made my way to Darwynyen. "Madigan will call a meeting at midday to further discuss the coming quest."

Darwynyen nodded, taking my hand.

"See you at midday." Madigan made his way to a bottle of scotch on one of the shelves.

Darwynyen glanced over his shoulder as he led me from the room. "Are you sure he is all right?"

"He will be fine," I replied. Eager to sleep, I pulled him down the corridor.

When we reached our abode above the keep, I rushed through the door and fell on the bed. Darwynyen joined me. "You did well." He pulled a strand of hair away from my cheek. "Do you feel better now that everything is out in the open?"

"Not entirely." I kissed him slowly. "I have missed your touch."

"As I have missed yours." He pulled me into his arms.

Exploring Their New Surroundings

When Sikes's breath deepened, Zenley squeezed through the opening in his pocket.

Teshna crawled up beside him. "Zenley," she whispered with anticipation. "Maybe we should wait!"

"Why?" he huffed, leaping into the air. "We have nothing to fear."

"The people of Aarrondirth," she spoke as she joined him in flight, "they might …"

"They might what?" He flew from the servant's quarters, where a few of the higher ranking elves had taken rest. "If we are discovered, we will announce ourselves as companions of Arianna."

"What if she finds out and becomes angry with us?" Teshna pleaded.

"It will make no difference." He fluttered his wings. "She is always angry with us anyway." Before Teshna could respond, he flew down the corridor. "Now come—let us explore our new surroundings!"

Who Will It Be?

I awoke in the later hours of the morn. Sleep had not come easily. I was overwrought with anticipation, and it would be impossible to rest deeply until the preparations for our departure were complete.

Darwynyen was restless as well. When he left in search of our lunch, I made way to the tower, to better survey the damage the city had sustained from the dragon's attack.

When I peered over the parapet, I noticed the northern courtyard was bustling with activity. The remainder of troops from the south must have returned in our absence. New rows of tents lined the pasture, along with several makeshift kitchens and armories.

Turning my gaze toward the city, I noticed that several laborers had already begun repairing the burnt-out rooflines along the main street. Carpenters worked to reinforce the beams, while others layered the completed work with bundles of fresh thatch. Relieved that most of the damage was not extensive, I left to join Darwynyen in the kitchen.

Once Darwynyen and I had eaten, we made way for the defense rooms in search of Madigan. As we walked the corridors, I wondered whom I would choose to accompany Darwynyen and me on this quest. Agreeing that Madigan should stay behind, I thought of Gin. Not only did he remind me of Madigan for his personal character, he was from the west, giving us an advantage when it came to navigating. I might also consider Sikes, because he had grown close to the fairies. Besides, it seemed best to allow Darwynyen one of his companions ... That left me one member to choose, perhaps a decision better made after the meeting, when those who Madigan had summoned became aware of our intentions.

From behind, I heard a hum echo down the corridor. When I turned, both Teshna and Zenley were hovering near my face. "Good afternoon, Arianna!" Teshna's wings fluttered.

"Why are you out in plain sight?" I snapped. "Have I not warned you that the people of this city might not understand your sudden appearance?"

They both fluttered their wings timidly. "Do not fear," Zenley appealed. "Thus far, the people of Man's Blood have been very welcoming. I believe they find us interesting." He paused in flight. "But there was a lady ... in the kitchen ... she tried to squash us with a broom!"

Darwynyen chuckled. "Evelyn was in a bit of a state when I arrived."

"Why did you not tell me of this?" I turned to face him.

He regained his composure. "Because she was fine after I explained their purpose." He looked at the fairies. "Going forward, you will no longer have to fear her."

Teshna flew to my face. "To be cautious, we will not leave for the city until the news has traveled."

"And we will not go alone," Zenley offered. "When Sikes forgave us for sneaking out, he agreed to accompany us."

"You snuck out!" I gave Darwynyen a fleeting look, wondering whether or not I should have left them in Sikes's company to begin with. Still, I was pleased that he had grown close to them, and if he had seen to forgive them, perhaps so should I. I changed the subject. "We are off to the defense area to find Madigan. We are to assemble a meeting, and I would like it if you were to join us."

"We would be honored, Arianna," Zenley replied, and both he and Teshna bowed their heads.

I nodded, leading them down the corridor.

As we turned into the main hall of the defense area, I was reminded of the secret meeting I had stumbled across before Darwynyen and I had left for Maglavine, the meeting where I had learned of the Amberseed, the ultimate power my father would seek once he had united the Stones of Moya. Overwhelmed by the thought, I brushed it aside.

When we entered the defense room, Madigan was sitting at the table, lost in thought.

"Madigan." I spoke softly, not to startle him.

He stood pragmatically. "I have been waiting for you." He picked up a map from the table. "I have changed the meeting location to the library."

"The library," I remarked. Although I had not seen the room, I remembered that Edina had spoken of it once before.

"Yes," he replied. "Morglafenn has found many resources there." He halted near the door, taking notice of the fairies that were hovering near the threshold. "Who are your companions?" he asked. "I heard there were fairies among us."

I held out my hand, beckoning Teshna and Zenley to land. "Aldraveena has asked them to assist us in the coming months ahead." The fairies landed on my palm. "Their names are Teshna and Zenley." Despite my doubts, having experienced their mischievous behavior firsthand, I reassured Madigan, "Not only is their bravery commendable, they are the finest of scouts."

"I am pleased to make your acquaintance," Madigan smiled.

Teshna flew to his face, bowing her head. "My brother and I are honored to be here, King of Aarrondirth."

When he reached out to touch her, she flew back to Zenley, who was hovering behind her. In response, Madigan turned and left the room.

"Madigan," I followed. "Could you tell me where Edina is?"

Madigan continued his pace. "I have given her a few days

to spend with her family. There was no need to keep her here in your absence."

"Of course," I smirked, knowing in truth that her time was being spent with her fiancé Stuart.

As we ascended the stairway to the study, I suddenly recalled my father and the time he had spent with the crone in the hidden room behind the bookshelf. Desperate to leave the past behind, I squelched the memory and distracted myself with thoughts of the library.

At the crest of the stair, we followed the southern corridor to the right of the study, where we came to an elongated threshold on the right. As we passed through the large wooden doors, Madigan lifted his arms and turned. "Amazing, is it not?"

I nodded, glancing over the area. The expansive ceiling rose well into the third level of the castle. Hundreds of books filled the shelves that encompassed the inner walls. Several ladders connected to a narrow walkway built along the beams on the second level. Colorful stained glass windows engulfed the south wall. Crimson curtains draped their sides. In the center was a huge wooden table. The top was layered with maps and stacks of old books that were open to different pages.

Madigan ushered us to our seats. "We have found great treasures in here." He pointed to the maps on the table. "There are many detailed maps on this table, including one of Cessdorn."

As I sat, I pulled one of the maps over to examine it. To my surprise, it was of the southern region where I had grown up in Hoverdire. Recollecting, I retraced the journey that had brought me to my homeland of Aarrondirth, recognizing the great distance my mother and I had traveled to get here. I put my finger on the mountains of Alcomeen, then to the rolling hills of Delfee. Last but least was the dreaded marshland of Gobbler, where the trolls, under the command of the Hynd, had attacked us. Then memories of the General resurfaced. A shiver swept through my body when I recalled the scar on his cheek. He had sustained the wound while defending us in the marsh, a wound he carried until the night Darwynyen took his life, as the General had so viciously done to my mother.

"The men should be here shortly." Madigan watched the fairies as they swept along the bookshelves above. "I have asked Dregby, Gin, and Morglafenn, among others." He paused and then looked toward Darwynyen. "I assume you have not yet heard from Shallendria?"

Darwynyen shook his head in response. "Do not worry, my friend; she will return with the rest of our armies, as promised."

Madigan nodded. "As long as she finds her way back, that is all that matters."

I was relieved that Madigan's focus was again on Shallendria. It was best that way, as Darwynyen would not understand Madigan's sudden and unwelcome declaration of love I had endured upon our arrival.

I was about to speak when I noticed Teshna and Zenley pulling a book from one of the shelves on the second level. It was plain to see that it was too large for their tiny bodies to carry. When I put my hand to my mouth, Darwynyen and Madigan turned. Weaving back and forth, the fairies flew in my direction. I stood from my chair as they neared, and I grabbed the book as it fell from their grasp. "What is it?" I asked, examining the cover.

"It appears to be a book about the dragons," Zenley replied.

Teshna flew to my face. "We may find some needed answers in its content."

Curious, I set it on the table and opened it. To my regret, it was in a language I did not recognize.

"It is written in elvish." Darwynyen spoke from over my shoulder. "What would a book—Arianna, may I?"

"Of course." I slid the book before an empty chair. Once he was seated, he started flipping through the pages. After scanning several of them, he paused for a moment and then began to read. Halfway down the first section, he looked up in a troubled manner.

"What is it?" I asked.

Before he could respond, Dregby trotted through the door. "Are we ready to begin?" To accommodate his boar-like lower body, he removed one of the chairs in order to take his place at the table.

"Quiet." Madigan silenced him with his finger. "We have found something."

Dregby nodded, taking notice of Darwynyen.

Darwynyen took a heavy breath. "It is an old dialect, one no longer used, but I think it states that the dragons were once of a kind nature." He finished skimming the page. "It seems they are intelligent beings, as well."

A look of doubt appeared on Madigan's face. "Perhaps we should seek the help of Morglafenn. He is versed in the old dialect."

Darwynyen did not respond, engulfed in the translations. As we watched with interest, he finished the page, and then he abruptly looked at Dregby. "What do you know of the dragons?"

"Nothing." Dregby shrugged, waving his tail nonchalantly.

Darwynyen pointed to the last inscription. "It is written here that the dragons stood in peace until the Four Sisters of Vidorr were sullied, that they believed their life's blood stemmed from the gold within the mountains." His eyes narrowed. "You must know something of this!"

"I know little," Dregby glared defensively. "Even so, I can assure you that they attacked us first and that the Miders were the ones to suffer the losses in the battle over the mountains!"

When Darwynyen looked at Madigan, Madigan took a step back, his hands raised, making it obvious that he did not want to take part in the exchange.

"Read further!" Dregby demanded. "I am certain there is more to this story, as it is common knowledge that the dragons sought both the elf and Man's Blood people as well."

In response, Darwynyen began to translate the next page.

Half way through, he closed his eyes in acknowledgement. "You are right. It seems our people and those of the Man's Blood came to your defense in these attacks." He paused. "It also states that the men of Man's Blood were responsible for the disappearance of their matriarch beast."

When I looked at Madigan in disbelief, I could not help but notice that Dregby appeared satisfied that the blame had been redirected. Darwynyen seemed to notice this as well, and he closed the book abruptly. To avoid an argument, I spoke. "We are too early in this discovery to draw any conclusions." I refocused on Madigan. "Whatever happened, I am certain our people took the only measures they could. The beasts are no doubt a force to be reckoned with."

Madigan nodded in agreement.

As the tension in the room eased, I drifted into thought, wondering why no one in those times had thought to negotiate with the dragons, if they were indeed intelligent. My heart skipped a beat. Was the dragon I encountered in Maglavine communicating with me after all? If so, had I unknowingly missed the opportunity to reason with it?

"Enter!" Madigan took his place at the head of the table. "Take your seats. We are about to commence this meeting."

I looked up to find Sikes, Falker, and Kendrick making their way into the room. Morglafenn entered shortly after. I smiled when I met his gaze.

"Who are we missing, then?" Madigan glanced over the room.

Gin rushed in. "My king." He put his hand to his chest. "Excuse my tardiness. I was preparing the northern field for the remainder of our troops."

"Is the task complete?" Madigan enquired.

"For the most part, my king." Gin bowed his head and then sat in an open chair.

Madigan nodded. "Shall we begin?"

"Yes." I winked at Gin.

"I am pleased by your return, my lady." Gin returned my wink with another.

Madigan sat back in his chair. "Arianna, you may speak first."

I stood to ensure that I had everyone's attention. "During my time in Maglavine, I met with the elvish queen Aldraveena, and through her visions she has shown me the way to Cessdorn. That is where my father will join with the Hynd. Upon his arrival they will reunite the stones. From there ..."

"We have already started planning for this!" Dregby stomped his hooves against the stone floor. "Did she give you a timeline?"

"If you would allow her to continue ..." Madigan's tone was condescending.

"Of course," Dregby nodded. "Please, excuse me."

I acknowledged his apology with a nod. "We have three moon cycles before my father is able to gain the full power of the stones. Should he reach the Hynd before the next cycle, the sky will turn dark to the north. If he does not, we will have gained another cycle, for he cannot join the stones without a full moon in his favor."

"So ... we must wait another two weeks." Dregby huffed.

"No," Madigan shook his head. "We must proceed with our preparations."

"Madigan is right. We cannot sit idle in hopes that my father does not succeed." I changed the subject. "Aldraveena also shared with me my future path, a path that will eventually lead me to my father. I must face him once again. To further my chances of success, she has asked that I first travel to the west coast in search of the great wizard Archemese."

"Archemese." Gin appeared perplexed. "I have heard of no such wizard."

"That is because his name has not been spoken for several years now. In fact, many believe him to be dead," Morglafenn explained. "To our good fortune, he is not."

Gin furrowed his brow. "Arianna, would your time not better be served here with your people?"

"Are you challenging the directions of our queen?" Darwynyen questioned.

Morglafenn interjected before an argument could prevail. "Arianna, who will you have accompany you on your journey to the west?"

"I have yet to decide, though I will need three who are willing." I glanced over the room until my gaze fell upon Dregby. "In an effort to show a united front, I will ask you to stand forward on behalf of the Miders." I paused. "I know this decision will be difficult for you, and I would understand your reasons if you were to decline."

"I would be honored." He put his hand to his chest with a look of pride. "My generals can see to my army while I am away."

"Thank you." I nodded and next looked to Gin, whose eyes were wide with eagerness. "In place of Madigan, I would like you to accompany us as well." From the corner of my eye I could see Darwynyen tense, and I ignored him.

"It would be my honor." Gin quickly glanced to Madigan for approval.

Madigan nodded.

Zenley and Teshna flew from the rafters. "What about Sikes?" Teshna exclaimed. "We cannot go without Sikes!"

Gin's mouth fell open when he saw the fairies. I could see that he was about to speak, and I put my finger to my mouth to silence him, returning my focus to the fairies. "Who said you were coming?"

"I thought …" she looked helplessly to Zenley, who had landed on Sikes's shoulder.

I sighed exaggeratedly. "If you are unable to follow simple instructions, how can I trust you?"

In response, Teshna flew to Zenley, slapping him on the head. "I told you we should not have snuck out!"

To make it clear that I was wavering on the decision, I bit my lip in contemplation until they became anxious. They needed to understand the potential for consequences should they choose to continue with their mischievous behavior. I relented. "I suppose your navigation skills would be an asset." Then I looked at Sikes. "Would you be willing to join us?"

Sikes turned to Darwynyen, who spoke on his behalf. "Yes, of course he will."

Madigan stood. "If we are finished here, I will leave you to chart your quest." Not waiting for a response, he made way for the door, followed by Falker and Kendrick. Morglafenn stayed behind.

Darwynyen began to rifle through the maps on the table. "This one will do." He pulled a map to the top of the pile. "It is of the west and details the quickest route to the river."

"Any suggestions on how we are going to procure a boat?" I asked, recalling Aldraveena's direction.

Gin sat back in his chair. "Why would we need a boat when we can travel by land on horseback?"

"Aldraveena was specific when she said we must take to the loch," I replied.

Rather than respond, Gin avoided Darwynyen's stare and began to survey the map. "There is a fishing village, called Brownen. Here." He pointed to a narrow inlet in the loch. "We can secure a boat there."

"Yes," Dregby chuckled. "It is a good place to start making use of Velderon's gold!"

Gin and Darwynyen ignored Dregby's attempt to lighten the mood. "How do you know of this village?" Darwynyen asked Gin, with some suspicion.

"I was raised in the west, along the shoreline you now seek, and stayed in that village once with my father during a hunting expedition." He continued quickly when Darwynyen raised his brow in doubt. "The population of Brownen is few. We should not attract suspicion there, should it be our motive to avoid doing so."

Morglafenn caressed his chin. "If the loch is your chosen path, you must stay on your guard until you reach the canyons."

"Why?" I asked.

"Because you will venture close to the land of the Gracken," he warned, moving his finger to a narrow point further west in the loch. "They dwell along the northern shoreline."

"Grackens!" I cringed.

"The water runs swift in that region," Gin countered with confidence. "If we travel under the cover of night we should go unnoticed."

"And the creatures fear water," Sikes concurred. "They will not attack us without an advantage."

When I looked at Darwynyen, he nodded with assurance.

Relieved, I urged the men to continue.

Once our route was mapped out, I glanced over the four I had chosen. Although each of the men differed in character, they shared one common bond: their strength and conviction to see this quest through. And their various qualities would only make us stronger, giving me the confidence I desperately needed at a time when I felt vulnerable and weak.

Darwynyen began to roll up the map. "If we are finished here, there are things Arianna and I need to tend to."

As I stood, I noticed Morglafenn. His fingers were on his temples.

"Quiet," Darwynyen whispered. "Morglafenn has made a connection." He looked at Sikes. "Quickly, find Madigan."

Sikes nodded and rushed from the room.

Several minutes passed. I kept looking to Darwynyen, worried. I was about to speak when Morglafenn released a heavy breath. "It was Shallendria," he said. "The news is good."

"What has happened?" Madigan ran through the doors. Sikes followed seconds later.

"Shallendria." Morglafenn closed his eyes for a moment, as though he were struggling. "She was able to persuade the elves in Tayri. A small army will set out tomorrow, arriving in Aarrondirth five days from now."

Darwynyen embraced Madigan. While they rejoiced,

Morglafenn put his hand on mine. "Whom have you told of this quest?" he whispered.

I was startled by his question. "Only those who were present … why do you ask?"

He stood and led me to one of the color-stained windows. "Something is not right here. Shallendria would agree. We have both felt an evil presence for some time now."

"What or who do you think it is?" I glanced over my shoulder to make sure no one was listening.

"Regrettably," he blinked, "we have yet to find the cause. It is well disguised. For all we know, it could be one of your father's guards who has lingered, or a spy in the form of an animal. Unfortunately, there is little we can do until the intruder becomes known." When I nodded anxiously, he continued. "Arianna, do not draw any unnecessary attention to yourself. Stay on your guard, and keep what I have told you secret."

"What about Darwynyen?" I asked.

"Shallendria has already approached him on the matter," he disclosed. "We decided it would be best not to frighten you until we knew more, but now that you are soon to be leaving, I thought you should know."

I glanced over my shoulder toward Darwynyen, wondering why he had chosen to keep this from me.

"Do not be angry with Darwynyen," Morglafenn implored. "I can assure you that there was no previous cause for alarm."

As I considered his request, I released a heavy breath. "Thank you for sharing this with me."

"Remember, stay on your guard." He squeezed my arm.

"I will," I nodded, determined.

"Very good." He turned and left the room.

Darwynyen approached "Arianna, is everything all right?"

"Yes." I kept my voice low. "Morglafenn was just telling me about the presence he and Shallendria have felt in the castle." I met his stare. "Why did you not tell me of this?"

"There was no need," he replied sternly. "I saw no point in

worrying you until something had been proven." He paused. "You are safe here, Arianna. If not, Aldraveena would have forewarned you during our time in Maglavine."

I released the tension in my shoulders. "I suppose you are right," I conceded. "Even so, I will take Morglafenn's words under advisement."

"As you should," he agreed. "I understand Morglafenn's motives, and if I had not forgotten, I would have cautioned you sooner myself."

I nodded, considering his claim. "If it does not weigh on your mind, then I will not let it weigh on mine either." I turned. "Will you join me in our quarters? I thought we could further settle."

"I will find you later," he winked. "Sikes and I must first make way to the courtyard to ensure that the elvish encampments have been erected."

"Very well," I replied, taking my leave from the room.

In need of a bath, I grabbed a few drying cloths from a rack beside the wardrobe in our quarters and made way for the stream.

As I passed through the wooded area in the eastern part of the lea, I felt as though I were being watched, and I halted. After carefully scanning the neighboring trees and shrubbery, I attributed the sensation to my overactive imagination, knowing that if the soldiers had stumbled across this place, they would have announced themselves upon my arrival.

When I reached the stream, the area was as serene as I remembered. As I knelt to unlace my boots, I heard branches above me snapping. Startled, I quickly stood. "Is someone out there?" I asked, my eyes darting to each of the branches. A gust of wind struck the trees, forcing them to crackle and grind. Dismissing what I had heard, which must have been the forces of nature, I continued to remove my boots. It was only after I began to release the tension that I felt the connection.

Arianna … that is your name, is it not?

Recognizing the voice as the Rinjeed's, the creature we had

released in the forest of Maglavine, I knelt to take hold of my weapons, the sais my uncle had given me before his passing. "Why are you here?" I demanded, slowly turning in place. "Have you come to finish me?"

"I am over here." I heard his feet hit the ground behind me. "Do not fear. I wish you no harm."

"How can I take you at your word when you admitted to me that you were the one who fired the arrow upon Darwynyen when he was a child?" I asked, turning to face him. When I met his stare and saw his shame, I no longer felt threatened. "Either way, your revelation has left me with few options. With that said, you must know that I can no longer protect you."

He appeared undaunted by my warning, and he smiled as the connection was restored. *There is no need. I can assure you that I am no longer a threat. When you defended me the other night, my desire for revenge suddenly faded. For once, I did not feel alone. Since then I have felt the need to repay you for your kindness.* He pulled a small sachet from his pocket. *I have brought you this.* When he extended his scrawny arm, I noticed that it was covered in scars, reminding me of the dreadful vision he had shared with me upon his capture.

Curious, I cautiously took his offering.

Keep it safe, he warned, *its contents are very powerful. It is a spell. When you sprinkle it on friends or foes, they will sleep for days.*

As I loosened the string to examine it, he grabbed me by the wrist. "You must be very careful. Only open it when you need it. If you feel yourself drawn in by its power, you must repeat these words three times."

"What words?" I asked.

He pulled a small piece of paper from his pocket and handed it to me.

It read "*Maznufaned Ieda.*" "These words alone will break its spell?" I asked with doubt.

"Yes!" He nodded confidently.

"Thank you." I looked at him with gratitude as I secured it to my waist belt. "Your gift is a generous one."

Without a response, he climbed back into the tree.

"Where will you go?" I called to him as he ascended.

He turned, looking down at me from one of the branches. "Do not worry, I will not be far. I have decided to stay and watch over you, my only friend." Not waiting for a response, he climbed to the next branch.

"Wait!" I moved to better observe him. "I do not even know your name."

As he leapt to another branch, he restored the connection. *My name is Ghezmeed,"* he replied.

"Perhaps you should stay and meet the others," I suggested. Although he had admitted to attacking Darwynyen, I had not sensed an evil nature about him. Instead, he had somehow put me at ease, and for doing so, I felt compelled to offer him shelter.

You know it is not possible for me to stay. He paused. *You said yourself your companions would see to the death of me.*

"I will speak to them," I pleaded. "You must be hungry, having traveled far in the past days."

I can take care of myself, he replied bluntly. *I do not settle well with others.*

I knew by the tone in his voice that his decision was already made. "Very well," I sighed. "If you should come to any trouble, you must speak my name. Have them bring me to you at once. I would hate to lose a friend so soon after meeting one."

He did not respond to my request, and I watched him retreat into the higher branches of the tree. During our short time together, I was quite taken by his character, and I wondered if I would ever see him again. If there was a possibility that my children would turn out like him, a result of the intertwined elves and Man's Blood's bloodlines, there would be no way for me to deny him, despite his clouded past.

"Arianna, where are you?"

"I am over here, Darwynyen!" I stood on a boulder. "Follow my voice!"

Moments later, he appeared on the bank downstream. "I was hoping to find you here." He rushed over. "You are not the only one in need of a bath."

Pleased to see him, I smiled, trying to quickly put my encounter with the Rinjeed behind me. "Are you to join me then?"

He pulled the shirt from over his head. "I want to feel you next to me, Arianna."

I blushed at his words. "Darwynyen, we cannot … not out here in the open."

"Come!" He threw his trousers aside, jumping into the stream.

Drawn in by anticipation, I quickly nodded, following his lead.

We waded in the current, and then he pulled my legs around his waist. I was secure in his arms, and he kissed my shoulder. "I love you."

"I love you too." I caressed his back.

In silence, we gently began to wash one another. Although I did not want to end our intimate moment, I could not get the Rinjeed out of my mind and felt I should tell Darwynyen. "I saw that creature again. He followed us from the tree line, and …"

Before I could finish, he pulled away from me harshly. "Where is he?" He scanned the trees. "Did he try to hurt you?"

"No." I wiped the water from my eyes. "Of course not. He only wanted to thank me for my kindness and leave me with a gift."

"A gift." He shook his head in disbelief. "What sort of gift?"

"There," I pointed to the waist belt on my trousers. "He left me with a small sachet of powder, claiming it is a spell. He said that whoever I sprinkled it on would fall asleep for days."

"How do you know he was telling you the truth?" he questioned, his tone sharp. "For all you know, it could be poison."

Right or wrong, I was insulted by Darwynyen's accusation. "If Ghezmeed's intention was to harm me, he could have done so easily. Instead, he came in friendship."

"I do not believe you," he responded wryly. "Have you already befriended this creature?"

"Yes." I nodded in defiance.

"Arianna …" He paused as if to find the right words. "The Rinjeed are known for their ability to influence the mind. For all we know, he may be manipulating you now." He moved toward the stream bank. "I will alert the others and have him detained before he can do further damage."

I took him by the arm. "Darwynyen, have you heard nothing I have said?"

He turned, furrowing his brow. "What are you asking of me?"

"I want you to forget what has happened." I met his stare. "You must believe me when I tell you that he is gone and will trouble us no further."

He took a moment before responding. "Very well, we shall leave it for now." He released a heavy breath. "I only hope I do not regret this decision."

"You will not." I spoke with assurance. "I promise."

A horn sounded from one of the towers, distracting us both. As I searched the skies, Darwynyen left the stream. He reached for his trousers. "Come, someone approaches."

"Oh!" I bit my lip, embarrassed. "I thought maybe it was the dragons."

He shook his head "No, an attack signal is more drawn out and aggressive."

With no way to conceal my naivety, I nodded humbly and then left the stream, reaching for my drying cloth.

Once we were dressed we ran toward the castle. A crowd had begun to gather in the courtyard. As we ascended the stairs to the main doors, the land beneath us began to rumble. When I looked for the origin of the tremor, I found a massive collage of metal making its way through the western fields. "Your armies are returning from Beckhurst and Rambury."

Darwynyen put his hand to his brow and looked. "Madigan has been anticipating their return."

"There are so many of them," I observed and I hesitated, in fear of once again revealing my naivety. "If our numbers are this great, why did no one revolt against my father sooner?"

"Soldiers follow orders," Darwynyen replied. "They live by the command of their leader, regardless of what they believe."

I was about to respond when Madigan appeared at the door.

The people around us bowed their heads.

He ignored them, looking at me. "Arianna, I will ask that you accompany me to the city gates."

"Why?" I asked, confused.

"To address the generals," he replied.

"Should you not see to them on your own?" I glanced to Darwynyen, in hopes that he would rescue me.

"Darwynyen has no say in this matter." Madigan spoke discreetly. "I need you. The people need you. These men will return to a home that is no longer their own. And the task of reuniting them with their forgotten foe will be a difficult one. With that said, a strong supporting leadership will be required if we are to find success." He ushered me down the stairs. "More importantly, I want you to get acquainted with these duties should anything happen to me."

When I turned back toward Darwynyen, he winked. "Go—you will be fine."

I nodded, following Madigan toward the stable.

We sat on horseback for some time. Bored, I was about to complain when I noticed two men appear over the crest of a distant ridge, kicking their horses with zeal.

As they neared, a large man, dressed in full armor, pulled the reins. "My king." He bowed his head. His lengthy ginger braids fell forward. His companion, a smaller man in similar uniform, also bowed, firmly holding the pike that held his banner.

"My king, General Braddim at your service." The larger man removed his helmet, exposing his brown eyes and ginger beard that was ruffled and full of sweat. "Speak your command."

Madigan smiled, rolling his eyes. "You may address me as friend, Braddim. There is no need for formalities here."

"As you wish." Braddim wiped his brow. "How are you, my friend?"

I looked at Madigan. "You know this man?"

"Yes." Madigan nodded. "We grew up together."

"I see." I looked at the man, observing him.

"This is Arianna." Madigan extended his hand toward me. "She is the daughter of Velderon, princess of these lands."

"I know who she is." Braddim bowed his head in my direction. "It is an honor to make your acquaintance, my lady."

"And you." I smiled, taking notice of the bronze beads that were woven into his beard.

"What news do you bring from the west?" Madigan asked.

"My men have grown fat and lazy," Braddim replied with a snort. "Velderon's only charge was for us to protect a land that did not require protecting."

"Those days are over." Madigan looked toward the troops as they approached. "I will brief you later."

"Of course!" Braddim nodded, returning his helmet to his head. "What are your orders?"

"We must first reintegrate the troops," Madigan replied. "Those who have family here in Aarrondirth may return home; those without will stay in the courtyard along with the rest of the accompaniments." Madigan turned his horse. "Give them two days. Once they are settled, they will be tested and, if necessary, retrained."

Braddim turned to his companion. "Why are you still here? You have heard your king's command!"

The man bowed his head and, kicking his horse, rode off.

When the procession of soldiers arrived at the gates, Madigan and I led them through to the city. The royal mile was lined with hundreds of people, the families of those my father had selfishly sent away during the time of his rule. Desperate to claim a view of their loved ones, they clung to one another with anticipation. They were not alone in their sentiment. As the first ensemble followed us in, the beating of the battle drums intensified, as though the men striking them were signaling to their loved ones. Overwhelmed by the moment, tears began to well in my eyes.

The heralds sounded their horns when we reached the castle barbican. Madigan turned his horse. I followed his lead. He raised his hand. "Men of Aarrondirth, as your king, I bid you welcome!" The men cheered in response. "Your time to sit idle is over!" His tone deepened. "War is at hand! Rest now, for you will be called to fulfill your duty soon!" In the silence that followed, Madigan looked at General Braddim to continue.

Braddim stood in his stirrups. "Those of you with family here are asked to return to your homes! Those without will stay in the courtyard! Rest now, for you will return to your duties in two days!"

Madigan nodded at the heralds. At the sound of the horns, the soldiers broke rank and began to disperse.

When the streets emptied, Madigan and I led the remaining troops into the courtyard.

Braddim rode up to meet us. "My king. I have counted over a hundred soldiers without family here in Aarrondirth." He removed his helmet. "From a distance, the courtyard appears to be full. Will there be room enough?"

"There is no need for concern," Madigan reassured him. "The men will be taken care of."

Braddim nodded, scanning the area beyond the bridge. "Do my eyes deceive me, or do I see Miders amongst our troops?" He winced in dismay.

"You will see elves among us as well," Madigan remarked,

pulling his horse's reins. "The matter of our future is serious, so much so, we have had no choice but to set aside our petty differences and reunite with the neighboring regions."

"Why would you put your trust in the elves?" he retorted. "The Miders I could understand, but the elves are not to be …"

"Choose your words carefully, Braddim," Madigan warned. "As you know, many of my childhood years were spent in Maglavine."

"Forgive me." Braddim blinked with humility. "I forgot your time there."

"There is nothing to forgive." Madigan sighed. "As your friend, I will not judge you on your personal feelings. However, as your king, I will ask that you set aside this ill sentiment and focus on strengthening our new alliances—if not for yourself, then for the others."

"As you wish, my king." Braddim bowed his head. "If you would point me in the right direction, I can lead the men from here."

Madigan nodded. "Take them to the west end of the courtyard. General Gin will be awaiting you there with further instructions."

"Understood." Braddim bowed his head again and returned to the soldiers.

When the procession began to move forward, I looked at Madigan. "May I ask the cause of Braddim's dislike toward the elves?"

"I cannot say for certain," Madigan shrugged, "but I believe it has something to do with the death of his grandfather."

"Will he be a problem?" I asked.

Madigan shook his head. "Despite his faults, Braddim is a loyal servant to Aarrondirth, and he can be trusted."

"Very well," I replied bluntly to conceal my doubt.

When Madigan nudged his horse across the bridge, I followed.

As we rode toward the stable, I glanced over the rows of tents that lined the outer courtyard, wondering if General Braddim's malcontent was shared by the others. If so, there was no indication. In the main staging areas the men of Man's Blood sparred with both the Miders and elves. The community food kitchens churned out meals for those who were taking a moment's rest from shared labor. Their mutual cooperation filled me with a sense of pride, reassuring me that, in time, General Braddim too would come to welcome these changes.

"Arianna." Madigan pulled the reins. "I will leave you here and tour the courtyard."

I nodded, guiding Accolade through the gate as he rode off.

A boy ran from one of the paddocks. "My lady, may I take your horse?"

"Yes," I leapt to the ground. "I am retiring for the evening."

When he took the reins, I left for the castle.

Famished, I made my way into the kitchen. The room was bustling with activity. Yearning for a moment on my own, I quickly filled a bowl with stew and then made my way to the dining hall.

As I pulled out a chair, I heard footsteps from behind; I turned to see Morglafenn. He slowly stepped across the threshold. "Arianna, excuse the interruption, but I was hoping to speak with you."

"Have you had further word from Shallendria?" I asked as I sat.

"No," he replied with a shrug. "Unless something unforeseen happens, she will not take the risk of disclosing her location while escorting our troops. It is too dangerous."

"Oh." I set my bowl of stew on the table. "How many of them are to be expected?" I expanded the conversation to conceal my naivety.

"Not many." He eyed the chair next to me. "I will assume that Darwynyen has made you aware of the detriments we have sustained to our population."

I gestured for him to sit. "To be honest, he has not been

as forthcoming as I would like." I paused. "Perhaps you could enlighten me further."

"It is complicated," he replied, gazing at a ring on his middle finger, which was similar to Darwynyen's. "It is ironic that we are envied for the magic we possess, when it has become the bane of our existence," he mumbled.

"What do you mean?" I asked.

"The powers we have manipulated to sustain us have in the end led us down a path that few will return from."

"Your words make no sense." I frowned. "The powers you possess have given you strength and endurance. I have often wondered why your people have not chosen to rule these lands rather than succumb to the regions around you."

"You are mistaken, Arianna." His eyes grew solemn. "Over time, the desire to expand our empire was lost to the promise of immortality; thus our populations have suffered. In truth, we have succumbed to nothing more than the simple will to live."

As I absorbed his words, the reasons for Darwynyen's indifference when it came to having children became unclear. Could it be that it had nothing to do with the Rinjeed and the mixing of our bloodline after all? Was it that he simply was complacent about something my people valued most, the passing of time?

I felt Morglafenn's arm on my shoulder. "Do not let what I have said trouble you. I feel certain that in time you and Darwynyen will both remove your jewels of eternal life and share a family."

At the mention of children, I immediately felt uncomfortable. "What gives you this certainty?" I asked. "I mean … how do you know such things, when it comes to our future?"

"You assume too much," he sat back in his chair. "Any fool could see the love you both share." He continued before I could respond. "When Darwynyen first returned from his encounter with you, he was overwhelmed by his emotions. He did not understand them. Eventually, he confided in me. Under the circumstances, I could offer no counsel. Frustrated, he made his way back to Hoverdire." My mouth fell open, but he persisted. "After watching over you for days, he selflessly released you and left unnoticed."

"Why?" I pleaded.

He took a weighted breath. "What Darwynyen carries in his heart is his own. You must seek him for these answers. You share a bond like no other." His eyes brightened. "With all that has happened, you have managed to find love in the shadow of darkness. That is why Aldraveena and I believe you are destined to be together."

"We are destined to be together," I responded. "I cannot imagine my life without him."

Morglafenn eyed the pendant that was hanging over my shirt. "That is a mighty gift you wear." He swallowed deeply. "It is hard to believe that a simple stone could hold such power."

"How do you feel about Aldraveena's offering?" I asked. "It is no secret that your people were displeased by her gesture."

"Forget the others." He lifted my chin to meet his gaze. "I can think of no other more worthy of her gift."

"Thank you." I smiled appreciatively. When I took the pendant in my hand, a vision of the dream I had experienced in Maglavine, the one of my father, flashed before me. "Do you know if it is powerful enough to cause dreams?"

He shook his head. "Dreams … foresight, maybe, but not dreams."

My stomach tightened. Could it be that the dream I had in Maglavine, the one where the ravens were attacking me, was a vision of foresight?

"What is it?" he asked.

"Nothing." I picked up my spoon casually and began to stir the stew, an attempt to sway his concern.

He nodded, placing his hand on mine. "Try not to focus on the negative. It will only cloud your judgment. Instead, focus on the good things in your life. You have much to look forward to. When this war is over, you and Darwynyen will be able to focus on each other and, as I mentioned earlier, share a family." He paused. "The union you and Darwynyen have shared in is more important than you realize, for the intertwining of your bloodlines will eventually forge a bond between our two people that will last an eternity."

At the second mention of Darwynyen and me sharing in a family, thoughts of the Rinjeed resurfaced, overshadowing my concern over the dream. Overwhelmed by uncertainty, I no longer felt in control. There were too many questions left unanswered. When my body tensed, I felt light-headed.

"Arianna." Morglafenn squeezed my hand. "Have I said something to upset you?"

I looked at him helplessly. "I am not even sure I want to bear Darwynyen's child, if …" I broke off, unable to speak of the Rinjeed.

"It was not my intention to pressure you." He smiled sympathetically. "There is plenty of time for you to make these decisions. As you know, you may not carry a child when you wear a jewel of eternal life. The rules of magic do not allow it."

"But our first night together I did not wear the pendant," I argued.

"Yes, but he wore his ring, did he not?"

I nodded. He was right, I was worrying over nothing. The tension in my shoulders eased. For now, I would forget about the Rinjeed and focus solely on my father. Until he had been apprehended I had no future, not one I could look forward to anyway.

Morglafenn stood. "I will leave you to eat before your dinner grows cold."

"Wait." I pushed the bowl aside. The thought of my father brought me to wonder about Darwynyen's. "Will you tell me of Darwynyen's father? Not once have I heard a mention of him."

He hesitated. "You should probably seek Darwynyen if you care to speak further about his past."

"Please," I begged. "Darwynyen is not as forthcoming on these subjects as you."

"I suppose I can share with you what is already common knowledge." He returned to his seat. "You may not like what you hear, but nevertheless, it should come from someone you know." A look of pride came over his face. "Darwynyen's father was a great warrior. He led the elves of Maglavine to victory many times."

"Where is he now?" I asked.

His eyes began to wander. "He was murdered by men of Man's Blood shortly after the death of King Alameed."

My mouth fell open when I realized the implications. "Do you speak of the king my father poisoned?"

When he nodded, I went numb with shock.

His tone deepened. "As I said, you should seek these answers from Darwynyen. I now feel that he would not approve of me telling you this." He abruptly left the room.

Thoughts raced through my mind. Was my father responsible for the death of Darwynyen's? If so, how could he bear to look upon me? Was this the reason he had kept the identity of his mother Aldraveena a secret? He must have known that I would have questions once I found out. Desperate for answers, I rushed from the room.

I searched the entire castle. Darwynyen was nowhere to be found. My last hope was that he was awaiting me in our quarters. As I made my way across the landing above the keep, I saw him standing alone on the northern tower, and I halted. My hesitation stemmed from the fear of having to confront him, but after Morglafenn's revelation, I had no choice on the matter. "Darwynyen," I called as I ascended the stair.

He did not respond.

"Darwynyen." I gently placed my hand on his shoulder. "What are you doing out here? I have been looking for you all over."

He broke from his reverie. "Forgive me. I was deep in thought."

Although I was curious about his contemplation, I gathered

my courage and persisted. "I have spoken with Morglafenn," I announced. "He has told me of your father, of how he died."

He turned sharply, startling me. "What exactly did he say?"

I took a step back. "He told me that your father was murdered by the men of Man's Blood shortly after my father had taken over rule of Aarrondirth."

"He had no right to speak to you about this," he exclaimed.

I blinked, attempting to block my forming tears. "I thought we were one," my voice crackled. "I thought nothing stood between us, but this secret, its implications, are far too significant to deny."

He embraced me with vigor. "Arianna, do not speak of us in such a way." I felt his lips press against my brow. "You are right, I should have told you, but I did not want you to worry. What happened is in the past and has no effect on my feelings toward you."

"Are you certain?" I asked. A part of me needed reassurance.

"Of course I am." He pulled back. "What can I do to settle this?"

"You can tell me the truth," I pleaded.

"Very well." His gaze wandered. "If you must know, my father was murdered on the streets of Aarrondirth shortly after the sudden death of King Alameed. To avoid mounting suspicion, Velderon redirected the blame for Alameed's death onto the elves. Because he was still in good standing, your father's lies were taken as truth, and any elves discovered in your land were executed on sight, without warning."

His words tore through my soul. It was confirmed; my father had inadvertently seen to the death of his.

"It is all right, Arianna." I felt his hand on my chin as he tried to direct my eyes to his. "What happened, happened for a reason. If not, I would not have joined the Men of Moya, nor would I be standing here with you now."

I received no comfort from his words and wondered if I was a constant reminder of something he would prefer to forget. "When you look upon me now, how will I know what you see?" I asked. Before he could respond, I continued. No longer could I leave the subject of children behind. "Morglafenn also spoke of our children." I paused. "You need to be honest and tell me how you feel about this."

"Children …" He furrowed his brow. "Why do you continue to dwell on this matter?"

"Because you refuse to discuss it." I searched his eyes. "Does your reluctance have something to do with who my father is, or is there another reason?" I asked obliquely, thinking of the Rinjeed.

"In a manner of speaking, yes, it does have to do with your father," he admitted. "But not in the way you think." He paused. "Until the war is over, I do not see the need to plan on a future that might never be."

"Is this your way of saying you never want children?" I crossed my arms.

He shrugged. "Either way, I can assure you that my end decision will have nothing to do with your father."

Unsatisfied with his answer, I narrowed my eyes. "Are you certain this indecision does not stem from another reason?"

"Another reason?" He frowned. "What do you mean?"

Not yet ready to speak of the Rinjeed, I turned the subject. "Have you ever considered removing your ring of eternal life?"

"Why would I?" A spark of greed appeared in his eyes. "Are you not pleased by the idea of us living together forever?"

Unsure as to whether or not I wanted to continue my life unnaturally after the war, I spoke bluntly to finalize the conversation. "You are right. Perhaps we should leave this discussion for another time."

"Nothing is lost, Arianna," he persisted with assurance "We have plenty of time to make these decisions." He lifted me into his arms. "This talk of children has left me with one desire alone."

When I realized his intention, I chose not to resist him.

Despite all the uncertainty, for the time being, his unyielding love for me was enough to carry me through.

† † †

I spent most of the morning in the library. Curious about the lands ruled by Aarrondirth, I meticulously went through each of the maps scattered along the main table. I discovered many places of interest and envisioned myself visiting each and every one of them. When I realized that my dreams were not unattainable, I selfishly pulled Aldraveena's pendant from my shirt. Its eternal life would allow me to not only investigate our lands but any of the other regions I chose, and during the journey I would never show my age. The thought overwhelmed me, for I had never imagined I would be given the choice to live forever.

As I rose from the table, I noticed the book the fairies had found that held a detailed account of the dragons. It was sitting on one of the chairs, where it had been left from our previous meeting, making it obvious that the others felt its contents held little or no value. If only I could read elvish, I could translate it myself, in hopes that it would hold the key to a successful reunion between our two kinds. Unfortunately I could not and frustrated that I had no control over the matter, I decided to visit the stables, and spend some time with Accolade.

After searching most of the stalls, I found him in the last one at the back; I approached quickly. "How is my Accolade doing today?" He nickered at my touch. "I regret you will not be joining me on the coming quest," I explained, even though I knew he could not understand. The one-sided conversation brought me a sense of ease, knowing that he would not be responding and adding pressure. "We will travel by water this time, and though I am sure you are a great swimmer, you would only impede our journey." When he stepped forward, I began to rub his neck.

"Arianna!" Teshna flew to my face. "We have been looking for you!"

Zenley arrived at her side. "Madigan has called a second meeting!"

"Where are they?" I asked, turning from Accolade.

"They await you in the defense rooms." Teshna fluttered her wings.

I nodded; brushing past them to make way.

When I arrived, Darwynyen, Madigan, Dregby, Gin, and Sikes awaited me at the main table.

Darwynyen stood. "Where have you been?"

Before I could answer, Madigan pulled out a chair. "It does not matter," he said impatiently. "She is here now. Let us get started."

As I sat, Teshna and Zenley flew into the room.

Madigan took his seat. "Now that the arrangements for your departure have been made, I would like to be briefed."

I looked at Gin to lead the conversation, because he was familiar with the region we were soon to be traveling through.

Gin cleared his throat. "Our intention is to leave tomorrow. The quest itself should take us no more than two and one half weeks," he explained. "To maintain our appearance of being commoners, we will travel on foot to Brownen." Gin pointed to the region on the map. "Should we come across anyone, we will state that we are distant travelers and introduce Dregby as our guide to avoid suspicion. When we arrive at Brownen we will secure a boat. And though time will be saved on the water, the return by land back to Aarrondirth will be more difficult, as we will have no choice but to navigate through the rugged forests along the loch until we reach open countryside."

Morglafenn appeared at the door. "It would be in your interest to leave Aarrondirth under the cover of night."

Darwynyen rolled his eyes. "Are you and Shallendria still concerned about this supposed presence?"

"Yes." Morglafenn sat in an open chair. "Until we learn of its origin, it is imperative that your quest be kept secret." His eyes scanned the room with intent. "Velderon must not learn of our intentions."

"What presence?" Madigan frowned.

"Shallendria and Morglafenn have felt a presence in the past weeks." Darwynyen sent Morglafenn a dismissive look as he spoke. "Shallendria warned me of it before we left for Maglavine."

"Why has no one told me of this?" Madigan huffed.

Morglafenn responded with wide eyes. "I thought Shallendria …"

"No, she did not." Madigan's tone was harsh.

"Forget your concern, Madigan," Darwynyen interjected. "What Shallendria perceives is not always accurate. If it were, Aldraveena would have warned Arianna during our time in Maglavine."

"Do what you will." Morglafenn appeared disheartened. "I will say no more."

"No." Madigan was not to let the subject rest. "Tell me more of this presence."

Morglafenn sat forward, reinvigorated by Madigan's interest. "Shallendria felt it first, but in the past week I have sensed it also. Still, we have not yet found the root. That is why I ask that you keep this quest in secret." He paused. "If our motives are to keep Arianna safe, I see no advantage in sharing our objectives at this point in time."

"Morglafenn is right," Madigan agreed. "Ultimately, this quest is no one's business but our own." His eyes scanned the room. "Rather than deliberate further, I think we can all agree that secrecy is warranted here."

When everyone nodded, Morglafenn eyed the map. "If you have no choice but to travel through the forest on your return, may I suggest the path leading to Iramak?"

"The little people." Darwynyen sighed. "I had almost forgotten about them."

"With good cause!" Dregby stomped his hooves. "Why

should we make the effort when they have not returned any of our previous communications?"

"Perhaps if you had not insulted them …" Madigan remarked. Before Dregby could respond, Madigan looked at Morglafenn. "Would our efforts not be better spent elsewhere?"

"All the regions must reunite if we are to be successful," Morglafenn urged. "Despite our reservations, it is in our interest to present them with the option, regardless of whether or not they choose to accept it."

"He is right," Darwynyen concurred. "Their part in this war is no less than ours."

"Who are these little people?" I asked.

"They are as their name describes them," Gin replied. "Even so, their size does not hinder them when it comes to their pride," he warned. "An unreasonable sort they are."

"That and they are devious," Dregby added.

"I disagree," Morglafenn spoke sternly. "In the end, they will only strengthen our cause."

"I say we stay on the route that follows the waterway," Gin stubbornly growled.

"I will not argue with you." Morglafenn crossed his arms. "Archemese will no doubt settle this matter once you have found him."

When Gin clenched his fists, I stood. "Let us not bicker and instead focus on the reason for this quest." In the silence that followed, I glanced around the room. "Archemese is the priority here, is he not?" I looked to Madigan for support.

"The subject is closed." Madigan eyed both Gin and Dregby before continuing. "As Morglafenn said, Archemese will be the one to decide this matter." He paused. "While you are away, I will continue with the preparations here in Aarrondirth. Before long, we will have to make our way to Biddenwade, and I want to make sure our armies are strong and ready beforehand, as we will not have the means to train the men en route."

"What if the war takes us beyond Biddenwade?" I asked. "Have we charted any of the maps we have of Cessdorn?"

"Arianna, until we know that Velderon has succeeded, there is no need to look beyond Biddenwade," Madigan contended. "Even now, the Hynd move quickly to secure the lands beyond the loch." He pointed to the map, directing his finger along the northern end of the loch. "In response, my only course of action was to send word to the settlers in those regions and have them abandon post immediately."

"I see." I considered his account. "Although these new developments are disheartening, there is still hope. My father might not make it to Cessdorn before the next cycle, giving us additional time to counter their advancements."

Madigan lifted his brow. "That is wishful thinking, but it changes nothing when it comes to where our people will make their stand. For now, the battlement at Biddenwade will sustain us." His stare intensified. "Leave the details of engagement to me, Arianna, and trust in the decisions I make."

"I will hope for his failure nonetheless," I mumbled, dreading the thought of having to face my father alone.

Madigan nodded. "As will we all."

Gin stood to roll the map. "It is to our good fortune that most of our armies are already stationed in Biddenwade." When I looked at him, confused, he continued. "There are many rogue warlords in the far northwest who have chosen to defy the laws of our kind, forcing us to defend our bordering lands with vigor."

"The outcome of these conflicts has worked in our favor, I might add." Madigan chuckled wryly. "I am sure your father toiled over the matter when he was forced to defend a region that in the end would only hinder his ambitions!"

The men laughed at his remark.

When Madigan moved to adjourn the meeting, I silenced him. "Before we adjourn this meeting, I feel it is my duty to remind you of my father's intentions. He is ruthless and will stop at nothing when it comes to reuniting the stones. His determination is great, and his power grows by the day. To thwart him, we must keep on our guard and give our trust cautiously. I can assure you that he will spare no time when looking to discover our weakness. Do not fear him. In the end it is we who will find success." I looked at Madigan. "We must guide our people with honor. Lead them with strength. Our union will instill fear in those who oppose us."

Madigan put his hand to his chest. "May victory soon be ours!"

"Here, here!" Gin and Dregby bellowed, as Sikes and Darwynyen bowed their heads.

Madigan stood. "This meeting is adjourned."

As the room emptied, Madigan took me by the arm. "Where did you learn to speak with such strength and honor?"

Humbled, I looked down, "I do not know—I only share the feelings within my heart."

"You did well." He released me. "I am proud of you!"

Relieved that he was not angered, I looked at Darwynyen and smiled as we left the room.

† † †

As I stood on the northern tower, reflecting on the outcome of our meeting, I noticed that a thunderstorm was brewing in the distance. Inhaling the crisp air, I looked over the courtyard. It seemed an injustice that the men would to have to endure a rain storm while completing a hard day of labor. I shook the thought, knowing the men would have grown accustomed to these kinds of conditions in the camps where they were previously stationed.

I was about to take shelter when I caught view of several dark silhouettes in the sky to the north. "Dragons," I whispered. The beasts were returning for another attack.

A horn sounded from the northeast tower. I immediately ran down the stairs in search of Darwynyen, who had left me earlier to address his men in the courtyard.

When I reached the main level of the castle, the area was in a state of turmoil. People were rushing in all directions. Through the confusion, I saw Edina entering through the main door. "Edina!" I waved.

She rushed over and embraced me. "Arianna, I am so very pleased to see you."

I pulled from her. "You must seek safe shelter! The dragons have returned for another attack!"

"I know, I-I was alerted," she stammered. "When did you return?"

"Hold your questions and hurry to the defense rooms." I nudged her toward the corridor. "I have to find Darwynyen!" Not waiting for a response, I made my way to the gated passage that opened from the foyer off the dining hall.

As I passed through the main archway, I noticed that Edina was following me, and I turned sharply. "Did you not hear a word I said?"

"I heard you!" She grabbed me by the arm. "But I would prefer to stay with you."

There was no time to argue. With pursed lips, I broke from her hold and ran toward the door at the opposite end of the foyer that opened off the dining hall.

Before I could reach it, it opened from the opposite side. Three soldiers ran across the threshold, followed by Zenley and Teshna. "Arianna!" Teshna cried, halting in mid-air. "We must find safe shelter!"

Edina gasped in alarm.

"Do not fear them," I said firmly. "They are our friends!"

"But …"

I silenced her and turned to the fairies with resolve. "Go to the defense rooms and take her with you." I gestured to Edina. "See that she is kept safe!"

"We cannot leave you!" Zenley flew to his sister's side. "Our queen would never forgive us!"

"Yes you can," I snapped. "Now go—you are no match for the dragons, for their fire will burn you to dust!"

Unlike Edina, they took heed in my warning, and did not argue, making haste toward the defense corridor.

"Are you not to follow?" I huffed.

"No." She stiffened her stance. "I will not leave you."

"Very well." I turned to peer through the open door. "I will see if it is safe to proceed."

When she nodded, I stepped through the doorway.

I had only taken a few steps when I felt raindrops strike my face. Frustrated by the unwanted impediment, I put my hand to my brow to observe the neighboring towers. To my relief, the attacks had yet to commence, and the soldiers, unharmed, were standing along the parapet with their crossbows and pikes aimed in readiness. I was about to turn and signal Edina when a beast flew overhead, scorching the area around the terrace with fire.

"Arianna!" Edina reached for me. "I beg you to come back!"

"I cannot." I edged forward. "I need to find Darwynyen!"

"How do you know he is out there?"

"Because he said that he was going to check on his men." I put my sleeve to my mouth when smoke from the burning shrubbery around the fountain began to creep onto the terrace. I coughed. "Stay here. I will return shortly."

Before she could respond, I ran toward the terrace stairs.

A haze of smoke was filtering through the courtyard. "Darwynyen!" I yelled, gasping for fresh air.

There was no response amongst the chaos.

When the smoke began to lift, I descended the stairs. Burnt corpses from the surprise attack were scattered along the ground. Those who had survived were seeking shelter. "Make your way to the castle towers!" I ordered. "You can do no more out here!"

A few of the men who heard me ran toward the gated passage.

To claim a better view, I ran to the fountain. As I stood on the ledge, a dragon dived from above, setting fire to a group of men as they fled through the west pasture. The creature's body was riddled with arrows; it was clear to me that its heart was consumed with nothing but hatred and revenge, if it were willing to give its life so readily. The thought, despite our predicament, saddened me.

Another beast swept the area. Its thunderous roar shook the castle's foundation.

I was about to return to the safety of the gated passage when the beast pounced to the ground. *You!* The creature growled.

"What do you want?" I stumbled backwards.

We know who you are! The connection was strong. *They will use you to destroy him.*

"Over here!" I turned to see a company of men approaching, their finger's clenching the triggers of their crossbows. "Ready and aim!" the general shouted.

"Hold your fire!" I raised my hands in an attempt to protect the beast.

The leading soldier raised the face shield on his helmet. "My lady, forgive me, but have you gone mad?"

I did not recognize him. "Stay your position," I demanded.

As I spoke, the dragon extended its wings, taking flight.

"Wait!" I called, running in the beast's direction.

The creature ignored my plea.

"Arianna!" Dregby trotted over, slinging his axe as he dug his hooves into the ground for traction. "What are you doing out here? You risk too much!"

Flustered by the mayhem, I found myself lost for words.

He turned to the general who had followed. "Leave us." As the man backed away, Dregby took me by the arm. "Come, I will lead you out of here."

"No." I pulled free from his hold. "I need to find Darwynyen."

He was about to argue when we both took notice of the silence. The dragons had fled. When I looked through the smoke-filled skies, I saw them retreating to the north. Around me, I heard the moaning of wounded soldiers. Darwynyen was forgotten. "We must help the wounded!" I exclaimed. "They will need to be seen to before nightfall."

Dregby nodded in agreement and then rode off in the direction of the Mider camp.

Many men had fallen in battle, and countless numbers of those who had survived were injured. Thankful that I was not one of them, I pulled Aldraveena's pendant from my shirt, wondering if it had again shielded me from the dragons' fire as it had done in Maglavine. Distracted by screams of pain, I put the thought aside and set out toward one of the main infirmaries.

Upon entering the tent, I immediately felt overwhelmed. Healers and their aides were rushing in different directions, flustered. There were too many patients for them to handle. "What can I do?" I knelt by an aide who was tending to a wounded soldier on the ground.

"There are too many." She wiped her brow with the cuff of her sleeve. "We are running out of supplies."

"I will return to the castle and see what I can find." I stood and ran from the tent.

Edina was approaching, carrying a soldier over her shoulder. "Take that man to the infirmary, and then enlist the help of those who are able," I ordered. "I will return with some fresh linens and water."

When she nodded, I made my way to the castle in search of Evelyn.

As I burst through the entrance near the paddocks, I shouted, "Evelyn!"

Moments later, the door to the inner food storage opened, and Evelyn timidly appeared. "Arianna, is …?"

"You are needed." I looked toward the cooks who followed Evelyn from the room. "The infirmaries require fresh water. Bring what you can. There are many wounded to contend with."

"Are the beasts gone?" one of the cooks asked.

"Yes." I took Evelyn by the arm. "You must find the seamstress Marion. Ask her to bring fresh linen."

"Of course." She bowed her head. "Where will I find you?"

I ignored her question. "Assemble what you can and deliver it to the infirmaries."

She nodded obediently and then rushed from the room.

I looked at the cooks. "Bring the water as I asked." When they nodded, I made my way back to the courtyard.

While the generals and commanders regrouped, Edina and I set out to organize a secondary infirmary for those in need of minor care. As we tended to the wounded, Marion and Evelyn worked steadily, delivering the needed supplies. I looked at Edina. "Hand me a bandage." As Edina tore pieces of cloth, I began to clean an open wound on the leg of a young soldier.

"Arianna!" Morglafenn rushed over. "Is there anything I can do?"

I stood, remembering his skills in healing. "Morglafenn, are you able to use your healing powers on these men?"

He glanced over the area. "You have many wounded here." When I tensed anxiously, he pulled a satchel of powder from his garb. "I will do what I can."

"Your efforts will be much appreciated." I changed the subject. "Have you seen Darwynyen?"

"He is with our people," he replied.

"How did they fare?" I asked, returning to bandage the young soldier's leg.

"They are fine." He glanced over the men again. "It seems the dragons spent most of their energy here." His eyes filled with regret. "If I had known, I would have come sooner."

"You are here now." I secured the bandage and then winked at the boy. "You will be fine."

The boy flexed his leg, "Thank you, my lady."

"There is no need." I looked at the man next to him. He carried a wound on the shoulder and was clutching the area, in pain. "I will see to you next."

When the man sat forward, Morglafenn left my side. "I will see to the men over there."

I nodded as he made his way.

After most of the men were seen to, I stood. "Edina, I must find Darwynyen. Can you handle the rest?"

"Yes," she replied. "If you see Stuart, will you send him my way?"

"Of course." I wiped the blood from my hands on a damp cloth. "I will return when I can."

"Take your time." She reached for a bucket of water. "We are nearly done here."

I threw the cloth in a nearby fire and then turned toward the castle. Madigan was addressing a few of his men near the fountain. "Madigan!" I waved, relieved that no harm had come to him. "May I have a word?"

Madigan turned from his men impatiently and pointed to the east. "If you are looking for Darwynyen, you will find him in the eastern part of the courtyard."

Although he misunderstood my intention, I nodded, taking my leave.

As I walked through the various encampments, I wondered why Darwynyen had not taken the time to find me, as he had always done. Had something happened to him? No. Morglafenn said that he was fine. He must have gotten caught up in the aftermath, as I had.

When I reached the elf encampment, I found him. He was busy with Falker, repairing one of the tents that housed their kitchen facilities. "Darwynyen!" I raised my hand as I approached.

He turned when he heard my voice. "Arianna!" He handed Falker the rope he was holding and rushed over. "Are you all right?"

"Yes. And you?" I asked, surveying his body for wounds.

"I sustained no injury," he replied. "The dragons, aware of our Hellum's Dew, avoided this area."

Annoyed by his response, I spoke. "Then why did you not find me?"

He looked to the ground. "I meant to, but I got distracted."

"Distracted …" I crossed my arms. "Are you saying your purpose here was more important?"

He took hold of my hands. "Never. The only reason I did not come was because I have grown accustomed to your strength and no longer worry for you as I once did. Besides, I know you would not take any unnecessary risks."

I was taken aback by his words. Although a part of me still wanted his protection, I was proud that he was finally trusting in my strength. I squeezed his hands. "Forgive me, for my exhaustion has led my emotions astray."

He took hold of my hair and smelt it. As he exhaled, his eyes narrowed. "Where were you during the attack?"

I spoke my words strongly, knowing he would not approve. "Like you, I was in the courtyard with my people."

As I anticipated, disappointment crossed his face. "You left the castle with all that is at stake!"

"My people needed me!" I rebelled.

"You are right, your people do need you," he agreed derisively. "And that is precisely my point."

Hurt by the truth in his words, I took a step back. "I should probably return to my work if we are to have the camps rebuilt by nightfall."

"Do what you must," he conceded reluctantly. "As soon as I am done here, I will find you."

I nodded and turned to leave.

When I neared the infirmary, I heard a woman crying out. It was Edina. I found her near a stack of dead bodies. My heart sank when I realized that she was kneeling next to one of them.

"No! No! It cannot be!" she wailed. "Stuart, not Stuart!"

I ran to her side. "Edina." I gasped at the sight of Stuart's body. It was severely burned. His char-covered face was almost unrecognizable. I gently put my hands to her shoulders. "I … I …" lost for words I could not help but shed a tear.

She turned to look up at me. "Why, why does this have to be?" Her voice was strained. "We were only just married."

"I do not know." I blinked heavily. "Come, let me take you inside."

"No," Edina cried. "I cannot leave him."

I nodded, brushing a wisp of hair from her cheek. "Should I send for both your families?"

"No." She slowly stood as she considered my question. "This dreaded news must come from me alone."

"I understand." I quickly blinked, to stunt the flow of tears. I knew from experience how difficult this would be for her. She was in shock. Only time would heal her wounds. Until then she would have to be strong for Stuart's family. "I will make sure he is prepared and ready upon your return."

She returned to Stuart, kissing his brow before leaving. "I will not be gone long, my love," she muttered.

"Would you like me to accompany you?" I offered in support.

"Thank you, but no." She slowly walked away in a daze.

I ordered two soldiers to take Stuart's body to the ballroom where they had laid my mother. As I walked behind them, I wondered why this had to be. Edina was such a gentle soul, who deserved nothing but happiness. Her pain restored the anguish I had felt in my mother's passing. Hatred filled my mind, for if it were not for my father we would not be in this predicament to begin with.

I felt a hand on my shoulder. "Arianna, what has happened?"

I turned to find Madigan. "Edina's husband." I choked on my words. "He did not survive the attack." Before Madigan could respond, I sought comfort in his arms, allowing the soldiers to carry on without me.

When I felt his embrace, I immediately felt comforted.

"He has died in the attacks then," he sighed.

"Yes." I allowed the tears I had held back in Edina's presence to trickle down my cheeks.

Madigan gave me his warmth for a moment. "You know her better than anyone." He hesitated. "Is she to be all right?"

"Perhaps in time." I pulled away to wipe my eyes. "When she returns, I will release her to her family."

He nodded, leading me toward the gated passage.

As he sat me on one of the benches in the foyer that extended from the dining hall, Darwynyen appeared from the gated passage. "Arianna, I came as quickly as I could." He entered the room slowly. "Word has traveled. I understand your lady in waiting has lost her husband."

"Yes." I brushed my nose with my sleeve. "Stuart is dead."

Darwynyen looked at Madigan. "I can see to Arianna from here."

Madigan took a few steps and then turned. "Arianna, if there is anything I can do, you need only to find me."

"Thank you." I managed a smile.

After sharing in a nod with Darwynyen, Madigan took his leave.

Darwynyen sat next to me. "I should have been there for you. Forgive me."

"There is nothing to forgive." I blotted my eyes. "It is Edina who has suffered this loss."

He put his arms around me. "Yes, but I know she is dear to you."

"She is like a sister to me." I pulled his body close to mine.

"Where is she?" he asked.

"She has gone in search of Stuart's family." I stood abruptly. "I must await her return in the main foyer."

"Should I wait with you?" He followed me from the room.

"No." I halted to face him. "It is better that I do this on my own."

"Of course." He kissed my brow. "I will await you in our quarters at the falling of the sun."

I nodded, making my way toward the main doors.

Desperate for some time on my own, I exited the castle and sat on the edifice stair. Although the recent storm had passed without shedding more than a few drops, the drifting clouds had left a slight drizzle in their wake. The melody of droplets seemed to fit my mood, and as I inhaled the fresh air, I saw Edina making her way through the courtyard along with her kin.

In their approach, they showed little emotion. Even so, their pain was visible. Unsure what to say, I quickly embraced Edina before leading them inside.

When we reached the ballroom, I watched in torment as the family gathered around Stuart's body. They did not stay long. An older man, Stuart's father, I presumed, gathered him into his arms and retreated down the stair along with a woman I guessed to be Stuart's mother. Edina turned to me before leaving. Her eyes were red and swollen. Despite the urge to reach out to her, I decided it best to keep my distance. "Edina, I release you of your duties. Be with your family. If you need anything, I ask that you come to me." I took her by the arms when I saw her legs begin to waver. "I love you, my sister."

She reaffirmed her stance. "Take care Arianna."

"Our business is finished here," a middle-aged man with a limp took Edina firmly by the arm.

I nodded to the man and then watched Edina assist him to the stairs. A tear trickled down my cheek. I would miss her. Our friendship was something I had taken for granted. Only now did I realize it was ending. Based on the attitude of her family, it was obvious that they held me responsible for Stuart's death. I could only hope that the grieving process would help Edina see things differently. Until then, I would leave her be.

To fill the empty hole in my heart, I returned to the abode above the keep in hopes that Darwynyen was waiting for me.

† † †

Sleep did not come easily; in fact, it did not come at all. I felt different. Was my mind weighted by Edina's grief, or was it perhaps Aldraveena's pendant? Was its power of life forbidding me the escape of my dreams? Although Darwynyen spent his nights with me, he did mention once that elves did not require rest like the Man's Blood people. Either way, I had no time to waste. We were to leave in search of Archemese this eve, and I wanted to be prepared for our departure.

Darwynyen reached out for me. "Arianna, must you leave? Can I not hold you in my arms for another minute?"

"No." I rose from the bed. "There are things I must see to if we are to depart from Aarrondirth this eve."

"That is precisely my point." His hand caressed the mattress. "This will be the last of our moments in private." He paused. "Forgive me, I did not mean to be selfish. How are you feeling this morning?"

"I am fine," I replied, knowing that he was referring to Edina. "I will not tell a lie and conceal the burden that has been placed upon my heart. The pain is there, and it festers. Even so, I must move on, and I intend to do so as quickly as possible."

His eyes searched mine for a moment. "I see now that you understand the grief that comes in times of war."

"Is it that, or has my heart turned cold?" I asked.

"Do not misinterpret your strengths, for they only work to preserve your fragilities." He tossed the covers aside. "Shall we make our way to the kitchen?"

"Yes." I pulled my shirt over my head. "Not only am I famished, I must speak with Evelyn if we are to have the necessary rations prepared for our departure."

He looked back to the bed. "I still do not see the hurry."

As I stepped into my boots, I half yawned, an action that reminded me of the pendant. "It appears that I no longer have the ability to sleep," I remarked. "Would this have something to do with the pendant I now wear?"

He secured the belt on his trousers. "If the power of the pendant has taken effect, you will no longer require rest as you once did."

"But I look forward to my sleep," I huffed. "It gives me peace from my troubles."

"You will still require rest," he explained. "Only now it will come in a different form."

"What are you saying?" I asked. "I mean, it almost felt like I was asleep, though not the kind of sleep one awakes from."

"Do not worry." He smiled sympathetically. "You will grow accustomed to its effect in time and learn to appreciate the ability to settle your thoughts with more focus."

"Perhaps." I knelt to attach my sais. "Still, in many ways it does not seem right."

His hand graced my cheek. "Are you telling me you do not feel its energy? Is your mind not alive, alive in ways you have not felt before?"

When he spoke of the energy, I could not help but sense it. Although my body was tired, my mind was sharp, clearer than it had been for weeks. "You are right, I cannot deny its effect," I relented. "And I will try to accept it for now, but when I no longer require the pendant's protection, I cannot promise you that I will continue to wear it."

"Then let us leave this conversation and wait to address it at that time." He kissed my hands and then moved to the door.

Although I was bewildered by his response, expecting him to argue the point, I was relieved that he had chosen not to, and I followed him through the door.

When Darwynyen and I entered the kitchen, I saw Marion sitting at a small table near the inner food store. "Marion!" I rushed to her side. "It is good to see you!"

She smiled, swallowing the food that she had been chewing.

"It is good to see you, my dear!" Her eyes quickly scanned my body. "I am pleased to see that your outfit has kept its form."

"It has." I returned her smile, thinking back to the day when I first saw it on the mannequin in her room. "For all the days I have worn it, it still feels like new."

"If you need any adjustments, you know where to find me." When I nodded, she continued. "Did the infirmaries receive the required linen yesterday?" Her eyes dulled. "I understand we lost many men in the attack."

"Yes." I released a weighted breath. "However, now is not the time to dwell on the past, for there is much still before us."

"Your lady in waiting …" Her words broke. "I am sorrowed by her loss."

"As am I." I looked down as the memories of Stuart's death resurfaced.

"Do not fret." She took my hand, "Edina is strong and will soon recover from her grief."

"Arianna." Evelyn appeared at the door that led from the paddocks. "I have received instruction from the king to prepare a week's worth of rations that you are again to take your leave from Aarrondirth." She furrowed her brow. "Is this true?"

I quickly glanced around the room in search of prying ears. "Evelyn, you must not speak of the quest as though it were public knowledge."

Her eyes widened. "Forgive me, I did not know."

"It is all right." I sighed. "The instruction was correct. If you could see to the food and have it ready by nightfall, that would be greatly appreciated."

"Consider it done," She nodded sternly and then looked over my shoulder. "I believe your fellow awaits you."

When I turned, Darwynyen lifted two bowls of porridge from the cutting table. "You may join me in the dining hall when you are ready."

"I will be there in a minute." I turned to both Evelyn and

Marion. "Take care." I met both their gazes. "Upon my return, we will take the time to visit."

"Of course, my dear," Evelyn smiled.

"Be safe on your journey." Marion stood with open arms.

After sharing in a loving embrace, I looked at her with feelings of guilt. A part of me felt responsible for her well-being. How could I not after learning of my father's indiscretion toward her?

She returned to her chair. "Arianna, my child, there is no need for you to linger, for I despise long good-byes."

"As do I!" I winked. "See you soon." I waved to both her and Evelyn as I took my leave from the room.

Darwynyen was halfway through his meal when I found him. "Who was that woman?" he asked when I sat next to him.

"Her name is Marion." I took hold of the bowl he had prepared for me. "She is the royal seamstress."

He closed his eyes in realization. "Then she is the one who crafted your outfits."

"Yes." I dug my spoon into the porridge. "Regardless of what you believe, do not think poorly of her, for she is very dear to me."

He wiped his mouth. "I think nothing. A friend of yours is a friend of mine."

Although I was taken aback by his reaction, I nodded, and then began in my meal.

Once we had eaten, Darwynyen and I went to the northern terrace. When Darwynyen opened the door to the gated passage, I immediately recognized Madigan's voice. "Bring the catapults out from the castle!" He spoke sternly. "This time we will strike the beasts as they approach!"

"What is going on?" I looked at Darwynyen with concern.

"In light of the last attack, the city of Aarrondirth has been declared no longer safe," Darwynyen replied. "Madigan has no choice but to make ready the battlements."

I quickly made my way across the terrace. To my dismay, construction in the courtyard was well underway. What remained of the greenery was gone. Several catapults had been placed along the castle, protected by a line of mantlets. Men were cutting away the dead trees around the fountain, while others dug trenches. "Madigan!" I shouted, interrupting his work. "Please, I would like to speak with you."

He trudged over with an annoyed look. "What is it, Arianna?" When he saw the hurt on my face, he continued, "You must understand the urgency in what I now do. There is little time to waste."

"Yes, but is all of this necessary?" I asked.

"Would you have me leave this city unprotected?" He paused. "While we are on the subject of leaving, I have been thinking. I feel that your quest might be better served if it were to end in Walferd."

"Walferd?" I frowned. "What are you saying?"

"I have decided that our time here is spent," Madigan replied. "No longer will we delay. I plan to assemble the troops and set off for Biddenwade immediately."

Apprehensive, I took a step back. I was not yet ready to face the inevitable. "But th ... this is our home," I stammered.

"And it will stay our home." He stiffened his stance, looking to Darwynyen. "My friend, if Arianna will not listen to reason and admit that returning to Aarrondirth is a wasted cause, I will ask that you take up the charge and lead her safely to Walferd."

"Forgive me, Madigan, but need I remind you that you are no longer a soldier?" Darwynyen challenged. "Send forth the armies, yes, but under the command of another. Until the defenses in this region have been fortified, is your duty not here with your people?" He continued before Madigan could protest. "Besides, the soldiers will have to cross the land on foot, an endeavor that will take time, something a small company like ours could easily undertake on horseback upon our return from the island, thus eliminating the need for several days of travel."

Madigan considered Darwynyen's suggestion. "Perhaps you are right. There is no need to be hasty. For the time being,

Biddenwade is protected. In your absence, I will only send half the troops on to Walferd."

I bit my lip. "Are you saying that you will stay here until our return?"

"Yes." He glanced over his shoulder toward the courtyard. "General Braddim will lead the first battalion forward, and I will stay on with the castle guard to ensure that our home is protected from the dragons."

The mention of dragons reminded me of the beast I had encountered yesterday during the attack. Was now the time to reveal the creature's elusive warnings to Madigan and Darwynyen? No. As on previous occasions, they would probably dismiss my revelation as nonsense. "Thank you, Madigan." I changed the subject. "Will I see you again before we leave?"

"I will meet you at the stables at the falling of the sun." Not waiting for my response, he returned to the soldiers who had been awaiting him near the catapults.

"Darwynyen!" Sikes shouted from the courtyard. "If you have a moment, we could use your guidance."

I waved to Sikes and then turned to Darwynyen. "It seems you are needed."

"I will find you later." He kissed me on the cheek and then ran toward the stairs.

As I watched him leave, I thought of Shallendria. If only she were here, I could have her counsel me on the dragons. And if she believed me, I would ask her to teach me how to speak with them through the mind, as she had previously done with me. Because she was not, in her place I would seek Morglafenn. If anyone in Aarrondirth would understand my predicament, it would be him.

After searching several of the main rooms, I found Morglafenn in the library.

When he saw me, he stood up from the table. "Arianna, did you need something?"

I entered the room. "Yes. May I speak with you?"

"Most certainly." He escorted me to an open chair. "I was hoping to have some time with you prior to your departure."

I nodded, taking hold of the book the fairies had found that detailed the history of the dragons. "Before I begin, I must tell you that I have spoken of this to no one."

"Your confidence is safe with me," he assured.

I sat, placing the book in front of me. "As incredible as this may sound, I believe that the dragons have been trying to communicate with me."

"Communicate with you … If so, where and when did this happen?" he asked calmly.

Bemused by his indifference, I paused to find the right words. "The first encounter was in Maglavine. During the attack there, a beast spoke to me in my mind, like Shallendria and Aldraveena." I paused. "For a time, I denied what had happened, and I had almost forgotten about it until I had another encounter yesterday."

He sat back in his chair. "How can you be certain that it was the beasts that made these connections?"

"Because," I tensed. "Who else would it be?"

His hand caressed his chin, considering. "What exactly did they say?"

"For the most part, they spoke in riddles." I shrugged. "It was as though they were warning me."

"Warning you." He puckered his brow.

I nodded. "Yes. They said that the Hynd would use me against him."

"Arianna," his tone deepened, "I must ask again. Are you certain that it was the beasts that made this connection?"

Insulted by his inability to trust my judgment, I said harshly. "As certain as I can be under the circumstances!"

He did not react to my outburst. "Who have you told about this?"

"No one but you." I looked down. The insecurities I had felt about revealing this to Darwynyen and Madigan resurfaced.

"That is probably for the best." I felt his hand on my shoulder.

"Until I have spoken to Shallendria there is no point in raising concern among the others."

"What about Darwynyen?" I asked, hoping that he would persuade me to reveal this secret to ease the guilt.

"Say nothing. Darwynyen has been very resistant toward my warnings as of late and …" He broke off.

"Are you referring to the presence you and Shallendria have felt?" My eyes widened. "Do you believe that it was this presence that connected to me?"

"It is too early to say," he replied. "We must wait until I seek Shallendria's counsel."

"Very well." I slid the book toward him. Despite his reservations, I needed to believe that it was the dragons that made those connections. "During my absence, I ask that you read this book. Its contents may hold the answers we seek."

He placed his hand on the cover. "I will have it finished on your return."

"Thank you." I stood up from the table.

"Wait." Morglafenn took hold of my wrist. "It is not my business, but I wonder if you have spoken to Darwynyen about our last conversation?"

Morglafenn was right; it was none of his business. "Why do you pursue this?" I questioned, suspicious of his motives. "Is it out of concern, or is there more to the story."

He appeared uncertain as to whether or not he should continue. "I fear Darwynyen is angered by my actions, and I …"

"Should he not be?" I interrupted in a harsh tone. "Should I not be?"

"Why are you being defensive?" he asked.

"Because," I huffed, "now that I know the truth, I wish you had never told me."

"You cannot hide from this, Arianna." He released his hold on me. "Are you willing to risk Darwynyen's sanity?"

"What are you implying?" I asked impatiently. Deep down, I

knew he was referring to the blame Darwynyen carried regarding the death of his father.

Morglafenn responded with a sigh. "Darwynyen has held much pain over the years. As you know, he and his mother are not close. It was after his father's death that things began to deteriorate between them. I know he does not share these feelings easily. That is why I turn to you. Now that you have joined as one, I thought you could … Aldraveena and I feel that it is important for Darwynyen to rid himself of this hatred soon. If not, his heart could be tampered with."

I immediately felt anxious. "What hatred?" I asked, in denial.

Morglafenn looked at me with disappointment. "You know what it is I speak of."

"Why do you burden me with this now?" I crossed my arms. "Do I not already have enough to contend with?"

"Can you not see what is at stake?" He paused. "Elves are not used to the emotions shared by your people. The more we are exposed to them, our sense and logic begin to dissipate. If Darwynyen allows this to happen, his anger may soon overwhelm him."

Morglafenn was right; Darwynyen had been allowing his anger to surface, not for extended periods of time, but it was there, a characteristic I had not seen in his companions, except for Shallendria, the only other elf who had been intimate with my kind. "What are you asking of me, Morglafenn?"

"Speak with him," he pleaded. "If his ill emotions are brought to the surface, they will soon come to pass."

"What goes on here?" Darwynyen appeared at the door, startling us both. His repugnance was obvious, and it compounded Morglafenn's warning.

I gave Morglafenn a quick glance. "Darwynyen, I did not expect you so soon."

"Morglafenn, leave us." Darwynyen clenched his fists.

"Of course." Morglafenn lifted the book from the table, as if it were a measure of distraction. "Darwynyen, I was …"

"Save your words," Darwynyen glared. "I am not interested!"

When Morglafenn abruptly took his leave, I turned to Darwynyen. "What is the matter with you?" I huffed with frustration. "Morglafenn is only trying to help. He loves you. Can you not see that?"

Darwynyen sighed heavily. "His meddling, it aggravates me."

"He meddles because he is concerned." I spoke with conviction.

"For what reason?" he asked.

I took a moment to choose the right words. "Do you remember when you forced me to tell Madigan of my bloodline?" When he nodded, I continued. "Do you recall what you asked me afterward?"

"I see now where you are taking this." Darwynyen sat in a chair.

"Your father …" I hesitated. "Perhaps if you would share more of his story, it would ease your pain and help you come to terms with his death."

"There is little more to tell," he replied. "Yes, I was deeply wounded by my father's death and grew cold to your people for a time. But in my darkest hour I was introduced to the Men of Moya. They looked to me to take my father's place. That is when I met Madigan. Between him and Morglafenn, my life once again found its path, a path that led me to you."

As he spoke, I was reminded of Morglafenn's revelation about Darwynyen returning for me in Hoverdire. "Do you speak of the time we met again at the den, or are you referring to the occasion when you returned for me in Hoverdire?" I asked.

His eyes widened. "How do you know of this?"

"Morglafenn," I replied.

"I should have known." He sighed heavily.

"Why did you leave me in Hoverdire?" I asked, now that things were out in the open.

"I do not know." He bit his lip.

When I looked down, he put his hand under my chin. "If we had not met again, I would have come back for you, I swear." There was intensity in his voice. "As I have told you before, your father has no impact on my feelings toward you."

Comforted by his words, I began to wonder if Morglafenn's warnings were somewhat exaggerated. In the end, Darwynyen's hatred toward my father was justified, and it was something I could not find fault with, as I carried the same ill sentiment. I could only hope that this common attribute between us would make us stronger, not weaker.

I felt his arms around me. "Trouble yourself no further. Let us look to the future and not speak of this again."

"Agreed." I took him by the hand, pulling him to his feet. "Come, it is time for us to pack."

"But it is not even midday!" He frowned.

"Was it not you who requested a last moment in private this morn?" I asked playfully.

With little more than a smirk, he led me from the room.

Lost in the passion of our lovemaking, Darwynyen and I held one another in silence as the minutes slowly passed. We each seemed to need to savor the moments shared between us, knowing there would be no intimacy during the time of our quest. As I caressed his chest, a knock came on the door.

"Who is it?" Darwynyen shouted.

"It is Morglafenn," the voice replied. "I need to see you."

Darwynyen tensed.

"Go to him," I rose from the bed, reaching for my dressing gown. "Make your amends before we leave."

Although reluctant, he pulled his trousers to his waist and made his way to the door, opening it slightly. "What is it?"

"No urgency comes with this visit," Morglafenn stated in

a humble manner. "I am only here because I felt the need to apologize for my indiscretions before you left."

In response, Darwynyen opened the door fully to face him.

Seizing the gesture, Morglafenn took him by the wrist. "I know my actions have reopened your wounds, but you must understand that I do it out of concern alone."

"If you must know, you have accomplished your goals." Darwynyen gave me a fleeting look. "As of now, Arianna and I hold no secrets."

Morglafenn's relief was apparent. "Nothing could please me more." He peered over Darwynyen's shoulder. "Take care of him, my dear."

I nodded. "I will."

Morglafenn took a step back. "May you find success on your quest and return swiftly."

"We will," Darwynyen concurred.

When Morglafenn turned to leave, a pang of sadness swept through my heart. Although our time together had been brief, I had grown quite fond of him.

Darwynyen shut the door. "We should go to the stable. The sun has made its descent."

With little more than a nod, I began to pack my belongings.

When Darwynyen and I arrived at the stables, we found a single horse, loaded with the necessary supplies for the first part of our journey to Brownen. Darwynyen examined the saddlebags. "It looks like we will have enough food." He gestured to his quiver. "If not, we can always hunt for our meals."

Madigan approached from the stable gate. "Are you ready for your journey?"

"Yes," Darwynyen nodded. "I am glad you are here. I have something for you."

"There is no need for a kiss good-bye!" Madigan snickered. "You will only be gone for a couple of weeks!"

I tittered, and Darwynyen spoke in his defense. "You must

have dreamt such a thing, for I would not kiss your unshaven mug if it were the last face left in these lands!"

Amidst laughter, Madigan embraced Darwynyen. "Be careful, my brother. Take care of Arianna."

I was not finished with the banter. "I think you meant to say that I should take care of him!"

We again broke out in laughter.

Madigan nudged Darwynyen aside and took me by the shoulders. "Take care, my sister. I do not wish to finish this war without you!"

"You do the same." I blinked away the forming tears. "I will miss you in our absence."

Madigan turned to Darwynyen. "You said you had something for me."

"Yes." Darwynyen reached into his pocket. "I will leave you with my Hellum's Dew," he handed Madigan a small bottle. "Use it wisely," he advised.

Madigan took it with widened eyes. "Thank you. Your gift is a generous one." When they embraced each other for the last time, my heart warmed to Darwynyen's selfless gesture.

"Are we ready?" Sikes shouted from the stairs. Gin followed.

"Only you can answer that question," Darwynyen smirked, "as you are the last to arrive."

"I had to find the fairies." Sikes rolled his eyes. "They take their rest in the oddest places."

"Where are they now?" I asked.

"They are gathering their belongings and will join us en route." Sikes replied.

I nodded, and then I looked at Gin. Not only was I proud that he was to accompany us, I was again thankful that he had survived the beatings he had endured from General Corbett to do so.

"Arianna." Gin looked at me oddly. "Is everything all right?"

"Yes." I smiled. "Excuse me. It was not my intention to stare. I was only thinking about the past for a moment."

"It seems I was mistaken." Darwynyen scanned the area. "We still wait on Dregby."

"I will find him." I headed for the servant's entrance.

Darwynyen followed me for a few paces. "He is in the quarters next to Gin."

"I know the way." I nodded, rushing up the stairs.

When I reached Dregby's door, I knocked lightly.

"Enter!" he yelled.

I opened the door to find him filling one of his satchels. "Arianna, I was just going to look for you. Are we ready to leave?"

"Yes." I glanced over the room. "We have been waiting for you at the stable."

"For one reason or another, I overslept," he said, exasperated, and he began to rush. "I will not be a minute."

I nodded, examining his pickaxe that leaned on the bed. "May I?"

When he noted my stare, he nodded. "Of course, my dear, but be careful, for the blade is very sharp."

His caution reminded me of my uncle, and for a moment I almost saw a likeness. "I will," I replied, and I knelt to observe it. The neck itself carried a string of engravings, and the grip was wrapped in an intricately braided leather strap. "It is beautiful—I mean, for a weapon, that is." I led my finger across the symbols.

He joined me, kneeling on his forelegs. "This axe has been in my family for countless generations. The training that came with its inheritance will allow me to defend you with my life." His brow lifted. "As you know, this quest will no doubt lead us to one danger or another."

I was taken aback by his words. The thought of looming danger had never occurred to me. "What … what do you mean?" I stammered.

"There are many possibilities to consider," he replied. "For one, on our return back to Aarrondirth we will travel through the forests that surround Iramak, an area that is heavily guarded by the little people." His tone deepened. "If they do not welcome us, we will have no choice but to navigate our way through their traps unassisted."

"What kind of traps?" I asked objectively, assuming by his manner that his only intention was to try to dissuade me from choosing that path.

"There are too many of them for me to describe." He stood. "But know this; each of those snares will be well hidden and fatal to any who stumble upon them."

Although my first instinct was to challenge him, I decided to continue the conversation in an amicable manner. "How is it you know of these things?" I asked. "You speak as though you have traveled through this region before."

"No," he returned to fill his satchel. "My forefathers, who once traded with their grand master, spoke of this. They also said that their main settlement, Iramak, is carved deep into the cliffs of the river Tanmeen and that their dwellings look like pigeonholes to the untrained eye." He winked. "What I am trying to say is that, despite their best efforts, they got lost several times."

I chuckled. "Do the little people have a name for their kind?"

He secured his axe to his back. "If they do, I do not know it."

Realizing that we had wasted more than enough time, I moved to the door. "Are you ready then?"

"As ready as I will ever be." He finished securing his satchel around his torso, and then he followed me through the opening.

When we arrived at the stables, the men were standing around impatiently. "What has taken you so long?" Darwynyen looked sharply at Dregby.

I put my hand to Dregby's shoulder when I saw him angering. "If there is blame to be placed, let it fall to me, for I was the cause of his delay."

"Little time has been lost," Sikes remarked, leading the horse through the stable gates. "Let us not bicker and instead make way."

Dregby kicked his hooves then trotted off in the direction of the barbican.

"Wait for us!" Zenley appeared from above the stable roof. Teshna flew up behind him.

Sikes opened the pocket on his jacket and allowed them to fly in. "Stay out of sight while we travel through the city."

Teshna nodded, closing the flap on the pocket once Zenley was inside.

As we walked through the courtyard, I could not help but feel anxious. Not only was I traveling to lands I had not seen before, the journey was in search of a wizard who for one reason or another had sent himself to self-exile. I could not help but wonder, under the circumstances, if Archemese would accept our proposed union or even welcome us, for that matter. Either way, there was no turning back now. With that in mind, I glanced over at my companions, they who would stand by me whatever the outcome, and reassured myself that this was indeed our path.

† † †

Night was once again upon us. It had taken two days of travel to reach the little fishing village known as Brownen, the place where we would sell our horse and secure a boat that would see us through the remainder of our journey.

The small settlement itself was nestled in an inlet that would take us directly to the loch of Walferd. Several meager establishments and a few row houses lined the one and only street. As we passed by the local pub, a few patrons standing near the door turned with looks of suspicion, making it apparent that strangers were not welcome. "Pull the hoods on your cloaks," Darwynyen directed. "We do not want to attract any unnecessary attention."

As we concealed ourselves, an older man approached from

one of the row houses. Darwynyen halted. "If you would be kind enough to direct us, we are in need of a boat."

"Why?" The man placed his hands over his large belly. "What is your business here in Brownen?" His eyes wandered to Dregby. "I see you travel with a Mider. We have not seen his kind for …"

"Our business is our own to contend with," Darwynyen replied sternly.

"I was only asking." The man adjusted his trousers when they began to slip from his waist. "If it is a boat you need, stop at the last house on the right, just before the docks. The people who live there will be able to assist you."

"Thank you." Darwynyen nodded, ushering us forward.

When we reached the house across from the docks, Darwynyen stepped up to the door and knocked on it briskly.

Moments later the face of a middle-age woman appeared through a window to the right. "What do you want?" she growled, lifting a small axe into view. "We do not take kindly to strangers!"

"We are in need of a boat," Darwynyen explained. "Where is the man of this house?"

"He is at the dock." She took a step back, gripping the axe tensely.

Darwynyen raised his hands, stepping back.

She quickly closed the curtains.

"They are not a welcoming sort, are they?" Dregby huffed.

"Perhaps we will have better luck at the docks," I sighed.

"We shall see," Darwynyen mumbled as we took our leave.

When we reached the dock, we found a single lantern hanging from one of the posts along the main plank, and through its flickering glow, I saw the outline of a man. He appeared to be unraveling a rope.

"You there!" Darwynyen raised his hand.

Gin took Darwynyen by the arm. "Allow me."

And though Darwynyen appeared offended, he stood aside.

"You, sir." Gin made his way across the dock. "We are in need of a boat."

"There are no boats for sale here," the scrawny man replied, tossing the rope aside. "You should best be making your way to the next village."

"That is not an option." Gin extended his hand in my direction. "The woman we travel with is very ill. We need to get her to a healer immediately." Gin looked at me with widened eyes. Acknowledging his ploy, I put my hand to my stomach and started coughing. "This ailment is like nothing we have seen before," he warned. "If we do not get her to Walferd, there is no telling …"

"Will it spread?" The man took a step back.

Gin ignored his question. "If you sell us your boat, we have gold to offer in trade." Gin gestured to Dregby, who in turn handed him a small satchel of gold. "If that does not satisfy you, then think of your people. If we are forced to stay …"

"Enough!" The man shielded his mouth with his sleeve. "Twenty gold pieces will do."

"We will give you fifteen pieces and our horse, nothing more," Gin bargained, looking at me sharply as he pointed toward the horse. In response, I continued to cough.

"Done!" The man took another step back. "Take this boat." He gestured toward the one next to him. "It is yours for the horse and fifteen gold pieces."

As Gin settled the debt, we began to stow our belongings. The man, eager to be rid of us, kept silent during the transaction, and then he ran off when his gold was in hand.

In his absence, we shared a laugh to ease the tension before setting off.

Darwynyen and Sikes took lead in the boat. Their elvish eyes could see things under the cover of night that we could not, making it easier for them to paddle us through the marsh-like passage that followed the narrow inlet.

"We are lost," Dregby grumbled. "You can tell by the lag in

the current that we have drifted off course. We should wait until first light before proceeding."

"No." Darwynyen lifted his oar from the water. "We are not far. I can see the loch up ahead."

"Your eyes, despite their ability, deceive you, my friend," Dregby countered. "If there were open water ahead, the estuary would have widened by now."

Gin anchored his legs and stood at the stern. "Quiet, I hear something!"

"You hear the current where the inlet connects to the loch," Darwynyen huffed. "As I said, we have reached our destination."

When we passed through the last bushel of reeds, the loch came into view. Its reflection appeared like a slab of muted glass on the horizon.

"We have made it to the loch of Walferd!" Gin bellowed, reaching for an oar. "Let us make way!"

Zenley and Teshna emerged from Sikes's pocket. "Where are we?" Teshna yawned.

"We have arrived at the loch," Sikes replied.

"May we offer our service and scout the land ahead?" Zenley asked, stretching his limbs before taking flight.

"Yes," Sikes nodded. "We will need your eyes during this part of the journey."

Teshna flew to my face. "We will meet you on the loch at midday, unless of course we find something."

I nodded. "Be careful."

"See you soon!" Teshna replied as they disappeared into the darkness.

Before long, the sky began to turn sapphire, shedding its light on the unknown landscape around us. Eager to better acquaint myself with the surroundings, I began to scan the banks. Waterfowl drifted among the reeds that sprung from the shallow pools of water along the shoreline. Kingfishers jumped from limb to limb, searching for their breakfast, while crickets chirped in the thicket. Beyond the banks, fields of green extended as far as the eye could see.

Gin rested his oar when he saw two ducks take flight in the distance. "Perhaps we should forego our rations and take advantage of what nature has provided us."

Appalled by his proposal, I looked at him with disgust. "Why would you say such a thing?" It was difficult for me to see a meal within the splendor of nature I was now witnessing. "There is no need to spill any blood when we have plenty of food to sustain us!"

Gin and Dregby chortled obnoxiously.

Frustrated, I looked at Darwynyen. "Have you nothing to say on this matter?"

"Nothing you would care to hear," Dregby grumbled.

"We will not hunt unless we need to." Darwynyen eyed both Dregby and Gin. "Is that clear?"

Gin and Dregby glanced at one another and then shrugged. "I suppose there is no need to argue this point until we have run out of food," Dregby relented.

In the silence that followed, I drifted into thought. Was I being irrational? There were, after all, many variables on this quest to consider. We could run out of food at any time should we get lost or hindered by the weather. And with no healers, soldiers, or magic to protect us, it might be wise to prepare for the worst, regardless of my hopes for a positive outcome.

Gin pointed to the northwest. "Look, we have reached the forest of Naksteed."

When I saw the jagged cliffs that rose among the forest, a chill ran over my body, a sensation I had long forgotten. We had come to the place that Aldraveena had shared with me in her vision, the place where we had stumbled across my father. "My father …" I hesitated. "If I am not mistaken, this is the route he traveled on his way to Cessdorn."

"How do you know this, Arianna?" Darwynyen furrowed his brow.

"I saw him. I mean… Aldraveena and I saw him in a vision she shared with me in Maglavine."

"Why did you not speak of this before?"

"With everything else that was happening, I guess I forgot." I bit my lip.

"It would be reasonable for him to take this route," Sikes remarked. "It is the quickest way outside of the Man's Blood region."

"If we had known sooner," Darwynyen huffed, "we could have tracked him."

"How?" I challenged defensively. "We were in Maglavine at the time."

Sikes put his hand on Darwynyen's shoulder. "Velderon was lost to us the moment he fled Aarrondirth. There was nothing we could have done about it, then or now."

Darwynyen calmed. "Forgive me, Arianna. It was wrong of me to react that way."

I nodded, returning my gaze to the forest. If I was right and this was the place I saw in the vision, I wondered how far my father had gotten in his journey. The terrain in the north was unfamiliar to me, but when it came to reuniting the stones, his determination was enough for me to believe that he was nearing Cessdorn. I could only hope that his ambitions were delayed when he attempted to assume control over the sorcerers. It was not that I favored their control over his, but at this point in time they were the last obstacle I could foresee in his path.

"Arianna." Dregby shifted his forelegs to lean on one of the benches. "I see now that you enjoy the wilds."

Although I was not in the mood for conversation, I turned to face him. "I do." I managed a smile. "The simplicity of nature brings me ease."

When he shifted again, it was plain to see his discomfort. His boar-like body would not allow him to sit on the benches like the rest of us. Instead, he was forced to lie in the hull of the boat, a factor I should probably have taken into consideration when I invited him. "Does my love of nature surprise you?" I asked, making my way unsteadily toward the middle bench. If I could not hasten the journey, the least I could do was give him more room.

When I stumbled, Sikes reached out to assist me.

"Arianna, what are you doing?" Darwynyen asked sharply, steadying the boat.

"If you must know, I was seeing to another's comfort," I replied sternly, eyeing Dregby.

Dregby slowly stretched out his hind legs. "And your gesture is most welcome."

Darwynyen dug his oar into the water, ignoring us.

"I hope you can forgive me." I glanced over Dregby's lower extremities. "When I asked you to accompany us, I overlooked your ability to travel by boat."

"I can travel by any means," he replied boldly. "The boat itself is not the issue, it is the size of it."

"Of course, and if we had …" I broke off and then diverted the subject before I unintentionally insulted him. "Will you tell me about your homeland?" I asked. "As you know, I have not been to your region before."

"Well, let me see …" He began to caress his beard. When I prodded him impatiently, he chuckled. "Patience, my dear. I am trying to think of something that might interest you."

I shifted in my seat. "You could tell me about Vidorr."

"Now that is a story in itself." He tapped my hand. "We Miders live deep within the ground. Our cities are vast, far larger than Aarrondirth." I saw a spark in his eyes as he spoke. "Our bodies are built for hard labor, and the ability to haul heavy loads on our backs has allowed us to develop an enormous region of the underworld."

"Why would you choose to live underground?" I frowned. "Do your people not miss the light of day?"

He cocked his head. "We utilize sunlight through our shafts. We capture its rays through carefully placed mirrors and route them into various parts of our keep." He paused. "Besides, sunlight is of little importance to us. As you know, our main ambition is our treasure, and that is why the Miders are the wealthiest of men in these regions."

"Yes." I rolled my eyes. "I know of your love for gold, but what about your family? Do you have a wife … children?"

"I have both." He pulled out a handful of trinkets. "My wife has borne me nine children. These are the birth symbols for each of them." As he shifted the tiny pieces around with his fingers, sadness appeared in his eyes. "To my regret, I have not seen them for over a year now."

Sympathizing with his pain, I felt compelled to reach out to him. "You must miss them terribly."

"I do, but I am very fortunate." He returned the trinkets to his pocket. "Despite our time apart, my wife continues to support me." He winked. "And that is a miracle in itself, for Mider women can be very demanding!"

"I see!" I giggled. "How long have you been married?"

"Sixteen years," he boasted, and then he paused in reflection. "That woman means everything to me."

"Then why have you chosen to be here?" I asked.

"The decision was not mine to make," he replied. "As the eldest brother of four, I was given no choice but to take my father's seat on the Mider council at the time of his passing, a seat that was bound to the Men of Moya. Thus I am also bound to them."

"Are you saying that you are here for duty alone? I asked.

"You misunderstand." He put his hand to his chest. "To continue in my father's legacy was an honor."

"Does your sentiment extend to the Men of Moya?" I searched his eyes.

"No one wants this role, my dear." He took my hand in his. "Like you, I do what I must. The shadow of the stones extends well beyond your people. It is a burden we all share, a regretful outcome of the last war, when only one of the three stones was recovered."

I asked, "Do you know why only one of the stones was recovered?"

"I can only tell you what is written in the scriptures." He gave Darwynyen a fleeting look before continuing. "The elves who wrote them stated that the armies were unable to reach Cessdorn before the eve of the third and last cycle." His eyes darkened. "Thereafter, the repercussions came swiftly. The sorcerers did not sit idle. When the stones were reunited, they conjured creatures known as Fegas from the sands."

"What are these creatures you speak about?" I asked.

"The Fegas are unnatural, brought about to serve their masters alone," he replied. "And the sorcerers were to show no mercy. The attacks thereafter were relentless, for the creatures do not tire as do you or I, nor do they feel pain." He lowered his voice when Darwynyen glanced over his shoulder. "Outnumbered and fatigued from the previous battle, our forces had no alternative but to retreat once the three chosen ones had been escorted to the realm." He raised his brow. "Do you know of the chosen ones?"

"I know little," I replied. "Who were they?"

"They were simple men. Two were farmers, I believe." His hand caressed his beard as he thought. "It came as a surprise when a seer, one who had the ear of the king, had claimed to see them in a vision. The seer stated that their lives were somehow tied to the stones and that they would see us to victory if we could somehow get them into the realm of Cessdorn." He gave Darwynyen another fleeting look. "You did not hear this from me, but some believe that this seer was an impostor."

"Why?" I sat forward with interest.

"Because when the chosen ones arrived at the altar, the sorcerers were awaiting them," he explained. "The men, with no means to protect themselves, were overcome by a spell that slowly began to turn them to stone. Despite the excruciating pain, one of the men did not give up and lunged toward the stones, clutching the one nearest to him, securing it within his arms before the transformation was complete." Dregby's eyes lightened. "At that moment the Fegas dissolved back into the land. With no one to stand in their way, the armies set forth immediately, leaving the sorcerers with no choice but to flee with the remaining two stones."

"Where did they go?" I asked.

"No one knows." He shrugged. "They disappeared without a trace." I was about to respond when he raised his hand to silence me. "It was this outcome that led to the creation of the Men of Moya. Not only are we bound to these stones, we are also bound to the Amberseed, for those who seek the stones only do so in hopes of utilizing their power to search for the seed. Something we cannot allow to happen."

As I absorbed his words, I thought of my father, whose motivations had suddenly become clear. The stones were only a means to an end. To obtain the ultimate power, he would do as Aldraveena had warned and take over the Hynd. After that he would conjure the Fegas, a distraction that would allow him to pursue the Amberseed. His arrogance would demand it. This overconfidence, however, appeared to be a weakness, one I would use against him when opportunity allowed.

"Arianna, are you all right?" Dregby frowned.

"Yes." I grabbed the ledge of the boat as I stood. "I think I have heard enough."

He swallowed deeply. "I did not mean to upset you."

"You did no such thing." I spoke with assurance. "In fact, you have empowered my will. And for that, I thank you." With nothing left to say, I slowly stepped to the bow of the boat and joined Darwynyen, knowing his presence would comfort me.

Warning

Morglafenn sat up in his bed in a panic. Something was wrong. "Was I sleeping?" he gasped. "Impossible, I have not slept for years." As he tried to recall his thoughts, he realized that they were lost to him. Unsettled, he put his hand to his pendant of life, wondering if it was still working. He shook the thought, knowing there was little point in dwelling on something that would be revealed to him with a little patience and time. He was an elf after all, and succumbing to emotions was forbidden.

After dressing, he made his way to the kitchen. He found the porridge pots empty. Irritated, he turned impatiently to one of the cooks. "Is there more breakfast to be served?"

The man glanced over his shoulder with a perplexed look upon his face. "We finished serving breakfast over an hour ago."

Morglafenn's chest tightened. It was very unusual for him to rest past sunrise. "What is the hour?" he asked.

"We will be serving midday dinner soon, if you care to wait," the man offered.

Morglafenn released a heavy breath. "Is there any fruit in this kitchen?"

The man shook his head and then continued chopping the carrots that were laid out on the cutting board.

"Very well." Morglafenn reached for a knife. As he began

to cut off slices of cheese, thoughts of Darwynyen and Arianna entered his mind.

Madigan appeared at the door. "Morglafenn, Kendrick is looking for you."

Despondent, Morglafenn slowly turned to him with glazed eyes.

"Morglafenn!" Madigan took a small loaf of bread from the baked goods bucket. "Did you hear me?"

Morglafenn dropped the knife.

"What is it?" Madigan frowned.

"The evil presence," Morglafenn whispered. "It seems to have vanished."

"Is that not good news?" Madigan bit into the loaf.

"Perhaps." Morglafenn turned to cut his cheese. "Did you say Kendrick was looking for me?"

"Yes." Madigan finished swallowing. "He is on his way to the library."

Morglafenn nodded. "I will see to him now." Not waiting for a response, he set down the knife, took the cheese, and then left the room.

Rough Water

When I opened my eyes, rays of sunlight blinded me. To my dismay, evening twilight was still a few hours ahead. Frustrated by my inability to sleep, I placed my hand on the pendant, wondering if its power would ever allow me a moment of repose.

As I stretched my limbs, I noticed that Dregby and Gin were sound asleep at the stern. Envious, I focused on Darwynyen and Sikes, who were manning the boat. The exhaustion on their faces was obvious. And though I was concerned, I chose not to speak about the matter, for trying times such as these were to be expected. When I reached for my satchel, Darwynyen glanced over his shoulder.

"Did you rest well?"

"Yes." I pulled out a wrap and then sat next to him as I secured it around my shoulders. "How are you faring?"

"I am fine." He managed a smile.

I was about to respond when I saw an outline of a man on horseback on the northern side of the loch. He was leading his horse to the water's edge. As my eyes focused, my stomach tightened. It was no man—it was one of those creatures who had attack Darwynyen, Shallendria, and I at the farmhouse on our way to Maglavine.

"Grackens," I said.

"Where?" Darwynyen asked, steadying his oar.

"Over there on the horizon." I pointed.

He looked, and he put his hand over my mouth. "Keep quiet. With the glare of sunlight in our favor we may go unnoticed."

Sikes slowly reached for an arrow.

"What is going on?" Dregby sat up groggy.

"Quiet!" Sikes turned sharply. "We see a Gracken on the northern bank."

Darwynyen slowly pulled his oar from the water. "If the Gracken sees, smells, or hears us, it will follow our path and wait for us to make landfall."

"Then put your oar back in the water," Dregby insisted. "We must hasten our pace!"

"Have you heard nothing I have said?" Darwynyen glared. "Keep quiet, or you will put us all at risk."

When Dregby nodded, we returned our focus to the Gracken.

As we watched its silhouette disappear on the horizon, Zenley and Teshna emerged from over the bow of the boat. Zenley flew to my face. "Did you see the Gracken?"

Darwynyen asked, "Was the creature traveling alone?"

"Yes." Zenley nodded with conviction.

Teshna landed on Sikes's shoulder. "Do not fear, the Gracken was not alerted to your presence and now makes its return to the forest."

"Come." Darwynyen put his oar back into the water and began to paddle. "We must hasten our pace." Sikes followed his lead.

In response, Dregby woke Gin and handed him an oar. "The time to rest has ended, my friend."

As Gin took hold of the oar, I continued to scan the banks. Although the potential for conflict was behind us, there was no telling what could be waiting for us up ahead.

† † †

After another day of travel, the landscape began to change. The green pastures and bordering forests that I had grown accustomed to had given way to massive sandstone cliffs. For the most part, the landscape was desolate. Clusters of driftwood and dead foliage had gathered along the banks; the loch had begun to close in around us. As we entered the mouth of the canyon, the echo of rapids could be heard up ahead, and the water lightened to a pale shade of green.

"The current is growing swift." Sikes looked at Darwynyen. "Perhaps we should wake the others."

"Let us give them a few more minutes." Darwynyen dug his oar deep into the water.

Sikes nodded reluctantly. "A few more minutes they shall have," he mumbled.

When we passed the first bend, the flow of the current intensified. Jagged boulders protruded from the water along the banks. In the calmer pools, blankets of foam had accumulated. Trapped in the narrow canyon, we were soon forced into the rapids, and the boat began to sway and grind. "Gin, wake up!" Darwynyen demanded. "Take hold of your oar!"

Gin sat up in a flustered state. When he saw our predicament, he grabbed his oar, digging it deep into the aggravated current.

Dregby opened his eyes. "Where are we?"

No one responded, and Sikes glanced over his shoulder. "Stay in the center of the boat!" he ordered. "We must maintain our balance!"

As Dregby steadied himself between two of the benches, Darwynyen looked at me. "Arianna, move to the stern and help Gin steer!"

I nodded, stumbling to the back of the boat.

Gin fought to keep our direction straight. "Arianna, I can do most of the work. When I tell you, put your oar flat in the current. If you are able to slow us, it will help me turn."

I took hold of the remaining oar in anticipation. I had never seen rapids such as these and was too frightened to speak.

As we approached the next bend, riled waves began to strike the boat. Splinters of water pelted my face. Up and down, up and down—the constant movement was stirring my stomach. When I wiped my eyes, I saw a massive boulder in the distance, protruding from the centre of the waterway. Darwynyen and Sikes saw it too and looked at one another apprehensively. "Which side?" Sikes shouted. "Either way looks deadly!"

"Where are the fairies?" Darwynyen growled. "Why are they not here to guide us?"

"Forget the fairies!" Sikes snapped. "Make your decision!"

When Darwynyen looked at me, I nodded in support.

"We shall go right!" Darwynyen tightened his grip on the oar. "There are not as many rocks that way!"

As we frantically paddled, the undertow began to pull us toward the boulder. "Harder! Paddle harder!" Darwynyen demanded.

Our attempts were in vain. The boat struck the boulder hard. Darwynyen turned. "Gin, use your oar to push us free!"

Before Gin could take action, Dregby jumped up and kicked his hind legs against the rock face. It was enough. The force pushed us back into the current.

The boat began to swirl. While Gin fought to regain our bearings, I noticed a cloud of mist before us. It was accompanied by a dense rumbling sound that was echoing down the corridor. Realizing what was ahead, I grabbed Gin by the arm. "The water drops ahead! I have seen this once before at Lake Vanderbrood with my uncle. We must make way for the bank!"

"Not now, Arianna!" Gin pulled from my hold. "We must first get our bearings!"

Darwynyen stood unsteadily, gripping the bow tightly. "No, she is right. There is a fall up ahead!"

"Look!" I pointed to the east, where the cliff gave way to a narrow strip of land. "We could go ashore there!"

The men nodded in agreement, and Gin and I fought to slow

our speed in the current while Darwynyen and Sikes paddled us into a calmer pool of water near the bank.

My arms had begun to weaken as the current finally released us. Out of danger, Gin anchored the boat with his oar, enabling Dregby to jump into the shallows and lead us in.

Once the boat was secure, we stepped onto the sandy embankment and took a moment to recover. And though I could not speak for my companions, I for one had never been so relieved to have my feet on solid ground.

"I was not expecting an obstacle such as this," Darwynyen remarked. "While light is still in our favor, we should see what lies ahead." Not waiting for a response, he turned and began to climb the embankment that led to the crest of the waterfall.

With little more than a nod, we followed.

When we reached the plateau, Dregby stomped his hooves. "There is nothing to be seen from here," he huffed, eyeing the cliffs on the opposite side of the fall. "The path before us is hidden beyond that bend."

Darwynyen looked at Sikes. "Where are those fairies?" he grumbled.

Sikes raised his hands helplessly, "How am I to know where they have gotten to?"

Gin nudged Dregby. "Your strength is impressive, my friend. If it were not for you, we might still be stuck on that rock face."

Dregby blinked. "It is a shame that you only recognize my strengths during a time of weakness." He gave Darwynyen a fleeting look. "My body may be different from yours, but those differences should only add value to what I am already able to offer."

When I saw Darwynyen tense, I stood forward. "That is precisely why I asked you to join us on this quest." I met each of their stares before continuing. "We all have our uses."

"Does that include the fairies?" Darwynyen retorted, eyeing Sikes.

"Why do you look to me? I am not their keeper," Sikes replied defensively. "Need I remind you that they are very fickle in their ways?"

When Darwynyen crossed his arms stubbornly, I stepped toward the fall. "Is there any need to bicker?" I asked, as I led my hand through the lingering mist that hovered over the precipice. "Instead, we should be thankful, for I fear that we would not have survived the plummet if we had not set aside our differences earlier and chosen to cooperate." The tension seemed to ease as I spoke. "If we can place our trust in one another when the situation is dire, there is no reason why we cannot do it now."

In the silence that followed, the men looked at one another uncomfortably. I was about to continue when Dregby stepped forward. "Perhaps we should set camp," he offered. "The hour is late, and it will take time to move the boat down this embankment."

"You are right," Darwynyen concurred. "There is little time to waste if we intend to set out first thing in the morning."

When the others nodded, we slowly began our descent down the embankment.

† † †

After what seemed like an eternity of constant bickering, the men managed to haul the boat to the other side of the waterfall. And though a part of me was finding humor in their escapades, I worked steadily to make sure the camp was prepared for their return.

When their silhouettes appeared at the top of the embankment, I began to divide our rations. The conversation was minimal as they sat and began to eat.

Because there was no wood, we had to forgo a fire, and without its enchantment we had no choice but to take an early night.

Now that sleep had forsaken me, my thoughts were disrupted by a resonating snore from the opposite side of the camp. It was Dregby, and in the passing minutes, his grunts slowly deepened, echoing throughout the corridor. At first I was annoyed, but after a while, the constant hum allowed me to focus and eventually succumb to the trancelike state that was brought on by the magic in Aldraveena's pendant.

Ill at Ease

Darwynyen stirred before the others. Although his first impulse was to reach out for Arianna, he chose not to and instead moved toward Sikes. He wanted to speak with his trusted companion alone. After a gentle nudge, Sikes opened his eyes. Before Sikes could speak, Darwynyen put his finger to his lips, and in silent agreement they both set off in the direction of the waterfall.

As they climbed the embankment, Darwynyen spoke. "I wish to speak with you about Gin."

"What about Gin?" Sikes glanced over his shoulder toward the camp.

"The more time I spend in his company, the more I grow wary." Darwynyen held out his hand to assist Sikes to the plateau. "It is difficult to explain, but something about him troubles me."

Sikes released a heavy breath. "I would be better able to sympathize with you, my friend, if I were certain that these ill feelings did not stem from another reason."

Darwynyen's eyes widened. "What exactly are you implying, Sikes?"

"Nothing." Sikes blinked heavily. "Perhaps you are being too hard on the boy. From where I stand, he has done nothing but prove himself." He held out his hands helplessly. "Either way, there is nothing we can do now that Madigan and Arianna have placed their trust in him."

After considering Sikes's appeal, Darwynyen conceded. "You are right. Our options are few when it comes to Arianna. Besides, she has been through enough."

Sikes knelt to move his hand through the mist. "Is it conceivable that you have overlooked the fact that Gin is very young in our terms and that with his youth comes naivety?"

"His youth has nothing to do with the way I feel," Darwynyen insisted. "It is his character that brings up these suspicions."

"Then we do not see eye to eye on this matter." Sikes stood. "I quite like the lad and will not give into your conjecture until it has been proven."

Frustrated, Darwynyen left the plateau. "Let us return. If you will not listen to reason, there is no point in drawing any unnecessary suspicion."

Sikes imperviously and then followed.

The Journey Continues

When I opened my eyes, I was surprised to find that Darwynyen was not at my side. Sikes was missing also. They must have left to survey the land. As I sat up, I noticed that Gin and Dregby were still sleeping. And though I was jealous of the peaceful look upon their faces, I decided not to wake them. After all, it was no fault of theirs that I could find no slumber. Instead, I quietly stepped toward the river, to wash myself free of the journey's grime.

After removing my boots, I pulled up my trouser legs and stepped into a shallow pool of cold water along the bank. I immediately stiffened, resisting the impulse to flee. After a few moments, my body adjusted. As I splashed some water on my face, I saw Darwynyen and Sikes returning from the direction of the waterfall, waving as they approached.

Darwynyen met me near the water's edge. "Good morning, my love." He kissed my brow. "Were you able to find some rest?"

"For the most part." I stepped onto a flattened stone near the bank and began to shake the water from my feet. "My body appears to be adjusting to the pendant."

He nodded and then turned to the others. "Time to wake!" He clapped his hands. "We have a long day ahead of us!"

Dregby and Gin began to stir, and before long everyone was up and about. As Sikes and I packed our belongings, Gin took a dip in a calmer part of the river. "You can take this one." I handed Sikes a satchel. "I will meet you at the boat shortly."

Sikes nodded, securing his bedroll under his free arm before making way.

"I will haul the rest of the satchels on my back." Dregby winked as he swallowed the last of his rations. "There is no need to make extra trips when I am around."

I smiled as I stood. "Thank you."

As I helped him stow the rest of our belongings, I noticed Darwynyen standing on a boulder near the bank. He was watching Gin with an intense look upon his face. Curious, I left Dregby to join him. "Is everything all right?" I stepped onto the boulder.

"Why do you ask?" He took my hand in his.

"You seem a bit distracted this morning." I tightened my hold.

He looked down to avoid eye contact. "I am fine."

Although his mood concerned me, I did not have the patience to confront him, and I released his hand. "Gin!" I stepped forward to wave him in from the river. "Come, we need to be on our way."

"Of course." He wiped his eyes and then headed for the bank.

"Are we ready?" Sikes shouted from the plateau.

"Yes." Darwynyen helped me from the boulder, and after quickly surveying the remnants of our camp, he led me in the direction of the boat.

Gin followed shortly.

† † †

To my relief, the water on the opposite side of the falls was calmer. And though the corridor was misleading and our predicament could change without warning, I was determined to enjoy the quiet time while it lasted.

As I stretched my legs out along the middle bench, I saw Teshna and Zenley appear from around the bend.

"The fairies." I pointed as they neared. "They have returned!"

When Teshna and Zenley landed on Sikes's shoulder, Darwynyen bluntly set his oar across the bow of the boat. "It is typical of you to return at a time when we do not need you."

"We were scouting the land." Teshna fluttered her wings. "It will please you to know that your journey through this corridor is soon to end."

"What do you mean by 'soon'?" Darwynyen grumbled, placing his oar back into the water.

"One more day, and you will arrive at the coast," Zenley replied.

"Shall we expect any more waterfalls in the interim?" Darwynyen's tone was condescending. "Where were you yesterday?"

Teshna put her arms around her waist. "As I said, we were scouting the lands."

"Then why did you not warn us of the waterfall?" Darwynyen glared.

When Sikes looked at Darwynyen oddly, I was reminded of Morglafenn's warnings.

Teshna shrugged with a look of bewilderment. "I suppose we never thought to look for that sort of danger."

Darwynyen stiffened. Before he could respond, I changed the subject. "Can you tell us more about the land up ahead? Are there trees? Will we have the luxury of a fire tonight?" I glanced to Darwynyen with an enthusiastic smile. "If so, perhaps one of us could catch some fish."

Zenley nodded. "If fire and fish are what you seek, I can assure you that you will not be disappointed."

"Excellent!" Dregby chuckled. "I despise the thought of another night of rations."

The others laughed at Dregby's remark, but I noticed that Darwynyen still appeared frustrated.

I rubbed his back. "Darwynyen, does the thought of freshly cooked fish not entice you?"

"Of course it does." He managed a smiled.

"Then let us hasten our pace." Dregby clasped his hands together. "My stomach rumbles as we speak!"

In response, Darwynyen and Sikes dug their oars into the water.

Twilight was upon us when we found a suitable shoreline to moor the boat. While the others surveyed the banks, Gin and I set camp.

"Dregby, get out of the water!" Sikes taunted as he removed his boots. "Your soiled hooves will only scare the fish away!"

"I think not!" Dregby challenged. "Do you banter because you are afraid that I might catch more fish than you?"

"Do I sense a wager brewing?" Darwynyen raised his brow.

Sikes rolled his eyes. "Darwynyen, please. Despite Dregby's strengths, there would be no contest should he attempt to match my hunting skills."

"You are right." Dregby picked up a dead branch and began to sharpen its end with a knife. "There would be no contest where you are concerned."

Darwynyen crossed his arms smugly. "Arianna, do you care to make a wager?"

I bit my lip for a moment and then conceded. "I suppose it would do no harm."

"I will place two gold pieces on Dregby." Gin dropped the bundle of wood he was carrying to the ground.

Undecided, I looked at Darwynyen. "Who do you favor?"

"Sikes, of course." He pulled two coins from his waist purse.

Dregby turned to me in a coy manner. "My dear Arianna, do you have no confidence in me?"

"Of course I do." I finished placing the last stone on the fire pit. "Forgive me, Sikes …" I hesitated in a moment of guilt, "but my gold will be placed on Dregby."

Pleased by my decision, Dregby tested his makeshift spear in an ostentatious manner.

"So be it," Sikes accepted flippantly. "You will come to regret your decision."

Before I could respond, Teshna and Zenley flew to my face. "Did we hear you speak of a wager?" Zenley asked.

"Yes," I replied. "Dregby and Sikes will vie for fish." I gestured toward Sikes and Dregby. "Who do you believe will win?"

"We have no money for a wager." Teshna fluttered her wings. "And even if we did, it would not be spent foolishly on a game of chance."

"Are you certain?" I jingled my change purse. "Should you change your mind, I have two gold pieces to spare."

Zenley pulled Teshna aside, whispering in her ear. After several moments of deliberation they returned. "We choose Sikes," Zenley stated with confidence.

Sikes eyed Dregby, who had positioned himself on a flattened stone that extended over the bank. "Are you ready, my friend?"

When Dregby nodded, Gin and Darwynyen stepped forward with anticipation.

Minutes later Sikes pulled a fish from the water, throwing it to land. Annoyed, Dregby plunged his spear into the pool next to him. When he withdrew it, there was a fish upon the end. Before he could revel in his accomplishment, Sikes tossed another fish into the air. I was unaware, and it struck me in the head. Disgusted, I glared at Sikes. "I hope that was not on purpose!"

Sikes ignored me, slowly placing his hands back into the water.

Darwynyen tried to take hold of the fish that was flipping on the ground next to me, but it slipped out of his hands and back into water, quickly disappearing.

"That one does not count!" Dregby remarked as he moved to spear another fish.

"I am not bothered," Sikes replied smugly. "There are plenty more where that one came from."

Gin knelt on the bank. "Dregby, stay focused, there is …" Before he could finish, a fish struck him in the chest. "What was that for?" He narrowed his eyes at Dregby. "If you have forgotten, my wager was placed on you!"

"And so you have received your reward," Dregby chortled, his eyes fixed on the pool of water.

Before long there were six fish to account for. "Consider this wager over." Darwynyen raised his hands. "It is not the elvish way to waste what nature has given us."

"Darwynyen, I …" Sikes stepped from the water, abashed. "Forgive me. I was carried away by the challenge."

Dregby continued to survey the water. "We will not finish until there is a winner!"

"You have tied." Darwynyen's tone was direct. "We are done here. There is no way for us to preserve what we cannot eat." He knelt at the fire pit. "Instead, let us be grateful as we work to prepare this feast."

Dregby's expression changed to a look of hunger. "You are right, my friend." He threw down his spear. "Allow me to assist you with that fire."

Sikes extended his hand toward Dregby. "Good challenge, my friend. May this be the first of many!"

"Indeed." Dregby squeezed his hand. "Until then, we shall share in the spoils."

Famished and with nothing left to say, we assembled around the fire pit as Darwynyen began to strike the flint.

† † †

Well rested, we again set out in the early hours of the morn. Thankfully, the weather was still in our favor. The crystal blue sky, free of clouds, allowed us to bask in the sunlight as the winding river led us along.

Sikes pulled his oar from the water as we turned the next bend. "There is a fork in the river up ahead."

"Do not allow the path on the left deceive you. Despite its direction, it will steer us away from our destination." Gin stretched his arms before digging his oar back into the water. "We must take the path on the right."

"Gin speaks the truth," Dregby concurred. "If we go left, we will arrive at the city of Iramak, for that watercourse is known as the river Tanmeen."

I closed my eyes, recalling Dregby's tale of the little people and how their city was carved into the cliffs. "If only we could take that route," I sighed. "The closer we come to finding this wizard, the more anxious I become."

When Gin puckered his brow, Darwynyen spoke. "Arianna, try not to worry. What is meant to happen will happen."

I nodded and took one final glance at the southern passage. Darwynyen was right. There was no point in dwelling on things that were, in many ways, beyond my control. I needed to face the future with optimism if we were going to see this quest through to its end.

As the fairies had promised, we arrived at the coastline by midday.

Unlike other places I had visited, the air was heavy with humidity. When I licked my lips, I tasted salt, something I had not experienced before. As I savored the taste, I found myself swept away by the breathtaking beauty. White beaches extended as far as the eye could see. One after another, rolling waves crashed upon the shoreline. As they drew back, the dampened sand appeared like shiny jewels. In the distance, islands jutted through the mist that had settled over the western horizon.

"We must find a way past the reef." Darwynyen lifted his oar from the water. "Any suggestions?" He immediately looked toward Gin.

"We should lead out directly from here," Gin replied. "Otherwise we might capsize."

Darwynyen lifted his brow. "Is that all you have to offer?" His eyes narrowed. "I thought you said you were from this region."

"I am." Gin pulled his oar from the water. "Are you implying that I am not?"

"Darwynyen …" I interjected before they could argue. "We need to stay focused if we are going to find the copper island before nightfall."

"Arianna is right—now is not the time to sit idle." Sikes began to paddle. "Let us be on our way."

"Very well." Darwynyen turned abruptly, digging his oar into the water.

When we were safely beyond the reef, I slid to the end of the bench and slowly leaned overboard. Having never traveled across a sea before, I was curious about its hidden secrets. To my delight, the water was not deep, and the bottom was still visible. Immediately enthralled by the creatures I did not recognize, my heart skipped a beat. It was a world of its own, a circle of life that was almost incomprehensible. "There is plenty of life to see along this reef," Gin remarked with a smile. "It is home to thousands."

"I had no idea." I continued to gaze into the water. "This place is a wonder to me."

"Look over there, Arianna." Dregby pointed off the bow. "There is an octopus floating near that boulder."

When I spotted the creature, I cringed. "Its legs—there are so many!"

"Eight to be exact," he replied. "Be careful. If it is hungry, it might reach out for you!"

I quickly sat back, "I, I do not …"

"Do not tease her!" Gin glared.

"I was only having a little fun," Dregby quipped.

Darwynyen turned, oblivious to our conversation. "Arianna, do you know where this island is?"

"No." I shook my head. "Aldraveena was unable to take me this far in her vision."

He nodded and then looked at Sikes. "Let us make our way around the first island and see what we find."

"Agreed." Sikes began to paddle more vigorously. "We must be swift; the tide is working against us."

As Darwynyen and Gin followed his lead, I picked up my oar to assist them.

Further into our voyage, the concealing haze around the islands slowly dissipated. As I surveyed the landscape, I again found it breathtaking. Each island protruded from the water like a sword. Cliffs of black stone were blanketed with pale green shrubbery that could easily be mistaken for moss. Purple flowers bloomed around the outcroppings that extended from an array of narrow waterfalls. Birds of various colors danced in the mist that hovered over the treed areas beneath them.

Realizing that I was parched, I reached for a mug, dipping it into the water. "You cannot drink from the sea," Darwynyen warned. "The salt will poison you. Take your water from the canteen in the stern of the boat."

I quickly emptied the mug with widened eyes. How could water hold poison, I wondered? To conceal my ignorance, I shrugged it off. Gin passed me the canteen. "Thank you." I took it nonchalantly.

As I sipped, I noticed a faint echo of song along the breeze. "Does anyone hear that?" I searched the area.

"Hear what?" Dregby asked.

"That singing." I put my finger to my lips. "Listen. It is very faint."

Gin put his hand to his ear. "You hear the Sirens. That is how they communicate with one another above water."

"Sirens." I furrowed my brow. Although the name was familiar, I could not place it.

"They are water-dwelling women whose legs give way to scales and fins," Darwynyen replied. "It was a Siren that held the key to Naksteed. Do you remember?"

"Yes." I closed my eyes, recalling the conversation I overheard in the study, when the crone had shared the information about their capture with my father.

Darwynyen surveyed the water. “Do not let their song sway you, Arianna. These creatures are not to be underestimated. As you know, they were responsible for the release of the dragons.”

“Responsible, yes, but not to blame,” Gin countered. “If you knew anything about the Sirens, you would know that they cannot leave the water for an extended period of time. Therefore it is easy to assume that they were tortured, for they would not have relinquished the key without a fight.”

“How do you know this?” I asked. “Have you met one before?”

Gin looked down in his response, “No, I …”

“You defend something you have never seen,” Darwynyen huffed. “I thought you said you were from this region.”

“If you have not already noticed, this region is vast.” Gin glared. “The village where I was raised is further south.”

I was about to speak in Gin’s defense when Zenley flew over the bow. “We apologize for our late arrival.”

“Your arrival is welcome nonetheless.” Sikes rested his oar. “What have you found?”

“Nothing of this copper island you have spoken of.” Zenley glanced toward Teshna, who had flown up next to him. “I fear you will not find your destination before nightfall.”

“Are you certain?” Sikes asked. “There are many small islands in this area. Perhaps you have overlooked one.”

“You misunderstand,” Teshna replied as she landed on Sikes’s shoulder. “There is a hefty crosswind ahead. A storm might soon be upon you.”

“Nonsense.” Dregby put his finger to the air. “I say we push on.”

“You should make your way ashore.” Zenley landed next to his sister. “This boat may not withstand the swells.”

“Have you seen the Sirens?” Gin asked, changing the subject.

"No." Zenley cowered. "By the command of our queen, we are forbidden to seek them out."

"Why?" Gin frowned. "If we had the opportunity to reason with them, they might choose to help us."

Sikes eyed Darwynyen anxiously. "You must not ask the fairies to disobey our queen."

"Your queen is not here," Gin scoffed. "And if she were, I am certain she would make an exception."

Frustrated by the direction of the conversation, I sat forward. "Perhaps we should listen to the fairies and make our way to one of these islands."

Gin was about to respond when a strong nudge hit the hull of the boat. The men quickly stabilized us. "What was that?" Sikes slowly peered overboard.

Darwynyen did the same. "I see nothing."

The force struck again. This time we saw a large tail retreat into the depths of the water near the stern. We had stumbled across a Siren. Unsure what to do, we looked at one another with trepidation. Darwynyen dug his oar into the water. "Paddle—paddle hard! Head for the nearest shore!"

It was of no use. Before we could make way, two hands appeared on the bow. When the Siren lifted her torso over the rim, I gasped in awe, for she was beautiful. Her hair was lengthy and red, her skin like porcelain, and her green eyes shimmered like jewels.

Darwynyen and Sikes sat back, apprehensive. "What do you want?" Darwynyen reached for his quiver. "Leave us now or suffer the consequences!"

"Wait!" I slowly stood to face her. "We mean you no harm." I pulled Aldraveena's pendant from my shirt. "We are here by the request of Aldraveena, queen of the elves. She has asked us to find the wizard Archemese who dwells on one of these islands."

The Siren looked at me oddly for a moment and then pushed herself away from the boat. I helplessly watched her drift away.

"Darwynyen, will you not call to her in elvish? She might not have understood me."

"There is no need." Gin put his hand to his brow. "I can assure you that they speak our language just fine."

With a subtle splash, the Siren descended deep into the water and out of view. "What are we to do now?" I asked in defeat.

"Make our way to shore." Sikes dug his oar into the water. "We have little time, should she decide to return."

Darwynyen followed his lead. "Sikes is right. If she is unwilling to communicate with us, there is no telling her intentions."

Although I was disappointed, I kept silent. In the end, our quest to find the wizard far outweighed my desire to seek the Siren's alliance.

As we paddled toward the nearest shoreline, I caught a glimpse of a large tailfin in the distance. "She returns!" I pointed toward the stern.

The men pulled their oars. Dregby shifted in his seat. "Where?"

I was about to respond when the Siren appeared with another. Her companion was just as beautiful. Atop her head a crown of pearls was woven intricately through her lengthy black hair. Assuming her to be their queen, I nodded when her pale blue eyes fell upon me.

Anxiously, Darwynyen and Sikes grabbed for their weapons.

"Stow your weapons!" the Siren who wore the crown commanded. "If it were our wish to harm you, we would have done so by now."

The men looked at one another with distrust. I spoke to avoid a confrontation. "Why have you returned?" I kept my tone formal. "What do you want, if not to harm us?"

The Siren wearing the crown eyed her companion. "Zhendon has told me that you are here by the request of Queen Aldraveena." Her eyes narrowed suspiciously. "Is this true? Do you carry her pendant?"

"Yes," I replied, lifting it from my shirt. "As I told your companion, the elvish queen has sent us here on a quest in search of the wizard called Archemese."

After examining the pendant, she nodded in acknowledgement. "I am Xiandera, queen of the Sirens." She paused. "You must excuse our suspicion. Our last leader was tortured to death by strangers such as you."

I glanced at the others with a look of affirmation, for we all knew what she spoke about.

"What is it?" she scanned our faces. "Do you know of what I speak?"

I nodded. "Yes. That is why we are here. With the help of Archemese, we hope to put an end to such evil atrocities."

Xiandera sent Zhendon a fleeting look. "Your knowledge of these matters gives me pause." Her tail slapped the water. "How do we know we can trust you?"

I looked down. "Regrettably, we can give you no more than our word."

When she appeared dissatisfied, Darwynyen extended his hand toward my pendant. "Does this pendant mean nothing?" he asked. "Is it not enough that my mother has given up her immortality to protect Arianna and see her through this quest."

Xiandera mouth fell open, "Are you the son of Aldraveena?"

"My lineage is not important." Darwynyen placed his hand on Dregby's shoulder. "As you can see, we have not come on Aldraveena's behalf alone. Now, in a time of uncertainty, forgotten alliances have been reforged." His tone deepened. "If we do not stand as one, then we might as well yield, for the sorcerers of Cessdorn will have already won."

Teshna and Zenley flew to Xiandera's face. "Are you to refuse the son of Aldraveena?" Zenley fluttered his wings.

"You travel with fairies." Xiandera's eyes widened. "They do not mingle with your kind!"

"Have you heard nothing Darwynyen has said?" Teshna huffed.

Xiandera nodded and then turned to Zhendon with resolve, "Zhendon, return for the others."

When Zhendon disappeared, Xiandera looked at Darwynyen. "As a gesture of goodwill, I will have my maidens guide you to your destination."

Before we could respond, she disappeared.

In the silence that followed, Dregby cleared his throat, "An odd encounter indeed, that was."

"Why?" I chastised. "Can you honestly blame them for their caution? What would you have them do, when Darwynyen and Sikes's first reaction was to draw their weapons?" I released a heavy exhale to ease my frustration. "Is it not plain to see that friendships such as these do not transpire in such a manner?"

Gin sat next to me on the bench. "Arianna, what more would you have them do? For all we knew the Siren's hearts could have been filled with hatred and revenge."

As I considered Gin's suggestion, Zhendon emerged from the water. "By Xiandera's command we have returned to escort you." There was a look of disdain upon her face. "Before we proceed, let it be known that the wizard you seek does not welcome strangers."

Although my first instinct was to confront her, I instead acknowledged her warning with a nod. Either way, she was bound by the command of her queen and had no choice but to oblige us.

With a snide look, Zhendon took hold of the stern. Her companions joined her. "Steady yourselves." Her tail nudged the hull. "I would hate to see one of you fall overboard."

I pursed my lips before I could blurt something I would regret. When Zhendon realized that I was not going to engage her, she propelled the boat into motion.

The fairies, oblivious to the tension, danced in the wake behind us. As I watched over them, I felt a hand on my shoulder. Darwynyen turned me to face him. "Arianna, are you all right?"

I shook my head, eyeing Zhendon. "What are we to do? If her words are true, the wizard may refuse us."

"Refuse us maybe, but not you," Darwynyen winked as though to lighten the mood. "Those you meet are drawn in by your kindness, a trait that could warm the coldest of hearts, including that of this wizard."

I smiled at Darwynyen's gesture. On the inside, I was struck with dread, unable to shake Zhendon's warning. A part of me wanted to turn back, and if I were alone, I might have done just that. When I looked at the others, I knew I had no option but to summon my courage and see this quest through, despite the uncertainty of its outcome.

I was about to kiss Darwynyen on the cheek when I saw the outline of an island in the distance. Its beaches sparkled like copper. "There!" I pointed, "The island of copper sands. We will soon reach our destination."

As we neared, I examined the narrow coastline. For the most part it was desolate. Bunches of seaweed flirted with the breaking waves, while gulls scavenged through the shallow pools that remained after the previous tide. Further inland, a dense cluster of trees lined a cliff that spanned the entire length of the inlet.

"Prepare to disembark." Darwynyen reached for a bundle of rope near the bow and began to unravel it.

"Our work here is done." Zhendon clung to the stern. "We can take you in no further." When I nodded, she heaved the boat forward. "Allow the waves to guide you in." As I steadied myself, Zhendon and her companions disappeared under the water.

"They are not a friendly sort," Dregby grumbled.

"No," I agreed, "they most definitely are not."

Minutes later, the hull of the boat began to drag along the bottom. When Sikes and Darwynyen jumped into the surf, I tossed my satchel ashore. I scanned the landscape that had already fallen under shadow. "Light is fading fast. We must act quickly if we are to set camp."

Zenley flew to my face. "Now that the storm clouds have passed, Teshna and I will take our leave and explore the mainland."

I jumped into the surf. "Very well, but you must promise to return should you find anything." My concession was of a selfish nature, for I was too exhausted to search for the elusive wizard myself.

They agreed, flying off.

When the boat was secure, the men left in search of wood for the fire. Rather than assist them, I took hold of their satchels and made way for the tree line. Once I found a suitable place, I assemble some rocks and gathered a couple handfuls of kindling. As I searched for a flint, I could hear the chattering of birds in the distance, or at least what I hoped were birds.

Darwynyen dropped a bundle of wood near my feet. "Arianna, are you having trouble with the flint?"

I scanned the surroundings. "No, I have only gotten a bit distracted."

"Allow me." He took the flint and knelt next to the outline of the fire pit I had created. When the kindling was lit, he stood. "Forgive me, but I feel compelled to ask again. Are you sure you are all right?"

"There is no need for you to worry about me," I replied reassuringly. To further persuade him, I opened my satchel and pulled out our rations. "The only thing that troubles me now is my growing hunger."

"Then I will ask you no more," he sighed.

After consuming my portion of the rations, I stood up from the fire. "The moon is bright this eve." I stretched my limbs. "Before retiring, I will take a short walk along the shoreline."

"Would you like me to accompany you?" Darwynyen asked, setting his rations aside.

"No." I took a step back. "Finish with your meal. I will not be gone long."

Darwynyen slowly found his footing. "Long or not, I do not like the thought of you out there on your own."

"I will walk with her," Gin offered, swallowing the last of his rations.

Although my preference was to go alone, I nodded grudgingly. "If I cannot be trusted, then allow Gin to escort me."

Darwynyen released a weighted breath. "Very well. If that is your wish, then so be it."

Gin took my arm in his. "Do not fear. I will see that no harm comes to her."

As Gin led me away, I glanced back at Darwynyen. The disappointment on his face was obvious, leaving me to wonder if I had misjudged his motivations. Perhaps his insistence had little to do with his lack of confidence in me and instead stemmed from a desire to spend some time with me away from the others.

"How about we head for that boulder?" Gin suggested, pointing down the southern part of the inlet to an outcropping of stone along the shoreline.

"Lead the way." I extended my hand.

When we reached the boulder, he assisted me to the top. As I sat on the ledge, I could not help but notice the surf as it churned over the jagged stones below. "It is beautiful here," I shouted over the reverberations. "I have only ever dreamed of such places."

"As have I," he replied.

Confused by his remark, I turned to face him. "What do you mean?" I asked.

"You misunderstand." He chuckled lightly. "What I meant to say was that I have always yearned to explore these islands."

I nodded. "Oh, I thought ..."

"You seem a bit distracted." He changed the subject. "Would you like to tell me what is troubling you?"

I returned my gaze to the sea. "If you must know, I carry doubts when it comes to this quest." I paused to find the right words. "I am not saying that I do not trust the queen, because I do. It is the burden she has placed upon me that is difficult to bear."

He nodded understandingly. "If you wish to be alone, I can find another rock to sit on."

"No, of course not." I smiled, trying to distinguish his face through the darkness. "I welcome your company."

"I wish I could say the same for Darwynyen." He picked up a few pebbles and tossed them into the surf. "If only I could find the cause of his intolerance toward me, perhaps your burdens would be lessened."

I sensed his frustration, and I tried to reassure him. "Do not lose hope when it comes to Darwynyen. Situations such as these have a way of mending themselves with time."

He nodded and then stood. "Come, we should make our return before he begins to worry."

In response, I extended my hand. And once I was on my feet, we leapt from the boulder.

† † †

Startled by a bird call, I opened my eyes. They were struck by rays of sunlight, and they burned. As I wiped away the tears, I heard the sound of waves crashing in the distance. To my dismay, I had not been dreaming. We were still on the island, and the quest to find the wizard was still before us.

Darwynyen knelt by my side. "Arianna, you have rested late this morn." He handed me a portion of the rations. "Eat now while we finish packing."

"Thank you." I quickly kissed him on the cheek.

As I picked at the dried fruit, I surveyed the cliff of stone that encircled the inlet. "I wonder if there is more to this island than what we have witnessed," I remarked.

"There must be." Gin reached for his boots. "I took a walk this morning and found no sign of the wizard."

"Then why would the Sirens have left us here?" Dregby huffed.

"To hinder us," Darwynyen replied bluntly.

"I suppose we have no choice but to wait for the fairies," Gin sighed. "With this cliff in our path we will be in need of their guidance."

Sikes ignored him, scanning the length of the inlet. "I say we take a route southward. The cliff does not appear to be as steep that way."

"Until our course has been plotted, we should leave our belongings here," Dregby suggested. "The added weight will only deter us."

"Agreed," Darwynyen replied, tossing his satchel near a tree. "We can always return for our supplies later."

"There is no need." Zenley spoke as he and Teshna emerged from the trees. "We have found a cave that leads through to the other side of the island!"

"Your time in this inlet has been wasted." Teshna fluttered her wings. "The island is deceiving. On the opposite side of the cliff the landscape changes."

"Changes how?" I asked.

"There is no time to explain," Zenley urged. "Come, we will show you."

Without further question, we followed them to the cliff.

When we arrived, we found a cave concealed by a blanket of vines. "How did you find this place?" I asked.

"Bats," Teshna replied. "We saw them taking flight after dusk."

I cringed at the thought. "How do you know it leads through?" I asked apprehensively.

"Because we came out on the opposite side, silly," Teshna mocked.

Darwynyen's eyes turned cold at Teshna's response. "How can we trust you, when in our previous travels, you neglected to warn us of any unforeseen danger?"

"What do you mean?" Zenley frowned.

"Need I remind you of the waterfall?" Darwynyen questioned.

"We should choose this course," Dregby interjected. "Either way, our chances are better here than on the cliff."

Gin pulled his sword. "I agree."

After a moment of consideration, Darwynyen nodded reluctantly. He reached for his daggers. "Arianna, ready your sais."

When I knelt to take hold of them, he pulled aside the vines. A whisper of chill escaped from the darkness.

"Sikes, take one of my axes." Dregby pulled a small battle axe from his waist belt. "If the area is as slight as it appears, your bow will be of no use to you."

Sikes took the axe and followed Darwynyen through the threshold. I went next. Gin and Dregby were in quick pursuit behind me.

Unable to see, I tripped on a stone. Before I could fall, Sikes took hold of me. "Arianna, allow me to guide you."

I kept silent, taking hold of his arm for stability.

After passing the first bend, we saw cracks of sunlight. "You see!" Teshna buzzed around my face. "Despite its appearance, this passage holds no danger."

Although I was relieved, I hastened my pace to avoid a possible encounter with the bats she had previously spoken of.

I brushed past Darwynyen when the path became visible. As I exited the cave, I pushed into a web. While I brushed it away, I was taken aback by the landscape. What appeared to be a rugged island from one side was completely different on the other. The area was filled with lush trees and shrubbery that left a rich smell in the air. Birds sang as they danced among the branches in the higher reaches. The tranquility of the place immediately put me at ease, assuring me that we had finally found the realm of this elusive wizard.

"I would never have imagined this side to be so different," Gin gasped.

When Darwynyen ignored his remark, I smiled to ease the

tension. "Nor would I, my friend, nor would I." I squeezed Gin's arm.

"Enough talk." Darwynyen turned. "We should move on."

Sikes turned from a fallen tree he was standing on. "Darwynyen, there is something ahead." Before Darwynyen could respond, Sikes disappeared through the shrubbery.

When we followed Sikes's lead, we came to a ring wall. Unlike the one I had seen in Maglavine, this one appeared to be made of fire.

"I have never seen a protection wall such as this," Sikes remarked. "Perhaps the wizard has cursed it!"

"If he has, the flame may devour us!" I recoiled.

Without hesitation, Darwynyen moved his arm through the flames. When he drew back, no harm had come to it. "It should work the same as ours," he shrugged, stepping to the other side. He turned in place. "You see, like ours it only works against evil."

Dregby stowed his axe and stepped through next.

Once he was on the other side, I turned to Gin. There was panic all over his face. I tried to reassure him. "Do not worry. I have done this once before. You will be fine."

"No." Gin stepped back abruptly. "I am not accustomed to magic and do not trust it." He continued before I could respond. "If you have no objections, I would prefer to wait for you back at camp. Someone should keep watch over our supplies."

Puzzled, I tried to persuade him. "Can you not see that there is nothing for you to fear? You have seen Darwynyen and Dregby pass with no harm."

Sikes stepped through the wall carrying the fairies. "Listen to Arianna," he encouraged him. "I can assure you that this wall will not harm you."

"I … I would rather not risk it," he stammered. "You forget that I once served in your father's elite royal army, a deception this magic may still sense." Beads of sweat had begun to form on his brow. "Your sudden silence only confirms my suspicions.

More importantly, I feel that someone should keep watch over our supplies, especially now that our search has led us to this part of the island."

I looked at Darwynyen for support. He shook his head impatiently. To avoid an argument, I turned back to Gin. "I will not force you to pass." I put my hand on his arm to settle him. "Return to the camp if you wish. We will join up with you later."

Gin nodded and then fled in the direction of the cave. And though I was concerned by his actions, we had no more time to waste on the matter.

When I leapt through the wall to join the others, I was relieved to find that the sensation was no different from the one I had experienced in Maglavine, bringing me to the realization that the wizard had only conjured the flames as a means of dissuasion.

As I emerged from the flame Darwynyen spoke. "There is something not right about that lad." He took me by the arm. "Do you not see it?"

"No, I do not." I spoke in Gin's defense regardless of my suspicions. "Can you not see that he is only frightened?" Before Darwynyen could argue, I continued. "I do not wish to speak on the subject further. Should we not seek out this wizard while light is still in our favor?"

"Arianna is right." Dregby trotted off. "Let us move on before another day is lost."

Frustrated, Darwynyen stomped off in Dregby's direction. With nothing left to say, Sikes and I followed.

Soon after, Dregby and Sikes decided that it would be more productive for us to search in groups of two. Darwynyen and I would explore the lands to the south, while Sikes and Dregby headed north. We would each follow the rim of the cliff until we reached the water and then walk the beach on our return. The fairies would search from above. "If you find the wizard, do not approach him," Darwynyen said to Dregby and Sikes, giving me a fleeting look. "Arianna will need to speak on our behalf."

They nodded in agreement. Teshna and Zenley flew around Darwynyen and then disappeared. "This way, Arianna." Darwynyen led me into the adjacent shrubbery.

We had only taken a few steps before I halted. Questions needed answering. "Darwynyen …" I hesitated, fearing his reaction. "Why do you carry these ill feelings toward Gin?"

"Because I do not trust him. Whether or not you choose to accept it, your friend has other plans!"

Rather than argue, I tried to reason with him. "Perhaps you should have more patience where Gin is concerned." I took hold of his hands. "Not only is he unfamiliar with magic, he does not have your trust as I do. In many ways he is on his own."

"Perhaps." He turned to leave. "Only time will tell his tale."

Defeated by Darwynyen's stubbornness, I silently followed after him.

Dusk was upon us when we found Sikes and Dregby along the shoreline. As we approached, it was obvious that their success was no greater than ours. Darwynyen looked at Sikes as we met. "What did you find?"

"Nothing." Sikes shrugged. "Elusive or not, I begin to wonder if the wizard is even here."

"He must be," I countered. "Otherwise, Aldraveena would not have sent us."

"Where are those fairies," Darwynyen grumbled. "They are never around when you need them."

"That is not entirely true," Sikes said in their defense. "If it were not for them we would not have gotten this far to begin with."

"You are right," Darwynyen conceded. "We should make our way back." He glanced over his shoulder toward the cliff. "There is little chance of us finding the opening to that cave under the cover of night."

In agreement, the men set off. I was about to follow after them when I caught sight of what appeared to be a man sitting at the end of a stone dyke.

Sikes returned to my side. "Arianna, what do you see?"

"Do my eyes deceive me …" I squinted, pointing toward the dyke, "or is there someone sitting on the end of that dyke over there?"

"I think you are right, Arianna." Sikes put his hand to his brow to shield the sun. "It appears to be a man." He paused. "I think he is fishing."

"Why do you delay?" Darwynyen asked impatiently.

"I believe we have found the wizard," I gasped. "He is over there on that dyke."

"Then let us make our way." Dregby trotted off in the direction of the dyke.

"Wait," Darwynyen called after him. "You cannot go. Arianna must undertake this task alone."

I turned sharply. "What do you mean? I cannot go alone!"

Dregby pulled his axe. "What if the wizard attacks her?"

"Why would he?" Darwynyen argued. "He is a man of magic, not a warrior."

"What do I …" I broke off. "What if he refuses me?"

Darwynyen took me by the arms. "Aldraveena has sent you on this quest, not us. We are only here to guide you." By the look in his eyes, I knew that he was right, and I turned to the dyke, summoning my courage. "I will not be gone long," I said.

As I climbed onto the dyke, Zhendon's warning resurfaced. What if she was right and the wizard did not welcome us? My heart pounded with anxiety. If she was right, would he even give me the opportunity to speak? I brushed the thought from my mind and instead focused on my footing as I leapt from one boulder to another. The only certainty I could cling to was my determination to see this through.

The wizard did not move as I approached. When I stepped onto the last boulder, I halted for a moment to take stock of him. His long hair was silver, like my father's. It spread on the rock face behind him. He wore a plain cotton robe, and on his feet were leather sandals. A basket sat at his side, and a spear lay before him.

"I know why you have come," he said, motionless. "Aldraveena should have known better than to send you."

"We are here because we need your help." I slowly took a step forward. "Are you the wizard called Archemese?"

"Even if I were, I would have no help to offer you, nor would I choose to." He kept his gaze on the sea. "People believe I am dead, and despite the circumstances, I wish to keep things that way."

His selfish attitude angered me. "Will you not even hear me out before you make your decision?" When he did not respond, I continued. "If there is one thing I have learned in the past, it is that you may not always have what you want." I paused to calm myself. "I did not ask for this task, yet I have taken it."

He abruptly stood to face me. "Will you stop at nothing to clean your conscience of your father?"

Stunned by his words, I began to tremble. "Unlike you, I will not deny who I am. Besides, if you know of my bloodline, then you know that it was not of my choosing." I stiffened my stance. "Although I am ashamed of my lineage, the only matter of importance here is what I am willing to sacrifice in an effort to bring about his downfall."

He considered my declaration for a moment and then spoke. "I see that Aldraveena has made a wise decision in you." His hand ran the course of his lengthy beard. "Even now, your strength shines through you."

"These strengths you speak of were thrust upon me, with little or no warning." I glared. "Like you said, I have much to atone for."

"Forgive me." He sighed heavily. "It was wrong of me to speak to you in such a manner." His blue eyes grew solemn. "I fear my lack of respect is a result of the many years I have spent in solitude on this island. It seems I no longer have the ability to interact with others."

"Then why do you choose to live here?" I asked as the tension eased. "Is it because you fear the future?"

"I fear nothing." His eyes began to wander. "If you have taken pity on me, then you misunderstand. It is my sanity that I cherish, and without solitude it will not last." He picked up his basket and spear. "With that said, it is time for you to take your leave."

Before I could respond, he brushed past me.

I followed. "Please," I begged. "Archemese, can you not see that we need you!"

He halted, looking down. "You are mistaken," he said. "I am nothing more than an old man, one who does not want the burden of your troubles."

I grabbed his arm. "If you choose to do nothing, my troubles will soon find you … for there will be no escaping them if my father succeeds with his plans." I released him and began to weep. "I will say no more. If your decision is made, then my companions and I must find our way to the cave before nightfall."

He reluctantly set down his bucket. "If I offer you shelter for the night, you must promise that you will take your leave in the morning." His eyes narrowed. "Do you promise?"

"Yes." I nodded, wiping my tears. "Thank you."

In response, he eyed the basket.

"Of course." I managed a smile as I took hold of it.

When Archemese and I neared the shoreline, the men were eagerly awaiting us. As I jumped from the last boulder, I warned them with a stern stare and then quickly made the introductions. Although each of them had a perplexed look upon their face, they were polite and somewhat humble.

"This way." Archemese set off across the beach.

I nodded, leading the men forward in silence.

We were well into the treed area when Archemese reached into the basket and pulled out a small lamp. "The sunlight fades fast in the shelter of the trees. If we are to proceed, we will need unnatural light to guide us," he remarked as he struck the flint.

"Where is your dwelling?" I asked, stepping under a branch.

"Not far." He lit the wick and then led us between two bushes.

Minutes later, we came to a small clearing. In the center, the ground gave way to stairs. The rock around the opening immediately reminded me of Aldraveena's realm in Maglavine. "I live underground." Archemese made his way to the stairs. "The weather is not always as kind as today."

The narrow door at the bottom creaked when Archemese opened it. Musty air escaped from the darkness. "Give me a moment to light a few candles." He handed me his spear.

I nodded, trying to manage it and the basket. Darwynyen assisted me. "What is happening?" he whispered.

"Not now," I winced, shaking my head.

Darwynyen pursed his lips anxiously. Like the others, he was confused as to whether or not Archemese had decided to join us.

Moments later a soft glow filled the room. To avoid Darwynyen's stare, I stepped inside.

The area was small and unkempt. A fireplace was carved out of a slab of rock near the door, the only place where he could properly ventilate it. Several tree stumps were placed around a square table that had been made from branches, something he must have crafted himself. The kitchen was barren, and a few belongings were scattered about the bed. I could not help but pity the way he lived and felt the urge to reach out to him. Before I could speak, he entered my mind. *Do not pity me. I do not require the necessities of man, for I am comforted by the land alone.* He lit another candle. "Make yourselves comfortable. I will tend to a meal." He indicated for me to set the basket upon the table.

As I set it down, I lifted the cloth that was covering its contents. To my surprise, I found that he had caught several fish. "I see you are a skilled hunter," I winked. "A match for those I travel with."

"There are plenty of fish to be found along that dyke." He

took hold of a knife. "So much so, they have become a main part of my diet."

When the tension eased, Darwynyen and Sikes sat on the tree stumps. Dregby took comfort near the smoldering fire.

I was about to offer my assistance to Archemese when I thought of Gin. I glanced back to Darwynyen. "Archemese, we have a friend on the other side of the cliff. He is alone and waits for us."

Archemese dropped the knife on the table. "I do not sense another. Who is this person?"

"He is a friend," I replied. "Could it be that the cliff dulls your powers."

Archemese shook his head. "That is not possible."

"Have you sensed the fairies?" I asked, in hopes that Gin was not the only companion he had failed to sense. "They too travel with us and scout this island as we speak."

He furrowed his brow, giving me the impression that he did not sense them either. "Aldraveena has sent fairies to accompany you?"

"Yes." I nodded. "Their names are Teshna and Zenley."

"That would explain things." He caressed his beard. "I felt something earlier, but excused it as the Sirens." His eyes darkened. "Your friend, however, seems to elude me."

"There must be a reasonable explanation for this," I pleaded. "Perhaps you should meet with him."

"That is not necessary," Archemese replied bluntly. "Your friend's chosen path has no bearing on mine."

When I felt Darwynyen's eyes on me, I ignored him, turning to Sikes for support. "Perhaps we should return through that cave and find him."

"For what purpose?" Sikes sat forward. "You know as well as I that Gin has no intention of passing through that ring wall."

"Either way, you should wait until morning," Archemese urged. "Elvish eyes or not, it is unlikely that you would find the opening to that cave under nightfall."

"Archemese is right," Dregby concurred. "Besides, Gin is skilled enough to manage the night on his own."

Sikes looked at Darwynyen, and then headed for the door. "If you will excuse me, I am in need of some fresh air."

When Darwynyen nodded, disappointed, Sikes's decision to leave became clear.

Rather than dwell on the matter, I turned to Archemese. If I was going to sway him, I needed to stay focused. "How long have you lived here?" I asked.

"Too many years to remember." He raised his sleeve to show me his bracelet. "Like you, I wear an eternal pendant."

I took hold of his wrist, my eyes wide. "I knew you were old, but … Why do you choose to live unnaturally if you are unable to share your life with others?"

"To be honest, I do not know." He looked down. "I have tried to remove it several times, only I cannot find the will to do it."

In my heart, I knew the reason. This was his destiny. That was why Aldraveena had sent me to find him. She had seen it in her foresight. Although I wanted to share my revelation, I decided to leave it for now, and I extinguished the thought before he could sense it.

In the silence that followed, I set the table, while Darwynyen assisted Dregby with the fire, making it ready for our coming meal.

As Archemese skewered the last fish, Sikes burst through the door. "Something is not right here," he exclaimed. "There are ravens among us! I saw them through the moonlight. They were fleeing in the distance."

"Did you see Gin?" Darwynyen quickly stood.

"No, of course not," Sikes huffed. "Forget Gin! I fear the Hynd is watching us!"

"If they are here, then it is not by chance," Darwynyen countered. "Someone has alerted them of our quest!"

Archemese entered my mind. *If your friend was of good nature, I should have felt his presence by now.*

When he severed the connection I shook my head. Darwynyen took my arm. "I do not wish to upset you, Arianna, but we can trust Gin no further. Ravens are the spies of the Hynd. If Gin is conspiring with them, there is no telling about his intentions!"

"The Hynd could indeed be spying," Dregby agreed. "However, if Sikes did not witness the ravens in the company of Gin, we cannot judge the lad so quickly."

With reluctance, Darwynyen conceded. "Because we have no proof, we shall leave it for now and question him in the morning." He looked at me. "Whatever his response, we have no choice now but to observe him more closely."

I nodded with a heavy heart. Although I did not want to admit it, Darwynyen was right. If the Hynd had found us, there were questions that needed answering, and, to my regret, the only person to look to in our company was Gin, who from the start had been very elusive about his history. Even so, my decision to stand by Darwynyen did not come without guilt. Gin, after all, was the only person I could trust when I first set out from Hoverdire. He was a true friend, one I had chosen to embrace as a brother. As I recalled those memories, I could only hope that Darwynyen's misgivings would be proved wrong.

When Archemese laid out dinner, we all joined him at the table. "Thank you for sharing your food with us." I reached for a potato.

He raised his brow. "Your gratitude is most appreciated; it is plain to see that I have little to offer."

Dregby swallowed his first bite. "A meal fit for a king, this is!"

"Here, here!" Sikes smiled, raising his fork.

In the conversation that followed, I saw the tension leave Archemese's face, as though he was enjoying the companionship he had shunned so many years ago.

Before long our bellies were full. As I gathered the plates, Archemese moved to the fireplace. "My dear, have you had the pleasure of witnessing the spell of warmth?"

"Yes." I placed the cutlery into a pail. "I have seen it once before."

"It is not cold enough in here to warrant a magical fire," Dregby grumbled. "The place has warmed nicely."

"The damp strikes hard." Archemese dug his hand into a bowl on the mantle. "We must weed it out." He tossed the powder onto the outer stones, blanketed in embers. "My old bones can no longer handle the chill."

Unlike Shallendria, he did not chant a spell. The stones turned red regardless, making it clear that his powers were not to be underestimated.

"Very well," Dregby grumbled, taking comfort on a rug near the door. "You are not the first man to admit this weakness. Most men cannot handle the depths of the land as do we Miders."

"You boast about nothing." Sikes rolled his eyes. "Who would want to live underground except a savage such as …" He stopped and looked at Archemese. "I did not mean …"

"I hope not." Archemese moved his stool closer to the fireplace.

After stacking the last of the plates, I joined him. "If you do not already know, I grew up in the south, in a village called Hoverdire." I held my hands out toward the stones. "I cannot explain why, but it seemed much warmer there."

"Because it was," he winked. "The mountains of Alcomeen keep the lands in the north cooler."

"Where are you from?" I asked.

He paused to think before responding. "I can say little more than that I was born in Biddenwade. Beyond that, the memories seem lost to me."

"How old are you?" I asked.

"Too old," he chuckled. "To be honest, I have lost count."

"Did you live in the times …" I hesitated. "What I mean to ask is, did you witness the last war, after the stones fell from the sky?"

He stood in anger. "How dare you speak of those times to

me!" His voice cracked. "Why could you not leave things well enough alone?" He grabbed a wooden staff from near the door and left without another word.

His absence large, the men looked at me. "What was that about?" Darwynyen questioned.

I blinked heavily. "I do not know how to tell you this, but Archemese has no intention to join us."

"Well, that is no good." Dregby stood on his forelegs. "What are we to do?"

"Persuade him." I spoke with conviction. "Archemese is in denial. Given some time, I feel certain he will change his mind. " I looked at Darwynyen. "He may not yet know it, but this is his destiny. Why else would he have kept his pendant?"

Sikes began to pace the room. "Although I sympathize with you, Arianna, how much longer must we wait? As you know, time is not in our favor."

Darwynyen interjected. "Let us not forget that it was Aldraveena who sent us here. For now, we must trust in her foresight."

Dregby eyed the door. "If he does not come around soon, we should make our return. Sikes is right. Time is not in our favor."

"We will give him another day." Darwynyen took my hand. "If his resolve holds strong, we will honor his decision and leave respectfully."

When there was no argument, Darwynyen led me outside. At the crest of the stair, he halted. "Are you certain about the wizard?" I could feel him searching my eyes in the darkness. "Despite his wisdom, from what I have seen he seems a bit unstable, and may be difficult to sway."

"What other choice do we have?" When he did not answer, I continued. "We must keep strong, Darwynyen. As I said before, I am confident he will change his mind."

He nodded. "What happened when you first met him on the dyke?"

"He was as cold and unwelcoming as Zhendon had warned," I admitted. "After speaking ill to me, he insisted that we leave immediately. I was about to concede when he, for whatever reason, took pity on me. His offer of shelter and food was the only thing I had to cling to, in hopes that he would eventually change his mind."

"How adamant was his refusal?"

I shrugged. "I do not know him well enough to say. Yet, I feel there is more to this wizard than what we now see."

He embraced me. "I trust in your instincts. Unfortunately, I cannot speak for the others."

"It is an anxious time. If the wizard should refuse us, your strength will be enough to see them through this." I held him tightly.

"As will yours." He drew back and kissed me.

Lost in the moment, I yearned for his intimate touch. If only we were alone, I would have allowed him to take me there, then. "I love you, Darwynyen."

"I love you more." His lips brushed my cheek. "I know my temperament has been challenging as of late. And you know the reasons." He paused. "Still, now, when I have the opportunity to prove the truth, I find myself dreading the outcome."

"As do I." I rested my head on his chest.

The Presence

Like most days, Morglafenn spent a majority of his time rummaging through the books in the castle library.

As he lit a candle with magic, an overwhelming sensation broke his concentration. He moved to the window, confused by the ill feelings that had returned so suddenly. Only when Darwynyen and Arianna came to mind did he realize their origin. The evil presence had vanished on their departure, and though they were not the cause, this being was either traveling with them or following. Could it be there was a spy clever enough to evade the power of the elves?

Madigan entered through the door. "Morglafenn, I should have known I would find you here."

"What is it?" Morglafenn turned impatiently.

"I have come to seek your wisdom." Madigan settled in a chair. "Like Shallendria, I know you can sense the presence of evil."

"What has happened?" Morglafenn asked with worry.

"Nothing." Madigan lifted a satchel on the table. "We found these supplies in the caverns. Someone has been hiding down there for some time now."

A tinge of fear struck Morglafenn. "The spy," he muttered.

"What spy?" Madigan stood.

"It follows Arianna." He put his hands to his brow. "Save your searches—you will no longer find him there."

"What do you speak of, Morglafenn?"

"The evil presence that I told you about. Although I did not realize it before, I see now that it has left to track the others." Morglafenn began to pace.

Madigan took Morglafenn by the arms. "We must warn them!"

Morglafenn pulled away. "There is nothing we can do. Darwynyen will defend her."

"How can he defend an enemy he is unaware of?" Madigan argued.

"You forget Darwynyen's skills," Morglafenn replied. "Trust in them, Madigan."

Madigan pursed his lips and then stomped from the room.

Off To Find Gin

A pale dawn light was breaking through the cracks in the door. Archemese had yet to return. Plagued with guilt, I began to pace the room, knowing that we had taken his only means of shelter. "There was a storm last night," I muttered. "He is old. What if something happened to him?"

"He will be fine." Darwynyen moved to block my path. "I am sure there are many places on this island for him to take shelter in."

When the door swung open we all turned. "What are you still doing here?" Archemese's eyes fell upon me. "You gave me your word that you would be gone!"

"Where have you been?" I turned the subject. "We have been worried for you all night."

"Do not try to control this conversation!" Archemese warned. "You do not have the skill to outwit me!"

Darwynyen stood in between us. "Do not accuse her of such things, for she has not taken rest on account of you!"

"I did not ask you to stay." Archemese gripped his staff. "Is it not clear that nothing can be said here to alter my decision?"

"So be it." I reached for my cloak. "We will leave you now."

Dregby found his footing, "Arianna, are you certain?"

"Yes." My tone was harsh. Deep down, I had to believe that

Archemese did not want us to leave. "It is plain to see that we are not welcome here." I stomped from the abode, waiting for Archemese to call after me. He did not.

Darwynyen rushed up the stairs. "Arianna, what are you doing?"

"Leaving." I crossed my arms. "We have done all we can here."

Dregby and Sikes appeared at the top of the rise. "The wizard appears upset." Sikes adjusted the belt on his quiver. "It might be in our interest for you to return and speak with him."

"No." I stiffened my stance. "The quest has failed. It is time for us to move on." I pushed my way through the bushes in the direction of the cave. "Let us make our way to the cave."

The men followed without further question.

In the passing minutes, I began to regret my actions. A part of me wanted to turn back. No. Archemese was the one who needed to apologize, and I could only hope that my instincts were right and that he would make the effort before we disembarked from the island.

When we arrived at the opposite side of the cave, we proceeded to the makeshift camp in search of Gin. Upon our arrival, he was nowhere to be found. "Where is the lad?" Dregby scratched his head.

"He has not been gone long." Sikes knelt at the fire pit. "The coals are still warm."

As I surveyed the camp, I noticed that all the supplies had been packed and were ready for our departure. "Perhaps he has grown bored and taken a walk," I remarked.

Darwynyen scanned the beach. "Then let us go and find him."

"Considering the hour, we should probably split up," Sikes suggested.

"Agreed. I will go with Sikes." I did not have the strength to endure another confrontation between Gin and Darwynyen. "We will search the north."

When Darwynyen looked at me oddly, I casually picked up a branch that Gin had been using to stoke the fire and began to test its strength.

Darwynyen gave Sikes a fleeting look. "Arianna, I would rather you came with me."

"Darwynyen, please." I moved to take Sikes's arm. "Sikes and I will be fine."

"Is there something wrong with my company?" Dregby put his hands to his waist, eyeing Darwynyen.

"Fine." Darwynyen trudged off. "If you should find Gin, set off an arrow to alert us."

"We will," I replied as Sikes and I set off in the opposite direction.

"Clever you are," Sikes put his hand to my back when we reached the beach. "Like you, I would prefer not to be in Darwynyen's company should he find Gin, as I suspect the exchange would not be agreeable."

"Were my intentions that obvious?" I asked.

"Not to Darwynyen." Sikes glanced over his shoulder in the direction of Darwynyen and Dregby. "His focus is on Gin."

"It has been for some time now," I remarked.

"We will resolve this matter soon, Arianna." Sikes spoke with assurance. "I promise you."

"Thank you." I released a heavy breath, and we made our way to the northern part of the inlet.

I was about to give up in our search when Sikes put his hand to his brow. "Over there." He pointed. "I see the outline of a man in the distance."

When I followed his direction, I immediately saw Gin. He was standing on the crest of a boulder that extended from the cusp of the inlet.

"What is he doing all the way out there?" Sikes huffed.

"Let us find out." I began to run toward the boulder. Sikes followed.

As we neared, I saw a raven leave Gin's arm. As though sensing our presence, Gin turned. A faint glow of red slowly disseminated from his eyes in the bird's retreat. "Gin," I gasped. "What are you doing?"

"Arianna." Gin slowly drew his hand behind his back. "It is not what you think. I had no choice, the bird …"

"Do not move!" Sikes reached for an arrow.

"Or what?" Gin flung a dagger through the air, striking Sikes in the neck as he took aim.

I cried out when Sikes fell backward. I could not believe my eyes. Instead of defending myself, I knelt by him. "Sikes." I put my hands around the wound in an effort to slow the bleeding, eyeing the blade.

"Leave it," Sikes choked.

I was about to scream out when I was tossed to the ground. Gin sat upon me. "I do not wish to harm you, Arianna." He took hold of my flailing arms. "Accept it now. There is nothing you can do for Sikes. Instead you must save yourself and come with me, for others have insisted on your capture."

"Never!" The death of my mother flashed through my mind as I fought for my escape. "I will never go with you!" I glared when Gin engaged my stare. "Darwynyen will see to your death when he finds us!"

"Arianna, will you not accept defeat, even when it has been thrust upon you?" Gin snickered, undaunted.

His mannerism instantly reminded me of my father, bringing me to the realization that he had been working for him all along. Why had I not listened to Morglafenn when he had warned me of a spy? Still, I never would have guessed it to be Gin. Again I had been deceived.

Gin lifted me to my feet. When I struggled to break free, he pulled another blade, holding it to my neck. Helplessly, I watched Sikes gasping for air as he lay on the ground next to me. "Start walking!" Gin nudged me forward. "We have little time."

"What about Sikes?" I tried to turn back. "We cannot leave him!"

"Forget him!" He pushed the blade against my skin. "Do not fight me, Arianna. You are of no use to me dead!"

Sensing the pressure of the blade, I followed his instruction. From the corner of my eye, I saw the fairies descend upon Sikes. I could only hope their magic gifts would be strong enough to heal his wound.

Instead of returning to camp, Gin pushed me to the boat. His plan was to escape and take me with him. I could not allow this. As we maneuvered through the surf, I kicked backward at his legs. He reaffirmed the pressure on the blade. "Do not push me, Arianna." The skin on my neck began to sting. "If I must harm you, I will!"

"Please," I begged. "Loosen your hold. I cannot breath!"

"Do not fear. I will not allow you to die." He snickered again. "The others would not have it." The blade loosened. "Get into the boat!"

Before I could respond, he pushed me in. I was about to jump overboard when he grabbed me by the hair. "Not so fast." He tried to position himself and reached for an oar.

I felt hair rip from my scalp. Desperate for release, I pulled at his leg. Unstable, he strengthened his grip on my hair.

Unable to bear the pain, I screamed out.

"Damn the gods!" he shouted toward the sky.

I tried to turn and see if he was hurt.

"Get out of the boat," he growled, pulling me upward. "We must return to the camp!"

He had forgotten something. Relieved, I did as he asked.

As he led me back across the beach, I tried to plead to his conscience. "Why are you doing this, Gin? After all we have been through, does our friendship mean so little?"

"Oh, Arianna, I gave you all the chances in the world to love me." His tone was patronizing.

"What do you mean?" I asked. "I gave you my love unconditionally!"

"You gave me nothing more than friendship," he scoffed. "I

tried to win your affections, but you would not have me! Instead you gave your love to that elf!"

As we approached the camp, I felt Darwynyen's presence and looked toward the trees. He was nowhere in sight.

"I knew you were not to be trusted." Darwynyen appeared through the shrubbery with his bow aimed in readiness. "That is of no consequence," he smirked. "It ends here now!"

"Darwynyen, I …" Gin dug the blade into my skin.

"Sikes," Darwynyen called out. "We are over here!" When there was no response, he looked at me. From my expression, he knew that his friend was in trouble.

"Darwynyen," Gin cackled. "You are no threat to me. The general was weak in his ways. I will not falter as he did." When Darwynyen did not respond, he continued. "Before these events unfold, you must know that I have no qualms about killing Arianna. The others do not care if she is dead or alive as long as she arrives in Cessdorn!"

"If you kill her, I will finish you next," Darwynyen countered.

"Then so be it!" Gin slowly pulled the knife across my neck. In that instant, I felt a warm sensation on my skin. He had drawn blood. Unsure of my fate, I closed my eyes.

"*Zechrendef dun a forthen*!"

I recognized the voice immediately—Archemese. Thereafter, time seemed to stand still. When I opened my eyes, Darwynyen rushed over. "Do not move. The blade still breaks your skin!" Before I could respond, he turned to Archemese. "What do we do?"

"Give her a moment." Archemese moved to get a better look.

"What is happening?" I cried.

Darwynyen put his hand under my chin. "Archemese has cast a spell on Gin. He is frozen in time. You must try and free yourself!"

Taking heed, I slowly began to wriggle free. The task was

difficult. Gin's hold was strong. Desperately, Darwynyen pulled at Gin's hands. Droplets of blood trickled down my neckline. "I cannot do it," I whimpered.

"Yes, you can!" he insisted. "Lift up your chin, and pull yourself under."

I tried to gauge the depth of the blade. When I relaxed my muscles, I was able to tilt my head high enough to free myself. As I fought for breath, I immediately tested the wound.

"The spell will not last." Archemese glanced over our belongings. "We must find some rope and secure him!"

Darwynyen pulled a dagger from his waist belt. "We should kill him now, before he can cause any more harm!"

"No, death is not the answer here," Archemese insisted. "When Gin sees that the odds have turned against him, he will give us needed information." He paused. "Think back to your elvish ways, Darwynyen, and you will see things more clearly."

Before they could argue, I took Darwynyen by the arm. "Sikes!" I choked back the tears. "Gin struck him in the neck with a blade!"

Darwynyen blinked as though he did not comprehend my words. "Where is he?"

"Over there!" I pointed to the northern part of the beach. "He did not look well. I saw the fairies descend upon him as I was taken away!"

Darwynyen ran off just as Dregby emerged from the trees. "What has happened here?" Dregby asked.

"Find some rope," Archemese ordered. "We must tie up your companion before the spell weakens!"

Dregby began to search our belongings. I wanted to help, but I did not have the will. Archemese came to my aid. "Let me tend to your wound."

I nodded, lifting my chin.

After carefully examining the area, he sighed. "The cut is not deep. I will be able to heal the laceration with magic." He pulled out a cotton cloth from his pocket. "Hold this to the wound. It should stop the bleeding."

"Thank you," I placed the linen against my neck and then turned to the beach, in hopes that I would see Darwynyen returning with Sikes. They did not come.

Shallendria's Return

Lost in thought, Madigan gazed over the courtyard. The conversation he had shared with Morglafenn was so unsettling he was finding it hard to concentrate. Until now, Arianna's fate was of little concern to him; he had assumed that, if nothing else, her quest for the wizard would lead her away from immediate danger.

"My king." Evelyn approached from the stair that led to the paddock. "Excuse the intrusion, Your Highness, but I was wondering if you have heard from Arianna."

"No." Madigan turned from the ledge. "There is no news to share."

Evelyn nodded. "I was told that a portion of the armies will set out tomorrow."

Madigan nodded. "Yes, Aarrondirth will begin to empty."

"And what of Amstead?" Her eyes began to wander. "He has yet to receive his orders."

"He will stay behind." Madigan's tone was direct. He did not want Evelyn to see his doubt in her husband. "Someone will need to look after the remaining troops."

"Thank you, my king." Evelyn bowed and retreated.

As he watched Evelyn leave, he again thought of Arianna but in a more positive manner, certain that she would approve of his decision. When his heart warmed, he wondered when he would see her again. If Morglafenn was right and a spy was following them, he could only hope that Darwynyen would protect her, for the thought of never seeing Arianna again was unbearable.

For a distraction, he focused his energy on the armies. The union of the troops was going better than expected, despite the cultural differences. He smiled, knowing it was Arianna's determination that had eventually changed their vision.

A horn sounded from the northern tower. It was signaling the arrival of an accompaniment. Thinking of Shallendria, he left, knowing her arrival was soon to be anticipated.

In his ascent up the tower stairs, he collided with Morglafenn.

"It is Shallendria." Morglafenn brushed past him. "She returns from Tayri with the others!"

"I suspected as much." Madigan turned to follow him down the stairs. "Come, we will ride out together."

In agreement, they made their way to the stables.

As they rode through the city gates the horn sounded again, this time a warning. Their first reaction was to search the sky. To the north, four dragons had swiftly emerged through the clouds.

"Dragons!" Madigan looked at Morglafenn. "Alert the troops. Have a small contingent meet me in the fields!"

"You must stay in the city!" Morglafenn insisted. "Your duty is to your people!"

"Duty or not, I cannot leave Shallendria out there to fend for herself!" Madigan tried to steady his horse. "Go now, before more time is wasted!"

Morglafenn nodded reluctantly and turned his horse. "Do not let anything happen to Shallendria. Our future depends on her survival!"

"If it takes my life to save hers, then consider it done!" Madigan kicked his horse and rode off.

Although frustrated by Madigan's neglect of his own self-preservation, Morglafenn made his return to the castle.

† † †

Shallendria pulled the reins when she sensed a presence closing in. "Dragons!" With dread, she looked over her shoulder to find four beasts emerging from the clouds in the distance. "Elves!" she shouted. "Prepare for battle! Dragons approach from the north!"

The men and women around her quickly dropped their belongings and readied their bows.

Deep down she knew their attempts would be futile. They were defenseless out in the open. Without another thought, she jumped from her horse and began to rummage through her satchel. "Gather around me!" she ordered. "I will conjure a spell of protection!" She quickly tried to remember the words to the spell, knowing that magic was their only hope.

As the elves began to assemble, she pulled out an orb and some powders.

An elf knelt to face her. "Shallendria, a horseman approaches from the south."

When she looked up, she saw Madigan. There was no time to alert him. She could only hope that he would pull back when he saw the beasts. "*Dolraden*!" she shouted. "*Dolraden!*" The orb in one hand, she released a handful of powders with the other. Moments later, the wind began to stir. "*Dolraden un forgeth*!" The winds formed into a far-reaching whirlwind around them. Again she called for their speed. "*Dolraden!*" The tempest began to reach for the sky. "*Forgeth, un forgeth*!" Her last command would sustain them.

Safe within the spell, she watched the beasts begin to circle. Madigan was still out in the open. "Madigan!" she screamed. "Make your way back to the city!" Her voice was unheard through the wind.

Madigan pulled the reins when he saw Shallendria's magic at work.

Before he could retreat, the dragons diverted in his direction. As he frantically rode toward the city gates, he saw Morglafenn leading out a small battalion. "Morglafenn!" he shouted. "Turn ba—" He was thrown from his horse, unable to finish. A talon had pierced his left shoulder. The dragon turned in the air. As it descended, Madigan pulled his dagger. With vigor, he thrust it into the air, piercing the beast in the eye. In agony, the creature attempted to claw out the blade. Its efforts were of no use. Seconds later it fell to its death.

"Madigan!" Shallendria mounted her horse, kicking it in his direction.

Clutching his shoulder, Madigan unsteadily found his footing. The beast had only fallen a few steps away from him.

As he searched for his horse, Shallendria rode up.

"Madigan, you have a wound on your back. Try not to move." She dismounted and tore off a piece of her gown, holding it to the gash on his shoulder.

"We have no time." Madigan pointed to the west. "Morglafenn is under attack!"

"Come." She helped him onto her horse. "If we are to protect your men, he will need my assistance." As she took the reins she glanced toward her companions. To her relief, the spell was still holding. Madigan winced as he wrapped his arms around her. She took no heed and kicked her horse.

When they arrived, Morglafenn was trying to erect a protection spell. Shallendria left Madigan to join him. She reached his side. "Morglafenn, it is of no use. The men are spread out beyond our reaches!"

He ignored her pleas, continuing with the spell.

Daggers of fire pierced through the smoke around them. The smell of death was in the air. If she did nothing, she realized that their demise was inevitable.

"*Noryndyffaron!*" she shouted.

Morglafenn turned sharply. "Shallendria, no! You are not strong enough!"

She ignored him. "*Noryndyffaron, Stellnyn un Fietnen*!" With power, she lifted her eternal ring to the sky. "*Noryndyffaron!*"

A ray of lightning burst from the clouds. The fury of energy pierced a dragon, hitting one of the men on the ground beneath it. Both were burnt to cinders. When the beast fell from the sky it landed on another man. Although she felt remorse for these unnecessary deaths, she stiffened her stance and directed her ring toward the remaining dragons. Without hesitation, they fled. It was over. Drained of her power, Shallendria fell to the ground.

Good-bye, My Friend

When Darwynyen found Sikes, there was nothing left for him to do. The fairy's magic was not powerful enough to heal his wound. Filled with despair, Darwynyen fell to his knees. Sikes was nearing his last breath. "Arianna …" He choked on his words. "Is she all right?"

"Yes." Darwynyen nodded, examining the wound. "Do not worry, my brother, you did well and have kept your honor."

Sikes struggled to nod. He was losing strength. "Take care of the fairies." He eyed Teshna and Zenley, who were hovering next to him. "I have grown close to them in the past days."

Darwynyen nodded, giving the fairies a fleeting look. "I give you my word."

As Sikes attempted to respond, blood trickled from his mouth.

Overcome with grief, Darwynyen took Sikes's hand in his. "Do not leave me, Sikes. Please, I beg you."

"You have Arianna now." Sikes coughed, fighting to breathe. "She needs you more than I." Before Darwynyen could respond, Sikes's head fell to the side. He was dead.

"No!" Darwynyen looked to the skies. "Why is this to be?"

When Teshna and Zenley flew off, Darwynyen gathered Sikes into his arms and trudged toward the camp.

Numb

Darwynyen had yet to return. Although Dregby had many questions, I silenced him with a stare. I was not in the mood for conversation, and I was not feeling well.

With a look of doubt, Dregby brought forward a rope. "If we must secure our companion, how should we do it if his hands are still in the air?" he huffed.

"The spell is weakening." Archemese took hold of Gin's wrists. "If I hold him down, you can use the tension of the rope to bind him."

"I will say no more." Dregby began to tie Gin's wrists. "Until we can settle things, I will do as you ask."

It was plain to see that Dregby still felt loyal toward Gin, a realization that sickened me. "Dregby, if you must know, Gin has proven to be an imposter." I paused, feeling a little light-headed. "Whether or not you chose to accept it, you must do as we ask."

"Arianna speaks the truth." Archemese struggled to keep hold of Gin's arms. "Gin is your enemy now."

I was about to check my wound when I saw Darwynyen returning from the beach. In his arms was Sikes. Clinging to hope, I ran over. "Is he to be all right?" When I saw the tears trickling down Darwynyen's cheeks, the answer was clear. I continued, in denial. "But I saw the fairies." I hesitated when they came into sight. "Was there nothing you could do?" I scowled a reprimand. "What good is your magic if it cannot even save a life?"

"How dare you?" Teshna wailed. "It was not us who led him down this path!"

When they flew off, I turned back to Darwynyen in desperation. "If only I had listened to you, we …" I felt numb. My legs began to waver. Darkness was all around me.

Deceit Prevails

When Arianna collapsed, Darwynyen placed Sikes next to a tree and rushed to aid her.

"You fools!" Gin fell to the ground cackling as the spell dissipated.

Dregby rushed over to further secure Gin's bonds. "How could you?" He grabbed Gin by the jaw. "I should kill you now!"

"Archemese!" Darwynyen beckoned, in despair. "Arianna—what has happened to her?"

Gin continued to cackle. "Is this how it is to end?" He struggled against his restraints. "Dregby is right. You might as well kill me now, for I will not speak a word!"

Darwynyen instinctively lunged toward him.

Archemese pulled Darwynyen back. "You have more important things to worry about." He eyed Arianna.

When Darwynyen returned to Arianna, Dregby kicked Gin in the face. "For your own sake, I suggest you keep your silence."

"What is happening to her?" Darwynyen knelt to touch Arianna's face. "She turns cold!"

"There is nothing the wizard can do," Gin taunted in a superior tone. "My blade held the essence of dregseed. The poison is already in her blood! She will die shortly." He cocked his head. "You are nothing but fools! I am far more powerful than any of you!"

"You may have knowledge of the poisons," Archemese lifted his brow, scornful, "but you lack the intelligence to truly understand them." He directed his staff toward Arianna, "*Sedamine! Sedamine*!"

A radiant glow emanated from Arianna's body.

"You must bring her now." Archemese gestured to Darwynyen. "I have a remedy for dregseed at my abode."

Darwynyen, confident in Archemese's abilities, lifted Arianna into his arms. As he set off toward the cave, he glanced back toward Sikes, hoping that Arianna would not be another victim of Gin's deceit.

Archemese put his hand to Darwynyen's shoulder when they entered the cave. "Arianna will be fine."

"If we act fast." Darwynyen led him through. "I know the remedy you seek!"

"I suspect you do." Archemese followed.

As Darwynyen carried Arianna into the abode, Archemese strode toward a shelf near his bed. "I see now that trouble follows you everywhere," he remarked, rummaging through a collection of small bottles. "I suppose that is to be expected in times such as these."

Darwynyen placed Arianna on the bed. "You must save her!" A tear trickled down his cheek.

"Do not worry." Archemese spoke with assurance and continued to search through the contents on the shelf. "As I said before, she will be fine."

"I trust you." Darwynyen kissed Arianna on the brow before stepping aside.

"Here it is!" Archemese reached for a narrow green bottle at the back of the shelf and then sat next to Arianna on the bed. "It is by sheer luck that I kept this resin, for its uses are limited." He looked at Darwynyen. "I will need you to hold her mouth open. I can assure you that unconscious or not, she will not welcome its contents."

When Darwynyen took Arianna in his arms, Archemese

pulled the cork from the bottle. The aroma was sickening, forcing Darwynyen to put his sleeve to his mouth.

Archemese chuckled. "Come now, it is not that foul." He held the bottle to Arianna's mouth, draining the contents.

Arianna immediately began to choke.

Darwynyen lifted her head. "Give me a cloth to wipe her mouth."

"Here." Archemese pulled a piece of linen off the table, handing it to him.

"How long will it take?" Darwynyen blotted Arianna's lips, supporting her lifeless neck.

Before Archemese could respond, Arianna's eyes began to flutter.

Moments Lost

"Where am ..." I began to choke. There was a bitter taste in my mouth. "What happened?"

"Save your strength." Darwynyen brushed the hair from my face. "You were poisoned."

I was about to ask how, when I realized that Gin was to blame. "Where is he?"

"He is with Dregby," Darwynyen replied. "You are safe."

My safety did not concern me. "I need to see him." I sat up.

Archemese put his hands on my shoulders. "And you will, once you have rested."

Darwynyen stood. "Arianna, if you are feeling better ..." he hesitated. His eyes red and glassy, he murmured, "I will need to tend to Sikes."

My chest tightened at his grief. Until now, Sikes's death had almost felt like a dream. "Darwynyen ..." I reached out to him. "Forgive me, but I do not know what to say."

"There is nothing to say." He leaned to kiss me on the brow. "I will return when I can."

Archemese followed him to the door. "Have Dregby return with our prisoner." His eyes narrowed. "It is time for Gin to atone for what he has done."

Darwynyen nodded and then left through the door.

A tear escaped from my eye. "I fear Darwynyen blames me for Sikes's death." I swallowed deeply with remorse. "And in truth, he has every right to."

Archemese put his hand to my shoulder. "There was nothing you could have done for Sikes. His wound was fatal."

To hold back my grief, I put my hands to my face. "I could have listened to Darwynyen. He did not trust Gin from the beginning."

"I see." Archemese sat next to me. "If you are to accept all the blame, perhaps you should take it a step further and damn yourself for his mere existence."

"I would not go that far." I pulled my knees to my chest. "But if it were not for my reckless decisions, Gin would not have accompanied us on this quest."

"Did anyone argue your decision besides Darwynyen?"

"No." I shook my head.

"Then are you suggesting that Sikes and Dregby are simple-minded?" He met my stare. "You must be, because like you, they did not see through him either. In the end, it seems that each of you is to blame."

"You are twisting my words!"

"Am I … or are you?" he asked.

I stood unsteadily, still weakened by the poison's effect. "I am not in the mood for your conundrums."

"You are right; it was insensitive of me to push you." He took my arm to steady me. "In future, I will do what I can to see that no harm crosses your path."

I nodded, not fully understanding. When realization finally struck, I looked at him eagerly. "Have you changed your mind?" I asked. "Are you to join us?"

"Yes." He smiled and gently nodded. "No longer will I deny my destiny. I see now that it is intertwined with yours, as well as your father's."

Relieved by his decision, I forgot Sikes for a moment and embraced him. "Thank you, Archemese." I slowly pulled away.

"I wish I could say that you will not regret your decision, but as you know, I cannot do that." Unable to control my emotions, I began to cry.

"What is it, my dear?"

"I am finding it difficult to look forward," I admitted, wiping my eyes. "How can I when there is so much deceit in my past?"

"Evil will always be around you, Arianna," he counseled. "There is no escaping it. Any man is susceptible to its power. Though with that said, I suspect that Gin is only a pawn doing the will of others."

"Gin chose his own path, as did my father." I clenched my fists. "And because of their decisions, I have not only had to endure the death of Sikes but the death of my mother."

"For now, you must forget your father," Archemese urged. "Our focus must remain on Gin alone, if we are going to find the truth behind his motives."

"Do you honestly believe that Gin will be forthcoming and divulge his secrets?" I asked, doubtful.

"It does not matter what I believe. One way or another, Gin will serve his purpose." He set a narrow green bottle on the shelf near his bed. "In the meantime, if you have any more doubts, know that I will be here for you, should you want to share them."

"Thank you." I managed a smile. It was strange, but a part of me felt close to him. It was as though he was meant to be my father, unlike the one I was born to. Bewildered by my thoughts, I shrugged them off and stepped into the kitchen.

"There is a bucket of water under the table." He pointed. "You may use it for washing."

When I knelt to reach for the bucket, he began to collect his belongings. "In the interest of time, we should leave first thing in the morning," he suggested.

"I agree." I gently patted the wound on my neck with a damp cloth. "Have you been to Aarrondirth before?"

"Yes," he smiled, "many years ago, though I am certain that the city has gone through many changes since then."

"I am sure it has." I began to wipe my face.

Archemese was about to respond when the door opened. It was Darwynyen.

"Darwynyen!" I pushed the dampened strands of hair from my cheeks. "I was …" I paused when I saw the anguish in his eyes.

Archemese approached him with concern. "Where is Gin?" he asked.

"Dregby brings him." He threw down his quiver. "Apparently I am no longer to be trusted where the traitor is concerned."

Archemese nodded. "What are your intentions when it comes to Sikes?"

Darwynyen stiffened, fighting his emotions.

Archemese cleared his throat and then continued. "He deserves a proper burial, and I would like to offer my assistance if it is needed."

"I will place him in the ground," Darwynyen replied. "I have only returned for linen."

"Of course." Archemese withdrew some fabric from below his bed. "Take this. It is all I have."

Darwynyen snatched the offering and then left without another word.

Moments later Dregby appeared with Gin. Secured in his bonds, Gin tripped on the last stair. Maddened, Dregby pushed him through the threshold with vigor, forcing Gin to fall forward. "I now understand his fear of the ring wall, for it turned bright red as we passed through it." Dregby eyed Gin with disdain. "For a moment I thought he might burst into flame."

"You overestimate my powers," Archemese remarked humbly.

"If I have, then it is unfortunate," Dregby mumbled. "Gin deserves no less of a death."

"Are you so blinded by your hatred that you cannot see?" Archemese questioned harshly. "Whether you like it or not, Gin will give us valuable information, should our intention be to bring about Velderon's downfall."

Dregby, as though puzzled by his words, looked at me.

"You are not mistaken, my friend." Archemese put his hand on my shoulder. "I have decided to accompany you on your quest."

"Well!" Dregby's eyes lightened. "That is wonderful news."

"We shall see." Archemese sighed.

"Do you really believe that this washed-up old wizard will do you any good?" Gin struggled to free himself. "I would not count on it! You are the fools, not me!"

Before he could say another word, Dregby hit him over the head with the butt of his axe. Stunned by the blow, Gin instantly fell unconscious. Dregby immediately looked at Archemese. "You said to keep him alive, not awake!"

"I cannot argue with you." Archemese shrugged. "I have heard enough from him as well."

When the tension eased, we silently became absorbed in our own thoughts.

The Burial

When Darwynyen returned to Sikes, his body had grown cold in the absence of the sun. Unable to face his grief, Darwynyen turned away. He would not allow himself to weep. Sikes deserved an honorable burial.

He set off to find a shrub, a natural marker for the grave. He would plant it over the body, following the traditions of the elves. Because the vegetation differed here, it would be difficult to find something similar to the shrubs used in his homeland, Maglavine. Even so, he searched with determination.

No matter which direction he took, his subconscious led him back to the area where he had found Sikes. His heart was desperate for some closure. Although few signs of the tragedy remained, he recognized the spot immediately. The blood-soaked ground had turned black. Images of death swirled through his mind. He would not stay long. Near the discoloration he found what he was looking for. The shrub was small, and though it had just begun in its life, water and sun would allow it to flourish in time. Certain that Sikes would rest easy beneath it, he carefully loosened the roots. Once it was free from the ground, he returned to Sikes's body and began to dig a hole.

Resistance

Shallendria awoke in a panicked state. "Morglafenn!"

"I am here, child." He took her by the hand, attempting to calm her.

Madigan sat at the foot of the bed. "Rest now, my love. The battle is over."

"I know," she replied coldly, and then she looked at Morglafenn. "The presence—I no longer sense it."

He nodded in acknowledgement. "It left with Arianna and Darwynyen."

"Who do you believe it was?" She slowly sat and faced him.

"I have my suspicions." Morglafenn lowered his voice. "We can talk about it later."

"No!" Shallendria began to weep. "I can feel it. Something terrible has happened."

"My heart carries the pain also." Morglafenn squeezed her hand.

"Are you going to share this conversation?" Madigan interrupted. "What upsets you, Shallendria?"

"There has been a death among the elves," Morglafenn replied.

"Who?" Madigan asked desperately, Darwynyen his first thought.

"We do not know," Morglafenn confessed. "To my regret, we can only sense it."

Madigan stood anxiously. "Please tell me you are not referring to Darwynyen."

"No." Shallendria shook her head. "Our bond is close. If it were him I would know it."

Madigan sighed in relief. "If anything were to happen to him on this quest …"

"The quest is not over, Madigan." Morglafenn's eyes bore through him. "The spy is still out there!"

"You keep speaking about this spy," Madigan huffed. "Even if there were one, they would not stand a chance against the others. As you know, Arianna travels with the most skilled companions."

"What if this spy was close to them, someone they did not expect?" Morglafenn raised his brow.

"What are you implying, Morglafenn?"

Morglafenn blinked. He had hoped to avoid this conversation. "I fear it is Gin."

In disbelief Madigan shot forward. "You are mistaken! Apologize now, and I will forget your accusation!"

"I can do no such thing." Morglafenn did not recoil from Madigan's intimidation.

"Morglafenn is right." Shallendria inhaled deeply. "It all makes sense now."

"Why must you push this?" Madigan argued. "Can you not give the boy a chance?"

"Nothing we feel is based on chance, Madigan," Morglafenn countered. "Is our word no longer good enough?"

Shallendria put her fingers to her temples, distracting them both. "The pain is overwhelming." She closed her eyes. "And now that we have spoken, I am certain that it is linked to Arianna's quest."

Morglafenn returned to Shallendria and began to comfort her. Madigan immediately thought of Arianna. To conceal his emotions, he left the room.

At Their Beckoning

Velderon held a hand to his chest; his heart was pounding from the exertion. Only a few more steps, he told himself, as he struggled to reach the crest of the bluff he and the trolls were climbing. On the other side, he was hoping he would find the borders of the Diamyn desert. He was mistaken. When he glanced over the rolling hillside beneath him, he realized that his intended destination would be impossible to reach before nightfall. Out of breath, he sat on a rock. "We will stop here for the night." He summoned the head troll. "Hunt me some rabbit. I am hungry."

The troll bowed obediently and grabbed his crossbow and set off. In their travels they had grown more timid of Velderon, as though they could sense his inner changes.

While the rest of his minions set camp, he pulled out his looking-glass and scanned the horizon. When he found the mountain of Cessdorn, he lowered his gaze to the desert, realizing then that he still had several days of travel ahead of him. Even so, he was certain that he would arrive in Cessdorn before the next moon cycle.

Thinking of his arrival, he brought forward his shoulder bag and began to caress the outline of the stone, knowing that boundless powers would be at his fingertips once it had been joined to the others. As he reveled in the notion, he reached for the twig he had torn off at the beginning of his journey. It was no longer a simple strand of wood; it was now a wand, one he had been developing during his travels. He chuckled when he envisioned the sorcerers' faces when he was finally able to use its power against them. After all, he was attempting a feat unheard of, something that they would probably dismiss as ludicrous. Still, what did they know? Little, he decided. If only they could see him now, they would not dare challenge him. When his hatred peaked, he realized that he had yet to contact them, and he reached into his pocket and pulled out a small fragment of bone that had been delivered by a raven in the early hours of morn. The bone itself had come from the spine of a Rinjeed and was used as a form of secure communication. Its energy would not allow any unwelcome listeners. As he examined the fragment, he wondered if he should make them wait, knowing that his disobedience would anger them. No. What if they had news of importance? It was likely. Why else would they have initiated contact in the middle of his travels?

With that in mind, he snapped the fragment of bone in two. Seconds later, he felt the connection in his mind. *Velderon, why the delay?* the voice questioned. *We sent you the bone of the Rinjeed several hours ago.*

"You are not in command of me!" Velderon snapped.

We have taken control of the dragons, and we intend to send one for you, in an effort to save you time in your journey, the voice growled. *Unless you wish to continue by foot, tell me where you are!*

"I have taken refuge on the last bluff of Naksteed where the foothills bleed into the desert." Velderon replied, half surprised by their generosity. "Send a beast now!"

You do not rule us, Velderon, the voice warned. *I would choose a better tone if I were you!*

"I will do no such thing," he snapped. "It is I who carries the last stone, not you! Without me you have nothing!"

Moments passed before the voice responded. *Very well. Light a fire when you reach the plateau that opens to the Labyrinth.*

"The Labyrinth," Velderon gasped. "It will take me more than a day to reach that destination!"

Two days it should take you, the connection began to weaken, *two days for you to remember your place.* The connection was severed.

Velderon thrust his fist into the air, displaying the wand. "You may speak to me that way now," he wailed. "Things will change when you see what I have planned for you!"

As he regained his composure, one of the trolls knelt by him. "As you requested, we have slain you a rabbit, sire." The creature lowered his head. "Shall we cook it for you?"

"Why do you ask useless questions?" Velderon stood over the creature in a haughty manner. "Have I not already told you that I am famished?"

"Of course, sire. We will prepare it for you now." The troll scurried away.

"Useless creatures," he muttered. As he secured his wand to his waist belt, he again thought to the future. This time, he wondered about his daughter. Although the impression was slight, he could almost feel her, giving him the certainty that she had survived. And if he was right, he knew it was only a matter of time before she would seek him out, leaving only one question—how was he going to tame her?

Darwynyen

Dusk was upon us. Darwynyen had yet to return. Worried, I decided to go and find him. "I will return shortly." I stood away from the table.

"Where are you off to?" Dregby queried.

"She goes to find Darwynyen," Archemese replied.

"Would you like me to go with you?" Dregby asked, setting down the axe he was sharpening.

"There is no need." I opened the door. "I will be fine on my own."

"How will you find your way?" Dregby stepped away from the table.

"Leave her." Archemese handed me a lantern. "Once she has found Darwynyen, he will guide her back safely."

"Very well." Dregby nodded in defeat.

"I will not be gone long," I reassured him, and then I ascended the stair before he could respond.

When I arrived at the camp, I found a freshly dug mound of soil next to a tree. A small bush had been planted upon it. It was Sikes's grave. The pain in my heart resurfaced. Out of respect, I knelt. A tear fell from my cheek as I remembered the events that led to his death. Unsure what to say, I sang a hymn my mother had taught me as a child. As I finished, I placed my hand on the soil. "Rest easy, my friend." I whispered. "I will take care of Darwynyen in your absence."

At the thought of Darwynyen, I realized the lateness of the hour and stood, knowing I only had minutes left to find him.

To my relief, the task was not difficult. As I stepped onto the beach, I saw his silhouette. He was standing at the crest of the rolling surf, looking out. "Darwynyen!" I shouted, waving my arms.

When there was no response, I rushed over. "Darwynyen …" I gently put my hand on his back. "I have been worried for you."

He turned to me with a stare somber enough to be apparent in the darkness. "I have seen to Sikes. He now rests comfortably." His voice was dry and raspy. "You may say your good-byes in the morning."

"I have already said good-bye." I glanced back toward the camp. "I saw the burial mound upon my arrival."

He nodded, returning his gaze to the sea.

Desperate to ease his pain, I tried to embrace him.

To my dismay, he shunned me. "The moon will show its entire face within days." His eyes scanned the northern horizon. "If your father has reached Cessdorn, the sky will soon grow dark to the north."

My chest tightened. His divergence from the subject could only mean one thing … he blamed me for Sikes's death. "I am sorry for what has happened." I looked down. "If only I had listened to you, things would be different."

"It is over now." His response carried little emotion. "Only time will heal my wounds, and until then, I do not wish to speak of Sikes again."

His demeanor left me uneasy. My eyes began to tear. "Darwynyen, if you blame me for Sikes's death, you must tell me."

"Blame you?" He turned. "I do not blame you."

"Then why do you shun me?" I cried. "Can you not see that I need you?"

He immediately turned. "I had no idea you were carrying this guilt." Before I could respond, he embraced me with vigor. "What happened was not your fault."

"Yes, but …"

"There are no buts, Arianna." He released me. "What is done is done. There is no turning back."

Although a part of me wanted further reassurance, I nodded. When I reached for his hands, I noticed that they were covered in dirt. "Your hands!" I gasped.

"Yes." He began to rub them together. "In accordance with elvish custom, the burial process must be kept as natural as possible."

Despite the urge to question this custom, I took his arm in mine. "Come, we must get you cleaned up."

"I am not ready." He stepped back.

Empathizing with his pain, I took him in my arms. "I am here for you, my love, and always will be."

He did not speak. I could feel his body begin to tremble as he gave into his emotions.

The moments that followed were silent. Together we would grieve; together we would find a way through this.

They Grieve in the Shadows

Zenley and Teshna descended upon Sikes's grave when Arianna disappeared into the distance. Overcome with grief, they held one another. "It is all right, my sister," Zenley sobbed. "We will not forget him."

"Forget him!" Teshna cried. "I do not wish to go on without him!"

Zenley rubbed the base of her wings. "Neither do I."

"I am finished with this quest!" She pulled from his hold abruptly. "We should leave now and return to Maglavine!"

"No." He shook his head. "We must finish what we have started. Besides, Aldraveena would never forgive us if we fled."

"Why should we stay?" She crossed her arms. "Arianna has made it clear that she no longer welcomes our company."

"Arianna is our friend," Zenley replied bluntly. "If you speak of her prior actions you have misjudged her, for she was only distraught with grief."

"Did you feel that?" Teshna flew into the air. "We are being summoned."

Zenley turned. "Yes, I feel it too."

Without another word, they sped off in the direction of the cave.

THE TRUTH REVEALED

When I opened the door to the abode, Archemese and Dregby stood. Darwynyen did not acknowledge them and rushed immediately toward Gin. "Wake up, you coward!"

Dregby hurried to take hold of Darwynyen. "Leave him!"

"Wake up!" Darwynyen tried to kick at Gin.

Dregby winced as he struggled to restrain Darwynyen. "My friend, Gin is unconscious for a reason."

"He should be questioned now!" Darwynyen broke free of Dregby's hold. "Once he has confessed to his crimes, we can execute him for treason and be rid of him!"

Archemese intervened, using his staff to block Darwynyen. "Whether Gin confesses or not, we need to learn all we can from him."

When Darwynyen shoved the staff aside, Archemese looked to me for assistance. "Darwynyen, please." I stepped forward. "We must trust Archemese on this matter."

"If you will not listen to me, then listen to Arianna," Archemese pleaded. "If you do not allow Gin to serve his purpose, your friend's death will be in vain."

Darwynyen relented. "Very well, if you require time, you shall have it."

"I will not ask for much, only enough to exact my spell,"

Archemese promised. "And before any more time is wasted, I need both you and Arianna to answer some questions." Darwynyen stubbornly put his hands to his waist. "Darwynyen, follow your elvish traits and do not give way to anger."

Darwynyen released the tension in his shoulders. "What do you need to know?"

"Everything," Archemese insisted. "The smallest piece of information could be vital."

"Then let us proceed." I made way to the kitchen and found a few plates.

Archemese sat at the table. "Arianna, this may be difficult for you, but we must first begin with your father." He hesitated. "Will you share with me what you know of him?"

"To be honest, there is not much to tell." I began to dish out dinner. Not only was I famished, Darwynyen needed a distraction. "My father was very elusive. Only when I met the Men of Moya did I come to realize his intentions."

Archemese slid the water bucket from under the table and then gestured to Darwynyen. "No, my dear, I need to know what magic he possesses," he explained. "Not the white, the dark, for I have not sensed him for several years now."

"We know little." Darwynyen began to wash the dirt from his hands. "He did, however, have a crone in his council, a powerful one."

"Did you learn her name?" He looked at each of us, seeking the answer.

"No." Darwynyen dried his hands and took a seat. "He went to great lengths to keep her identity a secret."

"There is more." I handed Darwynyen his plate. "Before the rebellion, I overheard a conversation she shared with my father in his study that confirmed that she was in contact with the Hynd."

"I see." He glanced over at Gin's motionless body. "And where does this fellow stem from?"

"Unfortunately, we know little of his past." I took a seat next to Darwynyen. "I first befriended him on my journey back to Aarrondirth, but when we arrived in the city, he disappeared." I stirred my stew with a spoon. "After the rebellion we found him in the dungeon. He was badly beaten and claimed it was by the hand of my father's general. Trusting his word, I nurtured him back to health."

"How did he come to be in your fellowship?" Archemese furrowed his brow.

I looked down, ashamed. "It was I who asked him."

Dregby turned from the fireplace. "We had no reason not to trust him," he said in my defense. "At that point Madigan, the new king of Aarrondirth, had placed him in charge of one of the battalions."

"Which was an odd move," Darwynyen remarked. "In the many years I have known Madigan, I can tell you one thing for certain—the man gives his trust sparingly."

"His decisions may have been influenced." Archemese released a heavy breath. "Gin is not only a skilled deceiver—from what we have learned today, he has had the resources of the Hynd behind him."

"Are you saying that Madigan was put under a spell?" Darwynyen asked.

"It is conceivable." Archemese sighed. "In any case, it is the Hynd's misfortune that I have now joined your cause, as their spells and trickery will no longer go unnoticed."

"Have you changed your mind?" Darwynyen puckered his brow. "Are you to join us?"

"Yes." Archemese put a finger to his lips. There was movement on the other side of the room.

Darwynyen immediately stood, rushing over to Gin. "Do not try to escape! Such actions would only lead to your death!" He kicked Gin in the stomach.

Gin groaned and rolled onto his back. His mood appeared to have changed. He was not as high-spirited or confident as before.

This seemed to bother Darwynyen. He yanked Gin up from the ground and forced him to sit on one of the stools near the table.

Archemese nudged Darwynyen aside with a look of intent. "Darwynyen, you must allow me to speak with him."

"I have nothing to tell you," Gin moaned.

"But you do!" Archemese took hold of Gin's chin. "And once I have placed an anaesthetizing spell on you, you will share it."

Darwynyen raised his brow. "Can you do that?"

"Yes." Archemese moved to the fireplace and began to remove one of the stones. "I hold the Book of Eternal Lights." When the stone gave way, he reached into the cavity and pulled out a dust-covered book. "These pages contain numerous spells, many of which I already know."

"You have the Book of Internal Lights!" I saw a spark in Darwynyen's eyes. "If I am not mistaken, I think the elves believe that book to be lost."

Archemese blew the dust off the cover. "Not lost. Appropriated perhaps, but not lost."

Darwynyen stiffened his stance. "That book belongs to the elves."

Archemese shook his head. "It belongs to me." His grasp on the book tightened. "I am the only one who sees its complete translations."

"That is not true." Darwynyen leaned over Archemese's shoulder to better observe the cover. "Aldraveena has utilized its magic before."

"Aldraveena can only decipher the spells the book will allow." Archemese opened the book and began to flip through the pages. "Its pages show me everything."

"But the pages are blank!" Darwynyen's eyes widened.

"Exactly my point," Archemese remarked wryly as he browsed an open page. "Only those gifted in magic can see what is written, and even then access is limited. In the end, the book itself decides what will be revealed."

Although Darwynyen appeared wary, he conceded. "Whatever

your skills, I suppose it does not matter now. We have more important things at hand."

"Will someone open the door?" Archemese looked up from the book. "The fairies have arrived."

Without question, I nodded. As I reached for the handle, I saw it turn. Seconds later, Teshna and Zenley flew through the narrow opening. "Master, we have found the ingredients you have asked for." Teshna flew to Archemese's face.

Taken aback by her words, I frowned as I secured the latch. "What did you call him?"

"Your fairies have sworn their allegiance to me." Archemese winked. "Do not misunderstand. They are attracted to those who delve in magic."

I nodded, realizing then that there was still much to learn from my little companions.

Zenley dropped a piece of dried root onto the table. "Will this be enough, master?"

"Yes." Archemese placed the root into a bowl. "May I have some of your dragon claw shavings?"

"Of course." Teshna landed next to Zenley. "How many will you require?" She reached into her satchel.

"At least three," Archemese replied.

"Then I will give you four." She fluttered her wings.

Archemese gently tickled her stomach with his index finger and then took the shavings and placed them into the bowl.

"Please!" Gin begged. "Do not use that spell on me. I swear, I will tell you everything!"

"Save your pleas. They are no longer warranted." Archemese began to grind the contents. "Instead, take your punishment with courage. The spell should not kill you in the end."

Gin began to sob uncontrollably. "Do not do this, I beg you!"

Archemese ignored him. "Darwynyen, you will need to take hold of Gin's head."

"Say no more." Darwynyen put his arm around Gin's neck to secure him.

Archemese poured the powder into a narrow glass tube. "This mixture will take effect in his eyes." He gestured to Dregby. "To ensure that none of it goes to waste, we will need your assistance."

Although Dregby appeared reluctant, he moved to Darwynyen's side and propped open Gin's eyelids.

"Stay still!" Darwynyen tightened his hold.

"Please," Gin begged again. "Let me go!"

"Do not resist me!" Archemese leaned over Gin and quickly drained the powder into his eyes. When it made contact, it began to fizzle. Gin screamed out in pain. For a moment, I pitied him. The sentiment vanished at the thought of Sikes.

"What is happening?" Dregby stepped back frantically. "We are not barbarians. There is no need for torture!"

"Silence!" Archemese demanded. "You will influence the spell!"

Dregby stamped a hoof in protest.

After several moments, Archemese indicated that Darwynyen could release Gin's neck. Gin's head fell to his breast. Drool trickled from his mouth, and he mumbled incoherently.

Archemese took hold of the book and began to read from it. "*Yaltemel*, you are mine. Yaltemel, I hold power over you." Gin screamed out. When his lungs would give no more, Archemese placed his hand over Gin's eyes. "Gin, can you hear me?" There was no response or movement, and he continued. "Yaltemel, I hold power over you." As he spoke, he dug his hand into the bowl and blew the remaining powder over Gin's face. "Gin, can you hear me?" he asked again. "Raise your head. I command you!"

Gin slowly lifted his head. When his eyes opened, I gasped. The green had vanished; all that remained was the white.

Darwynyen took my hand in support.

"Gin." Archemese sat to face him. "Tell us your plans for today."

"I was to take Arianna from this island and make way for Cessdorn." His words were slurred. "The sorcerers have insisted on her capture."

Archemese looked at me before continuing, "Is Velderon aware of this?"

"No," he mumbled; his head fell back.

Archemese persisted. "What do the Hynd want with Arianna?"

"I do not know," Gin choked.

As Archemese brought Gin's head forward, Darwynyen whispered something in his ear. Archemese nodded. "Gin, how do the sorcerers know of Arianna's survival?"

His head flopped to the side. "After the rebellion, I snuck into the study and contacted them with the eye."

"What did you tell them?" Archemese lifted Gin's head again.

"I told them that she had survived the rebellion, nothing more," he replied. "The conversation was brief. I had to break the connection before I was discovered."

Archemese pushed on. "What has led you down this path of evil? Moreover, where are you from?"

"I am the son of the sorcerer Goramine," Gin replied. "He sent me to watch over Velderon, when his trust in Velderon's leadership had begun to waver."

The tension in the room thickened at his revelation.

Archemese frowned. "If you speak the truth, how did you end up in the dungeon?"

"Velderon insisted I stay." Gin cleared his throat. "After the trolls gave me a beating in the cavern, I took refuge in the dungeon, where I was found the next day."

Sickened by Gin's deceit, I felt the urge to strangle him.

Archemese hesitated. "Velderon knows of your identity, then?"

"Yes, he knowwss," Gin slurred.

Archemese stood to examine Gin's eyes. "What are your father's plans in the coming months?"

"He will use the stones to seek the Amberseed." Gin tried to close his eyes. "His sole desire is to delve into its power."

"Where will they lead their attack?" Archemese began to speak quickly, as though he feared the spell was weakening.

"They will lead three attacks from the north. Most of the forces will assail Biddenwade, while smaller battalions make way for Walferd and then Aarrondirth, in an attempt to weaken the flank."

Dregby looked toward Darwynyen with dread. "Their plans have changed," he whispered.

"It was to be anticipated," Darwynyen replied. "As you know, Shallendria was not unnoticed by the eye."

Dregby began to pace the room. "Even so, how does Gin know of this?"

"My father sent word shortly after the elf wench left for Tayri," Gin replied. "There is no escaping him." A tear fell from his eye. "He is always watching over me."

"How does he communicate with you if not with the eye?" Archemese sent Dregby a sharp look, requiring he stay silent.

"With the bones of the Rinjeed." Gin's head fell to the side again.

"I have never heard of such things," Archemese scoffed. "Tell me more."

Before Gin could respond, the door was pummeled. Startled, I leapt from the stool. Darwynyen rushed over to the door, opening it enough to peer through it. "Ravens!" He grimaced, slamming it shut. "There are many of them!"

"Spies." Dregby pulled his axe and met Darwynyen at the door. "The Hynd, aware of our deeds, must have sent the ravens to hinder us!"

Archemese examined Gin, who had suddenly become unresponsive.

"What is happening to him?" I began to shake Gin's shoulders.

Archemese pulled me back. "It is the will of the Hynd. To protect him, they have taken control of his mind."

"What are we going to do?" I cried. "There is evil all around us!"

When Darwynyen noticed the door latch begin to turn, he snapped, "Not now, Arianna!" Dregby quickly grabbed it.

"Are they trying to enter?" I slowly reached for my sais, stunned. "How can they do that? They are only birds!"

Dregby leaned into the door. "Birds or not, they will soon break through!"

The pummeling ceased.

Cautiously, Darwynyen slowly opened the door. "They are gone," he sighed.

"That is because their work here is done." Archemese lifted Gin's head. "Gin has been taken into a trance conjured by the sorcerers. The spell is powerful and will hold strong for hours, maybe even days."

Darwynyen propped Archemese's wood axe under the latch. "Despite our situation here, it is in our interest to advise Madigan of the Hynd's battle plans, so that he can ready the troops in our absence." He looked at Archemese. "Are you able to connect with my cousin Shallendria?"

Archemese shook his head. "It is too dangerous. The Hynd will now be watching, waiting to intercept our thoughts."

Dregby stowed his axe. "Then we should leave tonight and immediately set forth for Aarrondirth."

"There is no need." Archemese gathered some rope, eyeing Darwynyen. "I will call upon the Sirens in the morn. They will expedite our travels then."

Darwynyen nodded reluctantly and held Gin while Archemese secured him.

I yawned. "If we are in agreement, we should rest now, while we can."

"Very well." Dregby took his comfort near the door, where he wedged the wood axe more firmly with his hooves. "Let us hope our feathered friends do not return in the interim."

Darwynyen gave him a snide look and then led me to a rug near the fireplace as Archemese settled into his bed.

A Secret Left Untold

It was early. The others had yet to stir. Silently, Archemese made his way across the room. There was something he needed to do, something secret.

Ever so slowly, he pulled out a stone from the opposite side of the fireplace and removed a small case. Before opening it, he made sure the others were still resting. They would not understand. Even he was frightened by it. So much so, he had not disturbed its contents for years. Only now, when the times were changing, did he understand that he would need to use it.

When he opened the box, he immediately felt the power, and quickly closed it. As he placed it into his satchel, he heard movement. To his relief it was only Dregby. "Is it time to wake?" Dregby mumbled, stretching his hind legs.

"Not yet." Archemese whispered, picking up a kettle. "Sleep now, while I warm some water for the morning."

In response, Dregby turned onto his side and fell back into slumber.

Our Return

Gin was still unconscious when we set out, leaving Dregby and Darwynyen no option but to drag him to the boat. Meanwhile, Archemese and I prepared and stowed our belongings for travel.

"Arianna, make sure there is enough room in the stern." Archemese tossed one of the satchels into the midsection. "We will need a place for Gin."

"Of course." I shifted the supplies. "Do you see them yet?" referring to Darwynyen and Dregby.

Archemese put his hand to his brow. "Yes," he nodded. "They have just broken through the tree line."

"Do they require our assistance?" I jumped from the boat.

"No." he grabbed his staff. "They seem to be doing fine on their own."

"What about Teshna and Zenley?" I asked, glancing around the island.

"Under the circumstances, they were eager to leave and have already made way for the mainland."

"I cannot blame them." I knelt to pick up a handful of sand. "They were close to Sikes." I paused. "As strange as this may sound, it almost feels as though we are abandoning him."

"He will not be alone for long." Archemese spoke reassuringly. "When the war is over, the elves will return for him."

Comforted by the thought, I nodded.

Minutes later Darwynyen and Dregby approached, Gin's motionless body in tow. As they fought with the surf, Dregby reared up on his hind legs, thrusting Gin into the boat. As Gin's body fell into the hull, his head hit one of the benches with force. Dregby smirked. "Someone is going to wake with a sore head!"

"It is nothing less than he deserves." Darwynyen jumped into the bow. He extended his hand. "Arianna, come. We must be on our way."

Once in the boat, I shook the water from my boots and then moved to the stern. Darwynyen took Archemese by the arm, assisting him onto the bench beside him.

Dregby leapt into the midsection. "Did either of you grab my leather waist belt?"

"Yes." I pointed to my satchel. "It is safe within my belongings."

"Thank you, my dear." Dregby slowly nestled into the hull.

Darwynyen stood, taking hold of an oar. "Ready your oars while I push us off."

Archemese and I nodded as we positioned ourselves, and as the boat swayed, we began to paddle.

When we reached the mouth of the inlet, Archemese pulled a small, peculiar-looking shell from his pocket. He cleared his throat. "Our work here is done. Now, I will summon the Sirens."

I watched him, intrigued, as he blew into the shell; no sound came from it. "I fear your device is broken," I teased.

Archemese chuckled as he caught his breath. "I can assure you that it is working just fine."

"But there is no sound," I argued.

"Things are not always as they appear, Arianna." Archemese winked. "See for yourself." He gestured toward the bow.

When I turned, I saw three Sirens swiftly approaching.

Seconds later, Zhendon appeared at the side of the boat. "Do you require our assistance, my lord?"

"Yes." Archemese stiffened his shoulders. "You must take us to the mainland."

"Why?" Zhendon frowned. "Are you leaving us?"

Archemese nodded. "My time on this island has ended."

"You cannot mean what you say!" Her tail slapped against the water. "How could you leave us now, at a time when we need you most?"

Archemese's eyes softened. "If I am to protect you, I must first set right the atrocities that have taken place here, whilst bringing about the downfall of your enemies."

Zhendon was about to respond, when her companions emerged from the water. Archemese put his hand to his temple, as though he was speaking to Zhendon through their minds. At first she appeared frustrated. Only after several moments of what I guessed to be deliberation did she seem to resign, gesturing to her companions. As the boat was propelled into motion, Archemese looked at me and nodded. Thereafter, we continued in silence.

When we were safely on the mainland, Darwynyen, Dregby, and I began to unload the boat. Archemese left to speak with Zhendon. The tension in their body language was obvious. When Archemese turned, she grabbed his arm. With compassion, he put his hand to her cheek. She wiped her eyes without words and then immersed her body in the water. Archemese watched as she swam away.

Concerned, I left Darwynyen and Dregby to join him. "Is everything all right?" I put my hand to my brow to shield the sunlight. "Does it grieve you to be leaving?" I continued before he could respond. "If it does, then perhaps you can take comfort in the thought of your return when the battle over the stones is over."

"There is nothing here for me to return to." He looked down. "The only thing I grieve is the years I wasted on that island. I should have acted sooner. I knew the Sirens were in trouble, yet I did nothing." I felt his hand on my shoulder. "Forget my ramblings. Now is not the time to dwell on the past. From this moment forward, we must gaze upon the future alone."

As he finished, an orchestra of song began to echo amongst the breaking waves. It reminded me of the day Darwynyen and I arrived at Maglavine, only this time the song was disheartening. "Do not let the melody sadden you," Archemese remarked. "It is a song of farewell and good fortune."

"Arianna," Darwynyen shouted. "Come ashore!"

"Is there a problem?" Archemese asked, taking my arm in support as we left the water.

"Yes." Darwynyen knelt by the supplies. "We must lighten our load. There is too much here for us to carry." As his eyes scanned the mound, he frowned. "Arianna, did you bring Sikes's belongings?"

I nodded uncomfortably. "I suppose I did."

He lifted Sikes's satchel with a huff. "Arianna, Sikes is no longer in need of this stuff. You should have left them. The only thing of importance was his eternal ring, which I now carry." He pulled the ring from his pocket.

"I know." I blinked heavily. "I apologize. I was not thinking."

"There is no harm done." Dregby eyed the ring greedily. "We all make mistakes."

When Darwynyen saw Dregby's gaze, he returned the ring to his pocket and lifted Sikes's satchel. "How is his family to find this?"

Dregby reached for the satchel. "How about I take his belongings to the tree line and bury them with a marker?"

Darwynyen stepped back. "No, I will do it." Before Dregby could respond, he ran off.

Ashamed of my actions, I turned away. "Why did I …" I hesitated.

"There was no malice in your actions, Arianna." Archemese freed the hair from around my shoulder. "What has happened here will soon be forgotten."

"Listen to Archemese, Arianna." Dregby began to rummage through the remainder of our belongings, and then he paused. "I see Gin's satchel is also here."

"I brought that," Archemese declared. "When Gin awakes I intend to examine its contents in front of him." He knelt to pick it up. "Until then, I will carry it."

Dregby's eyes began to wander. "Archemese, as you are familiar with this region, I will assume that you know the river passage." He paused nonchalantly. "Do you have a suggested route for us to take?"

"To be honest, I have not thought about it." Archemese shrugged.

I looked sharply at Dregby; I realized that his intention was to have us avoid Iramak. "You know our destination," I spoke bluntly. "We are going to Iramak."

Archemese leaned on his staff. "Why would we go to Iramak?" he questioned.

"To seek the alliance of the little people," I replied. "If we are to succeed against my father, we must unite as one."

Archemese nodded. "I suppose the little people would have their uses. There is no doubt the Hynd would underestimate their abilities when it comes to warfare."

"Many traps surround that city." Dregby spoke, attempting to dissuade him. "Despite your powers, will you be able to lead us there safely?"

"Yes," Archemese replied. "My magic will help us evade the traps you speak of." He paused. "With that said, the river passage is no longer an option."

Dregby gave in. "Very well. Iramak it is, then."

Darwynyen rushed over. "Are we ready?"

Dregby turned to the boat. "We first need to retrieve Gin."

"Him!" Darwynyen tensed. "I had almost forgotten."

"If only we could." Dregby stretched his hind legs, as though preparing for the added weight. "Asleep or not, it is best not to leave him unattended."

"Shall I help?" Archemese dug his staff into the sand. "The rolling waves might hinder you."

"There is no need," Darwynyen replied, trudging through the surf. "We can manage."

Dregby nodded in affirmation and then turned to follow Darwynyen. When they reached the boat their actions became agitated.

"What is it?" I yelled.

"He is gone!" Darwynyen shouted. "I do not understand. We only left him for a minute!"

As they frantically searched the water around the boat, I looked at Archemese. "Call upon the Sirens," I pleaded. "We must find him!"

"It would be of no use. If he has fled, he will stay in the shallows." Archemese closed his eyes. "I will summon the fairies instead. They will be of more use to us."

While Archemese made the connection, I frantically scanned the shoreline, unable to accept the notion that Gin had gotten away. Darwynyen was right—we had only left him for a minute … or had it been longer?

"Stay calm, Arianna." Archemese slowly opened his eyes. "The fairies come to us now."

"We have no time to waste!" I began to run south along the beach. "Let us search the shoreline while we await them. The veil of the surf will not hide him for long."

Archemese nodded. "I will go this way," and he ran in the opposite direction.

In the end, our searches proved futile. Even with the help of the fairies, Gin was nowhere to be found. Darwynyen was furious. Archemese tried to reason with him. "Darwynyen, we can search for Gin no longer. The lad is lost to us!"

"No!" Darwynyen insisted. "We must keep searching." He kicked the sand in frustration. "Sikes's death will be in vain if we do not recapture him. Gin must pay for what he has done!"

"And he will." Archemese gestured toward the forest. "Passage through those woodlands will be trying with no compass to guide him. Furthermore, he has no weapons or food. The odds of him succeeding are minimal. Alone and starving, he will succumb to the elements and eventually be forgotten. A dishonorable death few would wish upon another, even their worst enemy."

"If he has entered the forest, we can track him." Darwynyen picked up his satchel and stomped toward the tree line, making it apparent that he was not interested in Archemese's reasoning. "This debate is over. It is time for us to set out."

"Tracking him will only take us off course," Archemese insisted, following after him. "If your intention is to honor your friend, would it not be better served if we were to reach Aarrondirth before the next moon cycle?"

"Archemese is right." Dregby trotted after them. "Darwynyen, you must listen to reason."

Archemese grabbed Darwynyen by the arm. "Gin's destiny no longer lies in our hands. We have other priorities now."

Darwynyen halted, keeping his gaze on the forest. "Very well, we will continue with our quest."

When Archemese and Dregby returned for their belongings, I looked at Darwynyen. His pain over having to surrender his vengeance against Gin without any closure was plain to see. Even so, Archemese was right. It would be difficult for Gin to survive in the elements, especially with no food or weapons. And if he should find a dishonorable end, I strongly felt that he deserved it, despite Archemese's beliefs.

"Darwynyen will be all right." Dregby tried to reassure me, gently patting my back in passing.

"I know." I managed a smile and then rushed after Darwynyen.

Before stepping into the forest, I hesitated. Unlike the other regions I had visited, the shelter of this woodland was foreboding. Long, lanky trees made the area dark and gloomy. It was dense with vines and shrubbery, and the air was thick and heavy on my chest. Pollens and spores tickled at my senses. Insects buzzed all around us. "This should be interesting," Darwynyen grumbled sarcastically.

Teshna and Zenley descended from one of the branches. "We are here, master!" Teshna fluttered her wings to attract Archemese's attention. "If it is your wish, we will find a safe route for you to travel."

"You will only get us lost!" Dregby huffed.

Archemese took lead. "No, they will guide us through. Our connection is strong. Their minds show me the way as we speak."

"Then what are we waiting for?" Darwynyen put his hand on my back, nudging me forward.

"This way," Archemese directed us. "The fairies have found a path up ahead."

As I followed in Archemese's footsteps, I anxiously observed my surroundings. Sounds I had not heard before echoed throughout the trees and shrubbery, making their source impossible to find. "Do not fear the creatures that inhabit this woodland, Arianna." Archemese glanced over his shoulder, making it obvious that he had been reading my mind. "I can assure you that they are far more timid than us."

I stiffened when a flock of birds, alerted by our presence, scattered from the higher branches. "Even so, they might not take kindly to trespassers." I swiped at the insects.

"If we keep moving, we will be safe." Dregby took the lead and began to slice away at the undergrowth.

"Not if these insects choose to follow us." Darwynyen pulled up the hood on his cloak.

I slapped my arm, squishing a tiny black bug. "They are no doubt relentless." I continued to swat my arms; I next stepped into a cluster of tiny green bugs. "If only we could seek their allegiance, the war might turn in our favor."

When the others chuckled, the tension eased. Thereafter we continued on in silence.

When we came to a clearing, dusk was upon us. It opened

onto a shallow stream. Small waterfalls drained from the iron-crested stones that almost appeared as a footbridge. The melody of the current was welcoming and immediately brought me ease. Darwynyen dropped his satchel. "We should set camp here. We are soon to be without sunlight."

"Agreed." Archemese glanced over the area. "Despite the fairies' guidance, it is too risky for us to carry on without injury."

"I wonder where they have gotten to?" I wiped the sweat from my brow.

"They are exploring." Archemese dropped both his and Gin's satchels. "It is their nature."

Dregby pulled a small axe from his waist belt. "While you prepare camp, I will cut some wood for a fire."

"Then I will see to the fish." Archemese unfastened the end of his staff, revealing a spear. "It is one chore I am good at," he remarked lightly.

While Darwynyen retrieved some stones for a fire pit, I sat on a boulder on the edge of the stream and slowly removed my boots. My feet were aching. To ease them, I placed them in the cool water. As I adjusted to the temperature, I noticed my reflection. I still looked the same on the outside, no different than I did after a day of hard work in Hoverdire; it was the inside that was changing. Lost in my thoughts, I retraced the route that had brought me here. We had been through so much that I began to wonder where I had gathered my strength. When I looked at Darwynyen, I knew the answer. Gin then came to mind. His deceit was unforgivable. Tears welled in my eyes at the memory of Sikes. I had lost many people whom I knew and loved. The real shame came with the fact that mourning now somehow seemed to come easier. Could it be that my heart was turning cold? Unsettled by the thought, I grabbed my boots and returned to camp. There was no point in dwelling on a question I could not answer.

Upon my arrival, I was surprised to find that Archemese was already cooking the two fish that he had caught upstream.

Darwynyen was sharpening one of his blades. As I sat next to him, I took notice of Dregby, who was searching through Gin's belongings. I assumed his actions had come with Archemese's approval.

"Ah," he smirked. "Gin was kind enough to leave us with a bottle a spirits." He extracted the cork and took a swig.

"Is there anything else of interest?" Darwynyen accepted the bottle when Dregby offered it.

"Only this odd-looking fragment." Dregby held it toward the fire.

Darwynyen took it. "If I were to make I guess, I would say it was a piece of soft stone." He handed it to Archemese.

Archemese carefully examined the piece until the fish began to burn. "My fish!" He dropped the fragment to the ground and then lifted the spit from the flames to blow on it.

Darwynyen picked up the fragment and returned it to Dregby with a shrug. "Do what you will with it."

Dregby placed it in one of his pockets. "Do not tell me the great wizard, Archemese, has burned a simple dinner!" he bantered.

"A little." Archemese began to remove the fish from the spit. "It is still edible."

I heard a sharp cry echo from within the trees. "What was that?"

Dregby tossed some wood onto the fire. "If I am not mistaken, it is the call of fire beasts. They are common in my region as well." He took a step back when the smoke hit his face. "They howl when the moon nears the completion of its cycle." He coughed, wafting at the flames.

I turned to Darwynyen. "When is that to be?"

"Soon." He looked down. "Let us not worry about it now."

"What are fire beasts?" I asked.

"They are wild felines who hunt in the night." Dregby continued to cough. "Do not worry, Arianna. They are skilled hunters who will only attack when they have the advantage. As long as we stay together, they will be no threat to us."

I nodded amidst the howling.

"Perhaps one of us should stay awake and keep watch." Archemese eyed Darwynyen. "Not only for the fire beasts."

Darwynyen nodded. "I will go first, as I require the least amount of rest."

"You forget I also wear a pendant. Even so, I will not argue with you, as I must admit that I am a little exhausted by these travels." Archemese stretched his arms.

"You are not alone." I yawned as I leaned into Darwynyen's chest. "I also yearn for rest."

"Because I do not have the luxury of your pendants, you will get no complaints from me." Dregby curled up near the fire. "Wake me when it is my shift."

"With that said, I will go next," Archemese offered.

Darwynyen ignored Archemese. "Do not get too comfortable, Dregby," he teased. "One of us will call upon you soon." He winked at Archemese, who was readying his blanket.

Dregby mumbled something before turning onto his side.

When Darwynyen covered me in his blanket, I closed my eyes, too exhausted to partake in the banter.

The Final Escort

It was midday when Velderon reached the plateau that extended onto the labyrinth, the location that was given to him by the Hynd. Eager to reach Cessdorn, his final destination, Velderon put down his satchel and began to start a fire with magic. Despite the keen eye of the dragons, he would not risk the chance of going unnoticed.

"Why are we stopping here?" One of the trolls approached him, confused. "We should keep moving. Cessdorn awaits us, master!"

"Speak again and I will cut out your tongue," Velderon growled.

The troll backed slowly away. "Forgive me, my lord." He gestured to his companions. "Perhaps our master requires some time on his own." One by one the creatures retreated from the bluff.

"Wretched trolls," he mumbled, blowing on the wood as it began to spark. "They should be punished for their lack of respect." As he pulled out his wand, he heard the roar of a beast. "At last!" he cried. They were finally coming for him.

To be certain he was seen, he stood at the crest of the bluff and began to wave his arms. "I am here!" he yelled.

Before he could continue, he was struck from behind. He

saw the ground disappear beneath him and realized what was happening. Safe in the dragon's talons, Velderon broke into a sinister laughter, confident that there was no means to thwart him now.

BORDERLANDS

As we progressed in our travels, the landscape began to change. The rich air slowly lost its humidity, and the terrain became more rugged. Pine and spruce trees sprung from the dry undergrowth, which was blanketed in a cushion of dead needles that crunched beneath our feet.

When we reached the crest of a bluff, I heard an odd sounding chime. "What is that sound?" I halted.

"Over there," Darwynyen pointed.

My heart stopped when I saw a collection of bones hanging from a distant tree.

"What …?" I stepped back; a gust of wind rattled the bones. "Have we stumbled across a burial ground?"

"No, my child," Archemese chuckled. "These bones are here to ward off intruders. It is the way of the little people"

"We must be careful in these parts." Dregby drew his pickaxe. "Many traps lay here."

Archemese brandished his staff. "As I said before, my magic will protect us."

Teshna and Zenley jumped from Archemese's shoulder. "Teshna and I will make way for Iramak, where we will alert the little people to your coming arrival," Zenley stated.

"If you are able, have them …" Before Archemese could finish they were gone. Archemese immediately put his hand to his temple and then changed his mind, instead kneeling to the ground. "I see now there is no controlling them," he muttered.

Darwynyen rested on a boulder. "Will you need some time to prepare your staff?"

"Yes," Archemese spoke harshly. "Leave me be, and I will get started." His tone made it clear that he was annoyed by the fairies' disobedience.

"As you wish." Darwynyen extended his hand. "Come, Arianna, there is room for you here."

I nodded as I took a seat. My feet throbbed. For relief, I again removed my boots. Dregby followed my lead and knelt on his forelegs, resting his hooves with a sigh. Darwynyen was quite the opposite and did not seem bothered by our travels. And though I was bewildered by his strength, I kept silent.

To my regret, only minutes passed before Archemese stood. The magic he had conjured illuminated his staff from top to bottom. "We must be on our way." He scanned the trees with confidence.

Darwynyen handed me one of my boots. "How long will the spell last?"

"Only an hour, maybe two." Archemese reached for his satchel.

"Can you not recast it?" I asked as I secured my boots.

He shook his head. "Not until the morn. My powers have already been weakened."

"Understood." Darwynyen collected the remaining supplies. "Lead the way, my friend."

We had only taken a few steps when Archemese stopped. "My staff is vibrating." He scanned the area. "There is a trap up ahead."

Darwynyen reached his side. "What should we do?"

"Nothing." Archemese lifted his staff in the air, *"Stonemf!"* Seconds later a barrage of tiny arrows sped through the air ahead of us. Dregby and Darwynyen pulled me to the ground.

Archemese smiled. "Do not fear, the magic will warn us well in advance." He extended his hand. "Now come—there is little time to be wasted."

As we walked deeper into the unknown, I noted every step. Dregby put his hand on my forearm. "Calm yourself, my child. These traps will dissipate in time."

"Are you certain?" I asked.

"No." He shrugged lightly and then joined Archemese, who walked before us.

Cessdorn at Last

With little respect, the dragon dropped Velderon on the stairs leading to the altar of Cessdorn. On impact, pain coursed through his bones, forcing Velderon to rest a moment before standing. As he ascended the final steps, he pulled out his wand.

When he reached the edifice, the sorcerers crept from the shadows. "Thank you, my lords." He sent them a superior smile. "I am most grateful to be back in Cessdorn." As the men nodded, he raised his wand. "I cast upon you *Z'rderven*!" A surge of green light bolted from his wand. Caught off guard, the sorcerers' bodies slowly began to turn to stone.

"Velderon, you cast a spell beyond your powers!" Goramine winced. His legs and arms were already transformed. "Retract it now, before I turn it upon you!"

"Do what you will," Velderon cackled. "I can assure you that you will not succeed."

In response, the sorcerers frantically tried to counter the spell.

"You waste your time!" Velderon circled them. "This wand is not to be underestimated." He raised it as evidence.

"What do you want?" Goramine growled, as the spell overtook his torso.

"I do not like your tone." Velderon raised his brow. "Perhaps I should use you as an example." He paused. "That may be necessary, should the others need reminding of their place."

"Do not be foolish, Velderon!" Goramine continued to fight the spell.

Angered by Goramine's insolence, Velderon directed his wand toward him. "*Z'rderven!*"

Seconds later, a bolt of green light consumed Goramine's body.

Powerless to counter the spell, Goramine cried out as the remainder of his body turned to stone.

Velderon looked at the others. "Choose your fate now, and choose it wisely!"

"We will serve you, if that is your desire," one of the sorcerers whimpered. Unable to move, he eyed the other sorcerers, who immediately nodded.

Pleased by their decision, Velderon released them from the consuming spell. He met each of their eyes as they recovered. "I warn you now, do not deceive me. If you do, I can assure you that you will suffer a fate far worse than Goramine's."

Terrorized, the sorcerers quickly swore their allegiance. When they finished, Velderon dismissed them. "Be gone," he demanded. "Do not return unless I summon you!"

At his words, the sorcerers scurried down the altar stairs. In their absence, he turned to the stones. There were more important matters to attend to.

Iramak

The terrain was unforgiving. After fighting our way through a dense cluster of bushes, we arrived at a steep incline. There was little to hold onto during our ascent; most of the shrubbery was riddled with thorns. My legs burned, and when I felt I could go on no longer the magic in Archemese's staff began to fail. "It is of no use." Archemese leaned against a tree when we reached a narrow ridge, and caught his breath. "The spell has run its course. We can go no further until morning."

Dregby stretched his hind legs. "I cannot speak for the rest of you, but this rugged terrain has left me in need of a rest."

"You are not alone, for I need rest also." I sat on a fallen tree to ease the pressure on my feet.

Darwynyen scanned the area. "If we cannot proceed without magic, it seems we have no choice but to set camp here."

Dregby took a sip from his canteen. "If we had known, we could have stopped back at that little creek. At least there we would have had some resources."

"We still have our rations." I dropped my satchel to the ground.

"Master!" Zenley emerged from the trees. Teshna flew up beside him. "The little people are not far behind us." He fluttered his wings. "They have come to escort you to Iramak."

Teshna landed on my shoulder. "We would have returned sooner, but we first had to negotiate their trust." She brushed my hair from around my ear. "Arianna, how are you faring?" she whispered. "Not once have I seen you this exhausted."

"I will be fine." I reached for my canteen and took a mouthful.

"Where are they?" Archemese asked impatiently.

"Over there," Zenley pointed. "They should come into view shortly."

Darwynyen put his hand on my back. "Arianna, you have grown pale."

"There is no …" I squinted when I saw movement in the distance.

"What is it?" He turned.

"I am not sure." I moved past him. At first I thought my eyes were deceiving me. No. There was no mistaking the two tiny individuals moving over the land toward us. They were real. "I do not believe my eyes," I declared as they approached.

"I said the same thing when I first saw them," Dregby chuckled.

No taller than my knees, they could almost be mistaken for young children. Yet their bodies were those of fully grown men. Their hair was matted and dark in color. They wore only loin cloths, and their arms, shoulders, and legs were covered with thick leather protectors. The exposed skin was painted in symbols I did not recognize. Unique in their own way, I wanted to touch them.

The lankier one waved, lowering his spear. "Archemese, I would not have believed it! We thought you would never leave that island!" He glanced at his companion. "In fact, many of our people had begun to believe in the myth and thought you were dead."

"As you can see, I am not." He knelt. "It is good to see you, Jeel. It has been far too long."

"What brings you to the lands of Iramak?" the other asked. He was a little shorter than Jeel and had a pouched belly.

"We can discuss that later, Naseyn." Archemese stood. "Everyone, I would like you to meet Jeel and Naseyn. They are the keepers of this territory."

"We are pleased to make your acquaintance." I smiled, glancing over the jewelry that adorned their necks and wrists. "This is Darwynyen and Dregby." I extended my hand toward each of them.

Naseyn gave them a fleeting look. "Who are you?" he asked.

"I am Arianna," I replied.

"You are a female." His eyes scanned the length of my body.

"Have you never seen a woman of Man's Blood?" Archemese chortled.

Naseyn looked down humbly, shaking his head.

"I have." Jeel nudged Naseyn aside. "It happened once when I was hunting in the eastern regions of our land."

"You have not!" Naseyn nudged him back.

Archemese raised his brow. "Gentlemen, is it not time for us to be on our way?"

"Of course." Jeel composed himself.

Naseyn looked over his shoulder and began to whistle in code.

Alerted by his call, two gigantic fireflies emerged from the trees. Apprehensive, I slowly backed away. As they approached, their massive wings fluttered in harmony, creating a slight breeze.

Naseyn tugged at my leg, "Do not be frightened." He ran over and mounted one of the creatures. "They are our friends!"

I nodded and observed the creatures. In their own way, they were beautiful. Dark bristle-like hair covered their bodies, which glistened silver in the faltering light, and an iridescent glow that churned like hot ambers in a fire emanated from their underbellies.

"Come!" Jeel pointed his spear forward. "Iramak awaits us!"

Archemese stepped forward. "Lead the way, my friend!"

The incline decreased as we traveled. We regained our strength, "Are there still traps in this area?" Dregby, carefully examining the surroundings, asked Jeel. "Or do you only set them in the outer-lying regions?"

"The traps are everywhere." Jeel waved his arm to and fro. "The ones near the outer rim are only meant to ward off intruders. Though if the intruder persists, the traps become more lethal." He paused. "It matters, nonetheless, for those who trade with us know the entrance to Iramak is by way of the river."

"I thought as much." Dregby looked back at me. "Do you see now that it would have been more prudent for us to have taken the river passage?"

I ignored him, and he returned his focus to Jeel. "Forgive me for asking, but if there are traps everywhere, how can you be certain that there are none on the path you now lead us on?"

"Because," Jeel laughed wryly, "we are the ones who built them, silly!" He put his hand to his mouth when Dregby glared.

"Do not fear," Naseyn interjected. "You are safe in our company." When Dregby nodded, Naseyn pulled his reins, a perplexed look upon his face. "Could it be that I met you once before?" He scratched his brow in thought. "Yes, I remember you." His eyes brightened. "You used to trade in our city."

"It is not me who you remember," Dregby responded in a proud manner. "I believe you speak of my father. He once traded with your people."

"Then you are most welcome, my friend!" Naseyn bowed his head.

"Thank you." Dregby bowed his head in return. "I look forward to the hospitality of your people when we arrive in Iramak."

"As we will look forward to the rekindling of forgotten alliances." Naseyn put his tiny hand to his chest before urging the firefly ahead.

Their conversation left me with questions. I took Archemese's arm. "If you knew Jeel and Naseyn before your time on the island, is it too much to assume that their people live extended lives? Do they delve in magic, as do the elves?"

"You are very observant, Arianna." Archemese used my arm for support. "Even so, I can assure you that the little people do not possess the magic of the elves. Still, for some reason their life span doubles or sometimes triples those of the Man's Blood. It is a mystery yet unsolved that many ponder."

"For their sake, perhaps it is a mystery better left unexplored." I glanced over Jeel and Naseyn. "As you know, eternal life can be very tempting, and I fear the greed of others would only end with their demise."

"Your wisdom in these matters is remarkable." He squeezed my forearm.

"Why do they cover their bodies in paintings?" I asked.

"I do not know." Archemese shrugged. "But if you are curious, you should ask them."

I swallowed deeply as I mustered up my courage. I released Archemese's arm. "Jeel, is there a reason you paint your bodies?"

"Why?" He raised his brow flirtatiously. "Do you like the designs?"

"Yes." I began to blush. "But what do they mean?"

"They are the markings of our families." He displayed his arms. "The dyes are bled into our skin on the day we reach our manhood."

"Does it hurt?" I bit my lip.

"No," he responded firmly, and then he shrugged. "Well, maybe a little."

Darwynyen put his hand on my back. "Where are Arnep and Sydnay? I have not seen them since their last trip to Aarrondirth."

"You ask of Arnep and Sydnay." He looked at Naseyn. "If I am correct, they are currently leading a hunting expedition in the north."

Naseyn concurred. "They follow the migration pattern

of a falcon that is only known to this region in the summer months."

Darwynyen appeared disappointed. "Is there no way to summon them?"

"Regretfully, no." Jeel shook his head. "It goes against our laws to interrupt a hunt."

Ending the conversation, Darwynyen kept silent as we pushed on.

† † †

We had completely lost sunlight when we reached the river of Tanmeen. The course of the moon, whether or not it was in our favor, was nearing the completion of its cycle, and its powerful beams were enough to light the vicinity around us.

"Tanmeen!" Archemese bellowed with elation. "No longer is our destination far from our reach!"

I smiled, once again taking his arm for support. The slopes before us were steep, and I would not allow him to maneuver them alone. Thankfully, the vines and dead roots aided our decent. As I struggled with my footing, I held tight to Archemese and supporting each other, we made it to the bottom safely, followed by Darwynyen and Dregby.

"This way!" Naseyn shouted, as he and Jeel directed their fireflies around a bend.

The canyon was deep and narrow. We were hidden by a wrinkle in the face of the land. After several turns in the winding path, we reached the great city of Iramak. It was just as Dregby had said. Carved out of the cliff bank, torch light flickered from the hundreds of openings that encompassed the area. The silhouettes of several little people walked the pathways that connected each level, while fireflies flew in and out of the caves in the higher reaches.

When the little people caught sight of us, they gasped in fear, each of them fleeing in opposite directions, clearly panicked.

Archemese halted. "Rather than cause alarm, we should settle here for the night." He pointed to a jut in the cliff. "We can take shelter over there."

"There will be no argument from me." Dregby dropped his satchel.

Darwynyen looked at Jeel. "Where is your leader?" he asked. "There is much we need to discuss."

"Our grand master will not address you until he is ready," he replied bluntly, and then he looked at Archemese. "You know our customs."

Archemese nodded. "We will wait until he calls upon us."

Jeel looked at Naseyn. "Shall we go to the stables?"

"After you!" Naseyn chuckled as he sped off.

"We will see you in the morning!" Jeel waved, following after him.

Teshna flew to Archemese's face. "If you do not object, we would like to take this opportunity to explore further."

Archemese rested on a boulder. "What is this? Are you not to flee without asking?" When she glared at Zenley, he continued. "Go. Enjoy yourselves. We are safe for now."

"Thank you, master." Zenley took hold of Teshna and flew out of sight.

Darwynyen knelt to face Archemese. "You should have demanded the grand master's counsel."

"Patience, Darwynyen." Archemese wiped his brow. "If we insult them now, there will be little hope for forming an alliance."

Darwynyen stood abruptly. "Do you forget Aarrondirth?" he challenged. "We must find our way back before Cessdorn is able to align their forces."

I took Darwynyen's arm. "Darwynyen, it is the middle of the night. Should we not rest now and wait until morning to discuss this?"

"Arianna, how much time do we waste here? Should our focus not be on Aarrondirth alone if the grand master chooses to stall us?"

"Darwynyen …" I paused, attempting to conceal my frustration. "No time is lost here, as we cannot set out in such an hour." I took a step back. "What is wrong with you?"

Darwynyen seemed to shake free from his mood. "I do not understand my persistence. I can only tell you that I have not felt this focused for a very long time."

"Then save your determination for the morning." I pulled out my blanket. "Not only am I exhausted, we need to be considerate of Dregby, who does not wear our jewels of eternal life."

He nodded reluctantly and then pulled out his blanket, leading me toward the cliff.

† † †

Arianna … The voice echoed in my head. *You must come to me now.*

I opened my eyes, which were struck by sunlight. It was morning. "Who are you?" I called out. "What do you want?"

Darwynyen sat up. "Arianna, who are you speaking to?"

"She is being summoned." Archemese stood. "I felt it as well."

Find your way around the bend in this cliff, and follow the stair, the voice commanded.

Curious, I immediately stood and made my way around the bend. When I reached the other side there were no stairs in sight. I was about to turn when the cliff began to rumble. Moments later, a staircase emerged from inside a narrow cleft. *At the top you will find me,* the voice whispered.

"Arianna, wait!" Darwynyen blocked my path. "It might not be safe."

"Leave her." Archemese nudged Darwynyen aside. "As I said, she is being summoned by the grand master." His brow rose. "Is this not what you have been waiting for?"

"She must not go alone," Darwynyen argued. "Who knows what might be waiting for her up there!"

Archemese put his hand on Darwynyen's shoulder. "She will not go alone. We will go together."

"Then what are we waiting for?" Dregby emerged from around the bend.

Darwynyen blinked and then looked at Archemese. "Forgive me. I did not realize."

"There is nothing to forgive." I took his hand. "You were only acting to protect me."

When Archemese extended his hand toward the stairs, Darwynyen squeezed my hand and followed me in silence.

At the crest of the rise, we saw an elderly man sitting on a throne made of stone. In comparison to Jeel and Naseyn, he was petite, and his hunched-over posture made it apparent that the years had taken their toll on his fragile body. He was dressed in a cotton garb; his hair was twisted into a bun atop his head. Tight within his boney fingers was what I guessed to be a wand. "Come closer," the man beckoned in a raspy voice.

"It is good to see you, my friend." Archemese knelt to face him. "It has been far too long."

Darwynyen bowed his head. "Grand Master, my name is Darwynyen. I stem from the bloodline of our elf queen, Aldraveena. I am pleased to make your acquaintance."

"My name is Dregby. I represent the Miders of Vidorr." The man nodded as Dregby spoke.

Before I could speak, he extended his hand. "Come, my child." His voice crackled. "I have been expecting you."

Startled, I looked at the others. Archemese motioned for me to kneel. I did so, and the man continued. "I understand you hold the pendant of Aldraveena."

"Yes." I nodded as I pulled the pendant from my shirt. "It was a gift, to see me through these troubled times that now beset us."

"I have intercepted many thoughts," the man remarked. "Even so, this offering made by the elf queen does nothing but bewilder me. Why did …"

"Evil lurks near," Darwynyen interrupted. "The sorcerers of Morne are close to obtaining the third stone of Moya. Once they have united it with the others, they will set forth in finding the Amberseed."

The grand master looked down. "I already know of what you speak."

Darwynyen knelt by my side. "Grand Master, excuse my ignorance, but if you are already aware of the sorcerers' intentions, I must ask the purpose of these questions?"

"I want to know what light Aldraveena has seen in this child that she felt deserved giving up her pendant," he replied.

I hesitated "If you must know, Aldraveena has foreseen the future, one that has been blackened by my father. It is no longer the sorcerers whom we need to contend with, for Velderon will soon overthrow them. He has grown very powerful and …"

"She believes you to be his only weakness." He finished my thought with a sigh. "And you are willing to accept this fate and fight against him?"

"Yes." I nodded with conviction.

"That is why we are here." Archemese stepped forward. "Regardless of whether or not Arianna finds success, we will still need to set aside our differences and reunite as one."

"I do not see the need for this union." The grand master narrowed his eyes. "The last time we joined with you, we lost many men, only to see the very evil you speak of set loose once again."

"I understand your reluctance." Darwynyen stood. "However, if you choose to do nothing, your people will not be the only ones to suffer the consequences."

The grand master raised his brow. "The bones of foresight tell me otherwise."

"Grand Master," Archemese interjected, "can you not see that Darwynyen speaks the truth? The decisions you make now will hold great weight on the future." He inhaled deeply in an attempt to calm himself. "I will say no more, as you know that I would not have returned from seclusion if the situation was not dire."

The grand master looked at me. "What have you to say on the matter?" Dregby was about to interrupt. The grand master raised his hand. "Let her speak."

When I looked into his eyes, my heart quickened. "To my regret, my future path has already been written. Still, despite my bloodline, I would not stand aside and allow my father to realize his ambitions." I paused. "If you choose to deny us, I can only hope that in time you will come to understand the sacrifices I have made, not only for my people but for yours also."

"We have all made sacrifices." Dregby stomped his hoof on the ground. "That is why my men stand ready in Aarrondirth as we speak, under the command of the new king, Madigan."

"I have heard enough," the grand master sat back in his throne. "Leave me to think now." His eyes met my inquiring look. "When I am ready, I will send for you."

Archemese accompanied Darwynyen and Dregby to the stairs. "We will be awaiting your decision, I can assure you."

I slowly stood. "Thank you for this audience."

When the grand master nodded, I turned and walked to the stairs.

As we descended, the men began to quarrel over whether or not we should wait. Unable to face another battle, when we reached the bottom, I headed for the riverbed. As I ran my fingers through the current, I contemplated the encounter with the grand master. Something did not feel right, and though I wanted to, I was finding it difficult to trust him.

Lost in thought, I nearly slipped into the river when Naseyn rapidly approached on a firefly. "Forgive the intrusion, Arianna. I did not mean to startle you. I have come on behalf of the grand master." He looked over his shoulder toward Archemese. "He has requested your presence … alone. That's the reason why he has not made the connection himself."

Apprehensive, I looked toward the others before responding. "Why only me?" I asked. "What about the others?"

"Do not worry." He smiled genuinely. "No harm will come to you."

Although I was reluctant, I conceded. There was too much at stake; after all, the alliance depended on our cooperation. "I suppose it would be all right."

Naseyn turned the firefly. "I will leave you now."

I nodded, making way for the stairs.

When I arrived at the altar, the grand master pointed to a stone seat next to his throne. "Sit with me, child. Tell me of your life."

I looked to the ground, unsure of his motives.

"There is no need to be frightened." He gestured again for me to sit.

"You misunderstand." I moved to join him. "I recoil because I am finding it difficult to trust you."

"I am sure you have your reasons." His expression became serious. "I know you have been through many tribulations, and as a result, you now give your trust sparingly." He paused. "I am not your enemy, child, and like Aldraveena, I fear this is only the beginning for you."

"I know," I sighed, and I began to relax. "There is still much left for me to do."

He reached out toward me. "Do you fear the future?"

Irritated by his brazen question, I replied in a stark tone, "Not nearly as much as you."

Hearing my words, he sat back. "My decisions are not based on fear."

"Then what are you reasons?" I challenged.

"I no longer wish to speak on the matter." He lifted a cloth that was concealing a plate on his armrest. Upon it lay three pieces of what I assumed to be dried fruit. "You are here to make a choice, nothing more." He held the plate out to me. "Through this choice a decision will be made."

"What are you asking of me?" I pushed away the plate.

"On this plate is your destiny. One of these berries awaits your choice." His eyes narrowed. "If your destiny is true, you will not choose one of the two that carry poison."

"Poison!" I exclaimed. "Are you asking me to risk my life for your allegiance?"

"Your life will not be at risk, if your destiny is true. If your fate is proven, we will unite with your people." He offered the plate again. "Will you accept the challenge?"

Unsure what to do, I looked away. Not only was his request audacious, it came with a hefty price if my choice was wrong. I was about to decline when I realized that he was right. My destiny was set, and no challenge was going to change that. Besides, in my heart, I knew my life would not end in such a manner. "All right." I swallowed deeply. "How could I refuse you if the end result means your allegiance?"

In response, he led his hand across the plate. "Choose the berry you prefer." He raised his brow. "Only one small bite is needed."

With a sigh, I nodded. Which one was I to take? Uncertain, I closed my eyes and extended my arm. When I felt a berry, I brought it to my mouth. As I bit into its flesh the taste did not change. Satisfied, I chewed it slowly and swallowed.

"What goes on here?"

When I turned, Darwynyen, Dregby, and Archemese were standing at the top of the stair. The grand master slowly rose from his throne. "Arianna has undertaken a challenge," he replied, eyeing the plate. "The tradition is not uncommon with my people."

"What kind of challenge?" Darwynyen rushed to my side.

Archemese knelt to the grand master. "Would this challenge have anything to do with poison?"

"Yes," the grand master replied and then he wrinkled his brow. "Archemese, do you love this child?"

Archemese nodded. "Has she passed the test?"

The grand master gave me a fleeting look. "She has."

"Did I choose the right berry?" I asked. The notion immediately gave me comfort, knowing then that my destiny was intact.

"There was no right berry, my dear." He stepped toward a narrow cleft in the wall. "My intent was not to harm you. It was to see firsthand what you would sacrifice." He halted. "In accepting the challenge, your courage and true heart have been proven. I know now you will make the right decisions when it comes to my people."

I closed my eyes in relief. The challenge had nothing to do with poison. It was a test of my will. "What happens now?" I bit my lip.

"Jeel and Naseyn will accompany you back to Aarrondirth," he replied. "Our armies will follow later."

"Thank you." I put my hand to my chest and bowed. "You will not regret this decision."

"We shall see." He turned back toward the cleft and then disappeared through the tiny opening.

When he was gone, Darwynyen took a deep breath. I could tell he was angry. "Arianna, regardless of the outcome, I need to know why you would take such a risk."

Dregby came to my side. "What would you have her do? If she had denied his request, there would be no alliance."

"You have failed to see the point!" Darwynyen argued. "Under no circumstances should she be risking her life!"

"Do you not trust in her decisions?" Dregby crossed his arms. "Is it not time for you to start believing in her?"

"Enough!" I left to join Archemese at the crest of the stair. "What is done is done. Rather than argue, should we not be packing?"

"Arianna is right." Archemese took my arm in his. "Enough time has been spent here. We should be preparing to depart for Aarrondirth."

When Darwynyen shook his head, I ignored him, leading Archemese down the stairs. Although there was cause for his concern, there was little I could do about it now. Instead, I would try to make better decisions in the future.

"You did well, my child." Archemese squeezed my arm. "Your self-sacrifice will save the lives of many."

"I hope so." I muttered. Although I was pleased by the grand master's decision, it came with consequences, for I had inadvertently lured his people into a battle that many would not return from.

Archemese released my arm at the bottom of the stairs. "If you would be kind enough to pack my belongings, I will go in search of Jeel and Naseyn."

"Of course." I nodded and then watched him make his way toward the city.

Once Darwynyen, Dregby, and I had packed the camp, I left in search for Archemese, who had yet to return.

When I found him, he was engrossed in a story he was sharing with a few of the children. They were transfixed by his every word. Rather than interrupt, I joined them. "A three-headed monster lurked in the cesspool." He raised his hands. "Unknowingly, the mighty hunters had awoken it from its slumber!" When the children gasped in awe, he snuck me a wink. "The water began to bubble and stir. With bravery, the men drew their swords. Their attempts were useless. Be …"

"What happened?" one of the children interrupted.

Archemese raised his brow. "If you choose not to listen you will never find out!"

The children began to laugh among themselves. Archemese continued. "As the monster moved through the water the heads lashed out at the men. Before they could attack, it plucked their leader from the ground, swallowing him whole!"

The children were again enthralled. As they held to one another with anticipation, the same child spoke out. "What happened next?" she asked.

"The monster swam to Iramak and ate all the children." Archemese glared. "That is the end of the story!" He looked at the others. "You may thank your friend for ruining my mood." He stood. "Now leave me to Arianna. I must speak with her!" Disappointed, the children jumped on the lone inquirer and began a playful bout of mischief.

Archemese guided me to the riverbank. "My apologies for the delay. As you can see, I got a bit distracted."

"Where are Jeel and Naseyn?" I asked.

"They are packing." He took my arm in his. "Are you ready for our departure?"

"Yes," I nodded. "And so are the others."

He looked at a shadow dial carved into the cliff. "Then let us make our return, for the hour is already late."

I looked at the sundial for a moment, wondering where the time had gotten to, and then followed him at his pace.

When we arrived back at the camp, the only things left were Archemese's and my belongings. "Where could they have gone?" I frowned.

"Arianna, we are over here!"

Confused, I turned to find Darwynyen and Dregby across the river. "How did you get over there?" I shouted, handing Archemese his satchels.

"There is a bridge!" Darwynyen pointed to a row of stones protruding from the current that had not been there previously. "When Jeel pulled a lever in the cleft, they emerged from the water!"

Dregby leaped to one of the stones, testing it with his hooves. "It is solid, I assure you!"

Archemese stepped onto the first stone. "Did you find a stair over there?" he yelled.

"Yes," Dregby nodded, making his way across the bridge to meet him. "Its tiny steps lead to the forest!"

"I was afraid of this," Archemese mumbled. "I should have known that the little people would select this route."

"What concerns you?" I asked, securing my satchels around my shoulder.

"The forest is very rugged in these parts." He used his staff to assist him onto the next stone. "I was hoping to take the river passage."

"Did I hear you mention the river passage?" Dregby extended his hand to Archemese when they met.

"Yes." Archemese took hold of him.

"Are you proposing that we take that route?" Dregby asked, assisting Archemese onto the next stone. "What has changed? The last time I suggested that path you both dismissed it."

"If you are waiting for me to declare that I made a mistake in my first judgment, you will be waiting a very long time." Archemese leaped onto the riverbank. "The only reason I suggest that passage now is because the forest between here and Aarrondirth is very rugged."

"We will travel through the forest," Darwynyen interjected. "The river leads close to the land of our enemies. Now that the completion of the moon cycle draws near, we cannot take any chances."

Jeel and Naseyn appeared from around the bend, their satchels in hand. "Why do you delay?" Jeel looked up at the sky. "If we wait any longer, we might as well stay in Iramak another night."

"Come, my friends!" Naseyn raised his spear. "This mighty adventure awaits us!"

"And so it does." Dregby pointed toward the north. "Should we not take the river passage?"

"No," Naseyn replied. "We should stay to the trees. Their shelter will keep us hidden from certain dangers."

Jeel stood forward. "Besides, that route will only double our footsteps." He held his hand over Naseyn's head. "You forget our size, my friend."

Naseyn kicked Jeel. "What about our size!"

"I was only stating the truth!" Jeel kicked him back.

Dregby released a sigh in defeat. "The forest it is, then."

It was settled. With nothing left to say, we made our way to the stairs.

In our ascent, Zenley flew to Archemese's face. "We will search the land before you." Rather than wait for a response, he and Teshna flew up the side of the cliff and then disappeared.

† † †

We walked a steady course for two days. The enchanted city of Iramak was nothing more than a distant memory beneath the pain of my aching muscles. Although the forest was sparse on this leg of the journey, it was rugged, as Archemese had promised. The landscape was riddled with steep hills and rubble. Dead branches and twigs left their marks on my limbs, leaving me with the sensation that I had been tortured. The soles of my feet burned. The only thing that kept me going was the fresh aroma of pine. It reminded me of the woodlands in Hoverdire, a place I had grown to long for in the passing hours. My life was innocent there, and I did not carry my present burdens.

When the falling sun brought an end to our travels, Archemese and I began to prepare camp while Dregby and Darwynyen set out to catch our dinner. Our food supply was bearing the brunt of our hunger, and we had little to spare. Teshna and Zenley followed after them.

Jeel and Naseyn's constant playful bickering was pulling at my nerves. I was exhausted and finding it hard to tolerate their childlike joy when all I wanted was the warmth of a fire. Archemese could see the annoyance on my face when they swept around me in a game of chase and capture, and he quickly put a stop to the madness. "Gentlemen, I believe Arianna requires some peace after the hard day. You should take to the trees if you wish to play."

They halted at his words. "We are not playing." Naseyn frowned.

"Well, whatever it is you do," Archemese growled, "do it over there!"

Undaunted by his tone, Jeel and Naseyn looked at one another and then shrugged before running into the bushes.

"Thank you," I sighed.

Archemese nodded and continued to gather kindling.

Chilled by the evening air, I began to assemble the stones for a fire pit; before long, the wood we had gathered was set aflame.

As Archemese and I relaxed, the men returned with the corpse of a rabbit. Pleased with their work, they quickly prepared our meal and positioned it over the fire on a makeshift spit.

After dinner, I removed my boots. Blisters had formed on my skin. The fresh air made them tingle. When my eyes began to water, Darwynyen put his hands on my shoulders. "This should make you feel better." He dug his fingers deep into my muscles. "I know this journey has been hard on you."

"Thank you!" I dropped my head forward. "I will never understand the depths of your strength."

"Forget strength," he whispered in my ear. "Pride is what you see. Your presence demands it. Otherwise, we would do nothing but moan."

I giggled in response.

Dregby poked at the fire. "What is so amusing?"

"Nothing." Darwynyen pulled me back to lean into his chest. "Eat the rest of that rabbit and do not concern yourself with us."

Dregby lifted the spit. "Here." He held it toward me. "Have a bit more. If nothing else, it will help to heal your burdens."

"Thank you, but I have had enough."

He reached for the satchel that carried our rations. "We should probably save some for tomorrow anyway." He winked. "If our hunting skills do not improve, we might grow hungry."

"We would not be in this predicament if you had not scared most of the prey away," Darwynyen mocked.

"I did no such thing," Dregby grumbled.

Archemese released the straps on his bedroll. "I think I shall retire for the night."

"As shall I." I yawned.

"Where are Jeel and Naseyn?" Dregby rose on his forelegs.

"They are behind you." Darwynyen pointed. "It seems they have run themselves ragged."

I turned to see them draped over the limb of a fallen tree, and I could not help but chuckle.

"With any luck they will sleep through the night," Archemese remarked.

I was about to respond when the fairies landed on Archemese's blanket. Once they were covered, he closed his eyes.

Darwynyen wrapped me in his cloak. "May your rest come easy, my love."

"As may yours." I nestled my head on his shoulder.

The Stones

The vigilant glow of the moon over Cessdorn was powerful. With haste, Velderon made his way to the altar. It was time for him to begin in the ritual that would eventually reunite the stones.

Upon his arrival, Velderon began to flip through the pages of a book the sorcerers had used to conjure their magic. He was searching for four specific spells. His survival depended on them. After reading a detailed account from the last ritual, he learned that several of the sorcerers had been vain and lost their lives after choosing not to shield themselves. When the stones were joined, their bodies had either been thrown from the altar or incinerated, and only those who remained were able to embrace its power.

When he found the section he was looking for, Velderon placed the book on a stone platform near the center of the altar. To keep his body grounded, he conjured the first spell by chanting for substance and solidity. He would not be flung to his death like the others. Once his body felt weighted, he exacted the second spell, one for protection; if it was not accurate, he would be reduced to ash. The third spell would shield his eyes. What good would his powers be if he was unable to see? The last consumed most of his strength. Although each spell was manageable on its own, binding them together would be difficult. Knowing this, he began to concentrate.

An array of color consumed the altar when Velderon had finished. With due care, he placed the third stone with the others. At the moment of inception, the ground began to rumble. As he steadied himself, rays of cerulean pierced through the cracks of the orb that had slowly begun to spin to life.

Velderon could feel his spells weakening. Desperately, he began to chant. As he spoke, a spear of cerulean sliced through the skyline, forcing the clouds above him to swirl. The orb began to rise. it revolved in the air with great velocity. The energy pounded against the magical aura that was protecting Velderon's body. It was when he felt he could resist it no more did it cease. All that remained was a faint hint of the power. The orb was patiently awaiting the next cycle.

Relieved that he had survived the ritual, Velderon took a moment to regain his strength. Still, he was finding it difficult to break his gaze. As he admired the orb, he felt compelled to touch it. "No!" It was too soon. He took a step back. The energy, however, did not release him; instead it drew him in. Unable to resist the temptation, he held his hand forward.

When the connection was made, he could not only feel the energy, he could hear its deafening hum. His skin tingled. Drawn in by the phenomenon, he caressed the orb several times, extracting whatever he could. He cackled as he felt the energy flow through his body. Only when the sensation dwindled did he pull away, determined not to weaken its potency until the coming of the third cycle. The final outcome far outweighed his immediate desires. And while he relished the thought of what he would inevitably accomplish, he continued to gaze upon the orb for several hours.

The Inevitable Awaits

It was late in the night when I stirred from my trance. Darwynyen was still resting. Rather than disturb him, I slipped from his arm and sat at the dwindling fire. As I inhaled the fresh air, I heard the sound of the trickling stream we had crossed over to get here, and its rhythm immediately brought me contentment. It would not last. When I looked at the moon, my chest tightened. The end of the cycle was upon us. And though no one acknowledged it, it had become clear that we would not make it back to Aarrondirth before its completion. Instead, we would be stuck out here in the wild, with no way of knowing what was happening.

As I stretched the muscles in my legs, the pain in my feet resurfaced. Tears welled in my eyes. Not only was the thought of another day of travel difficult to bear, I did not want to give the others the impression that I was weak. Under the circumstances we could not sit idle, and with that in mind, I decided to go to the stream, in hopes that the cool water would ease the strain.

When I reached the stream, I sat on one of the fallen trees along the bank. Trickles of moonbeam danced upon the current. As I placed my feet in the water, I heard branches snapping in the distance. At first I assumed it was Darwynyen. I was about to call out to him when the snapping became more sporadic. Caught off guard, I quickly stood and saw several beasts converging. "Fire beasts," I muttered.

Their fire-red eyes were the only way to discern them as their sleek bodies swept through the shadows with precision. As they neared, they began to hiss at one another, the larger beasts striking out with their razor-sharp claws. When two of the beasts became entangled in a scuffle, I crawled over the fallen tree in an attempt to find a way to shield myself.

As I tested my footing, I looked up to find a lone beast waiting for me on the other side. I was trapped. Forced to defend myself, I slowly reached for my sais. In response, the beast hissed in warning and prepared to pounce. Frozen in trepidation, I heard an arrow speed through the air. Seconds later, it struck the beast in the neck. As it fell lifeless to the ground, Darwynyen emerged through the brush. He fired another arrow, striking the beast closest to him. When it screamed out, the others became wary and scattered.

Relieved, I ran toward Darwynyen.

"What were you doing out here on your own?" he questioned me, taking hold of my shoulders. "Have you heard nothing of Dregby's warnings?"

I looked down. "It was not my intention to upset you. I was finding it difficult to rest and thought the stream would ease my burdens."

"I am upset by your disregard." He placed his hand under my chin, raising it to meet his gaze. "Why do you continue to take these unnecessary risks?"

My first instinct was to lash out. No matter what I did, it seemed I was always at fault. How was I supposed to know that the fire beasts would attack me? We had been in the forest for days now, and not once had we seen them. Even so, how could I be angry with Darwynyen when he was only trying to protect me? "Perhaps I was being reckless," I conceded. "In future, I promise that I will not wander on my own again." I changed the subject, glancing over my shoulder toward the beast that had fallen. "I thought Dregby said that the fire beasts were timid."

"They are if you are in a group." He took my hand, leading me back toward the camp. "On your own, you were easy prey." His grasp tightened, and then he continued. "I would never forgive myself if I were to lose you."

The latter part of his response left me to wonder if I was being selfish. Not once had I considered how my actions had impacted him. Was I taking him for granted? If I was, that was not my intent. Before I could reassure him, something flew around my head.

"Arianna!" I recognized Teshna's voice immediately. "We have been looking for you all over!"

"Why?" I gave Zenley a fleeting look when he flew up beside Teshna. "What has happened?"

"Hope has failed." Zenley reached out for Teshna. "Despite our efforts, fate is no longer ours to contend with."

Archemese appeared through the brush. "You must come with me now!" Not waiting for a response, he ran off in a northerly direction.

We followed Archemese to the crest of a bluff. Dawning light was breaking across the eastern horizon. "Why do you bring us here?" I took a moment to catch my breath. "If you are concerned about the fire beasts, you …"

"Over there!" Archemese interrupted, pointing toward the north. "Forget the fire beasts—our worst fears are now upon us!"

I saw the billowing clouds that were piling on top of one another along the northern landline and felt my knees weaken. "My father …" I put my hand to my chest in an attempt to ease the shock. "He has made it to Cessdorn before the completion of the cycle."

"It has begun." Darwynyen stepped back. "We never stood a chance."

"Velderon's determination, it seems, has far exceeded ours," Archemese remarked.

"I was not expecting such immediate signs of change." I continued to gaze upon the flickers of lightning that illuminated the clouds.

"There is no more time to waste!" Darwynyen raced from the bluff. "We must wake the others and set out immediately!"

Archemese took me by the wrist, leading me, still in shock, alongside him.

Confirmation

When dawn light appeared through the windows, Shallendria made her way to the balcony that opened from the royal suite. She had not kept hope like the others and knew this would be the day, the day that would change the fate of many. She shivered when she stepped through the threshold and onto the frigid stone blanketed in a thin layer of dew. Her discomfort was quickly forgotten when her eyes fell upon the northern landline. Although she was aware of the stones' power, she was not expecting a spectacle such as this, and she was almost mesmerized by the clouds billowing over Cessdorn.

Desperate for guidance, she tried to make a connection to her queen. Aldraveena did not answer. As she broke from the trance, Madigan appeared at the door. "Good morning," he yawned, stretching his arms. "What brings you out here?" He continued with a wink. "I missed your presence when I awoke."

When she did not respond, he moved to embrace her. "What troubles you?"

Shallendria abruptly stepped aside. "See for yourself." She pointed toward Cessdorn.

Madigan halted, his eyes wide. "In the name of the gods, tell me what I witness."

"Velderon was able to reach the Hynd before the completion of the cycle," she replied. "They have begun the ritual."

Unable to accept her words, Madigan stumbled backward.

"We knew this day would come," Shallendria stated. "Whether we like it or not, Velderon has proven to be a worthy opponent."

Madigan took a moment to regain his composure. "Do not mind me. It is the people I worry for. They will not take this easily. Even I was not expecting such a drastic display of force."

"There is no doubt the power of the stones will be hard for them to comprehend." She took his hand. "That is why you must now address those loyal to you."

"I am not ready." He stiffened. "I would prefer to wait for Arianna."

"Why?" She frowned. "It is you who rules the people."

Madigan exhaled heavily. "As you know, it is not that simple."

"Whatever do you mean?" She took him by the arms. "You said yourself her father was an impostor."

"I was wrong," he confessed. "Aldraveena forced Arianna to see the truth during her time in Maglavine."

"Then why has nothing been said?" Shallendria scowled. "This is the first I have heard of this revelation."

"I thought you knew." Madigan searched her eyes. "Did Aldraveena not connect with you?"

"No." She turned, embarrassed to admit the truth. "I have not sensed her for some time now."

Madigan gently put his hands on the back of her shoulders. "Although I cannot speak to this, I am certain that Aldraveena has her reasons."

"Perhaps," Shallendria replied half-heartedly. After sharing a moment of silence, she changed the subject. "If your words are true, does this mean that Arianna is your cousin?"

"Yes," Madigan replied with conviction. "And though I have chosen to deny it, I have seen strengths in her that are comparable to those of my forefathers."

"As have I. For a time, her qualities intimidated me."

Madigan took hold of her chin. "I must go."

"Where?" she asked, reaching out for him.

"By your counsel, I see now that I must attend to my people." He managed a smile.

She nodded. "In your absence I will seek Morglafenn."

He looked to the north one last time before taking his leave.

Shallendria, eager to speak with Morglafenn, quickly dressed and made her way to the library. She arrived to find him sitting at the main table, reading a book, as she expected.

"Morglafenn …" She cleared her throat. "Is there something you have been meaning to tell me?"

Morglafenn blinked. "Are you here to speak about the pendant?"

"No." She met his gaze. "What pendant are you referring to?"

"Aldraveena's." Morglafenn closed the book he was reading. "I meant to tell you sooner, only I did not want to upset you."

"Tell me what?" She scowled.

Morglafenn stood. "Prepare yourself, for what I am about to say will be difficult for you to accept." His voice deepened. "Aldraveena has relinquished her pendant and given it to Arianna."

Shallendria's eyes widened. "But that pendant is my birthright!"

"It is not my place to dispute her actions. Aldraveena's wisdom far outweighs mine in these matters." Morglafenn moved to face her. "Still, I am certain there was good cause for her to break with our traditions."

"Even if there was, I do not see it," Shallendria huffed. "Arianna knows nothing about magic, and therefore the pendant is of no use to her."

"I can only surmise that Arianna was given the pendant as a means to protect her," Morglafenn suggested. "Despite her strength, she will need it if she is to once again confront her father in Cessdorn."

Shallendria released a heavy breath when Aldraveena's motives became clear. "If you speak the truth, then Aldraveena has sent Arianna on a quest that she may not return from."

"Yes," Morglafenn nodded.

Ashamed of her behavior, Shallendria's eyes began to tear. "Forgive me for assuming the worst."

"There is nothing to forgive. I was also taken aback," Morglafenn admitted.

"At least now I know why the queen has yet to contact me." Shallendria blotted her eyes. "Without the pendant, she has for certain grown weak."

"In her absence the elves will look to you for guidance." Morglafenn took her hands. "You must be strong, child."

"I know." Shallendria squeezed his hands. "I will not let you down."

Before he could respond, she raised her hand. "Forget the pendant. There is something you must see." She turned to leave.

With a perplexed look upon his face, Morglafenn followed her from the room.

Seizing Control

Far across the horizon, Velderon could see the imminent rays of dawning sunlight. Above him hovered the beginning of eternal night. He smirked when he thought of his achievements, knowing that powers envied by many would soon be at his fingertips. The only thing left was to wait. While doing so, he would utilize the energy the stones had bestowed upon him.

A sorcerer beckoned from the crest of the altar stair. His companions were huddled tightly around him. "Velderon. May we grace your presence?"

"Ah!" Velderon turned. "My feeble servants! What do you want?"

The men glanced at the stone statuette of Goramine and then bowed. "We wish to honor you," the man replied.

"You may honor me later." Velderon's eyes began to glow. "Be warned. If you come to this altar again without being summoned, you will meet your death."

The men backed away slowly. The sorcerer nodded. "As you wish. Until then, we will continue your work. If there is anything you desire, let it be known, for your wish is our command."

"Enough groveling!" Velderon growled. "Be gone!" When he raised his hands, electricity began to flow through his fingers. Fear-stricken, the sorcerers ran off. As the energy intensified, a vision entered Velderon's mind. "Arianna," he muttered. For the first time, he could see her. "She lives!" His voice cackled with elation. As his heart began to warm, the vision extended to an elf, the one he had encountered in the cavern, the one who saw to the death of his crone and most likely the general. "That bastard!" He tensed, reaching for his wand. "I will soon take care of him!"

To Stand Alone

It was midday in the city of Aarrondirth. Throughout the morning people had fled to the castle gates in distress. They wanted answers, and though Madigan begrudged this aspect of his duties, he would abide by Shallendria's wishes. He strode to the barbican to address the people.

Making his way, Madigan felt anxious, and he slowed his pace. Because he was not a man of many words, he wondered what he would say. If only Arianna were here, he would have her stand in his place. Her unconditional love for the people allowed her to speak freely, a gift he almost envied.

"My king!" One of the city's councilmen approached from the gatehouse. "Have you come to address your people?"

"Yes." Madigan brushed past him and ascended the stairs to the wall walkway.

The man followed. "Pardon me, my king, but might I ask what you intend to say?"

"I will speak the truth," Madigan replied, signaling to the heralds when he reached the crest of the stair. "Perhaps this time the people will choose to listen."

When the horn sounded, Madigan moved toward the ledge.

"My people!" He raised his hands. "I know you fear what is happening, but you must keep calm!"

"Why does the sky turn dark to the north?" an older man shouted.

Madigan's tone deepened "As I warned, the sorcerers of Cessdorn have reunited the Stones of Moya!"

When the people cried out, he raised his hands again. "Do not fret! We have time to prepare!"

"Prepare for what?" a woman cried.

"War!" Madigan replied harshly. "And the sooner you accept it, the better." He paused to scan the growing crowd. "Those who are able to fight, make way to the gatehouse for further instruction! Aarrondirth needs your protection." When he saw the fear in their eyes, he continued. "As your king, I give you my word. The sorcerers will not succeed!" He stiffened his stance. "Now go! Prepare yourselves!"

Although the people had further questions, he put his hand to his chest and then retreated. Unlike Arianna, he lacked compassion and could not settle their fears as she would have done. Instead, they would have to look to one another for comfort.

Fields of Green at Last

Another day passed before we reached the fields of Aarrondirth. The sky above was a crystal blue that reminded me of a summer morning in Hoverdire. The north still dwelled in darkness. I shuddered at every glance, not because the mass of cloud had grown but because of the evil it represented.

In the distance, I saw a village and longed for its comfort. Not only had my feet grown numb, I was famished. To my relief, I was not the only one to succumb; when Jeel and Naseyn could carry on no further, Dregby had no choice but to carry them on his back. Archemese was also beginning to show signs of exhaustion and depended on his staff for support. The only one who had kept his strength was Darwynyen, and like the others, I envied his endurance.

As I reached for my canteen, a presence entered my mind. *You must be strong, Arianna! Your people await you, and it is your courage that they will draw their strength from.* Aldraveena's life force consumed me. *Do not fear what is happening in the north. Trust in yourself. You grow stronger by the minute. So much so, your father has sensed your presence! Be on your guard, for now he will seek you!*

"How do you know such things?" I cried.

The men halted, looking back at me. I silenced them with my hand.

I have seen it for myself, she replied. *As I warned, your father has taken control of the Hynd, and with his newfound powers he has chosen to place his focus on you.*

Rather than alarm the others, I attempted to respond through my thoughts. *Why have you not contacted us sooner? We have been in need of your guidance. Sikes has been murdered and Gin …*

Need I remind you of the dangers? Her voice deepened. *Even now, we are at risk, and I only reach out as a means to protect you.*

At first, it was hard for me to comprehend that she was able to answer my questions when I did not speak them. *Forgive my insolence, but are these risks not warranted should they save a life*?

The sorcerers prevented me from contacting you on the island. She paused. *With this distance between us, it is Archemese who you now must take direction from. Allow him to become your mentor,* she pleaded. *Trust him. He will protect you and*— The connection ended abruptly.

As my head cleared, I turned to Archemese. "It was Aldraveena."

Archemese nodded. "I also heard her words."

"What did she say?" Darwynyen looked at the both of us.

"The connection was brief," Archemese replied. "Not only has Aldraveena grown weak without the pendant, she knew that contacting us would come with great risk."

"Then the risk must have come with a warning?" Darwynyen raised his brow, questioning.

"Yes," I looked down. "She spoke of my father." I hesitated. "No longer must we speculate, for it has been confirmed that he has taken over the Hynd and is now in control of Cessdorn." I swallowed deeply. "There is more … It seems that his newfound power has given him the ability to sense me."

"Velderon's focus on Arianna will bring danger to us all." Archemese put his hand on my shoulder. "From this moment forward, we must keep on our guard."

"Why?" Darwynyen questioned. "We are far from his reaches."

"You underestimate the power of the stones," Archemese countered. "Despite belief to the contrary, Velderon is able to draw energy from them now, and it will be enough to sustain him should he choose to seek out Arianna."

"I do not fear him." I stood upright. "If his focus is on me, then so be it. In the end, it will give us the advantage."

"I have heard enough," Dregby interrupted impatiently. "Let us make our way to the village." He looked over his shoulder at Jeel and Naseyn, who were sound asleep on his back. "Once we have eaten and taken some rest, we can discuss these matters further."

"Dregby is right. There is no reason for us to linger when what we debate is beyond our control."

When Darwynyen and Archemese reluctantly nodded, I gestured them onward.

In the silence that followed, I thought back to the connection I had shared with Aldraveena, of how I was able to speak with her through the mind. Was it always that simple? If so, perhaps I could use the skill elsewhere. Until now, my conversations with the dragons had been one-sided—a situation I intended to change if given the opportunity. Unlike the others, I had not given up hope, and I was determined to seek their allegiance, regardless of their previous actions.

Keep your hope, Arianna. Archemese took my arm in his for support.

I nodded appreciatively and then assisted him down the small incline that led into the village.

As we walked the main street, some of the younger men began to gather. Those with families quickly vanished into their homes. "The people in this village are not very welcoming," I remarked.

"Pay them no attention, Arianna," Dregby huffed. "These folk are simple-minded and wary of our presence."

"And so they should be," Archemese sighed, "considering the company we travel with."

I nodded, avoiding the eye contact of those I passed.

"There is an inn over there." Darwynyen pointed to a wooden building on the left. "Let us go, and retrieve our needed supplies."

In agreement, we followed after him.

When we entered on the main level of the establishment, the tavern fell silent. Undaunted, Archemese and Darwynyen sat at the nearest table. Dregby nudged Jeel and Naseyn awake.

Jeel and Naseyn were slow to react, and as they found their footing, people began to murmur. Some stood to leave. Archemese stood too. "Is there something that troubles you?" He turned in place. "Is it your custom to deny the patronage of distant travelers?"

Those who remained kept silent. Archemese shook his head and went over to the tavern keeper. "Bring us a pot of your stew and some bread," he demanded.

"And some ale!" Dregby waved his hand. "We are thirsty!"

When the barman nodded, Archemese returned to his seat. "Something is not right here."

Darwynyen was about to respond when we saw two men approaching from the back of the room. "Make ready your weapons," Dregby whispered. "By their mannerisms, I do not believe it is their intent to welcome us."

The bulkier of the men pushed up his sleeves as they neared our table. "We do not want any trouble."

"Please leave!" The short man beside him cocked his head. "Your group is not welcome here."

"And why is that?" I stood to face them.

Darwynyen pulled at my arm. I broke from his hold. "Is it your intention to insult the king's cousin?" I met both their eyes. "Before you respond, let it be known that you are addressing Arianna, the princess of Aarrondirth."

The men abruptly stood back. "You are the child of Aarrondirth?" the shorter man uttered.

"I am, and we are here on a quest that in the end will secure your future! You must not be afraid of the different faces you see; instead be proud. If we do not stand as one, I can assure you that our defeat is eminent!" When they looked at one another in a perplexed manner, I continued. "Do you know nothing of what I speak?"

"We received word that a war is soon to commence," the bulkier one responded.

"Yes," the shorter one concurred. "And we have also seen the sky grow dark in the north."

"Then is the quest I have spoken about inconceivable?" I challenged. "If not, would you accept my word when I say that we travel on the king's behalf?"

The men seemed to relax as I finished. I was about to persuade them further, but I was distracted by a mocking laugh that came from the opposite side of the room.

"She tells you lies!"

My stomach tightened as I identified the voice.

"Like her father, her only allegiance is to the sorcerers of Morne."

I gasped in disbelief when Gin brazenly stepped onto his seat. He opened his hands to his audience. "If you follow her, she will see you to your death!"

Darwynyen and Dregby pulled their weapons, frightening those around us. People began to flee toward to the door. Surrounded by the chaos, we lost sight of Gin.

"Where is he?" Archemese scanned the crowd.

"Look," Darwynyen pointed. "There is a door at the back!"

As we struggled through the crowd, precious moments were lost. Darwynyen reached the door first and pulled an arrow, firing it. When I reached his side, I saw Gin fleeing on horseback. The arrow had just missed him.

"Although my arrow was steady, he somehow eluded it." Darwynyen slowly lowered his bow. "How could that be?"

"Someone is still protecting him," Archemese replied bluntly. "The question is who?"

Dregby rushed through the door and then halted. "The fool makes his way east!"

"Why?" I scoffed. "Is Gin that brazen that he will try to poison the mind of Madigan before our return?"

Archemese put his hand to his brow to watch horse and rider. "Let him. If Madigan is the man you have described, he will see past the lies."

"We should get word to him regardless." I thought of Teshna and Zenley.

"Agreed." Archemese nodded and then held out his arm. Moments later, the fairies appeared, landing on his forearm.

"You summoned us, master." Teshna fluttered her wings.

"Yes." Archemese pointed to the east. "We have just encountered Gin, and at this moment, he flees to the east. You need to make your way to Aarrondirth ahead of us and warn Madigan."

"But who will scout the land ahead of you?" Zenley crossed his arms in resistance.

"We will manage on our own." Archemese spoke with conviction. "Madigan needs you. Upon your arrival you must find him and tell him everything you know about Gin."

"Very well." Zenley glanced at Teshna reluctantly. "We will do as you ask."

"Make haste!" When the fairies took to the air Archemese lowered his arm. "Connect with me when you arrive in Aarrondirth."

"As you wish," Teshna replied, and she and Zenley flew off.

When we could no longer see them, I turned. "We should gather some food and be on our way. Once we have …" I stopped when I saw four men with weapons emerge from the side of the inn.

Darwynyen and Dregby pulled their weapons. "Are you here to show your allegiance, or have you chosen to follow the path of a traitor?" Darwynyen readied his arrow.

"Leave our village!" one of the men shouted. "We are aware

of your intentions. That poor boy you frightened off told us everything!"

Angered by the man's naivety, I stepped forward. "That 'poor boy', as you call him, is a murderer. After befriending him, we discovered his evil ways, but not before he took the life of one of our companions." I could feel my muscles tighten. "Only after interrogating him did we learn that he is the son of one of the sorcerers who has been actively plotting against us."

The men began to edge forward. "How do we know we can trust you?" The man I had addressed narrowed his eyes. "For all we know, it is you who are the deceivers!"

Darwynyen lowered his bow. "Forget us. Believe in Arianna, the one your ruler, King Madigan, has embraced as a sister!"

"I heard differently," one of the other men growled. "Was her father not an impostor?"

"Yes!" Another man nodded, pointing his blade in my direction. "She is the one. We would be insane to put our trust in her!"

Archemese slammed his staff on the ground. The top began to glow. "You may trust whom you choose. It is of little consequence to me!" His voice deepened. "Leave now and no harm will come to you. Anger me and you will witness my wrath!"

The men slowly backed away. "You do not frighten us, wizard!"

In response, Archemese raised his staff. "If death is what you choose, then death is what you shall have."

When the men scattered, Darwynyen and Dregby stowed their weapons. Archemese turned to me. "Now that things are settled," he grinned, "shall we acquire the needed food and make our way?"

I smiled as the tensions eased. "Yes, for I am famished."

"No more than I." He took my arm for support as we made our way back inside. Darwynyen and Dregby followed.

We found the tavern empty except for Naseyn and Jeel who, to my dismay, were hanging over a mug of ale. While Dregby saw to them, Archemese and I rummaged through the kitchen. Once we had enough food to sustain us on the final leg of our journey, we set out for the stable we had passed on our arrival. If Gin had escaped on horseback, we hoped to do the same.

"Where has everyone gone?" Dregby scanned the streets.

"I believe the wizard has frightened them away." Darwynyen chuckled wryly.

Archemese chuckled back as we entered the stable.

We found each stall empty. "Where are the horses?" I frowned.

"These people are poor," Archemese sighed. "They cannot afford the cost of keeping horses."

"I found one!" Dregby waved from the back.

I ran to the stall to find an old horse with a deep curve in its back. I rolled my eyes. "Dregby, a steed like this will only hinder our journey."

"I suppose you are right."

"We should be on our way if we have no choice but to travel on foot," Darwynyen urged.

"Someone in this village must own a few horses."Archemese leaned on his staff. "Perhaps we should keep looking. Gin was able to find one."

"There is no time," Darwynyen insisted. "Furthermore, we do not want to risk another encounter with these villagers, who are probably regrouping as we speak."

Dregby nodded. "I agree with Darwynyen. Besides, the worst of our journey is over. If we keep a steady pace, we will arrive in Aarrondirth the day after tomorrow."

Concerned for Archemese, I took him aside. "Are you able to proceed on foot?"

"Of course I am," he responded proudly, straightening his posture. "Let us be on our way."

A Discovery

Like birds on a migratory path, Zenley and Teshna swiftly flew across the open fields. The land was barren, and though their pursuit for Aarrondirth far outweighed their search for Gin, they could not help but look for him.

Before long they came across a deep gully that stretched across the land. "I bet he hides in there!" Zenley halted in the air. "If he had kept to the fields, we would have seen him by now."

Teshna scanned the area. "Even if you are right, there is no time to seek him out." She crossed her arms stubbornly when she saw the devious look in Zenley's eyes. "Not this time, brother. We must follow Archemese's command and make way for Aarrondirth as planned."

"But if we found him, our mistakes of the past would be forgotten. For once we would be seen as heroes!" He swirled in the air. "Come, I promise not to linger for long!" Before she could respond, he flew into the ravine.

Despite her reluctance, Teshna followed after him.

Before long, they came across a wetland that contained several tributaries. When Teshna's gaze fell upon the winding path of reeds that bordered the main waterway, her heart skipped a beat. "Look!" she pointed. "It is Gin! He has watered his horse, and now he heads north!"

"I knew it!" Zenley hovered next to her. "The boy may be bold, but he's not bold enough to return to Aarrondirth."

Teshna nodded in agreement. "He must have gotten lost in the woods, and the village was only a resting point before plotting his course to Cessdorn."

"And while he was there," Zenley huffed, "he took the opportunity to persuade those he could."

"It seems Gin is far more clever than we wanted to believe," Teshna remarked.

Zenley glanced toward the east. "Now that we are certain of Gin's motives, I no longer see the need to continue on to Aarrondirth."

"Why?" Teshna put her hands to her waist. "This outcome changes nothing. We must still do what was asked of us."

Zenley shook his head. "I think we should return to the others. They may need our guidance."

Unable to reach a compromise, an argument between the fairies soon commenced.

The Final League of our Journey

We encountered a ravine in our path at twilight. Unsure of its depth, we began our descent with caution. In the distance, a waterway reflected the afterglow. "Perhaps we should set camp here?" I halted. "Venturing into this ravine without sunlight could be dangerous."

"The danger is here, Arianna." Dregby brushed past me. "In the ravine we will keep safe."

"But we have …"

Darwynyen took my hand. "Dregby is right. In plain sight we are vulnerable. To go unnoticed, we must conceal ourselves."

I nodded and followed him in.

Near the bottom we found a clearing. The soil was damp and clung to my boots. "There is higher ground over there." Archemese pointed.

When we reached solid ground, Dregby kneeled on his forelegs. "Jeel, Naseyn, wake up!" He shook his hindquarters. "I have had enough of carrying you!"

"Where are we?" Jeel rubbed is eyes and then assisted Naseyn to his feet.

Archemese tossed a satchel in their direction. "A little further down the path."

"What is this?" Naseyn fussed with the latches on the bag.

"Food," Archemese replied. "I will assume, regardless of your inactivity, that you are hungry."

"You are right." Jeel grabbed the bag from Naseyn. "Famished would be a better word."

Infuriated by Jeel's actions, Naseyn fought for the satchel. Jeel pushed him back. "Wait your turn!"

"But I had it first!" Naseyn argued.

Exhausted and a bit annoyed by their bickering, I left in search of kindling, in hopes that a warm fire would ease my mood.

After tripping over several stones hidden in the long grass, I clenched my fists and suppressed an urge to scream. I was about to turn back when I heard voices in the distance. "You should go to Aarrondirth. I will return for the others!"

"No! We will both go to Aarrondirth together. That is final!"

"I am not going to Aarrondirth. The sooner you accept that, the sooner we can be on our way!"

The voices sounded familiar. "Teshna, Zenley—is that you?"

There was no response. Anxiously, I reached for my sais. Just then their shimmering bodies emerged from the shadows. "Now look what you have done," Teshna berated Zenley. "Your stubbornness has allowed them to catch up with us!"

"Calm yourself, sister," Zenley demanded. "When we tell them what we saw, they will not be angry." He slapped Teshna on the arm. "And when you see that I was right, I will twist your nose!"

I had not once seen them this agitated and almost laughed. Even so, I was curious to know what they had found. "What has happened?" I asked. "Why are you here and not in Aarrondirth?"

Zenley flew to my face. "We found Gin in the ravine several hours ago. He makes his way north." He looked at his sister. "As for us, well …"

Unnerved, I interrupted. "How can you be certain he is gone?"

Teshna buzzed around my head. "Because we saw him flee into the distance."

"Yes," Zenley nodded. "As I said, he makes his way north, and swiftly."

I glanced over the wetland and released a heavy breath. "If you are certain, I will take you at your word." I paused. "What troubles me is the trust we have placed in you. If you have been arguing all this time, how will anything we ask of you get done?" Before they could respond, I turned to leave. "Come. You must inform the others of what you have witnessed."

They silently followed after me.

Archemese was awaiting us upon our return. "I thought I sensed your presence," he huffed. "Why are you here and not in Aarrondirth?"

"We found Gin!" Zenley exclaimed. "He was in the ravine watering his horse."

Darwynyen abruptly rose from the fire pit, dropping his flint to reach for an arrow. "Where is he now?" he asked, readying his bow.

"He did not linger," Teshna replied. "Instead, he rode off in a northerly direction."

"Then he does not make his way for Aarrondirth as we suspected," Archemese remarked.

Dregby trotted into the camp, tossing a few dry branches near Darwynyen's feet. "Why have you not lit a fire?" he asked.

Darwynyen raised his hand to silence Dregby. "How can you be certain he is gone?"

"Who?" Dregby interrupted.

"Gin," Darwynyen replied impatiently. "The fairies stumbled upon him in the ravine."

Dregby instinctively drew his axe.

"There is no cause for your apprehension." Zenley flew to Dregby's face. "I can assure you that Gin is no longer in the vicinity."

Darwynyen scanned the area. “Regardless, we should keep watch through the night.”

“Agreed,” Archemese nodded. “Despite the fairies’ assurance, Gin is not to be underestimated.”

Dregby stowed his axe. “Who will take the first watch?”

“I will.” I stepped forward.

Darwynyen returned the arrow to his quiver. “Are you certain?”

“Yes.” I stiffened my shoulders. “I can manage a few hours on my own.”

After a moment of consideration, he exhaled heavily. “Very well.”

Pleased by Darwynyen’s agreement, I stood proud while he and Dregby built the fire. When it was lit, we consumed some of the rations. Conversation was sparse. In the silence that followed, one by one the men closed their eyes. As I watched over them, I found it difficult to stay alert, and I closed my eyes for a moment.

I opened my eyes to the sound of snapping twigs and froze in fear when I sensed danger. Darwynyen put his hand over my mouth. “Keep quiet!” he whispered. “We are no longer alone!”

I nodded, and he slowly reached for his quiver. I pulled out my sais. Through the moonlight we saw the shadows of horsemen. Unsure if they were friend or foe, we crouched in readiness.

As they neared, a cloud drifted over the moon. In the darkness, their silhouettes became more pronounced. My stomach tightened when I saw their piercing amber eyes and the horns that protruded from the hoods on their cloaks. “Grackens!”

“Wake now!” Darwynyen shook Dregby. “Grackens approach!”

Dregby leapt from the ground. “Where are they?” He reached for his axe.

“We are surrounded.” Darwynyen pulled an arrow. “Mind the periphery!”

Dregby nodded, assisting Archemese to his feet.

When the Grackens saw movement, they pulled their swords. One of the horses reared and turned violently. Darwynyen fired an arrow. It struck the animal in the neck, dropping it to the ground. The creature next to it was crushed beneath the weight. I turned to protect Darwynyen's flank when he pulled his daggers. Another Gracken was approaching on the right. Without a thought, I flung my sai into its chest. It had no effect. As the creature struggled to withdraw it, its beast emerged.

"Arianna, step aside!" Dregby yelled.

Before I could act, an axe flew by my head. With precision it split the Gracken's skull in two. When the creature fell, its beast lunged forward.

Archemese stepped in front of me. "*Venfynd*!" he shouted.

The beast curled up on the ground, screeching in pain. Dregby seized the opportunity and galloped over to finish Archemese's work. From above him leaped another beast. Before it could attack, I threw my other sai. The blade hit the beast in the eye, killing it. Dregby nodded in appreciation.

Darwynyen was losing ground. Two creatures were advancing from the opposite side of the camp. Archemese mumbled a few words and then reached into the fire, taking hold of an ember. "*Yemadomen nofaston*!" he shouted. "*Nofaston!*" At his words, the ember's glow intensified. With vigor, he tossed it in the direction of the creatures. The magic set them aflame. As they fought for their lives, Dregby decapitated them with his axe. Lost without their masters, the remaining beasts fled. It was over.

"How did they find us?" Dregby wiped the blades on his axe. "Moreover, who was to be on watch?"

I looked to the ground guiltily. "Forgive me. I had only closed my eyes for a moment."

Without words, the men looked at one another. Sensing their disappointment, my eyes began to fill.

Darwynyen embraced me. "It is all right. Nothing was lost."

Unable to face the others, I burrowed my head into his chest.

"The blame is not your burden alone." I felt Archemese's hand on my shoulder. "This trek has been tiring on us all."

Darwynyen tightened his hold. "So much so, we all took rest as though we were children."

As I pulled away from Darwynyen, Dregby spoke. "I do not sleep like a child!"

Zenley and Teshna crawled out from one of the satchels. "You are right," Zenley chuckled. "You sleep like a wild boar."

"Not a boar, a dragon!" Jeel giggled as he and Naseyn emerged from a tuft a long grass. "Your snore was fierce enough to shake the ground!"

Teshna flew around Dregby's face. "It makes me wonder how anyone can take rest in your company!"

Dregby, taken aback by their accusations, mumbled to himself while the rest of us shared in a laugh, leaving no room for arguments. When I looked to the sky, I noticed that it had turned sapphire.

"Dawn is soon to be upon us." Darwynyen remarked. "Now that we have horses we should be able to reach Aarrondirth before nightfall."

"Yes," Archemese turned. "We are fortunate. There appears to be one for each of us."

I looked at Dregby. "Will you be able to keep stride?"

"For the most part," he nodded. "Do not fear, for the hunger in my belly will be enough of an incentive."

Darwynyen took my hand. "Come, it is time we left."

Eager to reach Aarrondirth, we quickly packed our belongings. And once Dregby had corralled the horses, we were underway.

† † †

On horseback, we made swift progress in our journey. The stallions of the Gracken foe were feisty. Accustomed to the evil ways of their masters, they swiftly tore through the countryside.

Darwynyen, wary of retaliation, rode behind us while Dregby kept the northern flank. And though we had to allow Dregby a few moments of rest here and there, I was surprised by his agility and speed when it came to keeping pace with the horses. Naseyn and Jeel, unable to ride with Dregby, took refuge on Archemese's steed. Above, the fairies flew along the wind currents, directing us home.

The outline of Aarrondirth became visible late in the afternoon. Relieved by the sight, we hastened our pace. Our journey was drawing to an end. From this day forward, the strings of destiny would now lead me to my father. My future was sealed. Only one question loomed: was I strong enough to endure his powers? Uncertain of the answer, I shook off the thought as we rode onward.

Sunlight began to falter as we approached the city gates. The silhouettes of guardsmen lined the wall walks and towers. Anticipating our return, they opened the portcullis without question. The people took little notice as we rode through the city streets. Making their way home after a long day of labor, many looked exhausted. The vendors were packing up their carts, completing the last of their business.

When we reached the castle barbican, I kicked my horse toward the stables. The others followed my lead.

I saw Madigan and Shallendria awaiting us when we rode through the stable gates. "Welcome, my friends!" Madigan took hold of my horse's harness. "We have long awaited your return."

"It is good to be back." I dismounted.

"Where is Sikes?" Shallendria searched our faces.

Darwynyen leapt from his horse to embrace her. "Sikes is no longer with us."

"I knew it!" she cried. Tears began to stream down her cheeks as she held him.

Madigan broke in. "Where is Gin?"

Darwynyen pulled away from Shallendria. "The deceiver has eluded us!"

"Deceiver?" Madigan gave Shallendria a fleeting look. "Whatever do you mean?"

"He is a murderer!" Darwynyen bluntly stated.

Madigan's eyes widened. "You must be mistaken. I just finished telling Shallendria that there was no—"

"Accept what you have been told," Dregby interjected. "Darwynyen's words are true."

"What happened?" Madigan grabbed Darwynyen by the shoulders.

Darwynyen pushed Madigan away harshly. "Your trust put us in danger!" He tightened his fists. "I warned you about him, but you would not listen!"

"Darwynyen, Madigan is not to blame!" I exclaimed. I stood between them. "If you have forgotten, it was I who asked him to join the quest!"

Both Darwynyen and Madigan calmed. "It is over." Darwynyen backed away. "Until we find Gin, I will discuss it no further."

It was plain to see that Madigan was still in denial. And though a part of me wanted to reason with him, I was unable to comprehend his reaction, wondering if our word was no longer good enough. *The spell that was cast upon Madigan still lingers.* Archemese entered my mind. *Do not fear. He will see the truth shortly.*

Archemese slowly dismounted his horse. "King Madigan, my name is Archemese. By Arianna's request, I am here to assist you through the troubled times that now beset you."

Madigan gave Archemese a quick look and then glanced back at Darwynyen. Shallendria took his place and wiped her eyes. "Archemese, as a wielder of magic, I am most happy to make your acquaintance."

Archemese bowed. "Shallendria, I can assure you that the feeling is mutual, for I have watched over you for several years now."

Naseyn raised his hand, as both he and Jeel crawled from the saddlebag. "King Madigan, our presence here should speak for the grand master's renewed loyalty to this alliance."

Madigan nodded. "Your grand master was wise to reconsider."

"Their names are Jeel and Naseyn." I moved to help them down from the horse. "They are here as representatives. The little people's defense force will join with us later."

Madigan ignored me and looked at Darwynyen. To avoid an argument, I gestured for the others to make their way to the castle.

As we ascended the stairs, Shallendria took me aside. "Gin's path was in darkness then?"

"Yes, his loyalty lies with the Hynd." I replied cautiously.

She blinked heavily before continuing. "I understand the queen has given you her pendant."

Before responding, I searched her face for signs of anger. There were none. "It was a gift." I pulled the pendant from my shirt. "Aldraveena believes I will need its protection."

"And you will." She took my hands in hers. "The northern horizon you have witnessed is only the beginning."

My eyes begin to water. "I must tell you that I now fear the path that has been thrust upon me."

She embraced me. "Do not worry. I will see you through this challenge."

I held to her, comforted by her sympathy. She was strong, and I needed her now more than ever. "Thank you." I pulled away and managed a smile.

I felt Darwynyen's hand on my shoulder. "Come, let us retire. I am eager for some rest."

"We cannot." I took his arm. "I must see to our guests."

Shallendria interrupted. "I will see to them. Go now. We will speak first thing in the morning."

Eager to take his leave, Darwynyen did not allow me to respond and led me inside the castle.

In the Eyes of a Raven

Unable to contain his urges any longer, Velderon placed his hands before the stones, immersing himself in the dark magic. Around him the wind began to stir. While he chanted, he raised his hands to the sky. Lightning attacked the clouds above him. Through the lands he searched. He required a single entity, a carrier for his mind. When he found the raven it was pecking on the carcass of a small rodent that had been crushed on a roadway on the outskirts of Aarrondirth. At the point of contact the taste sickened him. His vision became hazy and lost color as he entered the creature's mind.

Once he had control of the raven, he sprung to the air. Beyond the trees he found what he was looking for. "Aarrondirth castle," he muttered.

As he glided through the towers, he felt his daughter's presence. The sensation directed him to a small abode atop the keep. Unsteadily, he landed on the windowsill. He peered inside, and though the room was dim, he saw her, asleep on the bed with another. Enraged by the sight, his emotions turned to fury. He may have hated his daughter, but a shimmer of humanity still remained. Unaware, he tapped the raven's beak against the window. When Arianna sat up from her slumber, he froze, in hopes that he would go unnoticed. But she saw him, proving that their connection was still strong. A part of him wanted to summon her, his only heir. The sentiment did not last. His anger quickly resurfaced when he saw her awaken her companion. He watched as the man took hold of a weapon and moved to the door. It was time for him to leave, but he could not tear himself away, so desperate was he to see the man's face.

"No!" He gasped when the man reappeared from around the corner. It was the elf from the cavern. Was there no being rid of him? The feeble creature was obviously in love with his daughter. The thought disgusted him. Her blood was not to be mingled with an elf—anyone but an elf. Distraught, Velderon's emotions overwhelmed the bird.

In a moment, the connection was severed. As the spell diminished, Velderon began to pace the altar. He needed to formulate a spell, one that would make his daughter despise the elf. And if her heart was hardened, the dark magic would be more enticing. Yes. It was the only way, if he wanted Arianna to himself.

"What troubles you, Velderon?" A sorcerer appeared at the crest of the stairs.

Velderon turned with fire in his eyes. "I thought I told you to never come here unless summoned!"

The sorcerer stood his ground. "I hope it is not your daughter that leads you astray."

Velderon took no disrespect from his servants. With no warning, he cast the sorcerer into stone. When the transformation was complete, he took his wand and began to flip through a book of magic.

Spies

I heard the raven shriek, and seconds later, Darwynyen returned through the door.

"Why did you kill that bird?" I cried.

Darwynyen sat to the bed fastidiously. "I believe it was your father's spy."

I shook my head in denial. "What purpose would he have here?"

"I do not know," he shrugged. "Perhaps he wanted to see you."

"How can you be certain it was him?" I asked.

"The bird was not well," he replied. "It was acting strangely, and like most wild animals would, it did not flee at the sight of me."

"What should we do?" I felt violated and pulled the covers up to my chest.

"There is nothing we can do." He embraced me.

"We could change rooms," I suggested.

"It would make no difference." He tightened his hold. "As long as we are in Aarrondirth, he will find you."

"I was not prepared for tactics such as this," I confessed. "I thought I still had time."

"As did I." He drew back. "In any case, I hope it bothers him that I rest with his daughter."

I managed a smile and caressed his cheek.

"Have you had enough rest?" he asked.

I nodded.

"Then let me hold you until sunrise." He stacked a few pillows.

When he was comfortable, I leaned into him, taking solace in the beating of his heart.

The Dungeons

Carrying a torch, Velderon made his way in the dim light through the winding corridors of the dungeon beneath the castle of Cessdorn. For the most part, the cells were empty. Rats scurried around the bones of the dead, the remnants of those who had not survived their capture. Undaunted by his surroundings, he allowed his senses to guide him, for he was not there to see the prisoners. He was there for another reason.

At the end of a winding corridor, he came to a stone wall, one that had been created by magic. With his free hand, he searched for the entrance. When his fingers disappeared through the illusion, he chuckled. The sorcerers were clever. Through a simple spell they had remained hidden during the last incursion. Biding their time, they waited until Cessdorn was once again abandoned and then had emerged from their hiding place with two of the stones. From that day forward they again sought victory—this time the victory would be his.

Once past the opening, he descended a broken stair to a large chamber. In the back lay one of his prize possessions. Guarding it was his most trusted servant, Fasken's brother.

"How is the creature doing, Besken?" He peered through the iron bars and gazed upon the creature curled up near the back.

The troll bowed. "She is fine. We will need more food. The supply room is nearly drained, and her appetite is relentless."

Velderon looked at the beast with a cunning smile. "Get what is needed. I do not intend to lose her."

Besken nodded, taking hold of a basket. Velderon gazed upon the beast again. For a moment he was struck with pity. She had grown weak over the years, and solitude was stealing her sanity. Disgusted by his empathy, he quickly brushed the feelings aside and turned to leave the room.

Guilt

Madigan and I spent the morning alone in the study. Hours elapsed before he would finally accept the truth. Not only was the spell difficult for him to comprehend, Gin's deceit ran deep.

When he looked at me, I saw the guilt in his eyes. "Do not punish yourself, Madigan." I reached out to him. "The blame is not yours alone."

He recoiled at my touch and moved to the window. "How can you say that? It was not you who gave him control of our armies."

I looked down. "No, but I was the one who ignored Darwynyen's misgivings and brought Gin on our quest." My eyes began to fill. "If I had chosen to listen, Sikes might still be alive."

He turned from the window. "I see now that there is no point in arguing over who is at fault. What is done is done."

"Agreed." I wiped my eyes. "Now we must look forward, to the future."

"The future is less unsettling than the past." He released a heavy sigh. "Although I have accepted what has happened, I still do not understand why I did not see through him."

"As I said before, Archemese believes you were put under a spell."

"Yes, but why?" he asked.

"To expedite Gin's rise in command," I replied. "With his given powers, he could eventually have brought about our downfall."

"This may not be over." Madigan clenched his fists. "You said that Gin made his escape to the north."

"Yes." I searched his eyes. "What is troubling you?"

"What if Gin seeks out the battalions that have already made way for Biddenwade?"

My chest tightened as he spoke. "That must have been his intention all along."

He frowned. "What are you saying?"

"When Gin eluded us on our last encounter, we first thought he would make his way for Aarrondirth," I explained. "After the fairies proved us wrong, we assumed that he was lost and was plotting a course for Cessdorn. We did not consider that the journey would lead him to Walferd and then Biddenwade, where he could once again cause dissention, this time among the troops."

Madigan strode to the door. "If that is the case, the generals must be warned. They trust him and believe him worthy of my command!"

Archemese and Morglafenn appeared at the archway. "Are we interrupting?" Morglafenn raised his brow inquisitively.

"I was just leaving." Madigan brushed past him.

Archemese barred Madigan with his arm. "What has happened?" He looked at me with concern.

"Madigan and I have come to realize Gin's true intention," I replied. "We believe that he will try to sway our battalions in Walferd and Biddenwade while on route to Cessdorn."

"Let me pass!" Madigan stared Archemese down. "I must send out a rider."

"There is no need." Archemese lowered his arm. "I will summon the fairies." He closed his eyes and put his fingers to his temples. "They should be the ones to go."

"Why?" Madigan snapped, a look of frustration upon his face. "My men will never listen to them."

"But the elves will," Morglafenn interrupted. "If the fairies go, we can stay in contact with them."

Madigan was about to respond when the fairies flew past his head. "What is it you need, master?" Zenley bowed, midair, in front of Archemese. Teshna followed his lead.

Archemese bowed his head in return. "I charge you with a quest of great importance. Gin will try to sway the armies to the north. They must be warned." He looked at Morglafenn. "Make ready a decree from the king."

Morglafenn removed a small jar of ink from a shelf, "Will the fairies be able to carry a scroll?" he asked, looking doubtful.

"Let me see to that," Archemese replied, placing a sheet of thatch paper in front of Morglafenn. "Command that Gin be detained should he show his face. Have them keep him prisoner until our arrival." When Morglafenn began writing, Archemese looked at the fairies. "When you reach Walferd, give the scroll to an elf. Elves will understand."

After Madigan reluctantly signed the scroll, I held a stick of red wax over a candle and then validated the decree with the royal seal. "Allow me." Archemese took hold of the scroll, "*Denadra, zuite.*" At his words the scroll suddenly shrunk to a size the fairies could manage.

Madigan gasped and then blinked his eyes. "I do not believe my eyes." Morglafenn carried the same expression.

My mouth dropped open. "Neither do I!"

Archemese ignored us, handing the scroll to Zenley. "Be swift in your travels," he urged. "Tell any who will listen of the threat!"

Zenley took hold of the scroll and then sped through an open window. Teshna followed after him.

Madigan stiffened his shoulders. "I will still send out a rider. I can assure you that my men will not easily accept the word of an elf."

Archemese nodded. "Send your rider. If nothing else, he will reaffirm the decree, should there be any indecision among the troops."

Before Madigan could excuse himself, I spoke. "While we are all here, there is another matter we need to discuss." I took a seat, gesturing for the men to join me. I could see that Madigan was eager to leave, so I got right to the point. "Darwynyen believes that my father sent a spy in the form of a raven last night." I tensed, chilled by the thought. "We found the creature peering into our bedchamber."

"Are you certain?" Archemese puckered his brow. "I know that I warned you to stay on your guard, but this move is bold, even for Velderon."

"Not if Aldraveena's predictions are coming true." Morglafenn took my hand in support. "Spies are to be expected. We should anticipate more as the cycle proceeds."

"Where is this bird now?" Archemese asked.

"Darwynyen took its life when it did not flee," I replied.

Madigan stood. "I will alert the guards to these intruders. The ravens shall be hunted until Velderon refrains from this sort of trickery."

"No." Archemese spoke with determination. "If they are seen within the castle, we must capture them."

I frowned. "For what purpose?"

"If your father is curious, he might want to communicate." He glanced at Morglafenn. "If Velderon is willing, we can use the raven as a medium."

Madigan raised his brow. "Is that possible?"

Archemese nodded. "Although the black magic is far more devious than the white, we can still use Velderon's powers against him."

Morglafenn acknowledged Archemese's ploy with a nod. "There is little danger," he reassured Madigan when he saw the concern on his face. "It will be no different than when Shallendria breached the portal and connected to the Hynd."

"Very well." Madigan stomped toward the door. "If the birds are seen within the castle walls, they will be captured."

The abrupt manner in which Madigan took his leave made his stress obvious. Deep down, I knew he was finding it difficult to cope with all the recent demands. I worried for him, knowing that if he were to succeed in his charge as king, he would have to set aside his misgivings and draw strength from his courage.

I was about to adjourn the meeting when I noticed that Archemese was gazing deeply into Morglafenn's eyes. They were communicating in secrecy, I was certain. Insulted by their lack of consideration, I was about to interrupt when Morglafenn stood, bowed his head, and then left the room.

"At last we are alone." Archemese clasped his hands together. "Since our arrival in Aarrondirth, I have been waiting for this opportunity."

"We have only been back a day." I turned in my chair to face him. "What more could there be to talk about?" I spoke impatiently. Madigan was not the only one feeling stressed.

He entered my mind. *You cannot run from your troubles, my dear. Facing them is the only way.* When I nodded, he continued. "What leaves you ill at ease?"

I released a heavy breath. "I am distressed by the recent events. First Gin and then the raven—I thought I would have more time."

"And what would you do with time if it were given?" he asked.

"I do not understand." I pursed my lips.

"Either way, your destiny is set." His brow rose. "Would it not be better for you to face it now, rather than later?"

"I suppose." I slowly nodded.

"Then you must forget Gin the traitor and stay focused." He pulled a small book from his robe. "With that said, I would like you to learn the skill of magic."

I shook my head in disbelief. "Did I hear you correctly?"

"Yes."

I greedily eyed the book. "But I thought it took years to learn such things."

"It normally does." He winked. "With me as your mentor, you will absorb the knowledge swiftly."

As I considered his proposal, my thoughts strayed to Darwynyen, who had discouraged me when it came to magic. "Darwynyen is unlikely to approve. I feel I should speak to him first before I make any kind of commitment."

"I understand." He placed the book in front of me. "While you make your decision, I would like you to read this book. It will explain all the elements in our land. You must understand these things before we can begin."

I took hold of the book. "Thank you, Archemese … I mean, for believing in me."

"Do not misjudge Darwynyen." He smiled sympathetically. "He too believes in you."

"I know." I nodded.

"Find me when you have finished." He stood and left the room.

I must have stared at the book for several minutes before turning the cover. My hesitation proved futile. From the opening line, I was captivated. Without the mention of magic, the pages explained the harmony of our world. It described how the sun was the orb of life, how every being relied on its energy. It also spoke of the moon and its effect on the tides; how they worked together to keep the fabric of life in motion. It then detailed how creatures great and small strived for equilibrium. Through the readings, I realized how precious my mere existence truly was, and I promised myself that in future I would make a better effort to respect the delicate balance that until now I had unknowingly taken for granted.

As I began the next chapter, Jeel and Naseyn ran through the door in what appeared to be another game of chase and capture. Flustered, I took a moment to compose myself. "Jeel, Naseyn. What brings you into the study?" I asked.

Startled, they halted. Naseyn said, "Arianna, what are you doing in here?"

I lifted the book. "I am reading, and I require peace and quiet to do so. If you would be so kind as to find another area to play in, I would be indebted to you."

Jeel assumed a defensive stance, "We are not playing, you silly girl. We are men, not children!"

Exasperated, I raised my brow. "Well, whatever it is you are doing, I would appreciate it if you would do it elsewhere."

They began to prod one another and then ran from the room. As I heard their laughter echo down the corridors, I smiled. They were so innocent in their ways. My heart sank when I thought of the coming times, wondering if they would be able to cope with the war when it was upon us.

Darwynyen appeared at the door. "Here you are! I have been looking for you all over." He took notice of the book. "What are you reading?"

Fearing his reaction, I quickly closed it, hugging it to my chest.

"What is it?" He tried to pry it from my hands.

"I am reading a book Archemese gave me." I reaffirmed my grasp.

He snatched it away and glanced over the cover. When he realized what it was, he looked at me with disappointment. "This book involves magic. Why would he give this to you?"

"He wants me to learn from it," I replied boldly. "He feels that I am not only worthy but ready."

"If you wish to learn such things I will not hold you back." He placed the book to the table. "I will only ask that you be careful, for I have seen magic destroy bonds that were once unbreakable."

Although I was hurt by his insinuation that I would choose magic over our love, I tried to reassure him. "It is not my intention to become a sorceress." I motioned for him to sit next to me. "Archemese will only show me what is needed to protect myself in the times ahead."

He nodded with little emotion as he sat. Relieved that we were not to argue, I pushed the book aside. "How about I take a break and we spend some time together?"

"It will have to wait." Darwynyen motioned toward the door.

When I turned, I saw Morglafenn. "Morglafenn!" I sent Darwynyen a fleeting look. "Were you looking to speak with one of us?"

"Yes." Morglafenn entered the room. "Excuse my interruption, but I have finished reading the book that you left me." He looked at me as he pulled it from his cloak. "If you have time, I would like to share what I have learned about our dragon foes."

Darwynyen moved, directing Morglafenn to sit in between us. "I hope your words are encouraging," he said.

"I can assure you that they are." Morglafenn sat in the open chair.

I tugged at his arm impatiently. "What does it say?"

"The dragons are extraordinary creatures," he remarked enthusiastically, opening the book near its end. "They are extremely intelligent. One should not be fooled by their inability to physically speak our language, as I can assure you that they understand it, and they are able to communicate through the mind."

Sharing in his enthusiasm, I was about to reiterate our prior conversation when I had disclosed my encounters with the beasts. As though sensing this, Morglafenn prodded my arm, eyeing Darwynyen.

I nonchalantly sat forward, staring at the book. Morglafenn was right; now was not the time to share this revelation with Darwynyen.

Morglafenn persisted. "Their tale is a sad one. During the last war their matriarch ..."

Darwynyen interrupted. "We are already aware of the matriarch's disappearance."

Morglafenn raised his brow. "Yes, but do you know who took her?"

"Of course," Darwynyen replied. "The text stated that it was the Man's Blood, which is one of the reasons why the creatures sought revenge upon us."

"No, Darwynyen." Morglafenn shook his head. "You are mistaken. The book goes on to tell a different story."

"What are you saying?" Darwynyen frowned.

"If you would allow me …" Morglafenn retorted.

Darwynyen gestured for him to continue.

"You may find this difficult to comprehend, but it appears that the creature was taken by the Hynd."

"For what purpose," I asked, stunned.

"It was a strategic move," Morglafenn replied. "When Cessdorn was losing ground in the war, the sorcerers found a way to capture the beast."

"How can you be certain?" Darwynyen's undertone conveyed doubt.

"The author of this book claims to have seen her." Morglafenn turned the page. "A minion of the sorcerers, he was charged with finding food for a beast that was locked in the dungeons at Cessdorn. Over the years, he came to realize that this beast was the matriarch dragon. Sometime later, he was permitted to see her. Sensing the man's humanity, the dragon began to communicate with him." His fingers swept the following page. "When the sorcerers learned of this, the man feared for his life. Under the cover of darkness, he made a daring escape that would free him of the sorcerer's rule. Thereafter he sought to liberate the beast. After his attempts proved futile, the years caught up with him, and he wrote this book, knowing that it was the only means for him to share in this legacy."

"If the author was a minion of the sorcerers, for all we know this book could have been written as a lie," Darwynyen rebuffed.

Morglafenn abruptly closed the book. "It is unlikely. There

is little chance the sorcerers would have freed the dragons unless they were certain that they had control over them."

When Darwynyen drifted into thought, I looked at Morglafenn. "If these words are true, then my father is now in control of this matriarch beast."

"Yes!" Morglafenn nodded intensely. "And he will use her to bring about our downfall." His voice deepened. "If the dragons are to protect their queen, they are unwillingly bound to your father's command."

"Not if we put a stop to this madness." I stood. "We must see to freeing this beast—not for our advantage, but for the dragons in Naksteed who are also held captive by this abduction."

Morglafenn turned in his chair. "I thought the same, my dear, but we are helpless until the war leads us to Cessdorn."

"There might be another way." I bit my lip. "We could try to communicate with them."

"It is unlikely that they would listen," Morglafenn replied. "We have one option, and that would be to seek the counsel of the matriarch's companion, who presently resides in Naksteed. He is the only one with the authority to make the final decision."

I looked at Darwynyen. "Then we must travel to Naksteed and locate their sanctuary. If they learn of our intentions they may assist us."

Darwynyen shook his head obstinately. "We do not have time! War is at hand."

"Darwynyen!" Morglafenn paused to gather his composure. "Whether you like it or not, these creatures are part of the war." He stood. "If nothing else we must try."

"This is not a decision we can make alone." Darwynyen stood to face him. "We must consult the others."

"Then let us gather them now," Morglafenn beseeched.

"It can wait." Darwynyen pointed to the bay windows. "We will gather them this evening when the sun is no longer in our favor." It was plain to see Darwynyen's motivation in ending the conversation. Seeking an alliance with the dragons was of no consequence to him, and it was obvious that he was going to do all he could to thwart us.

Morglafenn glanced at me before conceding. "Very well, I suppose there is no urgency in the matter."

Darwynyen headed for the door. He turned when he noticed that I was not following. "Arianna, will you not join me?"

"I will find you later." I sat back on my chair defiantly.

With a look of frustration, Darwynyen disappeared through the archway.

I felt Morglafenn's hand on my arm. "Arianna, are you all right?"

"Yes." I changed the subject, determined not to allow Darwynyen's hurt feelings to distract me. "When the matriarch beast was taken, why did the dragons not attempt a rescue?" I asked.

"Clever you are!" Morglafenn grinned, taking hold of the book. "I wondered the same thing, until I learned that the sorcerers had hidden her with magic." He paused. "That is why the beasts were easily deceived when they were led to Naksteed."

"Who led them to Naksteed?" I asked.

"Our people." He looked down with regret. "The king of that day forced the decision upon the elvish council, after the dragons renewed their attacks in our regions."

"I do not understand." I rested my head on my hands in defeat.

"Forgive me, I have not fully explained." Morglafenn smiled encouragingly. "Although the sorcerers had the matriarch, she would have initially resisted their command. Their plan was not flawless. When chaos broke out amongst the beasts, the sorcerers quickly redirected the blame onto the Man's Blood and elves. With few options, the king of those times ordered the queen of the elves to Naksteed, where she would summon the creatures through the mind."

I furrowed my brow. "Why would the dragons listen to her?"

"She did not call to them. Instead she deceived the creatures by calling to the wind, knowing that they would intercept the message."

"What was the message?" I asked.

"That the elves were losing control of the matriarch and they needed assistance. When the dragons followed the connection to Naksteed, our people locked them in the catacombs with iron and magic."

"Excuse my ignorance, but how have they survived?" I asked. "I suspect there was little food in these chambers."

"That chore was left to the sirens, along with the key." He opened the book to a drawing. "Naksteed was the perfect place to contain them. You see," he pointed to a map, "the catacombs are massive."

I glanced over the map. "How were they able to capture all the beasts at once?" I asked.

"They did not," he replied. "Only seven of the beasts fled to the cave, including the matriarch's companion, who was desperate to save her. Without their leaders, the remaining dragons became irrational, and killing them became easy."

"I have seen more than seven beasts," I challenged.

He chuckled. "The catacombs may have contained the creatures, but it most certainly did not prevent them from breeding."

"Oh." I sighed heavily. The thought of knowing that many of the captive dragons would not have seen the light of day until recently saddened me. "Will you tell me more of the matriarch?" I asked as a distraction.

He closed the book. "Certainly. She is kept somewhere deep in the bowels of Cessdorn. The text states that the room is bound by dark magic, hidden by a protective wall of stone. I also believe this place to be the sanctuary of the sorcerers. That is why the remaining two stones were never found, for it was a place for them to stay hidden until the day Cessdorn was once again abandoned."

"Are you saying that this one room has concealed them for all these years?"

"Yes, along with the dragon."

"We must find her, Morglafenn!" I spoke with fervor.

"We will." He paused. "But first, we must persuade the others."

"Leave that task to me," I responded firmly. "I do not intend to yield on this matter."

"Neither do I." He picked up the book. "I'd best be on my way—I understand you have some studying to do."

My eyes widened. "You know of my teachings?"

"Yes, my dear." He squeezed my hand. "Archemese informed me of his plans. Do not fear. I too believe you are ready."

"Thank you." I smiled. "If only Darwynyen thought the same."

He turned to leave. "Give him some time. He is only worried for you."

I nodded, and I watched him take his leave.

En Route

Exhausted from their travels, Teshna and Zenley rested in the hollow nook of a tree. The weather was turning for the worse. Despite all their efforts, there was still no sign of Gin. Hope remained. They were still in the early stages of their journey; because they did not have to follow the roadway there was still a chance they might arrive in Walferd before he did.

"We shall stay in the cover of this tree for the night." Zenley stretched out. "Walferd is not far. In the morning we will continue to seek out the battalions."

"I have no strength to argue with you, my brother." Teshna yawned. "Besides, tomorrow is not far away."

"Do you ever wonder about Gin?" He turned to face her.

"No." She pulled some food from her satchel. "I would sooner just forget him. His soul has nothing left but evil."

"You are probably right." He pulled a leaf around him. "Good night, my sister."

"Good night." She rested her head against his shoulder.

Seconds later they were both asleep.

To the Dragons

I was halfway through the book when I felt the connection. *My child, you must come to the library,* Archemese demanded. *Morglafenn needs your help! The men are discussing the dragons.*

When the connection ended, I immediately stood and made way, annoyed by the fact that I had not been summoned to begin with. Did Darwynyen's intention to thwart us outweigh his trust in me? If so, he was not going to be pleased by my decision.

As I walked the corridor that connected to the library, I could hear shouting. The men were in a heated discussion. Curious, I halted outside the doors. "Why should we trouble ourselves with the dragons?" Kendrick argued. "We have no allegiance to them!"

"I agree!" Dregby bellowed. "Do we not already have enough to contend with?"

"Everyone, we must stay calm!" The voice of reason was Madigan's. "We should wait—"

"We should finish this conversation now!" Darwynyen interrupted. "We have listened to Morglafenn's proposal, and no one has agreed." His tone was dry and condescending. "And why would we, when the dragons have done nothing but attack us?"

I stepped through the threshold. "They attack us because they have no choice."

The room fell silent. Having captured their attention, I continued. "Furthermore, why are you discussing these matters without me?"

Shallendria appeared from behind me. "I would like to know the same."

Madigan raised his hands defensively. "Do not look at me! It was Darwynyen who initiated this meeting."

I sent Shallendria a fleeting look. "Then may I ask why we were not invited?"

"Of course you were." Madigan eyed Darwynyen for a response.

When Darwynyen swallowed deeply, Archemese stood. "Now is not the time to bicker." His tone was stern. "If we are here to discuss the dragons, then let us proceed."

I acknowledged Archemese with a nod. If not for his connection, there was little doubt that Darwynyen would have succeeded in persuading the others. I moved to the open chair next to him. Shallendria glared at Darwynyen for a moment and then took a seat.

Madigan cleared his throat as I sat. "Arianna, am I to understand that you share the same viewpoint as Morglafenn when it comes to the dragons?" Before I could respond, he continued. "If so, what are your motives?"

"I will not deny that I feel compelled to reach out to these creatures and save them from my father," I admitted. "Even so, there are several other advantages to consider."

"Such as?" Madigan raised his brow.

"Is it not plain to see that the dragons' fate is in our hands?" Morglafenn interjected. "If we seize this opportunity and support their cause, I am certain that victory will fall to us."

Kendrick leaned forward. "Logic has eluded you, Morglafenn, if you believe that the dragons will ever agree to an alliance."

"Your opinion is of no importance to me." Morglafenn scanned the room. "I intend to travel to Naksteed, with or without this council's approval."

"As do I." I nodded with conviction.

Darwynyen's mouth fell open. "How can you commit to another quest when you know that your destiny lies elsewhere?"

"Forgive me, Darwynyen, but I must follow my heart in this matter."

Shallendria stood at Morglafenn's side. "If Arianna and Morglafenn are going to Naksteed, then I intend to accompany them."

Madigan shook his head. "Shallendria, do you even know what you are agreeing to?"

"Yes. If you would take heed of Morglafenn's words, you would see that he is right. If we do not seek out this alliance, the odds will undoubtedly turn against us."

Darwynyen sat back in his chair. "There is no point in arguing, Madigan. It will serve no purpose—their minds are already set on this outcome."

Archemese reached for a map. "If our destination is soon to be Naksteed, then let us make the arrangements."

When I looked at Archemese, he winked.

"Should we not discuss this further?" Madigan questioned. "How do you plan to make your way to Naksteed, when we have yet to secure that region?"

"That is of no concern." Shallendria confidently glanced to Archemese and Morglafenn. "The magic in our company will protect us."

Dregby chuckled wryly. "If the dragons are as intelligent as Morglafenn has claimed, why not connect to them when they next attack? That is, if you can outlast their fire."

Darwynyen and Madigan began to laugh mockingly. Morglafenn interrupted. "We will not forgo that option, if the creatures should return before our departure. However, we must accept the fact that they may not listen to reason. In the end, it is the eldest male of the beasts, the matriarch's mate that we must seek."

When there was nothing left to argue, Madigan, Dregby,

and Kendrick left the room. Darwynyen remained. Despite his resistance, I knew he would not allow me to undertake this quest without him. Pleased by his decision, I looked at him when making the initial decisions.

After several hours of deliberation, we decided that we would first make our way to Walferd. From there a small battalion of soldiers would escort us to the catacombs of Naksteed. We would undertake the remainder of the journey alone. Upon our success or failure, we would then reconnect with the soldiers and travel to the city of Biddenwade to prepare for battle. These arrangements seemed sufficient; we had no intention to linger, for there were more important things at hand.

I rose casually, to avoid attention. "If we are finished here, I will go to the study to continue my reading."

Darwynyen stood. "I thought we could first speak." His eyes bore into mine intensely.

I tightened my shoulders, knowing by his mannerisms that he wanted to discuss the lack of consideration I had given him when I abruptly made the decision to accompany Morglafenn. *Do not deny him, Arianna.* Archemese spoke in my mind. *It is Darwynyen's love for you, and his need to protect you, that brings about this discourse. Settle things now before they fester.*

I gave Archemese a quick nod, acknowledging his counsel. Although he did not fully understand the depth of the situation, his intentions were sincere. I turned to Darwynyen. "Would you care to join me in the study?"

Shallendria took Darwynyen by the wrist. "My cousin, I have wanted to speak with you. If you could spare a few moments it would be appreciated."

"Can it not wait?" he asked gruffly.

"Take the time, Darwynyen," I urged. "I will meet you in our quarters instead. I will not be long, and I will bring dinner for us to share when I am finished."

"Very well," Darwynyen conceded, returning to his chair.

I nodded, leaving the room before he could change his mind. If nothing else, the given time would allow his hurt feelings to settle.

Upon entering the study, I lit a few candles, determined to finish another chapter of the book before retiring. As I sifted through the pages, a knock came to the open door. I turned and saw Madigan. "Arianna, may I have a word?" he asked, stepping through the threshold.

"Yes, of course." I smiled to conceal my frustration. "Please come in."

He nodded and held out a scroll. "I am preparing an announcement about our departure from Aarrondirth."

"What do you mean by 'our' departure?" I asked.

"If you are to make way for Naksteed, then I no longer see the need to delay our plans," he explained. "In your absence, I intend to lead the remainder of our battalions to Biddenwade."

"Why would you take unnecessary risks now ...?" I hesitated when I realized the hypocrisy of what I was about to say. How could I expect him to stay behind after I had just taken on another quest? "Forgive me. It is not my place to question you." I set the book on the table. "Instead, I will respect your decision and take comfort in knowing that you will be accompanying me on the first league of our journey."

"Thank you." He paused. "Are you certain you are making the right decision?"

"I see no other way, Madigan." I held out my hands, beseeching him. "What else would you have me do?"

"It was not my intention to upset you, Arianna." His hand caressed his brow in frustration. "I am only concerned."

"You have not," I sighed. "But as you can see, I feel very strongly on this matter."

"As do I, though for different reasons." He began to pace. "Tactical moves must be decisive and direct. You, however, do nothing to follow these rules and are in many ways reckless. I find this very disconcerting when it comes to our people, especially now, when they need your guidance most."

"What I do is for the people." I took him by the arm. "In the end, they will see this." I released my hold. "If not, I will face the consequences then. Eluding my father is of paramount importance, and he will be the last to expect this sort of move. Moreover, if we are successful, the odds will turn against him. A risk worth taking, is it not?"

He considered my appeal for a moment and then nodded. "I see no need to discuss this further. When the speech is written I will consult you."

"Thank you, Madigan." I returned to my seat when he left the room.

Revenge

Overwrought by his daughter's relationship with the elf, Velderon returned to the altar. "Anyone but an elf," he grumbled as he ascended. When he reached the plateau, he opened the scroll he had been carrying. As he scanned the spell, he realized that he needed a few things before he could conjure it, and he set out in his quest.

He found a raven along the roadside and quickly took control of it. To avoid capture, he entered the realm of Aarrondirth under cover of twilight, gliding through the towers with precision until he reached the abode above the keep.

After peering through the window, he made for the door. He needed to be swift, knowing that Arianna or the elf could return at any moment.

Using the bird's weight and its talons, he popped open the door latch. When the door slowly creaked ajar, he flew inside. To avoid injuring the bird, he immediately landed on one of the bedposts and began to scan the room. He needed to find something of a personal nature that was small enough for the bird to carry.

To his dismay, their belongings were scattered everywhere. He was about to give up when he spotted a silver comb near the bathing tub. The design was elvish. Strands of hair were caught around the teeth. Ecstatic, he quickly snapped it up with the raven's beak and flew from the room to commence with his plans.

To Seek a Lost Friend

Despite my efforts, Darwynyen was still finding it difficult to cope with our coming quest and the approach through which it came about. Because of this, we had spent little time together. While he worked alongside Madigan, preparing our troops for their departure to Biddenwade, Archemese began to mentor me in the magic. And though I was concerned by Darwynyen's sudden withdrawal, Archemese's teachings were proving a compelling distraction.

"Concentrate!" Archemese demanded, pointing to a section of the book he had placed before me. "Draw the power from within!"

"I am trying," I huffed. "Only I feel nothing of which you speak." In frustration, I rose from the table. "I cannot do this. I am not strong enough!"

"Sit down," he insisted. "Try again!"

"No!" I crossed my arms. "Can you not leave …?" I broke off when the candle I had been trying so desperately to light burst into flame. "Did you see that?" I gasped in excitement.

Archemese blew out the candle. "I knew you could do it. You just had to muster the right emotions."

Troubled by the latter part of his response, I frowned. "If I must give in to negative emotions every time I need to conjure magic, I will not do it. Aldraveena told me I needed to focus on the positive, not the negative."

Archemese chuckled wryly. "Arianna, you do not derive magic from anger but from emotion alone. That is why I have pushed you. You must draw from your feelings, not your mind."

I realized then that he had angered me on purpose. He was trying to make me feel as I conjured the spell. "Why did you not tell me of this aspect?" I asked.

"Some things you must learn for yourself, my dear," he replied shrewdly. "Enough chatter. I want to see you do it again."

As I sat at the table, he handed me his small satchel. "Before you begin, you must release another pinch of this powder near the wick."

I nodded, sprinkling the powder as I repeated the words he had taught me. To my dismay, nothing happened. When I saw the look on his face, I grew annoyed. I was about to speak in sarcasm when the candle again came to life.

"Good!" He extinguished the flame with his fingers. "Now do it again."

As I began to understand the true meaning of his teachings, the task became easier. I lit the candle several times before tiring. "I somehow feel exhausted." I wiped my brow. For the first time I was experiencing the damaging effects of magic. "I must get some rest," I muttered.

"Of course." He smiled sincerely. "You have done well, my dear. Have your rest. We will meet again tomorrow."

"Thank you, Archemese." I took his hand. "If I appeared angry, it was only my frustration. I will try to do better in the future."

"I know you will." He rose and ushered me through the study door.

† † †

I awoke from a dream I could not remember. The trance had taken me deep into my subconscious. As I sat in the bed, my first thought was of Edina. I had to see her. Unsure of the hour, I moved to the window. The skies were lost to twilight. Convinced that there was still time, I made my way to the stables.

As I adjusted Accolade's girth, I again thought of Edina and wondered how she was coping with Stuart's death. I should have been there for her. Unfortunately my obligations had led me elsewhere.

"Where are you off to?" Jeel approached from the paddock rail.

"I am going to see a friend." I mounted Accolade.

"Can we go with you?" I looked down to find Naseyn jumping for the stirrup.

"Now is not the best time." I paused to find the right words. "The friend I seek is mourning the loss of a loved one."

Their eyes filled with disappointment. Struck with guilt, I found it impossible to deny them. "All right," I sighed. "You may come, but you must stay with the horse at all times." I steadied Accolade near the rail. "Under the circumstances, I do not wish to cause further alarm among the people."

"Of course." Jeel jumped onto the saddle. "There is no need for concern. We will do as you ask."

Naseyn jumped again for the stirrup, and when his hold was secure, he climbed my leg until he reached Jeel. When they had taken a hold of the lacing around the saddle horn, I nudged Accolade forward. "I hope I do not regret this," I mumbled.

As we passed through the gates at the barbican, I pulled the reins, realizing then that I did not know where Edina's family dwelled outside the castle.

"Why do you delay?" Jeel asked.

"It seems almost foolish to admit this, but I do not know where this friend lives," I replied humbly.

Jeel nudged Naseyn. "It seems our adventure has abruptly come to its end."

I kicked Accolade. "You obviously do not know me well enough if you believe that I would give up this easily."

When we arrived at the main square, I slowed Accolade to a trot. "If I am not mistaken, I believe her family lives off one of the main streets near the armory." I scanned the intersecting roads.

"Ask that vendor." Jeel pointed to a cart near the fountain. "He may know where to find her."

As I observed the man securing the shutters on his cart, I noticed that he was in a fuss and mumbling to himself. He must have had a long day and was eager to be on his way. Rather than risk his mood, I directed Accolade to the stables next to the inn.

A stable boy rushed over when we neared the entrance.

"Two gold pieces for the evening, miss."

I dismounted. "Give me a moment." I searched for my coin purse.

He nodded, gawking at Jeel and Naseyn.

"What is it?" I asked.

"Who … I mean, *what* are they?" He took a step back.

"They are my companions." I placed three gold pieces in his hand. "I will ask that you mind them, along with the horse."

"Wait a minute." He furrowed his brow. "Do I know you?"

I nodded. "My name is Arianna."

"Lady Arianna!" His eyes widened. He bowed. "Please, excuse my ignorance." He tried to return the coins. "Please, I beg your pardon."

I raised my hand. "Keep the gold. It is for your inconvenience. I shall return shortly." I turned to Jeel and Naseyn with a warning look. "Do not stray from the horse."

Naseyn put his arm around Jeel. "We will do no such thing. I give you my word."

Although I was reluctant to leave them, I was here to find Edina, and I set off to look for her.

After several enquiries, I began to lose hope. It was getting late. Perhaps my time would be better served if I returned in the morn, when there were more people about. As I turned toward the main square, I caught of glimpse of a man entering a building down one of the side roads. My intuition told me that it was Edina's father, and I immediately ran toward the door.

When I reached the building, I realized it was a community dwelling that housed several flats. As I pulled open the door, I saw a long corridor and a stair on the right leading upward. The man was nearing the top of the rise. I cleared my throat. "Excuse me, sir?"

He ignored me and limped down the corridor.

"Excuse me, sir," I said aloud as I climbed. "Are you the father of Edina?"

He paused for a moment and then turned. "Why are you here, Arianna?" His eyes were tired, almost lifeless.

"I am here to see Edina." I halted on the second-to-last step. "My duties have recently taken me away from Aarrondirth, and I would like to know how she has been coping in my absence."

He leaned against the wall. "You are wasting your time. Edina has not left her room from the day of Stuart's burial."

"Why?" I asked. "Is she all right?"

"No." He looked down. "She is not well. That is why I will ask you to leave. She receives no one, not even her own family."

"I am not leaving." I took another step. "Not until I see her."

He lifted his right foot. I could tell he was favoring it. Pain filled his face. "I suppose it is not my place to deny you." He sighed. "Still, you may regret your insistence."

"Thank you." I took hold of his arm, assisting him to the second door on the left.

Once inside, he led me to a door at the back of their main sitting area. "She is in there." He bowed his head and then left for the kitchen.

As he took his leave, I gave myself a moment to prepare, and then I knocked on the door. "Edina. It is Arianna. May I come in?"

"Go away!" she shouted.

"Edina!" I tried the handle. "I need to see you!"

There was no response. As I contemplated my next actions, I heard floor boards creaking from the interior of the room. Moments later the handle turned. She brushed the tangled hair from her face. "Arianna, why are you here?"

I reached for her hand. "I have come because I miss you terribly."

She flinched. "Now is not a good time."

"I will not stay for long." I put my hand to the door when she moved to close it. "I promise."

She backed away slowly, her body trembling with anxiety.

I glanced over the room as I entered. It was cluttered and filled with gloom. The furniture was old and held together by rusty nails. Her matted mattress appeared soiled. Clothing was scattered along the floor. The smell was foul. "How are you?" I asked, discreetly holding my breath. "I can only begin to imagine what you have been through."

She looked at me with resentment. "You know nothing of my pain!"

"Perhaps." I moved to the window for some fresh air.

Edina sat on the bed, her face in her hands. "I do not wish to live without him!" She began to sob.

I returned and embraced her. "Edina, you must not talk in such ways. I know you are hurting, but I can assure you from my previous experiences that these emotions will ease in time."

She rested her head on my shoulder. "Time will never heal these wounds."

Unsure what to say, I gave her a few moments. When she stopped responding all together, I laid her on the bed. Her eyes were still open, reminding me of my mother when she was in a daze. I shook the thought. Unlike my mother, I would not leave her here to die. I would do anything to see her free from this prison she had unknowingly created in her mind. I brushed the hair from her brow. "Edina, I command you to return to the castle." My tone was harsh. It had to be if she was going to listen. "You are needed. I will not accept no for an answer."

She snapped into consciousness. "No." She sat up and regained her composure. "You cannot come in here and order me about. I am not going anywhere. If anyone is leaving, it is you!"

"Are you refusing my command?" I stood and glowered over her, I hoped convincingly. "As your lady, I will not accept it. If you do not arrive in the morning, I will send the castle guards to collect you!"

She ran to the door and flung it open. "Get out! I tell you, get out!"

Although her temper disturbed me, I felt I had done the right thing. "As you wish." I moved through the archway and turned. "See you tomorrow."

"Get out!" she screamed, slamming the door.

I took a deep breath and nodded to her father, who stood in the middle of the sitting area with wide eyes, and I passed through the door.

On my way to the stables, I tried to reassure myself that I had done the right thing. Either way, my options were few. I was not about to leave her in that room to rot, as I had done with my mother. No. Edina was like a sister to me, and one way or another I was going to see her through this.

When I found Accolade, I quickly mounted. I was about to leave when I realized that something was missing—Jeel and Naseyn. Infuriated, I leapt from Accolade and went in search of the stable boy.

I found him mucking a stall in the back. "Where are my companions?" I asked impatiently.

Startled, he dropped his shovel. "Whom do you mean?" His eyes began to wander nervously.

I took him by the arm, "The little people—whom else did I arrive with!"

"I … I could not," he stammered. "They left, down the street. I saw them go into the tavern at the inn."

"I thought I paid you to mind them," I snapped. "Is this how you conduct yourself?"

The boy took a step back with raised hands. "My lady. I beg your pardon, but they would not listen!"

Rather than respond, I rushed from the stable.

When I entered the tavern, I hesitated, reminded of Edric. As I glanced over the room, I noticed a small crowd gathered around the bar. Otherwise, the place was empty. "Where are they?" I grumbled. I was about to turn when I spotted Jeel and Naseyn atop the bar. They appeared to be intoxicated, conversing with those who would listen.

To avoid a scene, I gathered my composure. I was about to interrupt when laughter broke out among the small group of men. Curious, I listened to the conversation. I realized that Jeel and Naseyn were sharing stories of their homeland and that the men around them were giving them their full attention.

As I stepped forward, the men burst out in laughter again. When one of them stumbled back, he caught sight of me, and he gestured to his companions. "Quiet, Lady Arianna is here."

The remaining men abruptly turned and then bowed.

Beyond the men, I met the gazes of Jeel and Naseyn. There was shame all over their faces. And though my first instinct was to reprimand them, I smiled to ease the tension. Despite their disobedience, there was no harm done in their actions. "Please, I did not mean to spoil your fun." I looked at the men, "These little people you converse with are my companions. I am only here to retrieve them."

Jeel and Naseyn excused themselves, moving to an open area on the bar. "Forgive us, Arianna." Jeel looked at Naseyn. "We could not contain ourselves."

Naseyn hiccupped, "Yes, we love the ale of the Man's Blood, so we do."

I extended my hands. "Come, we must return to the castle. I have much to do."

"Of course." Jeel took hold of Naseyn. "Are you ready, my spirited friend?"

Naseyn giggled as I scooped them into my arms. I turned to

the others. “Thank you for your kindness. We shall be leaving now.”

A few of the men nodded as we moved for the door.

A Weighted Encounter

In his search for Arianna, Archemese stumbled across Darwynyen in the study. He was alone, staring out the bay windows. Before interrupting, Archemese took a moment to observe him. Something was wrong. He could feel it. He slowly stepped forward. "Darwynyen, may I have a word?"

Darwynyen did not respond. It was as though he were in a trance. "Darwynyen." Archemese gently placed his hand on Darwynyen's shoulder.

Darwynyen turned abruptly. "What is it?"

Archemese took a step back when he realized that Darwynyen was holding a blade. "Is everything all right?"

"Why do you ask?" Darwynyen stowed the blade, keeping his hand on the grip.

"No reason." He looked into Darwynyen's eyes and found them lifeless and cold. Intimidated, he changed the subject. "Have you seen Arianna?"

"What do you want with Arianna?" Darwynyen's eyes narrowed. "Why can you not leave her alone? Can you not see that she is mine to govern?"

"I did not realize that Arianna required governing." Archemese reached for his staff, realizing then that he had not brought it. "Why do you speak of her in such a way?"

"Because I want you to cease your teachings." Darwynyen crossed his arms. "There is no reason for her to learn magic. Arianna is still a child in many ways."

Archemese shook his head, "No, Darwynyen, she is a woman. You of all people should know this."

Darwynyen put his hands to his head. "What is wrong with me?"

"There is nothing wrong with you, my friend." Archemese sighed, doubting his own words. "Your emotions are led by love." He leaned toward the wall. "Do not concern yourself with the magic. My intention is only to teach her how to protect herself, nothing more."

"How do you know that she will not delve deeper, like her father?" Darwynyen argued. "I do not want to lose her as I did my mother."

"I do not see that happening." Archemese straightened. "Your bond with Arianna is unbreakable."

"I hope you are right." Darwynyen returned is gaze to the window.

"I feel certain I am right." Archemese stepped back toward the door. "In fact, I know I am." When Darwynyen did not respond, he observed him for a moment and then took his leave.

Edina's Return

I waited over two hours for Edina and still there was no sight of her. I was about to send for the guards when I saw someone crossing the bridge over the outer lea.

"Edina!" I waved, rushing to meet her. "I am very grateful that you decided to come."

"What did you expect?" she scowled. "I had no choice in the matter. As your servant, I must obey you."

Although I was hurt by her resentment, I brushed the feeling aside. "Oh, Edina, that is not the reason I asked you back." I reached for her satchel. "No longer do I see you as my lady in waiting. I see you as a friend."

She pushed my hand away. "I can manage, thank you."

"As you wish. Come, let us get you settled."

"Settled," she huffed. "I was settled where I was."

"Please, Edina," I pleaded. "Are you willing to set our friendship aside so easily?"

Edina did not respond to my question; even so, she seemed calmer, and she followed me into the castle.

Thereafter we continued in silence.

When we arrived at her room, she waited a moment before opening the door. Her thoughts must have been on Stuart. "Would you like different quarters?" I asked.

"No, I will be fine here." As she stepped through the threshold, she noticed the flowers I had left for her.

"Do you like them?" I put my hand on her back.

"They are lovely!" She dropped her satchel near the bed and put her hands to her face. "Arianna, please, you must forgive me."

I took her into my arms. "Do not worry. We will get through this together."

She nodded, and then she pulled away.

"I will give you some time to unpack." I stepped back. "You may come and find me when you are ready."

She wiped the tears from her eyes. "Thank you. I will."

I observed her for a moment before closing the door.

As I neared the main foyer, Archemese approached from the rise. "Arianna, I have been looking all over for you."

I smiled as I began my descent. "I was just on my way to the kitchen. Would you care to join me?"

"No." He blocked my path. "There is something you should know about Dar—" He took a step past me."Shallendria! What have you done?"

I turned and saw Shallendria leaning against the archway at the top of the stair. "I have seen it," she whispered.

Archemese rushed to her side. I followed. "Seen what?" he asked.

"The dragon's lair." She fell to her knees.

Archemese lifted her, and we assisted her to a bench on the mezzanine. She took a moment to regain her strength.

Archemese knelt by her. "Did you use magic to take you to Naksteed?"

"Yes."

I looked at Archemese. "I will find Madigan."

"No!" She took my hand. "You must listen to me."

Archemese ushered me to the bench. "Let her speak."

I nodded as I took a seat beside her.

"As we have seen from the maps, the dragon's realm is beyond a labyrinth of dark crystal." Her head drooped.

Archemese knelt, lifting her chin. "Yes, I know the place you speak of."

She met his eyes. "Promise me now. Under no circumstances are we to take that route to Biddenwade."

"It was never my intention to lead you through the labyrinth, Shallendria. We will travel back through the forest as planned."Archemese sent me a fleeting look. "What did you see in your vision that has distressed you?"

"It is not what I saw, it was what I felt." She began to tremble. "Something terrible dwells in that labyrinth."

"Forget the labyrinth. As I said, we will not be traveling there anytime soon."

"I must rest." Shallendria tried to stand. Archemese assisted her.

I gestured to the guards standing next to the main door. "These men will see you to your quarters." I looked at Archemese. "I will take my leave now."

Archemese entered my mind. *Madigan is in the defense room.*

I nodded as I passed the guards on the stair.

As I walked the defense corridor, I could not help but wonder what Shallendria had felt in her vision. From the time I had met her, not once had I seen her so frightened. I brushed the thoughts aside, reassuring myself that it was of no consequence; we had already agreed on another route to Biddenwade.

On the final turn, I noticed that the door to the main planning room was shut. Rather than knock, I opened it slowly. I flinched when it creaked. Darwynyen and Madigan stood, indifferent to my presence. Baffled, I searched their faces. "What goes on here?"

Madigan looked at Darwynyen before he spoke. "Your friend is being detained."

"Why?" I frowned, assuming that he was referring to Edina. "What has she done?"

"He was lurking in the caverns," Darwynyen announced. "What else would you have us do?"

"The caverns …" I frowned. "There must be some mistake. Who do you mean when you say 'he'?"

"The Rinjeed!" Darwynyen snapped.

"Ghezmeed!" I gasped and looked at Madigan. "What is it you intend to do with him?"

"We will execute him." Darwynyen pulled his blade. "He is evil. All Rinjeeds are."

"No!" I begged. "He is different. Will you not listen, even to reason?"

Madigan put his hand on my shoulder. "I am sorry, Arianna, but the decision has already been made."

"Please, Madigan!" I took his arm. "You must reconsider."

Darwynyen interrupted. "I warned you of this, but you paid no heed. You should have told him to leave when you had the chance."

"I did ask him to leave, but he refused," I cried. "He wants to watch over me."

"The Rinjeed bides his time!" Darwynyen scowled. "His intention is to kill you."

"Why do you speak such lies?" I clenched my fists. "You deem him evil when you do not even know him." I moved toward the door. "I have heard enough. Tell me where he is."

When neither of them responded, I turned and ran down the corridor.

"Arianna, wait!" Madigan yelled from the door.

"Stay back, Madigan, I warn you!" Before he could respond, I turned the corner and ran toward the dungeons.

After searching each of the cells, I halted. Ghezmeed was nowhere to be found. I was about to search again when I heard screams coming from a room at the back. I dashed for the door. When I opened it, I gasped in horror. My little friend was shackled to the wall, and a guard was prodding him with his sword.

"Step away from him!" I growled.

The man turned. "Lady Arianna." He looked puzzled.

"I will not ask you again." I grabbed a pike from the wall.

The man backed away slowly. "What are you doing down here, my lady?" he asked. "This creature is dangerous."

"Get out of my way." I nudged him aside with the pike.

"Does the king know you are here?" He tried to take hold of the pike.

"Leave us!" Madigan appeared at the door.

The man obediently bowed his head and left the room.

I dropped the pike and rushed to Ghezmeed. His torso was beaten and bruised, reminding me of how I had found Gin. I brushed the thought aside. "Ghezmeed, can you hear me?"

"Arianna," he choked. "I knew you would come for me."

I snatched the key ring from the table, looking at Madigan. "Which one is it?"

"I do not know." He approached cautiously.

"Very well." I began to test each key. The third one worked.

Once Ghezmeed was free of the shackles, I took his limp body into my arms.

"I cannot allow you to leave with him." Madigan blocked my path.

"Madigan, I will not ask you to move again." My eyes transmitted my disdain.

"Why are you doing this?" he pleaded.

"I am doing what I must." When he lowered his arms I cautiously maneuvered past him.

Darwynyen was waiting for me in the corridor. "Arianna, I …"

"Leave us alone!" I warned, brushing past him. "You have done enough already!"

When I reached the third level of the castle, I opened the door to a room down the hall from Edina's and carefully placed Ghezmeed on the bed. "Ghezmeed, I am so sorry." I put my hand on his brow. "No one will hurt you again, I promise!" A tear fell from my eye. "Stay here while I retrieve some food and water."

"Thank you," he whispered.

After I slowly closed the door to the room, I took a moment to regain my composure. My emotions were vivid with hatred and anger. Not only did this situation remind me of Gin, but I found it incomprehensible that Madigan and Darwynyen had ordered the use of torture. Moreover, I did not understand Darwynyen. He knew about Ghezmeed and how I felt on the matter. What were his intentions? Was he planning to commence with the execution first and then advise me of it later?

As I wiped the tears from my eyes, Edina appeared in the corridor. "Arianna, are you all right?" She ran over. "What has happened?"

I rushed to embrace her. She comforted me as I wept. When I recovered, I pulled away. "Madigan and Darwynyen captured someone I have recently befriended. They were going to execute him without reason."

"Who is this person?" she frowned. "Please tell me it is not Gin you speak of. I know Darwynyen has not taken kindly to him."

At the mention of Gin, I nearly lashed out, before I realized that she was unaware of what had happened on the island. "It is not Gin. His name is Ghezmeed. I met him on the journey home from Maglavine." I paused. "His people, the Rinjeed, have a blackened history, so the men see him as evil, when he is nothing more than troubled."

"A Rinjeed." She glanced toward the door. "What are they?"

"They are creatures whose blood is a combination of ours and the elves. They are …" I paused, suspicious when I noticed that she had taken on a look of skepticism. "I can only hope you are not like the others. He means us no harm, I assure you."

She held out her hands. "You must excuse my ignorance. I am only taken aback."

"If you speak the truth, will you assist me?" I searched her eyes.

"Yes," she nodded. "What do you need?"

"If you could see to some food and water, I would be most grateful." I returned to the door. "I do not wish to leave him. I do not trust the others."

"Consider it done." She turned, making her way down the corridor. "I will return shortly."

I exhaled heavily before I pulled the latch. When the door opened, it was dark. For some reason, Ghezmeed had pulled the drapery. As my eyes adjusted, I found him. He was curled up in a blanket on the floor. While he wept, I lit some candles near the bed, and before long the room held a handsome glow.

"Arianna." He peered through his fingers.

"Yes, Ghezmeed, I am here." I managed a smile.

"You must let me go," he begged.

"I cannot." I knelt by him. "If I do, they will kill you." When he did not respond, I pulled the cover around him. "Ghezmeed, you must tell me what happened. Why did you not ask for me?"

"I do not want to stay," he cried. "Please, you must take pity on me and release me."

As I considered what to do, I gently put my hand on his back and allowed him to weep.

Minutes later I heard the door latch and quickly stood, expecting either Madigan or Darwynyen. To my relief it was Edina.

When she caught sight of Ghezmeed, she gasped.

"Edina!" I glared.

"I … I was not …" She unsteadily placed the tray on the table. "What would you like me to do?" She began to blot at the water she had spilled. "I do not know how to care for such a creature."

"It is all right—I will see to him," I replied. "You may go if you wish."

"No." She took a seat next to me. "I will stay … if you do not mind."

I smiled. "That would be nice." I pointed to the ewer. "May I have the water? His breathing is a bit rattled."

"How do you know that this is not normal for him?" she asked.

"Because," I replied. "Look at him. Is it not plain to see that he is frail and malnourished?"

"You are right." She handed me the ewer. "You must again forgive my ignorance."

"There is nothing to forgive." I turned to face her. "You are here, something I cannot say for the others."

Ghezmeed snatched the ewer from my hand. We watched while he emptied its contents. When he was finished, he chucked the ewer to the floor. Edina reached for it. "I will return shortly with more water." She stood and left the room.

As the door shut, I looked at Ghezmeed. "Are you feeling better?"

He entered my mind. *I am sorry for the trouble I have caused you. Would it not be better for you to release me?*

I shook my head. "You are safer here with me."

He did not respond, instead looking at the cracks of sunlight that pierced through the drapery. I took his hand, lifting him to his feet. "What is it?"

"I do not belong here." He met my look. "Nor did I belong in the caverns … only I could not bring myself to leave."

I pitied him. "You do not have to be alone." I squeezed his hand and helped him return to the bed. "In time you may grow used to the companionship of others."

"No." He took hold of a pillow as he sat. "The gods have forsaken me. They do not approve of my existence and have punished me with seclusion."

"How do you know that this is not your chosen path?" I asked. "Could it be that the gods have brought you to me for a reason?" I reached for the covers and placed them over him. "If you give it some time and consider what I have said, you may grow to like it here."

"What you sleep on is far too soft," he remarked, shifting on the mattress. "I am used to taking my rest on the ground."

"Perhaps in time, you may also grow to like comforts such as these." I winked.

"Perhaps." He fidgeted with the pillow.

Edina returned with the ewer and handed it to Ghezmeed with a smile. "My name is Edina. As a friend of Arianna, I offer you my trust."

Without a word, he snatched the ewer from her hands. Edina looked at me. "Did I say something wrong?"

"No." I lowered my voice. "Do not misinterpret Ghezmeed's actions. He is not accustomed to being around others." I gave him a fleeting look. "That, and he has been mistreated his entire life."

She turned to Ghezmeed with a sincere smile. "Do not worry. I will treat you with respect until you prove otherwise."

Ghezmeed looked at me for an answer. When I nodded, he began to drink the water. Edina took a bowl from the tray. "Would you care for some stew? It is no longer warm, but tasty nonetheless."

Ghezmeed nodded, draining the remaining water over his head.

The droplets of water streamed down his face and began to wash away the grime. I reached for a cloth to finish the work.

"What are you doing?" He tried to push the cloth away.

"You are in need of a bath." I gently lowered his hands and wiped his cheeks.

"I do not bathe." He squinted as I carefully swabbed around his eyes.

"You do now!" I playfully lifted an eyebrow.

"I am clean enough!"

He was growing anxious, so I beckoned to Edina. While she helped him with the stew, I hummed a song. He seemed to relax under the attention. As I looked at his fragile body, I was consumed with sadness. Would this be the result for my children? Would they be hunted, as he was? Moreover, could I bring myself to love a creature such as this? Yes, of course I could.

I put my hand on Edina's shoulder. "You may go if you wish. I will sit with him tonight."

She stood. "I would like to sit with him, if you do not mind."

Surprised, I wrinkled my brow. "Are you certain?"

"Yes. He needs me … or perhaps I need him."

I smiled and realized that her offer stemmed from a desperate need to save the life of another, one who could potentially fill a gap left by her beloved Stuart. "I will leave you, then." I moved toward the door. "If anything should arise, summon me."

"Of course." She returned to Ghezmeed's side.

Content, I left in search of Darwynyen and Madigan, hoping that we could work toward a compromise that might resolve this matter.

When I opened the door to the defense room, Madigan stood, eyeing Darwynyen. "Arianna. We were …"

I raised my hand, silencing him. "I am only here to advise you that Ghezmeed is recovering in one of the guest rooms. He will be staying with us until he is well enough to travel." I narrowed my eyes. "If either of you wish to challenge this decision, I suggest you do it now. Otherwise, I will consider the subject closed."

Darwynyen shook his head. "Your decision is not wise. He must go!"

I crossed my arms defiantly, "If he must go, then so shall I."

Madigan eyed Darwynyen. "Arianna, can we not discuss this?"

"How can we when Darwynyen will not listen to reason?" I backed away, training my eyes on Darwynyen. "If any harm comes to him, know now that I will never forgive you."

"No harm will come to him," Madigan interjected. "I swear. You are right to be upset, Arianna. We should have consulted you."

"Save your words. I am too upset to hear them now. I must go. There are things I need to do." I turned and closed the door before either of them could respond.

In need of Archemese's counsel, I made my way to the library. If anyone were to see things my way, it would be him. When I arrived, I found Archemese at the main table reading a book, and I cleared my throat to announce my presence.

Archemese looked up. "So, you have come to seek my guidance on the Rinjeed."

"How did you know?" I stepped toward the table.

His brow rose in his response. "Your anger is easily sensed."

"Then you agree with the others?"

"I have yet to draw any conclusions," he replied. "I can, however, tell you that creating a rift among those you care for is not the way."

Frustrated, I turned for the door.

"Arianna, wait!" Archemese demanded. "You will not dismiss me as you did the others."

I returned to face him. "What else would you have me do?"

"Calm yourself, child." His voice deepened. "You have not yet heard what I have to say."

I looked at him with a glimmer of hope.

He stood. "I feel that the others have chosen their way too quickly. Still, I am uncertain as to whether or not you should be taking on this burden." He paused as though to read my mind before he continued. "When Ghezmeed is well enough I will meet with him and seek the answers I require then."

"Thank you." I sighed in relief. "I knew you would understand."

"I am not the one who needs persuading. If you are going to have your way, you will need to mend these wounds between you and Darwynyen." He moved to the window.

I looked down. "I cannot face him right now. He is not himself."

"What do you mean?" Archemese turned suddenly. "I have also …" His eyes widened. "Darwynyen. Have you come for Arianna?"

I turned to find Darwynyen at the door. "No." He avoided my eyes. "I was looking for Morglafenn."

"Forget Morglafenn," Archemese huffed. "Take this time to settle your differences. If not, the rift between you and Arianna will begin to affect the others." He picked up his staff and left the room.

"Perhaps Archemese is right." I sat in an open chair. "I do not like this distance between us."

"There is no one to blame but yourself," he stated. "Despite my efforts, there is no reasoning with you. Instead, you expect me to abide by your decisions without question."

His response rekindled my anger. "How can you say that after you not only tried to thwart my efforts with the dragons, you also sought to execute Ghezmeed after I had explained his intentions?"

"It is not the quest for the dragons that troubles me, it is your sudden loyalty to the Rinjeed," he countered. "As you know, I have had a different experience with these creatures. Is it not enough that one almost took my life?"

Although a part of me felt guilty, I persisted, convinced that Ghezmeed was no longer a threat. "I understand your concern, but you must trust me. Ghezmeed is not our enemy." I held out my hands, beseeching him. "Give him a few days to prove himself. If your feelings do not change, we will revisit the subject then, I promise."

"Very well," he agreed half-heartedly. "In the interim, if you have no objections, I would like to post guards near his door as a precautionary measure."

"I suppose it would do no harm," I sighed. If we were going to settle our differences, we would need to find an adequate compromise.

"Where can I find him?" Darwynyen asked.

"He recovers two doors down from Edina's room," I replied.

He looked disgusted. "You have him staying in the royal wing of the castle?"

"Yes," I snapped. "Where else would you have me put him?"

"Why not have him stay with us?" he replied dryly, and then he walked to the door.

"Darwynyen, please." I followed after him. "I cannot take much more of this."

"Nor can I. I must go. I need to assign the guardsmen."

His response rendered me speechless. My heart sank as I watched him stomp down the corridor, and my frustration quickly resurfaced. Why was he being so difficult? Moreover, where were these dark emotions coming from? It was as though his love for me was lost. Disturbed by my thoughts, I left in search of Shallendria, hoping that she would be able to provide me with some answers.

I found her in the royal suite, but she was not alone. Madigan was with her. They were sharing in an intimate moment. Embarrassed by the intrusion, I backed away. It was too late. "Arianna, did you need to see me?" Shallendria nudged Madigan aside.

"Yes, but it can wait," I replied bashfully, turning to leave.

Madigan stood. "Please stay. I need to speak with you."

I tensed, presuming that he was referring to Ghezmeed. "If it is in regard to Ghezmeed, I have heard enough."

"Wait!" Madigan spoke sternly. "This behavior of yours must stop!" He paused to compose himself. "Arianna, can you really fault my suspicion after what happened with Gin?"

I blinked, absorbing his words. "No, I suppose I cannot."

"Good." He nodded. "Now tell me about this friend of yours."

"I met him on our return from Maglavine," I replied. "Darwynyen and his companions captured him when we found him lurking around our camp."

"Am I mistaken, or are you speaking about a Rinjeed?" Shallendria interrupted with a stunned look upon her face.

"Yes." I nodded firmly.

She sent Madigan a brief look. "Arianna, Rinjeeds are known to be deceptive. How can you be certain of his intentions?"

"He has no intentions," I pleaded. "If he had, would you not have sensed them?"

She considered my question for a moment before responding. "Unfortunately, I am unable to offer further counsel until I have met with him."

"Then you may do so at your convenience," I assured her.

"If you would like to sit with me while I finish my tea, we may go afterward."

Madigan gently kissed Shallendria on the brow. "Then I will leave this matter for you to settle." He looked at me. "Do not keep her for long—she needs her rest."

When I nodded, he left the room.

Shallendria sat upright and slid her covers off. "He worries far too much."

"That is because he loves you." I smiled sincerely.

"Perhaps." She paused. "Would you like to tell me what is troubling you?"

I looked down. "It is Darwynyen," I replied. "There is …"

A guard rushed through the door. "My lady! You must come!" He beckoned. "Your guest grows anxious!"

"What have you done to him?"

"Nothing," the man replied. "We heard screams, but we were ordered not to enter."

"I will come with you now," I replied with a nod, then I turned to Shallendria. "Are you well enough to join me?"

"Yes, of course." She reached for her robe. "Lead the way."

As we ascended the stairs, I asked the guard, "Did anyone emerge from the room?"

"Not that I saw," the man replied.

Concerned for Edina, I hurried.

When we reached the top of the rise, I heard Ghezmeed screaming, and I ran for the door. I pushed it open, to find Edina embracing him on the floor. "What upsets him?" I asked.

"I do not know!" she cried. "He suddenly became alarmed and began to scream out in terror."

"They wish to harm me!" Ghezmeed shrieked.

I knelt by him and spoke reassuringly. "If you speak of the guards, they are not here to harm you. They are here to protect you."

"No!" he protested. "I can feel their minds! They fear me and want me dead!"

I turned to Shallendria with desperation. "What should we do?"

Shallendria entered the room slowly, observing Ghezmeed. "If he can easily sense the thoughts of others, you may want to seek guards who are unaware of his presence," she suggested.

"Of course." I went to the corridor. "Gentlemen, you are dismissed."

One of the guards stepped forward. "My lady, we are here on orders."

"And I am ordering you to leave!" I countered.

He looked at his companion and then shrugged. "If that is your wish, my lady, then so be it."

"It is." I ushered them toward the stairs.

When they began their descent, I returned to the room.

Before I could speak, Ghezmeed entered my mind. *I beg you to release me. Can you not see that I do not belong here?*

Shallendria knelt by him. "Worry no further. You will be safe here. As an elf, I give you my word of honor." She pulled the hair back from her ear.

"You are an elf!" he exclaimed. "Why do you not fear me?"

Her brow rose. "Because your presence holds no evil."

"I am humbled by your generosity." He looked down.

When Shallendria stood, Edina covered Ghezmeed with a blanket. As I watched, I noticed a bond growing between them. "If you can manage, I will leave you on your own for a while."

"We will be fine," Edina replied as she helped Ghezmeed onto the bed.

I nodded and directed Shallendria toward the corridor.

After closing the door, I turned to her. "Thank you. I know I have put you in a difficult situation."

She placed her hand on my cheek. "It is you whom I should be thanking, for you have shown me how to be less judgmental and more compassionate." Her eyes filled with regret. "Until now, I have chosen to despise the entire Rinjeed population, unwilling to accept that there may be some exceptions."

"Not without good cause." I took hold of her hand. "Do not punish yourself. The Rinjeed population still has much to answer for." I tightened my grasp. "Even so, I am relieved that you saw no evil in Ghezmeed. It is difficult for me to explain, but I somehow feel compelled to protect him."

"Why?" She frowned. "What are you not telling me?"

I looked away uncomfortably. "The creature's origin leaves me unsettled."

"I see." She bit her lip. "You wonder about your children."

I nodded. My heart pounded.

She smiled sincerely. "Arianna, I can assure you that you have nothing to worry about."

"But how can that be, if the Rinjeed originated from the mixing of our bloods?" I argued.

"Because their origin resulted from different circumstances," she replied.

"How do you mean?" I asked.

She paused, clearly searching for the right words. "There was a time, long ago, when your people mingled together with ours. It was more commonplace around the villages that bordered both our regions, and no one thought much of it, until the elves began to share their magic with the people, not understanding the repercussions. As the Man's Blood's power grew, the elves became reckless with their emotions and were soon shunned. Expelled from both our lands, they set forth to the north where they would eventually settle. Their lifespan covered centuries. When they grew bored of eternal life, they removed their pendants to have children. The women were able to conceive, but without the magic of the pendants they aged rapidly. The children were born deformed, and soon after were named the Rinjeed, an ancient term for 'evil seed'. Despised by their creators, they were eventually banished and disappeared into the forest, where they would dwell for decades in solitude. In time, however, they learned of their heritage and sought revenge. Unfortunately there was none to be taken. Their parents were deceased. Unable to accept this, they turned to us, the remaining wielders of the magic they so despised."

Her words left me speechless. "That is a horrible story," I muttered.

"There are many undesirable things in our past, Arianna." She left for the stairs. "And to ensure that none get repeated, we must learn from them."

I nodded, and she took her leave. Although I was relieved, I also regretted that I had not asked the question sooner. I should have known that if there were a risk of my children turning out like the Rinjeed, Aldraveena would have warned me when she learned of Darwynyen's love for me. Still, I was not sure that I would have felt any different after meeting with Ghezmeed. Despite his outward appearance, I felt certain that in time I could grow to care for him as I would one of my own. I could only hope that Darwynyen would come to share in my sentiment. Thinking of him, I decided that I would once again try to mend our differences, and I set out for the northern courtyard to find him.

When I passed through the gated passage, I halted when I saw Darwynyen. He was standing with an elvish woman I had not seen before. My chest tightened when I saw the look of passion in his eyes. She playfully giggled as he caressed her lengthy chestnut hair. Unable to comprehend what I was witnessing, I gasped when their lips were about to meet.

Darwynyen nudged the woman aside. "Arianna, I was not expecting you."

His words echoed in my head. I backed away slowly. He turned to the woman. "Leave us."

When she nodded, he approached me in a casual manner. "Why have you come?"

Still in shock, I watched the woman make her way to the stairs. "Who is that woman?" I asked.

"A friend." He looked away. His response left me queasy. Fighting the sensation, I put my hand to my stomach.

"Why are you here?" he asked again. "Have you come to seek my forgiveness?"

"Your forgiveness," I scoffed. "I was here …" My words broke as images of him and the woman flashed through my mind.

"What is wrong with you?" he glared.

"How can you ask me that?" I cried and then ran from his sight.

When he did not follow, I slowed. Tears began to well in my eyes. There was something wrong with Darwynyen. His love for me was gone. I could no longer feel it.

Shallendria appeared from the corridor that led from the kitchen. "Arianna."

Madigan was behind her. "Is everything all right?" he asked.

I blotted the tears from my eyes. "Was there something you needed?"

"We were hoping to find you." Shallendria studied my face as she approached. "I thought you would like to know that I have spoken to Madigan, and he has agreed to allow Ghezmeed to stay on in the castle."

"Thank you." I nodded and stepped toward the foyer.

Madigan took me by the wrist. "What has happened? You look deeply troubled."

"I am fine." I pulled away.

Shallendria turned to Madigan. "Please, allow me to see to Arianna."

Madigan exhaled and then reluctantly took his leave.

"Come." Shallendria put her hand on my back. "We can speak in the courtyard."

"No." I stepped back. "Darwynyen might still be there."

She looked at me curiously. "Are you avoiding him?"

Unable to respond, I nodded.

"Then let us speak in the dining hall." She opened one of the main doors, ushering me through.

When she closed the door behind us, I began to weep. "Why is this happening?"

Shallendria led me to a chair. "What has my cousin done to leave you this way?"

"I found him in the outer ward with another," I cried.

She frowned. "Do you mean to say he was with a woman?"

"Yes." Tears began to stream down my face. "And if I had not interrupted, I am certain he would have kissed her."

"How do you know that was his intention?" she asked.

My breathing became erratic. "I know what I s-saw," I stammered.

She smiled sympathetically. "Arianna, that would not be unusual behavior for the Darwynyen I once knew, but it is incomprehensible for me to believe that he is acting this way now. Your love has made him whole. He is a different person, someone I have grown to admire." She paused. "I must ask you again … Are you certain what you saw?"

Thoughts raced through my mind as I analyzed the images. Doubt emerged. "Perhaps I have placed too much trust in my instincts."

"You must never doubt your instincts," she replied. "Even so, things are not always as they seem." Her look intensified. "That is why you must confront him. Give him the opportunity to prove you wrong."

I turned toward the table, leaning forward to rest my head on my arms. "If you do not mind, I would appreciate some time on my own."

She nodded understandingly and then left the room.

Keeper of the Strings of Love

Velderon cackled with satisfaction as he watched the events in Aarrondirth unfold. Not only was his daughter's heart in turmoil, the spell he had placed on the elf was having a greater effect than he had anticipated. He withdrew his mind from the small bird he had abducted and pulled another strand of hair from the comb, to further interfere with the elf's sanity. "When I am finished with you, elf, your mind will be spoiled," he mumbled, and he placed the strand in the potion. "In time I will have control over the one you love. Arianna will soon be mine."

A troll appeared at the altar stair. "My lord Velderon."

"Why are you here?"

"The last of the troll armies has arrived." He put his hand to his chest and bowed his head. "Honor us with your command."

Velderon moved to the stones. "Make ready the armory." He inhaled deeply, summoning the energy. "We require more weapons."

"As you wish, my lord." The troll bowed and slowly backed away, descending the stairs.

When the energy of the stones began to overwhelm Velderon, he took a step back.

As he recovered, he gazed over the southern horizon. At last, his plans were coming to fruition. Anticipation coursed through his veins. Soon he would have full control over the regions, and those who opposed him would have no choice but to bow down to his command. Unlike his father, who in the end abandoned him, he would become a great ruler. If only the pathetic bastard were still alive, he would have sought his revenge. Because he was not, the people of Aarrondirth would have to suffer in his place. With that thought in mind, he set out to conjure his next spell.

PERSUASION

After leaving Arianna, Shallendria made her way to the outer ward, hoping that she would find Darwynyen. Although it was not her place to confront him, there were questions that needed answering. She was dismayed that he was nowhere to be found.

As she sat on one of the benches, she began to wonder if Arianna had possibly misjudged the situation and was simply blinded by her emotions. Despite Darwynyen's past, it seemed unlikely that he would behave in such a manner.

Archemese spoke from the gated passage. "What brings you to these deep thoughts?" When Shallendria turned, he smiled. "Excuse the intrusion, but I could not help but sense your indecision."

Shallendria stood purposefully. "It is good you are here. There are things we need to discuss."

"Indeed." He sat on the bench, beckoning Shallendria to join him. "Although I know little of what has transpired, I can tell you that I have felt great pain from Arianna."

"To my regret, it seems my cousin Darwynyen is the cause." She hesitated. "I cannot say for certain, but I fear that something is not right with him."

Archemese blinked in acknowledgement. "You are not alone in your concern," he admitted. "The other evening I came across

Darwynyen in the study and noticed then that he was acting strangely. I also noticed a heavy weight when I entered the room, one I could not place. At the time, I did not take much heed, as the sensation quickly waned. Only now do I regret that I dismissed it."

"What would bring about that sensation?" Shallendria wondered, and then she quickly looked at Archemese. "Velderon!" they both exclaimed.

Archemese stood. "Find Darwynyen, and bring him to the study. I will meet you there." He grasped her arms. "Say nothing of our suspicions. If you confront Darwynyen now, it will only intensify Velderon's spell."

"I understand. The black magic is not to be underestimated."

Archemese released her. "Connect with Morglafenn; have him accompany you." He rushed toward the gated passage. "Go now! We have wasted too much time already!"

"I will not be long." She looked over the courtyard as she connected to Morglafenn.

Several minutes passed before Morglafenn appeared from the gated passage. "What is it, Shallendria?" He spoke impatiently. "I do not appreciate the disruption. I was reading about …"

"Forget your books," she snapped. "We must find Darwynyen!"

"And you needed me to do this?" He rolled his eyes.

"Yes!" She ran toward the stairs. "Darwynyen has been put under a spell conjured by Velderon."

At the mention of Velderon, Morglafenn rushed to join her. "How can you be certain?"

"There is no time to explain." She hurried, leaving Morglafenn to follow behind her.

When they reached the elvish encampment, they halted. "Where could he be?" Shallendria put her hand to her brow.

Morglafenn pointed. "Over there. I do not believe my eyes."

Lying under the shelter of a tree, Darwynyen was sharing a meal with a woman. They were flirting with one another as though they were a couple. Overcome by what he was witnessing, Morglafenn stomped over before Shallendria could stop him. "What goes on here?" he demanded.

Darwynyen stood abruptly. "Morglafenn, there had better be a good reason for this intrusion."

Morglafenn looked at the woman and ignored him. "Leave us!"

When the woman stood and ran off, Darwynyen took Morglafenn by the arm. "How dare you!"

Morglafenn pulled away harshly. Although he was accustomed to containing his emotions, he could not help himself. "How dare I?" He glared. "Have you nothing to say for yourself!" He sent Shallendria a quick look when she reached his side. "If not, then what about Arianna?"

Darwynyen shrugged, opening his hands. "Is it not plain to see that our love has been conquered by our differences?"

"Nonsense," Morglafenn retorted. "Whether you admit it or not, I know you still love her."

"No." Darwynyen's eyes grew cold. "I loved the idea of her. Now that I know her, I am no longer swayed. How can I be, when she gives no consideration to my feelings, doing only as she pleases?"

Morglafenn shook his head in disgust.

"Darwynyen." Shallendria placed her hand on his shoulder. "If your love for Arianna is lost, then so be it. It is no secret that I have not approved of your relationship."

Morglafenn looked at Shallendria oddly, before realizing her intentions. "Shallendria is right. Perhaps I have overreacted."

Darwynyen seemed to relax.

"Forget Arianna. We are here on a different purpose." Shallendria eyed Morglafenn. "Will you join us in the study?"

"Why?" Darwynyen asked suspiciously.

"Morglafenn has founds some documents in Velderon's belongings that pertain to your father," she replied casually, concealing the lie. "We thought you would like to see them."

"Why would Velderon have kept such things?" Darwynyen frowned.

"You ask what we cannot answer," Morglafenn replied, leading Shallendria toward the castle.

"Very well," Darwynyen huffed, following after them.

Hearts Apart

In a daze, I wandered down the corridors, unable to escape my thoughts about Darwynyen. How could our love have gone astray? If I closed my eyes, I could still feel his hands on my body. Was he going to leave me, and if so, could I live only with the memories of him? Why had I not listened to Morglafenn when he warned me about Darwynyen's emotions and the negative influence they were having on him? If I had, we might not be in this predicament.

Archemese entered my mind. *Come to me now, child. I await you in the study. Do not delay. Too much time has already been wasted!* The connection ended.

Confounded by his message, I immediately left to meet him.

When I arrived at the study, I opened the door without knocking. The curtains were drawn, and the room was dim. On the table a single candle was lit. "Archemese," I called.

Archemese emerged from the shadows with his staff in hand. Through the flicker of candlelight, I caught sight of his eyes and gasped. The color was gone. They were grey, like Gin's when we questioned him on the island. "Do not fear me, child. I have been delving in the magic."

"Why?" I asked, avoiding his stare. I found myself frightened of the magic.

"Velderon has cast a spell on Darwynyen," he replied bluntly.

"How can that be?"

"It seems we have once again underestimated him." From the corner of my eye, I saw him flipping through a book. The spell had not impeded his ability to read. "Shallendria and I have only just made the discovery," he explained. "Not once did I anticipate this sort of move." His staff began to glow as he spoke. "Either way, his boldness only proves that he has set risk aside and is manipulating the power of the stones ahead of the next cycle."

"Still, why would my father cast a spell on Darwynyen?" I asked with doubt.

"To hurt you." His eyes returned to normal. "Take your place at the table. We must get started."

Shallendria and Morglafenn appeared at the door with Darwynyen.

"What is she doing here?" Darwynyen scowled.

"Bring him to the table," Archemese ordered. "We have much work ahead of us."

Darwynyen stepped back. "What is this?"

"Darwynyen, sit!" Morglafenn demanded.

"No! How dare you lead me here with trickery?"

"Do not make us use restraints," Archemese warned.

Darwynyen pulled his blade. "I do not fear you, old man!"

Archemese raised his staff. "*Deydonas!*"

At his words, Darwynyen's hand began to tremble. He fought the spell, and as he lost control, the blade dropped to the floor. When he turned for the door, it slammed shut. Morglafenn and Shallendria took hold of him as he fought with the door latch, dragging him toward the table.

I watched helplessly as they secured him to the table top. He glared at me when he caught me looking. "I despise you!" Then his head fell back on the table.

Tears trickled down my cheeks. "Archemese, please, I cannot take much more of this!"

Archemese opened his hand, blowing a fine powder into the air above us. Darwynyen immediately closed his eyes and held his breath.

"From the skies of eternity, I beg the gods!" Archemese put both of his hands on his staff, clenching to it tightly. "*Zomerick! Zomerick un ou foslted!*"

Darwynyen fought to hold his breath. When Shallendria noticed, she pushed on Darwynyen's chest until it heaved, forcing him to inhale the powder.

Minutes later, a thin blanket of moisture appeared on Darwynyen's skin. "*Zomerick*!" Archemese yelled. "*Un ou foslted!*"

"Your spell will not work on me!"Darwynyen began to cackle deliriously.

"*Zomerick!*" Archemese persisted. "I command the release of this spell!"

Darwynyen mumbled in elvish.

"He is countering your spell," Shallendria exclaimed.

"No!" Archemese slammed his staff into the floor. "*Zomerick*, I command you!"

Shallendria raised Archemese's book and began to chant the spell in tandem. Darwynyen's head swayed back and forth.

I felt Morglafenn's hand on my shoulder. When I looked at him, he nodded reassuringly.

"I told you, your spell would not work on me!" I turned and saw Darwynyen staring coldly at the ceiling, a smirk on his face.

Archemese stumbled backward. "It is of no use. Velderon's spell has taken him."

"No!" I cried. "You must keep trying!"

Shallendria put her hands to her face and began to weep.

"Please," I begged. "Do not leave him like this!"

May the light of Cemenbar shield you! The bookcases in the room began to rumble. *Do not give up on my son. With the last power I hold, I now protect you. Cast your spell once more, Archemese.* Aldraveena's voice was as clear as if she were there.

Archemese reaffirmed his grip on his staff, and he and Shallendria repeated the spell. Defiantly, Darwynyen continued to counteract it. When I saw Archemese weakening, a shimmer of white light flashed through the room. As it dissipated, Darwynyen became motionless. I went to him and put my hand to his brow. "Is he …?" I could not finish, fearing the worst.

"It is over." Archemese slumped in a chair, exhausted.

I was about to scream out when Darwynyen slowly opened his eyes. "Arianna."

"I am here, Darwynyen." When our eyes met, I glimpsed the man I loved. He looked at me, confused. "What am I doing here?" He winced. "What has happened?"

"It is all right." I smiled lovingly. "My father placed a spell on you, but it has failed."

"Your father!" He tried to sit and discovered he was restrained. "What do you mean?"

Shallendria and Morglafenn began to untie the restraints. "We thought we had lost you." Shallendria kissed him on the cheek.

"I am fine." He sat, squinting when Morglafenn drew the curtains. "It feels as though I was in a dream." He paused. "The dream was not a good one."

"It was not a dream." Shallendria sat next to Archemese. The magic had also weakened her.

"It must have been, for I would not have acted in such a manner." He closed his eyes for a moment and then looked at me. "If Shallendria speaks the truth, then I have wounded you deeply."

I nodded, unable to speak.

"You are not at fault." Archemese stood unsteadily, placing his hand on Darwynyen's shoulder. "The spell was of great power."

Morglafenn lifted his brow. "If I am not mistaken, Velderon would have needed something personal of Darwynyen's to conjure it."

"Then he has once again returned to Aarrondirth," Shallendria remarked.

"Yes." Archemese moved to the bay windows. "He would also have required the power of the stones, which confirms that he has begun to utilize them." He leaned on his staff. "From this day forward, we must be more watchful. Velderon is cunning. This will not be the last of his trickery. He will do all he can to thwart us."

"With that said, it may be in our interest to take an inventory of our belongings," Morglafenn suggested.

Shallendria moved toward the door. "In the interim, I will speak to Madigan and tell him what has happened and request that he post guards at our doors." She glanced over the room one last time and then left.

Archemese looked at Morglafenn. "Will you assist me to my quarters?"

"Of course." He held Archemese by the arm.

Before leaving, Archemese turned and looked directly at Darwynyen. "You are safe now. By the will of your mother, the shield of Cemenbar now protects you."

"I know." Darwynyen slowly slipped from the table. "I have felt her presence."

Archemese nodded and allowed Morglafenn to escort him from the room. Darwynyen and I followed shortly.

When we arrived at our quarters, he sat me on the bed. "Now is probably not the time, but there is something I must confess."

My heart sank as images of that woman swept through my mind. "What is it?" I asked half-heartedly.

"It is regarding my previous actions," he replied with shame.

I took his hand. "You were not yourself." I squeezed it. "Unless you tell me otherwise, we should put the past behind us and speak of it no further."

His eyes filled with guilt. "If I were to have deceived you, would you be so forgiving?"

A knot formed in my stomach. "What are you saying?"

He looked down. “If my memories are accurate, I believe I kissed that elvish woman. It only happened once. She means nothing to me.”

“I see.” I released a heavy breath to conceal the pain within my chest.

His eyes filled. “Arianna, I made a promise to love you forever, and I meant it, only I could not control myself. I can, however, swear that it went no further. In the moments lost to her, I thought of nothing but you.” He spoke with conviction.

Unsure what to say, I looked away. He took hold of my chin. “Arianna, please tell me you forgive me.”

I waited a moment, to allow the pain to settle. “What is done is done.” I met his look. “In time I will forgive you … if there is anything to forgive. Until then, I have no choice but to believe that we will get through this.”

He stood. “If you need some time on your own, I can return for you later.”

I shook my head. “Our time should be spent together, not apart, if we are going to mend these wounds.”

“I am sorry for the pain I have caused you,” he said.

I wanted to reach out to him, but I was not yet ready.

He returned to me. “I want to make love to you. Never have I wanted you more.”

Unsure what to say, I searched his eyes. His pain was obvious. I knew then he needed me. Clinging to the remnants of our love, I slowly placed my lips against his. When I pulled away, a tear trickled down his cheek. “I love you, Arianna.”

“I love you, Darwynyen.” As I spoke the words, I once again felt whole.

He kissed me passionately as we renewed our connection; in our mutual embrace, it was not long before we once again became one. Despite my father’s evil intentions, this time was ours and forever would be.

CHANGED

Alone, Archemese sat in his room, considering what had happened in the study. He had risked much in conjuring such power and was concerned about the changes he was now experiencing. He had expected something entirely different. Even so, he was not disappointed. In fact, his mind felt alive for the first time in years. It was his body that was weak. Perhaps it was just part of the process. Regardless, he knew he could never tell the others about what he had delved into. They would never understand and might condemn him for his good intentions.

A knock sounded. "Archemese, are you in there?"

It was Shallendria. Had she discovered his secret? "I am here." He grabbed his robe to conceal his naked body and then opened the door. "Shallendria, Morglafenn." He took a step back, not expecting both of them. "Why are you here? Has something happened to ...?"

Shallendria moved through the archway. "No, we are here on a different matter."

Archemese tensed, convinced by her mannerism that he had indeed been exposed. "I see."

Morglafenn took hold of Archemese's staff. "We sensed the magical energy in that room and know it did not come from your staff."

Shallendria crossed her arms. "Are you going to reveal the source of your power?"

Archemese sat to the bed. "I hold an amulet, and though it does not contain the energy of the stones, it has its purpose."

"What kind of amulet?" Shallendria questioned.

"I cannot say. I found it on the island."

"On the island …" Morglafenn wrinkled his brow.

"Yes," Archemese replied, avoiding their stares. "That is why I was originally drawn there."

"Where is it?" Shallendria's eyes darted around the room. "I wish to see it."

Archemese stood and opened a drawer next to his bed, removing a small box. "It is in here." He opened the lid, revealing the contents. "It is a gem." He removed the item that lay in the velvet interior. "Whoever left it on the island went to great lengths to hide it from anyone not acquainted with magic."

Shallendria's eyes widened. "What do you mean by 'whoever'? Are you telling me that you used it without verifying its origin?"

"What if I could not learn of its origin?" Archemese snapped. "You should be grateful. As you know, the spell Velderon placed on Darwynyen was very complex. It is not easy for one to control the mind of another. If I had not taken this risk, Darwynyen would be lost to us—more importantly, to Arianna."

Shallendria sent Morglafenn a brief look. "Will you use it again?" she asked. "I mean, it might not be safe."

"If it means protecting Arianna, then yes." Archemese placed the gem back into the box.

"One thing is for certain." Morglafenn moved to the window. "Velderon's eye is no longer on his daughter alone."

"Regardless, Arianna is still the most vulnerable," Archemese commented.

Shallendria nodded. "How far has she gotten with the magic?"

"She learns quickly, as did her father." Archemese returned the box to the drawer. "Even so, it will not be enough. Despite our ambitions, we will not have enough time to see her through her studies." He turned the subject. "How apt is Darwynyen in the magic? Certainly his mother has taught him in the ways."

Morglafenn turned from the window. "He knows little. Aldraveena would only teach him how to counter spells, not cast them."

Archemese sat on his bed, contriving a yawn, hoping that they would leave. "His knowledge may still assist us."

"Perhaps." Shallendria moved to the door. "We will leave you to your rest."

"Thank you." Archemese reached for a blanket.

They both nodded and took their leave.

The Calm After the Storm

It was not long before Darwynyen and I found our love once again. Sparked by rekindled emotions, we tried to spend as much time together as possible. Despite this, I still had studying to do, and though Darwynyen did not approve of my new teachings, he supported me as best he could. Besides, we had bigger problems to face, especially when it came to my father.

We planned to leave two days after tomorrow, when the final preparations for our departure were completed. It was time for the castle to empty and for the king to make his way to Biddenwade to oversee the coming battles. If all went according to plan, we would travel, unnoticed, in his company until we reached Walferd. From there, we would set off for Naksteed in search of the dragons.

There was only one matter left to settle. If we were to leave soon, I needed to make a decision regarding Ghezmeed. Although he had begun to settle in his new surroundings, it was unlikely that he would choose to stay in Aarrondirth during our absence, and it would not be appropriate for me to bring him to Naksteed. Not only would Darwynyen disapprove, I did not believe that Ghezmeed would be able to cope with the sudden changes.

Archemese rose from the table. "Arianna! I do not know how many times I have to tell you!" His voice echoed throughout the library as he snatched the feather I was holding from my hand. "A small child could exact this spell if they put their mind to it!"

Startled by his tone, I looked at him with narrowed eyes. "If you no longer feel that I am worthy, then perhaps you should seek a student more to your liking."

He moved to one of the windows. "I apologize, my dear. It was not my intention to upset you. I only push you because I worry for your safety."

I stood, closing the book I had been reading from. "To be honest, I sometimes wonder why I am doing this. At the pace we are going …"

"We are doing this to save your life!" he exclaimed, abruptly turning from the window. "Can you not see that?"

"No." I moved to join him. "Can you not see that I will never be as strong as you or Shallendria, and that I do not want to be?"

"You put too much trust in people who might not be there when you need them, when instead you should be looking to yourself." He returned to gaze out the window. "Whether you accept it or not, uncertainty holds true for us all."

Confused by his pessimistic mood, I put my hand on his shoulder. "Is there something you are not telling me?"

"No, my child." He blinked. "As powerful as I may be, I have never sought to look into the future."

"Aldraveena has." I raised my brow.

"She has only seen glimpses of what is to be, nothing more," he countered. "The rest she decides for herself. Do not misinterpret what I am saying. I respect her judgment. Trusting it is another matter. Although our lives are written, the chapters themselves may lead us in directions that divert us from our main path. Magic may also change that path. It might make you stronger, or it might only save you once. Do you understand, child?"

"I believe so." I glanced over my shoulder toward the table at the book of magic that sat upon it. Archemese was right; I had to keep trying, even if the magic only saved me once. "If it is all right with you I would like to attempt the spell again."

Archemese nodded, indicating for me to sit.

When I was ready, I balanced the feather he had previously given me on my hand and closed my eyes. "*Domedar domedar!*" I shouted. "*Tefhare saire.* I command you!" Curious, I opened my eyes just enough to see the feather lift from my palm. "It is working," I whispered.

Archemese chuckled. "You may speak aloud. The feather cannot hear you."

Annoyed by his remark, I felt the energy intensify within my chest. The first thing I thought of was his nose. His sarcasm would not pass without retribution. Seconds later, my thought was realized, and the feather darted toward his face. I was unable to control it, and it quickly lodged in one of his nostrils.

He glanced down at the feather. "Clever, but by no means amusing."

Although my original intention was to tickle him, the end result was far more amusing, and I burst into laughter.

"I think we are finished for the day." He pulled the feather from his nostril with disdain and dropped it to the floor.

"Forgive me, Archemese." I desperately tried to hold back my laughter. "I promise I will not do it again."

"You are forgiven." He gave into a smile. "Return tomorrow and we will continue with your studies then."

"Thank you." I stood, changing the subject. "I am off to see Ghezmeed. If we are soon to be leaving for Naksteed, his future path must be decided."

"How do you mean?" he asked with a furrowed brow.

"I have a dilemma." I replied. "Although I have made a commitment to protect Ghezmeed, we cannot take him with us, nor can I leave him here in Aarrondirth castle." I could not help but feel guilty as I spoke. "If I have no other option but to release him, it must be done in a respectful manner, for I do not want him to suffer through another experience of abandonment and resent me for it."

"I suppose you are right. From what I have heard, he does not take kindly to others and reacts quickly."

"You judge him too quickly." I picked up the feather and placed it to the table. "Perhaps you should meet him before you settle on an opinion."

"I am not the one you need to prove his qualities to. Have Darwynyen accompany you." He moved toward a bookshelf.

"I cannot." My eyes began to wander around the room. "If truth be told, I have a confession to make."

Archemese ignored me, pulling a book of interest from one of the shelves.

"Did you not hear me?" I asked.

He looked up. "Yes. I gave you a moment, in hope that you would reconsider."

I took a moment before responding, realizing that he was again suggesting that I look to Darwynyen. And though I probably should have, the last thing I wanted to do was create another rift between us; we had only just mended the last one. Besides, what would it accomplish? Whether I liked it or not, Ghezmeed was soon to become part of my past. Darwynyen was my future, and I did not want to put him through any unnecessary pain when it could easily be avoided. "If you are suggesting that I speak to Darwynyen, then you misunderstand. Darwynyen must never learn of what I am about to tell you."

"Very well," Archemese sighed. "I will hear you first, and then we can decide how to proceed together."

Concerned about his reaction, I swallowed deeply. "When we first released Ghezmeed in the forest of Maglavine, he revealed to me that he once tried to end Darwynyen's life."

Archemese shook his head in disbelief. "I see now why you were disinclined."

"What should I do?" I asked desperately. "Despite Ghezmeed's past, I no longer believe that he is a threat."

"Perhaps I should meet him now," Archemese suggested. "Before I can counsel you, I must first be certain of his intentions."

My chest tightened with dread. After my confession, I was no longer eager to have them meet. Besides, Ghezmeed was timid, and I knew he would not react well to the pressures of being questioned. "Of course." I concealed my concerns and made my way to the door. "I suppose it would be better to settle this now rather than later."

Archemese set the book on the table and followed me from the room.

When we reached the third level, Archemese hesitated.

"What is it?" I asked.

He was about to respond when Edina opened the door. "I thought I heard you." She smiled, until she noticed Archemese. "Whom have you brought with you?"

"I am a friend of Arianna's." Archemese sent me a fleeting look. "I am here to see Ghezmeed."

Edina looked at me apprehensively. When I nodded, she reluctantly stood aside. "Then you are most welcome."

We found Ghezmeed sitting on the bed. His eyes were wide with anticipation. "Arianna, I have been waiting …" He paused when he saw Archemese. "What do you want with me?" He clenched the covers, pulling them up to his face, like a makeshift shield.

"We are here to discuss your future." I sat on the bed. "I would like you to meet Archemese."

"I know who he is!" Ghezmeed quickly blew out the candles and then slid off the bed.

Before he could crawl under it, I took him by the arm. "Ghezmeed, please, have you no confidence in me?"

He tried to pull from my hold. "The wizard hates me!"

"No." I tightened my grip. "You are mistaken. Not only is Archemese my mentor, he is a trusted friend." I looked at Edina for help.

She knelt by Ghezmeed. "Come, sit on the bed. I will protect you."

Her calm voice seemed to reassure him. With his eyes trained on Archemese, he slowly crawled back onto the bed.

Archemese stepped forward. "Trust what Arianna says. I will not harm you. As a wielder of magic, I give you my word."

Edina looked at me. "You said you were here to discuss the future."

"Yes." I moved to the window. "Things are soon to change. King Madigan will make an announcement the day after tomorrow. The city of Aarrondirth will empty, and the remaining battalions will make way for Walferd in two days' time."

"What does this have to do with us?" she asked.

When I turned from the window, my foot hit a stool. As I set it aside, I furrowed my brow, glancing toward Edina. "Why is this stool here?" I asked. "Has Ghezmeed been looking out the window?"

"Yes." Edina bit her lip. "He gazes upon the northern horizon, or what he can see of it from here. I try to dissuade him, but he refuses to listen. He stares as though he is in a trance and only when darkness takes over or daylight blinds him does he turn away."

Curious, I drew the curtains. Evening twilight was upon us. As I searched to find the northern horizon from this angle, Ghezmeed came to my side, stepping onto the stool. "Can you not feel it?" he whispered. "There is a great evil in the north."

"What do you know of the north?" Archemese questioned.

Ghezmeed put his hands to his face and began to weep. His body trembled.

"What upsets you?" I asked, gently placing my hand on his back. "Please, you must tell us what you know."

"I sense a man!" he cried. "His thoughts are full of vengeance."

Archemese took him by the arm. "Do you speak of Velderon?"

Ghezmeed shrieked at Archemese's touch and fell off the stool.

I knelt to pick him up, giving Archemese a sharp look of warning. "Ghezmeed, are you all right?"

"No." He clung to me. "My thoughts bring pain, lots of pain."

As I lifted him to the bed, his fingers dug into my skin. "Let me go, Ghezmeed!" I winced. "You are hurting me."

When Archemese stepped forward, I gave him another sharp look. "I can manage."

Ghezmeed released me and looked down. "Arianna, my uses may be few, but I can help you if you will let me."

I sat, lifting his chin. "Your offer is kind, but I see no way for you to do so."

"There is a way!" He smiled cunningly. "I could travel north to Cessdorn and offer my services to your father. He will not suspect me, and as his willing slave I can watch over him and listen until I learn of his battle plans."

Edina stood. "Arianna, you must refuse him!"

"Edina, please." I gestured for her to sit. When she nodded, I returned to Ghezmeed. "Why do you want to do this?"

He sat upright in a proud manner. "Not once in my life have I had a purpose. When you saved me in Maglavine, you gave me hope. The emotion warmed my heart, and I wept for several days as I began to feel whole for the first time. I am forever in your debt, Arianna, and I want to do right by you, if you will allow me."

Overwhelmed, my eyes began to fill. "I am honored by what you are willing to sacrifice." I paused. "But my answer is no."

"It is not your decision," he replied defiantly. "I will go with or without your approval." He turned to Edina. "Forgive me, but I have to do this."

Edina stood again, crossing her arms. "If he goes, then I will see him to Biddenwade." She spoke with determination. "I will not have him travel the extended journey alone. It is too dangerous.

If he is captured by our people, you know as well as I that he will be persecuted if no one is there to speak for him."

My heart sank at the thought. Edina was right. He could not go alone. Even so, could I allow my dearest friend to accompany him? If I refused her, there was little doubt that she would resent me. Like Ghezmeed, she needed a purpose. Besides, if they restricted their travels to our region, they would most likely go unnoticed. And if they were stopped, I could give her a royal decree that would allow her and Ghezmeed safe passage. "How will you return?" I asked. Although I could not find a flaw in their plan, I was not completely convinced and wanted to discourage her. "It will be a long journey back to Aarrondirth on your own."

"I will wait for you in Biddenwade," she replied. "I have an uncle there."

"What about your family?" I persisted, in need of further assurances. "They would never forgive me for agreeing to this. Moreover, I would never forgive myself if something were to happen to you."

"I appreciate your concern." She returned to Ghezmeed as though to display her commitment toward him. "Arianna, can you not see that I must do this?"

When I looked at Archemese for support, Archemese slowly held out his hand, placing it on Ghezmeed's shoulder. At the moment of contact, each of them closed their eyes. I knew then they were speaking within their minds. Moments later, Archemese opened his eyes. "Your friend is of a good heart. Trust him. With the help of Edina, he may be able to assist us."

Speechless, I nodded, taking a seat on the bed.

Archemese took a step back. "If you are to leave tomorrow, we must see to the necessary arrangements."

"Wait." I was still uncomfortable with the situation. "I am not yet convinced. Should we discuss this matter further?"

"What is there to discuss?" Archemese clasped his hands together. "As I told you before, each of us has a design, a path we must follow." He sent Edina and Ghezmeed a quick look. "This one happens to be theirs."

I had nothing left to argue, and I conceded. "Very well," I sighed. "Let us get on with it."

After hours of debate, we finally came to an agreement. The course was plotted. In an effort to keep Edina and Ghezmeed safe, they would take a route that led them away from the main cities. Their only concern would be food. In the wild, they would have to depend on rations and Ghezmeed's hunting skills. When they reached the high end of the loch near Direside, Edina and Ghezmeed would go their separate ways. Edina would take the trail to Biddenwade while Ghezmeed made his way to Cessdorn. During their travels through the region of Aarrondirth, Ghezmeed would stay in contact with Archemese, alerting us to their progress. The rest of the journey Ghezmeed would undertake alone. From there we would await his connection or return, hoping that his selfless act would be successful.

Archemese stood. "If everyone is in agreement, we should retire for the night." He looked at Ghezmeed and Edina. "Get plenty of rest. Tomorrow will be a test of your endurance."

Edina took Ghezmeed by the hand and nodded.

Exhausted, I stretched my limbs as I stood. "I will look forward to the day when there is nothing left to be done."

Archemese chuckled. "When that day comes, you may discover boredom."

"Perhaps." I moved toward the door.

Archemese entered my mind. *Try not to worry about your friends. They are stronger than you want to believe.* He paused. *As for the matter concerning Darwynyen, your secret is safe with me. I no longer see the need to trouble him.*

I nodded in acknowledgement, before taking my leave down the corridor.

Rage in Failure

Two moons would cross over the horizon before Velderon found time to return to the altar. Although the trolls were proving to be obedient servants, they were simple-minded and required constant direction. Even so, he could not help but feel proud. How could he not? His hard work had finally been realized, and his new found empire was slowly taking form around him.

As he trudged up the altar stair, the guards at the landing bowed. "Welcome back, my lord."

He ignored them when he caught sight of the stones. He had felt fatigued without them. Their energy was addictive, and he rushed to embrace them, knowing that their power would revitalize him.

After consuming most of their energy, he left to observe his potion, confident that he would be pleased by his findings. His eyes widened as he picked up the bowl. To his dismay, the spell he had cast upon the elf had turned black in failure. Infuriated, he tossed the bowl to the ground. "Curse the elves!" he screamed. He turned to make his way to the dungeons. "They will pay for this!"

When he reached the secret chamber, his rage boiled over. "See to another attack on Aarrondirth!" he commanded the matriarch dragon. "I want my daughter and her elvish companions killed!"

The dragon roared in defiance as it tried to break free of its shackles. Velderon eyed the cell on the opposite side of the room. "Do as I say or I will harm your child." The beast backed down immediately. "Hold those orders." Velderon began to caress his beard in contemplation. When the dragon attempted to enter his mind, he blocked her. "I have changed my mind. Do not kill my daughter, only her companions. I want her kept alive." Finished with his demands, he lifted his wand. "Make your connection now while I have dulled the chamber's powers." The land above the cell became visible with the spell. Obediently, the dragon closed its eyes.

To the Tower

After sharing breakfast with Archemese and Morglafenn in the library, I left in search of Darwynyen, who had set out early. As I passed by the study, I heard Madigan call my name and returned to the archway. "Was there something you needed?" I smiled when I met his look. "I was just on my way to find Darwynyen."

"He is in the northern courtyard with the Miders." Madigan stood from the table, lifting a scroll. "If you could spare a few minutes, I would like you to review the announcement I have prepared." He handed it to me. "Now that all the preparations have been met, it is time to advise the people of our departure."

I took hold of the scroll, reading it quickly. When I reached the bottom I frowned disapprovingly. "I see you are planning a celebration. May I ask your reasoning?"

"We will celebrate our coming victory," he replied. "Not only will it give hope to the ones we leave behind, it will strengthen the conviction of the soldiers who leave for battle." He shrugged lightly, "The city councilmen suggested it as a gesture of goodwill."

"I cannot say that I agree, though if anyone knows the minds of the people, it would be them." I placed the scroll on the table. "I suppose we could use the distraction."

He returned to his chair. "I will expect you on the balcony at the falling of the sun."

"I will be there," I nodded and then left the room.

I searched a greater part of the elvish encampment before finding Darwynyen. When he caught sight of me, he waved. "Give me a moment. I am almost finished here." When I nodded, he returned to finish instructing the Miders. Behind him was Dregby. I had not seen him for days. I was about to beckon him over, but he got distracted and trotted off.

Although I was disappointed, I shrugged and leaned against one of the neighboring wagons that had recently been stocked with supplies in preparation for our departure.

After examining the contents, primarily weapons and digging tools, I returned my eyes to Darwynyen. "Follow my lead when I extend my bow," he directed the Miders who stood next to him. "We must work together. As one we will be invincible."

With determination, each of the Miders retracted their bows. When they released their arrows, only half hit their mark. My eyes quickly darted to Darwynyen, assuming that he would be frustrated, a characteristic I had grown accustomed to in the past weeks. To my surprise, he appeared calm, approaching those who had missed with words of encouragement. His dark emotions, it seemed, were no longer present, and I could not help but feel proud, knowing that in the end my father's spell had only strengthened us. No one could tear us apart now.

"Lady Arianna."

I turned to see the elf woman that Darwynyen had been intimate with, and I crossed my arms uninvitingly. "What do you want?"

"May I have a word?" She glanced toward Darwynyen.

"Concerning what exactly?" I asked bluntly. An image of her and Darwynyen flashed through my mind.

"I would like to discuss Darwynyen." She cocked her head confidently. "You have no right to meddle in our affairs." When my mouth fell open, she continued. "Can you not see that we belong together?"

"It is you who meddles." Darwynyen rushed to my side. "Why are you here?"

"I am here to fight for you." She tried to reach out for him.

Darwynyen shoved her aside. "As I told you before, my heart belongs to Arianna, no other."

"But she is of Man's Blood," she argued. "She could never love you as I!"

"You are right, she could only love me more," he replied. "Can you not see that you are making a spectacle of yourself?" He eyed the Miders who had gathered to watch. "There is nothing left to say. Accept what I have told you and leave us."

Her eyes began to fill. "It is no bother. In time, you will see things clearly and come to me." Before either of us could respond, she ran off.

Darwynyen exhaled heavily and then turned to the Miders. "We are finished here for the day. You may take your leave."

When they began to disperse, he led me toward the castle. "Forgive me, Arianna. I cannot explain her actions."

"There is nothing to explain." I sighed. "She acts out of desperation, nothing more."

"Forget her," he urged. "She will not bother you again, I assure you."

I nodded and then changed the subject. "My purpose here was not to interrupt your work." I hesitated. "I have come to discuss Ghezmeed. There are things I must make you aware of."

"The Rinjeed." He halted. "I do not know whether to be upset or pleased." His tone was discontented. "Now, when you give me the consideration I desired, I find I no longer want it."

"You cannot mean that!"

"Do not misunderstand." He took hold of my hands. "You forget that my experience with the Rinjeed differs from yours, and one day you may come to appreciate this. Until then, you must respect my skepticism."

"Why must you always think the worst of him?" I asked. "Will you not even give him the opportunity to prove you wrong?"

Before he could respond, a horn sounded in the distance. Startled, we both looked to the sky. "Dragons!" he exclaimed. "They have returned for another attack!"

I turned toward the castle. "I must find Shallendria and Morglafenn. We were to meet at the northern tower should the beasts make their return."

"I will lead the men out here." He quickly kissed me on the cheek. "Be careful. I will find you when it is over."

When I nodded, he disappeared among the wagons.

As I opened the door to the northern tower, a dragon flew overhead. His force made the stone blocks rumble. I shuddered at its strength.

Morglafenn turned with wide eyes. "Arianna, stay back!"

Through one of the openings in the parapet I could see a dragon hovering near Shallendria. "Has she made a connection?"

He shrugged helplessly. "Where is Archemese?"

"I do not know." I slowly stepped through the door to gain a better view.

The air beneath its wings heaved outward as the dragon struggled to keep still. I was about to take another step when it let out a roar strong enough to pierce my ears. Moments later, another dragon flew to the tower. For some reason they had yet to commence with their attacks.

Shallendria cried out and then stumbled back.

I did not understand what was happening. As I clung to Morglafenn, the dragons growled at one another. Shallendria dropped to her knees, placing her fingers to her temples. When the dragons saw this, they began to fight amongst themselves. Fire bled through the sky. Morglafenn moved to cover Shallendria with his cloak. The dragons flew apart. One fled. The other returned to the parapet, attempting to land. The stone beneath it crumbled under the weight. As it fell backward, it lifted its wings to ascend and then flew off with a roar. In response, the remaining dragons followed the beast as it flew into the distance.

Shallendria cried out. Morglafenn immediately took her in his arms. She pulled away. "Leave me. I am all right."

Morglafenn nodded, assisting her to her feet. She took my hand. "Arianna, things are far worse than we first expected."

"What do you mean?" I supported her arm when she began to waver.

"What goes on here?" Archemese appeared at the door.

"The dragons." Shallendria winced, gathering her breath. "I was able to connect to them."

"They spoke to you?" Archemese puckered his brow in disbelief. "What did they say?"

"It is complicated," Shallendria replied. "It seems that during her captivity, the matriarch has given birth to a child."

"A child?" Archemese leaned on his staff. "Are you certain?"

"Yes."

"I see." Archemese blinked and looked concerned. "Unfortunately, this revelation changes everything."

"How do you mean?" I questioned. "Has learning of this child not put the odds in our favor?"

"To the contrary." Archemese leaned on his staff. "It is no longer conceivable that the beasts will listen to reason, especially if they intend to protect their heir." His eyes wandered toward the northern horizon. "Velderon has won this victory. Now we must reconsider our quest to Naksteed."

"I have not finished." Shallendria stood upright. "The dragons are divided. Despite the risks, many are willing to fight. Before the last beast fled, he requested I seek the counsel of their eldest beast, as we suspected. Until the matriarch returns, he is their acting viceroy. If any decisions are to be made, they will be done through him."

Morglafenn frowned. "If they are willing to negotiate, why can it not be done through your thoughts?"

"It is too risky," Shallendria countered. "Velderon watches, and should he discover our plans, the matriarch would be the one who suffers the repercussions."

"Can you not summon the viceroy?" Archemese asked. "If he were to accept our terms and meet with us, we could shield the connection with magic."

"As plausible as that sounds, it is not an option," Shallendria replied with regret. "Not only is the viceroy aged, his wings are tattered from his time spent in the catacombs, and he is no longer able to fly. There is more," her voice deepened. "Our arrival in Naksteed may not be welcomed. Nor will the dragons cease their attacks. Things must progress as they are now, if we are to go unnoticed in this quest."

Morglafenn nodded in acknowledgment. "Then it seems our choices are few in this matter."

Archemese stood aside, ushering us through the doorway. "If nothing has changed, then let us be done with this conversation."

When Shallendria nodded, I assisted her down the stairs. Morglafenn and Archemese followed.

After escorting Shallendria to her quarters, I went to the third level of the castle. Ghezmeed and Edina would soon be embarking on their journey, and I wanted to see that they had everything they needed prior to their departure.

As I stepped into the corridor, I noticed the guards were no longer posted at Ghezmeed's door. Confused, I hastened. When I entered the room, my chest tightened. It was empty. Distraught, I ran to Edina's quarters. They were also abandoned. On her bed lay a carefully placed note. My name was inscribed on the front. I realized then that they had taken their leave sometime during the night. The act was cowardly, and to make amends they had left the note to clear their consciences. Although I was disappointed and hurt, I slowly picked it up to read it.

Arianna,

If you are reading this note, then you know that Ghezmeed and I are already on our way to Biddenwade. You may not appreciate the reasons why we left as we did, and I understand if you are disappointed. I hope that in time you will come to forgive us. Remember our friendship, and know that we are doing this for you.

With love, Edina

A tear trickled down my cheek as I finished. Overcome with emotion, I unconsciously crumpled the note. As I tried to straighten it, I thought of Archemese and ran from the room.

When I reached the library, I burst through the doors. "Archemese!" I began to pace when I saw him. "Ghezmeed, Edina ..." I put my hand to my chest to settle my breath. "They are gone!"

Archemese's eyes filled with guilt. "I know."

"You knew!" I threw the note to the ground. "Why did you not tell me?"

"I was asked not to. Besides, they had their reasons."

"And you condoned this!" I spoke with disdain. "How could you?"

"It is not I who is in question here," he rebutted. "If you had known, would you have let them go?" He continued before I could respond. "It was not only Ghezmeed who could sense your hesitation. I felt it as well. In the end, you left us with no other choice."

"Your insinuations insult me," I glared. "Regardless of my doubts, I had given my word, and that should have been enough."

"Do not let your disappointment overshadow their good intentions," he pleaded. "I can assure you that there was no malice in their hearts when they made this decision."

I sat in a chair to consider his explanation. Was he right? Was I overreacting? If given the opportunity would I have changed my mind? It was conceivable. There was no denying that I had been dreading their departure. Good-byes were difficult enough on the best of terms, but the thought of knowingly sending two people that I cared for into the unknown was difficult to bear.

"Arianna, you cannot change what has happened. Instead,

take comfort in knowing that they will not undergo this journey alone, that through the mind, I have chosen to guide them." Archemese reached for a book. "For Ghezmeed and Edina's sake, you must set your ill feelings aside and commit to your studies." His stare intensified. "If learning one of these spells is enough to save you, it may also save another."

I released a heavy breath as I took hold of the book. "If I do this, you must promise to advise me of Ghezmeed and Edina's progress."

"Of course. I will not keep anything from you, good or bad."

Although the latter half of his words left me unsettled, I had no choice but to believe that he would do right by me, and I opened the book. "Where should we begin?" I asked.

"Turn the page," he replied. "We will continue from where we left off yesterday."

I nodded, following his instructions.

To Listen

It was midday when Teshna and Zenley arrived at the outer lying border of Walferd.

"We should keep moving." Zenley walked down a branch to meet Teshna.

"I am tired, my brother." Teshna held a leaf over her head, protecting the scroll. "Will this rain ever stop?"

"I know your rest last night did not come easy." He knelt to face her. "If Gin was the cause, then you must rid your thoughts of him."

"How can I?" she huffed. "The lad is unpredictable. There is no telling what he might do."

Zenley rolled his eyes. "You forget that he is only a man. Unpredictable or not, I fear that you give him too much power."

"Quiet!" Teshna put her fingers to her temples. "I sense something."

"You are right, the voice is faint, but I can hear it."

Where are you?

"It is Archemese." Teshna smiled when the connection intensified. *We have reached Walferd,* she replied.

Has your path crossed with Gin's? Archemese asked.

No, Zenley replied. *He is either before us or behind us.*

Keep looking, Archemese urged. *Until we know his intentions, the slightest bit of information could prove vital.* He paused. *In the meantime, I want you to listen for another voice.*

Whose? Teshna asked, looking at Zenley.

His name is Ghezmeed. Archemese replied. His tone deepened. *He is a Rinjeed, a friend to Arianna. He travels with another. Her name is Edina. If they come to any trouble you will alert me. They may need our assistance.*

A Rinjeed! Teshna cringed. *Why would you ask us to listen for him?*

The reason is not important, Archemese replied sternly. *Will you abide by my request?*

If we must. Zenley responded with little enthusiasm.

You must! The connection abruptly ended.

Frustrated, Zenley stomped his feet on the branch. "Wizard or not, he demands too much of us!" he growled. "Who is this Ghezmeed anyway?"

Teshna stood, letting go of the leaf she had been using for shelter. "He is the Rinjeed Sikes told us about, the one who attacked us on our way to Aarrondirth." Zenley's eyes widened with contempt, and she continued. "Do not allow the past to sway you, my brother." She shook her hands in Zenley's direction, hoping that the droplets of water would distract him from his mood. "If Archemese watches over this Rinjeed, we must trust that his request comes with good reason."

"His elusive behavior has not warranted our trust." Zenley retorted, raising his hands to shield her. "We could always choose not to listen … no one would be the wiser."

"Zenley!" Teshna shook a saturated leaf in his direction. "Never say such things unless you mean them!"

"All right!" Zenley covered his face with his arms. "I concede. There is no need to further drench me!"

Teshna flung the leaf aside and flew off. "Come," she beckoned, concealing the scroll under her body. "It is time we moved on."

Zenley fluttered his wings, expelling the water, before following after her.

Alone in the Unknown

In the shadow of the falling sun, Edina and Ghezmeed found their way to an abandoned barn. "Are you sure this is wise?" Ghezmeed pulled out his flint and lit a lantern they found near the entrance. "What if we are discovered?"

She unrolled her blanket. "The chances are few. Like this one, most of the settlements in this region have been abandoned."

"Why?" he asked.

"Because the area has endured a drought, and the land is no longer workable." She rummaged through her satchel,

"Where have they gone?" He took a seat next to her.

"I would guess to the cities." She shrugged. "It happens sometimes. Many blame it on the gods."

"The gods are mean!" Ghezmeed's eyes darted over the room. "I relate to these people. They have suffered. I know how it feels to be abandoned." He pointed to the rusted farm equipment.

Edina dropped her satchel to take hold of his hand. "I will not abandon you, I promise."

At first, he flinched at her touch, and then he relaxed. "I am most grateful, Edina."

She smiled to further reassure him, and then she reached for her book, opening it to the marker. "How about we finish the remainder of this book?"

Ghezmeed reached for his blanket. “Nothing would please me more. I love the story within its pages.”

“As do I.” She yawned with contentment. “It is one of my favorites.”

Ghezmeed adjusted the light on the lantern and then nestled on her arm as she began.

The Mounting of his Evil

After a short visit to the armory, Velderon quickly realized that there was still much work ahead of him. Only half the furnaces were lit, and the weapon store was nearly empty. The lack of production was not the fault of his minions. He needed more coal. He turned to Besken. "Take the wagons. Assemble those who are of no use to us in battle. Lead them to the mines," he ordered. "I want all of these furnaces lit and in commission as soon as possible."

"It shall be done." Besken bowed.

"Besken!" A troll in full armor rushed over. "We have had word from the goblins in Vidorr."

"Have they made their decision?" Besken began to drool greedily. "Will they join us?"

"Of course they will!" Velderon sneered. "Only a fool would deny me!"

The troll bowed. "You are right, they have not refused you, my lord, and they already make their way."

Velderon clasped his hands together. "The time has come! Besken, ready your troops. Have them make way for the region next to Direside. There is an old citadel near the loch. I want it reinforced and ready for the Goblin's arrival. No longer will our borders stand unprotected!" He paused. "While they are there, have a battalion sent over to the docks of Biddenwade. If we can stall the Man's Blood by sinking a few of their ships, it will be worth the losses."

"Yes, my lord." Besken bowed and then turned to leave with his companion.

Velderon cackled as they retreated.

The Announcement of their Departure

As anticipated, a mob formed at the castle barbican shortly after the herald's announcement. The people wanted answers, as was to be expected after word had traveled that we had begun to disassemble the encampments.

While the servant's made their final preparations in the lea, Madigan summoned the counsel of the city vendors. We met in the waiting room that connected to the main balcony.

Madigan approached one of the wealthier men who owned most of the establishments that encompassed the main square. "You know the people. What must we do to settle their concerns? Will they accept the announcement of my departure?"

The man bowed. "Forgive me, my king, but I do not have the answers you seek." He glanced at his companions. "The people are fickle. As their king, it is left to you to sway them."

"He is right, my king." The jeweler I had once met with my mother bowed and stepped forward. "The decisions have already been made. Their approval is not necessary. Be direct," he urged. "Divulge only what you must. If the people begin to waver, announce the celebration as a distraction."

I took Madigan aside. "Are you certain about this celebration?"

I asked. "What if my father is watching and sends forth the dragons?"

Madigan lowered his voice. "Arianna, this war cannot be won out of fear. If your father chooses to continue his attacks, let him. He accomplishes nothing. In the end, his cowardice will only serve to further unify us. Do you understand?"

I took a moment to consider his opinion. Although his perspective differed from mine, in many ways it made sense. Despite the loss of life, the dragon attacks had only made us stronger, despite the spell that was placed upon Darwynyen. "I may not fully agree, but I understand your logic." I glanced over to Darwynyen.

"Then trust it." Madigan turned to the councilmen. "Thank you for your guidance."

When they nodded, he gestured to the heralds.

At the sounding of the horns, my chest tightened. As though sensing my hesitation, Archemese emerged from the corridor and placed his hand on my shoulder, squeezing it with encouragement. "Excuse my tardiness," he smiled. "Do not fear, I will be here for you should you need me."

In response, I released a heavy breath and then followed Madigan to the balcony.

Several hundred people had gathered. My chest tightened again at the sight. Madigan leaned to whisper in my ear. "Do you see now what I spoke about?"

I nodded.

"Hail our king!" a man bellowed from below. "Hail our king!" The crowd slowly joined him.

Madigan gave them a few moments before raising his hand. "People of Aarrondirth, hear your king!"

In the silence that followed, he continued. "I have summoned you here to announce my departure from Aarrondirth." When the crowd gasped, he continued. "To ensure our victory, I will travel to Biddenwade, where I intend to personally oversee the coming battles."

"Why?" an elderly woman yelled. "As our king, you must not abandon us!"

Madigan was about to respond, but I silenced him when I saw a bird entangled in the matted hair on her shoulder. I pointed. "Look! There is a raven on her shoulder!"

Madigan leaned over the ledge. "Guards!" he commanded. "Seize that woman!"

The woman's eyes went blank. "People of Aarrondirth," she yelled, "do not listen to this man, I beg you! He is not our king, he is a traitor!" As the guards fought through the crowd, she continued. "Do not put your trust in a man from a broken bloodline. If you do, his rule will see you to your end!" As she finished, the raven flew from her shoulder, and the woman fell.

"Capture that bird!" Madigan ordered.

From the parapet above, the guards threw a net. The bird was swift and already beyond our reaches. When the mesh hit the crowd, panic broke out. People began to flee in all directions.

Archemese appeared at my side. "Citizens of Aarrondirth! I command you to listen!" His staff began to glow. Mesmerized by the spell, the people obediently halted. Archemese took me by the arm. "Speak, child!"

"People, I command you to stand your ground." I raised my hands. "Do not fear what you have witnessed. We are at war. Spies are to be expected. Now you must set aside your doubts and find your courage. Our victory depends on it." When the people began to reassemble, I persisted. "In the absence of your king, I charge you to protect this city." My tone deepened. "If you fail, his sacrifice will be in vain, for there will be no throne for him to return to."

"Hear your lady," Madigan beseeched. "Find your courage, for we are stronger as one. I give you my word." He put his hand to his chest. "Victory will soon be upon us!"

"To victory!" a soldier shouted from the fields.

"To victory!" The people raised their hands. "To victory!" they chanted.

To further persuade them, I leaned over the ledge. "Go now! Make your way to the lea, where we will celebrate this coming victory!"

"Yes," Madigan glanced at me. It was plain to see that he was surprised by my sudden change of heart. "Make your way to the lea. Let the celebrations begin."

When the people began to disperse, Madigan led me back into the castle. He frowned. "I thought you were against this celebration. What has changed your mind?"

"You," I smiled. "No longer will I fear my father. He is, like you said, a coward. As long as we remain unified, he will not have the means to thwart us."

Madigan moved to embrace me and then quickly stepped back, eyeing Shallendria, who had appeared at the archway. "Thank you for reconsidering, Arianna. It means a lot to me."

I nodded. Darwynyen followed in after Shallendria, and I took his hand. "Shall we make our way to the lea?"

"Of course." Madigan escorted everyone from the room. "The celebration of our victory awaits us!"

When we reached the main foyer, Jeel and Naseyn rushed to my side. "Will there be ale at this celebration?" Naseyn asked, excited.

"Yes!" Jeel began to jump up and down. "We love the ale of your people, so we do!"

I knelt to face them. "Under no circumstances are you to get carried away with the spirits." My tone was firm. "Do you understand?"

Jeel shook his head. "No, we do not."

"Need I remind you that you are here as representatives of your people? And I will expect you to conduct yourselves accordingly."

"Will there be ale at this celebration or not?" Naseyn took Jeel's arm in his. "If there is, then I feel that you have no right to deny us."

"Mind your manners." Dregby trotted into the foyer, nudging

them with his hoof. “You are here as Arianna’s guests. Show her the respect she deserves, or you will have me to contend with.”

They stumbled backward and then looked at me. “Forgive us, Arianna. We will abide by your wishes.”

“There is nothing to forgive.” I put my hand on Dregby’s shoulder to acknowledge him. “We are all friends here.”

When Jeel and Naseyn nodded humbly, I could not help but feel guilty. Deep down, I knew it was not their intention to cause trouble. They simply could not help themselves. Even so, I could not allow them to run amuck when there was a risk that it would undermine our alliances. “Jeel, Naseyn, you do not need the spirits to be merry.” I smiled. “To prove this to you, you will see no ale at the main table.”

Both Jeel and Naseyn’s eyes widened. “You will not take in the spirits either?”

“None of us will,” I replied, extending my hand toward the others. When Madigan and Dregby’s mouths fell open, I rolled my eyes. “If we are to travel tomorrow, is it not in our interest to forgo the spirits?”

Madigan and Dregby then glared at Jeel and Naseyn.

Shallendria took Madigan’s arm. “You are not going to cause a fuss over a little bit of ale, are you?” She raised her brow.

Before he could argue, I gestured to the guardsmen, who promptly opened the main doors.

Darwynyen took my hand and led me out, following Madigan and Shallendria.

As we walked through the courtyard, I glanced over my shoulder in search of Archemese. To my relief, he was directly behind us. I was about to smile, but I noticed that his face was pale and his steps were heavy. Morglafenn held his arm supportively. “Are you all right?” I asked.

“I am fine.” He steadied himself with his staff. “You forget that I am an old man.”

I was about to respond when I noticed Morglafenn looking over my shoulder toward Shallendria. His concern was obvious.

When I turned to Shallendria, she noted my stare and continued on, leaving me to wonder if they were hiding something.

When we reached the main table, the horns sounded.

One by one, we were announced and then escorted to our seats. Amid the resounding applause, Madigan took his place on the throne. I sat next to him. Darwynyen took the seat next to me. Shallendria and Morglafenn sat opposite Madigan. Jeel and Naseyn were led to their own shorter table. While Archemese slowly moved toward the seat next to Darwynyen, Dregby quickly trotted up, taking the open place next to him.

As Archemese sat, he let out a moan. I quickly turned to Morglafenn and Shallendria, who immediately looked away. They were hiding something. Was Archemese ill? Was his pendant failing? Unsure, I turned back to Archemese. To my surprise, the color had returned to his face. Could it be that I was overreacting? No, something was wrong, and I intended to find out what it was. I regretted that it would have to wait until the celebration was over.

Madigan stood. "People of Aarrondirth, as your king, I officially open this celebration!" When the crowd bellowed in joy, he took hold of his goblet. "You would not deny me a toast, would you?" he mumbled. Before I could respond, he continued addressing the people. "As you can see by the many faces here, we have successfully reunited with our neighboring regions, and we now stand as one." He raised his goblet. "Embrace your new brothers in arms, for we shall share in this victory together!"

Moments later, music filled the air. As I watched over the people, I was amazed by how quickly they had accepted their fate. The past had been forgotten, and with pride they welcomed their new allies. Their selfless actions warmed my heart; we would no longer be separated by our differences. "It is good to see," Madigan commented, drinking the last of his ale.

"I could not agree more." I sent a servant away when he approached with a flask.

Madigan set down his goblet in frustration. "I resent you for this."

"You will forgive me tomorrow." I winked.

"Where are those pests?" Madigan looked at the table that had been set out for Jeel and Naseyn.

I looked, and I found myself speechless, for the chairs were empty.

"It seems you have little influence over your friends," Madigan chuckled. "They are probably drinking ale as we speak."

"If they are," I huffed, "they should hope that I do not discover them."

Madigan waved for the servant. "Oh, Arianna, it is only ale." He raised his goblet, allowing the servant to fill it. "Would you deny us our last night of freedom before we head into battle?" He paused as though to find the right words. "We must embrace these moments while we still have the chance."

"You are right, Madigan." I put my hand over my goblet when the servant moved the flask in my direction. "I will say nothing further."

A single horn sounded, distracting us both. From the far side of the pavilion came the food. Roasted pig and venison were the main courses. Each platter was garnished with an array of colored vegetables that were hard to come by in this region, making it clear that Madigan had spared no expense on his people. "Let us feast tonight in celebration of our coming victory!" Madigan stood. "Victory to us all!"

The people raised their mugs in acknowledgment. "To victory!" they shouted.

When dinner was finished, we joined in the celebration. Not only was Madigan uncomfortable with the formalities, they seemed pointless now that war was upon us. As we mingled through the crowd, a man stood upon his chair and shouted, "Will the king not share a dance with the lady?"

Taken aback and somewhat embarrassed, I politely shook my head.

"My lady, do I ask too much?" He bowed before me.

"Of course not." Madigan held out his hand. "Arianna, would you honor me with a dance?"

I bowed to Madigan. "As your humble servant, how can I refuse you?"

"You cannot," Madigan replied with a grin, leading me to an open area near the main table.

When the music began, Madigan took me in his arms. His touch forced me to blush. I could almost feel his heart beating. To settle the uncomfortable emotions, I fluttered my eyes as he led me into the melody. After several turns, he spoke. "Have I told you how beautiful you look tonight?" Before I could respond, he led me into another turn and then brought me back to face him. "I believe your role brings you more happiness than you are willing to admit."

"I believe you are right." I smiled, relieved that he had not taken the subject in a different direction. "It brings me great joy to stand by your side."

"The joy is mine," he replied, looking deep into my eyes.

Trapped in his gaze, my heart skipped a beat. I almost felt faint. "Madigan, I …"

The music stopped before I could finish. As the people applauded, we bowed and then went in separate directions.

As I desperately searched for Darwynyen, one of the musicians approached. His eyes immediately reminded me of Edina. He bowed. "My lady, I am Percy, the brother of Edina." His eyes scanned the crowd. "Where is she?"

"Percy." I held out my hand. "I am most pleased to meet you."

He gently kissed my hand. "As am I, my lady."

In the awkwardness that followed, I looked down. "As for Edina …" I paused. "I do not know how to tell you this, but she is gone."

"No!" he gasped. "What have you done to her?"

"I have done nothing." I returned his look, insulted by his presumption. "When your sister left, it was by her will alone."

"Are you saying she is still alive?" he asked.

"Of course." I sighed, realizing that I had misled him. "Forgive me—I did not mean to give you the wrong impression."

"Where has she gone?" he questioned.

"She makes her way to Biddenwade," I replied.

He took a step back. "You allowed her to travel that distance in her state?"

"You judge me too quickly," I snapped. "As I said before, she left of her own free will. She did not even say good-bye."

He quieted down. "Why would she do so?"

"Regrettably, I am unable to divulge the reasons." I put my hand to his shoulder. "I can, however, tell you that this journey has brought new light to her eyes."

His demeanor softened. "I apologize. My sister is strong-willed. I did not mean to take her actions out on you."

"You are forgiven," I replied. "If I get any news, your family will be the first to hear it."

"Thank you." He bowed and retreated.

As I watched him make his way through the crowd, I caught view of Shallendria. She was leading Madigan to the dance area. Curious, I moved for a better view. "What are you up to?" I felt Darwynyen's hand on my shoulder.

"Look," I pointed. "Madigan and Shallendria are dancing."

"I cannot believe my eyes," Darwynyen said in disbelief. "Not once has she condoned the practices of your culture."

I was about to respond when I saw Shallendria abruptly break away from Madigan, clutching her stomach. Something was wrong. Darwynyen also noticed, and he rushed to her side. I followed.

"What is it?" Darwynyen took her arm in support when her legs began to waver. "What do you feel?"

"I sense a force," she winced. "It is powerful!"

Madigan left to silence the musicians. Confused, the people's faces became worried. I tried to calm them. "Do not fear," I spoke with conviction. "Everything will be all right."

Archemese approached from behind. "Beware," he warned. "There is a dark presence closing in around us."

"Lower your voice." I eyed the gathering crowd.

"Forget them." Archemese looked to the sky.

When I followed his eyes, I noticed that the clouds above us were swirling. "What is happening?" I stumbled back when a face took form in the billows. It was my father.

"Fools," he cackled. "You are nothing but fools!" His voice echoed like thunder. "Fear me now, for my power will crush you!" As he spoke, the winds gathered strength. Terrified, people began to flee. "You will suffer at my hands!" Lightning crackled from around his blurry image.

Archemese stepped away, raising his staff with determination. "Light of Cemenbar, I command you to expand your shield and protect these lands!" His staff began to vibrate.

"Wizard!" my father growled. "Whoever you are, your powers are no match to mine!" The distorted face swirled in my direction. The winds intensified. "My daughter, what shall I do with you?"

"Father," I shouted, clenching my fists. "Why are you doing this?"

His features became more pronounced. "Everything I do is for you, child."

Darwynyen pulled me aside. "Arianna, allow the wizard to do his work."

Archemese stood straighter. "Cemenbar, I call upon you now!" Seconds later a bolt of light surged from Archemese's staff. When it struck the cloud, the energy forced it to ripple. It was not enough. To my dismay, my father's face promptly resurfaced. Archemese lowered his head and began to chant. Shallendria joined Archemese, placing her hands on his staff, repeating his words as he spoke them. With their combined powers, the stream of light brightened. Moments later the clouds began to dissipate, and the sky quickly cleared. It was over.

Archemese and Shallendria fell to the ground.

Darwynyen released me, and we both rushed to them.

"We must get them back to the castle." Darwynyen helped Shallendria to her feet.

Madigan turned to the remaining guardsmen. "See to the people. Escort them to the gates."

I knelt to Archemese. "Archemese, can you hear me?"

He was unresponsive.

"Is he alive?" Madigan put his hand on my shoulder with a look of dread.

I placed my ear to Archemese's chest. "Yes. He is still breathing."

Morglafenn and Madigan pulled Archemese to his feet, leading him toward the castle behind Darwynyen and Shallendria. I took hold of Archemese's staff and followed.

As we ascended the stairs, I looked at Morglafenn. "Will Archemese be all right?" I asked.

"It is too early to tell," he replied, tightening his grasp on Archemese.

I nodded. When we reached the second level, I turned to Darwynyen. "Will you see to Shallendria?"

"Yes." he replied, leading Shallendria down the corridor that led to the royal suite.

I followed Madigan and Morglafenn as they dragged Archemese up the stairs to the next level.

In his room, Madigan placed Archemese on the bed. I took his arm. "Madigan, go to Shallendria. It is where you belong."

"Thank you." Madigan squeezed my shoulder and hastily took his leave.

Archemese began to moan. Unsure what to do, I put my hand on his brow. His skin was moist and heated. "Arianna," he muttered, slowly opening his eyes. "What happened?"

"You saved us." I managed a smile. "How do you feel?"

"Shallendria," he gasped. "Will she be all right?"

"She will be fine," I replied. "It is you I worry about." I turned to Morglafenn. "I will fetch some water."

"There is no need." Morglafenn sat on the bed. "With the use of a spell I may be able to heal him." He pulled some sachets of powder from his waist belt. "Leave us. If I am to be successful, I will need to concentrate."

Reluctantly, I slowly made my way to the door. "While you work, I will look in on Shallendria."

He ignored me, opening one of the sachets.

I hesitated at the door. "Morglafenn, you will save him, will you not?"

Morglafenn paused and looked at me. "I will do what I can."

With a heavy sigh, I glanced one last time at Archemese and left the room.

When I arrived at the royal quarters, I rushed through the door. "How is Shallendria?"

"She is weak but will recover." Darwynyen stood.

Madigan assumed Darwynyen's place at Shallendria's bedside.

Darwynyen extended his hands, beckoning me to join him. "Is Archemese to be all right?"

"I do not know." I fell into his embrace and started to weep. "He did not look well. I was about to tend to him when Morglafenn excused me."

"I see." Darwynyen tightened his hold. "Do not lose hope. Morglafenn is a gifted healer."

Although I wanted further assurance, I nodded, keeping silent.

Darwynyen sat me on the end of Shallendria's bed, where we would watch over her until we were summoned by Morglafenn.

Walferd

Morning light broke through the clouds on the eastern horizon. Dew shimmered on the wheatgrass and bushes that danced in the morning breeze. With caution, Teshna and Zenley approached the Aarrondirth encampment along the outskirts of Walferd. Flags whispered in the morning breeze. Smoke escaped from the dying coal pots. The soldiers were still asleep. “What should we do?” Teshna held out her hands helplessly.

“Listen!” Zenley put his finger to his lips. “I hear laughter.”

Teshna nodded. “It is coming from that tent over there.”

Zenley fluttered his wings and then flew off. Teshna quickly followed.

When they arrived at the entrance to the main tent, they halted, clinging to each other in midair. “It is him,” Teshna gasped, dropping the scroll.

“Quiet,” Zenley leapt to the ground. He picked up the scroll and crawled under the canopy.

Teshna met him on the other side. “What are you doing?” she whispered frantically.

Zenley looked at her impatiently. “Have you forgotten Archemese’s instructions?” He ran to the edge of a wooden crate, beckoning her to follow. “If we are to provide information, we must listen to what Gin has to say before interrupting.”

Welcoming Zenley's sudden change of heart toward Archemese's instructions, her eyes brightened. "I am proud of you, my brother."

He ignored her, looking at Gin.

When she followed his eyes, she scoffed. "Look at him! He is dressed in his military garb."

Zenley turned to her with dread. "This guise only proves that Gin has reassumed his command."

Before she could respond, Gin spoke in a raised voice. "I know it is difficult to comprehend. Still," he raised his shoulders and opened his hands, "you cannot deny me, when you know it was I who traveled with her to the island." He paused. "Trust me. Arianna is evil."

"I am not convinced." One of the generals shook his head. "Nothing you say makes sense."

Gin casually lifted his mug, taking a sip. "Need I remind you that she is the seed of Velderon, our sworn enemy?"

"He has a point." Another general shrugged. "What if Gin speaks the truth and our lady plots against us?"

Gin persisted, before the others could respond. "Whether you agree or not, are you willing to take the risk?" Gin set his goblet on the table. "If we allow Arianna to see her agenda through, the stones will be reunited, I promise you." His voice cracked. "While time is still in our favor, we must find a way to stop her!"

"Liar!" Teshna flew in the air. "Gin, how could you?"

"Hear my sister!" Zenley reached her side. "Gin is the impostor, not Arianna."

The generals abruptly stood. "Who are you?" one asked. "What is your business here?"

"We were sent to warn you!" Teshna replied.

"By whom?" One of the generals took a swipe at them.

Zenley offered the scroll, and then he spoke the magic word to increase its size. "At King Madigan's request, I serve you with this decree." He handed it to one of the generals.

"Do not pay any attention to the fairies." Gin rolled his eyes. "As minions of Arianna, they are only here to thwart us."

The general holding the scroll opened it. "This scroll bears the royal seal." He looked at Gin.

Zenley interjected. "Whom do you serve, Gin, if not the king?" he taunted. "Is treason not an executable charge in these lands?"

"If not, what about the charge of murder?" Teshna fluttered her wings.

"What does she speak of?" one of the generals asked.

"I cannot say," Gin stood. His eyes moved toward the entrance. "As I said, they are here by the will of Arianna."

"Ask Gin about his origins," Teshna insisted. "If he speaks the truth, he will tell you that he is from Cessdorn and that his father is the sorcerer Goramine."

Gin slowly stepped back from the table. "Nonsense!" Beads of sweat began to form on his brow. "She tells you lies!"

The generals looked at the fairies. "How can we trust you?" one asked.

Before Teshna and Zenley could respond, Gin ran from the tent.

"Detain him!" a general yelled.

It was no use. Like before, Gin's horse was ready and waiting, and with no one to stop him, he was once again able to make his escape.

The Amulet

Archemese sat up, panicked. "How long had I been resting?"

"Several hours." Morglafenn turned from the window. "What ails you, my friend?"

"The amulet." He pulled it from his robe. "It is somehow changing me."

Intrigued by his words, Morglafenn sat on the bed. "What do you mean?"

Archemese shrugged. "I am not sure, though I can tell you that I no longer fear the future. In fact, I fear nothing!"

"I cannot condone this sort of behavior. Magic should not be used without first considering the consequences." Morglafenn stood. "In the end, your actions are no less reckless than Velderon's." With a disappointed look, he made his way to the door.

Before he could leave, Archemese called out to him. "Please, do not tell Arianna of our words. She has enough to worry about for now."

"Is it Arianna you protect, then?" he remarked. "Does she not have the right to know?"

"She does," Archemese agreed. "Do I also not have the right to tell her when I am ready?"

With hesitation, Morglafenn conceded. "I will keep your secret when it comes to this amulet … for now." He turned and left the room.

Hearts Fail

The hour was late. Madigan approached Shallendria on the balcony of their quarters. "What brings you out here?" he asked, putting his hands around her waist. "You should be resting if we are to travel tomorrow."

"I have rested enough." She turned to face him. "It is my heart I must now contend with."

"What troubles you?" His hand smoothed her cheek.

"Something you are unable to mend." Her eyes began to fill.

"How do you know until you tell me?" He moved to kiss her.

She drew back. "It is over Madigan."

"What do you mean?" He furrowed his brow. "I do not understand. Are you angry with me?"

"No." She hesitated. Tears began to trickle down her cheeks. "I do this because I love you." When Madigan turned away, upset, she put her hand on his back. "Madigan, whether or not you choose to accept it, I know your heart lies elsewhere." She paused. "In truth, I have known it for some time now, only I could not bring myself to accept it."

He turned sharply. "You do not know what you are saying. Have I somehow misled you?"

She wiped the tears from her face. "If you search your heart, you will see that I speak the truth."

"I have searched my heart," he replied with conviction. "It belongs to you—it always has!"

"No, Madigan." She looked down. "It belongs to another."

"How can you say that?" Madigan took her by the arms.

She gently pushed him away. "I have seen into your soul, Madigan." Her eyes met his. "It speaks the name Arianna."

"No," he stammered. "I share only kinship with her! Why can you not accept this?"

"There is nothing to accept, for this would not be the first time those lines have been crossed," she stated. "You must follow your heart wherever it leads you."

"Why are you doing this?" He searched her eyes.

"Madigan, please." She turned toward the ledge. "My decision is final. It is only a matter of time before you come to realize these emotions, and I do not want to face this journey to Naksteed with false hope." She paused. "The next time we meet, it will be in friendship alone."

"Very well, if you wish to part in such a manner, then so be it." He shrugged. "I am a patient man and will wait for the day when you come to your senses and change your mind."

Shallendria put her hands along his face. "You are an honorable man, Madigan."

Distraught, he embraced her. "I will wait for you."

Unable to refuse him, she held him in what would be their last embrace.

Dunstirth

After another day of travel, Edina and Ghezmeed arrived at the small city known as Dunstirth. And though they had strayed from their original course, Edina was famished, and she longed for a proper bed to rest in. "Ghezmeed, we must enter the city," she insisted, stepping from the shelter of the trees into the neighboring field, where she was more visible. "If you have not noticed, we are running low on supplies."

"It is too dangerous," he contended, stepping back into the shrubbery. "If we are discovered here, your people will see to my death. I did not set out on this journey to have it end with my neck snapped!" He put his hand to his neck protectively. "I may be irrational at times, but I am not yet ready to die!"

"Why must you always fear the worst?" She raised the hood on her cloak. "If we make the effort to disguise ourselves, I can assure you we will go unnoticed." She paused. "Ghezmeed, trust me—you need not say a word. I am more than capable of speaking for the both of us when negotiating terms for food and lodging."

"You ask too much of me," Ghezmeed retorted. "If you must go, I will await you at the northern border of the city. Once you have eaten and taken a night's rest, you may collect me in the morning."

"No," Edina argued. "You cannot ask me to leave you. Besides, if we are captured, one mention of Arianna or Madigan and they will have no choice but to release us."

"You must not mention their names!" he gasped, his eyes bulging. "If you do, you will put us in danger. Spies lurk among the masses, and they will tell the sorcerers of our plans!"

"All right!" Edina crossed her arms stubbornly. "Would you at the very least agree to walk through the city? Either way, we still need to secure some food." She raised her brow. "And once we are there, you may even decide that it is all right to stay."

"I see now that there is no refusing you." He pulled up the hood on his cloak reluctantly.

Edina turned. "You will not regret this, I promise."

Ghezmeed released a heavy breath and followed her toward the city gates.

After walking the entire course of the main street, Edina decided that it was safe enough for them to stay the night, and she left Ghezmeed in the rear paddock of a barn while she set out to find suitable lodging.

Upon her return, Ghezmeed was nowhere in sight. "Ghezmeed?" she called, digging through the bales of hay. "Where are you?"

"We should leave." He clawed his way from one of the bundles. "I have an ill feeling about your plan!"

"No," Edina replied insistently. "I have seen to everything. We will be all right. You must trust me!" She brushed the strands of hay from his cloak. "Stay calm, and keep your head down until we reach the room," she instructed. "If we continue to keep to ourselves, we will go unnoticed, especially at this late hour."

He nodded, taking her hand.

As they walked the narrow streets, Edina felt confidence in her plan. To avoid suspicion, she smiled at any onlookers in passing. When they reached the inn, she peered through the main doors. Relieved to find that the place was still empty, she tugged on Ghezmeed's arm. "Come, it is safe."

They had only gotten a few a steps when the innkeeper

appeared. He cleared his throat, eyeing Ghezmeed. "Miss, your guest will need to sign the registry."

"Can it not wait until morning?" Edina shielded Ghezmeed with her cloak. "My friend is not well. He has grown weak on our travels."

"Registries must be kept, nonetheless." He tried to peer over her shoulder. "Does your friend have something to hide?"

Edina reached for her coin purse. "What will it cost me for you to look the other way?"

The innkeeper became agitated. "I cannot be bought!" He nudged Edina aside. "Let me see him."

Entangled in Edina's feet, Ghezmeed fell to the ground. His hood flew from his face.

"That is no man!" the innkeeper shrieked. "What have you brought to our city?"

Edina's first instinct was to mention Arianna. Ghezmeed's previous warning kept her silent. "I do not answer to you!" She escorted Ghezmeed toward the door. "Our business is our own!"

Before the man could respond, she took Ghezmeed by the arm and ran from the establishment.

"What are we to do now?" Ghezmeed cried out in panic, pulling from her hold when people began to stop and stare.

Edina quickly surveyed the area. "Make your way to that wagon!" She pointed to an unmanned wagon that was harnessed to a single horse. "Do it now!"

The innkeeper appeared at the door. "Stop them!" he shouted. "They are spies!"

At his words, Ghezmeed leapt into the back of the wagon. To hasten their escape, Edina released the reins and mounted the steed, kicking it with zeal. To her dismay, the horse did not budge. "That horse responds to no one but me." The innkeeper approached, ready with a crossbow. Edina and Ghezmeed slowly raised their hands in defeat.

† † †

Overcome with fear, Ghezmeed and Edina clung to one another as they were led through the dungeon at Dunstirth's citadel. The odor emanating from the underground chamber was putrid, smelling of feces. Men moaned and reached out through the bars. To avoid their stares, Edina kept her eyes forward. They reached the last cell at the back of the corridor.

"I hope you enjoy your new quarters," the guard chuckled, nudging them through the opening.

"What are you going to do with us?" Edina clung to the bars as the guard locked the door.

"Your fate has yet to be decided." The man smirked. "I would not cling to hope if I were you."

Before she could respond, he turned and left down the corridor.

Frustrated, Edina rattled the bars. "Will you not even listen to reason?" When the man ignored her, she sank to her knees. "What are we going to do now?"

"I am not sure." Ghezmeed sat, pulling his knees to his chest.

"We should speak Arianna's name." She tested the chain that fastened her wrist shackles. "Under the circumstances, I no longer feel we have a choice."

"It is too risky," Ghezmeed said with conviction. "We must find another way."

"Call to the wizard," Edina pleaded, crawling from the bars to face him. "If he learns of our predicament, he may be able to help us."

Ghezmeed shook his head. "I am not good with the power. Until recently, I have not had a reason to use it." He paused. "What if I connect to the sorcerers by mistake?"

"You must try!" She put her hands to her neck. "If you do not, your worst fears are soon to be realized."

"You are right." Ghezmeed reluctantly put his fingers to his temples. "As I told you before, I am not yet ready to die."

Edina sighed in relief as she watched him make the connection.

The City of Aarrondirth Empties

Time—the more I tried to delay its passing, the more it seemed to accelerate. It was morning again, and the day ahead would be difficult. To welcome us, the colors of the aurora were majestic. It was as though the clouds themselves were ushering us into a future where, in the end, we would claim our victory. As I stood on the tower, I wondered if this would be the last time I would see Aarrondirth Castle, my home. No. I would return, if it took my last dying breath. To distract myself from such thoughts, I inhaled the rich morning air that had been reinvigorated by a passing storm in the night, and I suddenly felt at ease.

Below me, the soldiers were dismantling the last of their encampments. The rows of tents I had grown accustomed to were now gone. As I watched, I wondered about the soldiers. Were their thoughts filled with anticipation? Did they fear for their lives, or did their duty surpass these kinds of emotions? My questions seemed pointless. War was inevitable. We were walking down a narrow path through steep cliffs. Many would be lost on the journey. Again disheartened, I turned and made my way down the stairs.

When I opened the door to our quarters, Darwynyen stood. "Are you ready?"

"Yes." I reached for my satchels. "Are you?"

He took hold of his quiver. "As ready as I will ever be. Shall we make our way to the stables?"

I nodded and glanced over the room. "I am going to miss this place."

"So will I." he kissed my brow.

I moved to the door. "Have we got everything?"

"Do you have your sais?" He reached for his bow.

"Yes." I pulled up one of the legs on my trousers. "I wear them now."

"Then it seems we have everything." He escorted me through the door, closing it behind us.

On our way to the stables, we encountered Archemese in the main foyer. "Archemese!" I rushed to his side. "How are you feeling?" I put my hand to his brow. "You look much better today."

"You must stop worrying about me." He took my hand and squeezed it reassuringly. "Did Morglafenn not come to see you last night?"

I nodded. "But he was brief, stating only that you were better and that I was to leave you to your rest." I looked at his satchels. "Are you sure you are strong enough to travel?"

"Of course, my dear." He turned toward the kitchen. "I will meet you in the stables shortly."

Darwynyen headed down the corridor. Before I followed, I took a moment to observe Archemese. Despite his reassurances, I did not believe him. There was something wrong with his health, I was certain. He entered my mind. *Arianna, I can feel your eyes on me.*

Frustrated that I had been discovered, I released a heavy breath and took my leave.

As I descended the stairway to the stables, Madigan approached from the paddock. He waved and then led me to a supply room near the farrier's den. "Arianna, if you are to accompany us to Walferd, you will need to assist me in leading the troops."

I slowed. "Why?" I asked with little enthusiasm. "Can you not manage such a charge on your own?"

He rolled his eyes. "Of course I can. I ask you because I want you to be prepared, should anything ever happen to me."

My chest tightened. "Are you asking me to prepare for your death?"

"In a manner of speaking, yes." His tone was firm. "Your duty is first and foremost to the people. If I were to fall in battle, it is you to whom they will look for leadership."

"Why are you burdening me with this?" I snapped. "As I told you before, I do not want the charge, nor am I willing to prepare …" I could not finish. The thought of losing him was too painful.

"Arianna, I need you to do this. Will you deny my one and only request of you?"

I swallowed deeply. "I will do it on one condition."

"What are your terms?" He released me.

"You must promise me that you will not die." I blinked to halt my tears. "I simply could not bear it."

His hand smoothed my cheek. "I promise." When I backed away, he changed the subject. "If you would step inside this supply room, I have something for you."

My eyes widened with anticipation as I recalled his last present, Accolade. "What is it?"

He opened the door, extending his hand.

When I entered the room, I saw nothing of interest.

"Over there." He pointed to a sack on the table near the back.

Curious, I rushed over and loosened the strings. When I reached inside, the contents were hard. As I struggled to pull it out, he assisted me. At the sight of the breast plate, I cringed. He ignored me and held it against my torso. "I had it sized to fit your body."

"I cannot wear this." I pushed it away. "I am not a soldier, Madigan."

"If you are to travel through the land of the Grackens you will need its protection."

"No." I crossed my arms stubbornly. "It will only hinder me."

"There is no negotiation, Arianna." He unbuckled the straps. "Try it on." I rolled my eyes as he secured it to my body.

"How does it feel?" he asked.

"Uncomfortable," I replied with sarcasm.

He reached for the sack and pulled out a helmet. "I will expect you to wear this also." Before I could respond, he placed it on my head. "Not only will your father not expect to find you in such attire, it will define your rank amongst the men." He held the white mane secured at the top toward me. "This mane is a symbol of leadership."

Frustrated, I turned to leave. Madigan took me by the arm. "Arianna, will you not do this for me?"

"You are taking advantage," I replied. "If I agree, what more will you ask of me?"

"I will ask that you find your way back to me … I mean to Biddenwade." He embraced me. "I could not bear to lose you, either."

"Excellent!" I turned to find Archemese at the door. "I could not have thought of a better disguise myself!" He chuckled. "My dear, you look stunning!"

Darwynyen appeared next to him. "What is going on in here?"

Archemese stepped aside. "See for yourself."

Darwynyen puckered his brow. "Arianna, what are you wearing?"

"A disguise," Archemese replied. "In this armor, Arianna will remain unnoticed by her father."

"Any measure taken to keep Arianna safe is worth the effort." Darwynyen smirked when he saw the look of repugnance on my face. "All you are missing are bracers."

"I have them here." Madigan pulled them from the sack.

My shoulders drooped. "Perhaps you should suit me up from head to toe—only then I would not be able to mount my horse, and you would have to drag me to Walferd."

When the men began to laugh, I trudged from the room.

Madigan rushed to my side. "Arianna, wear the bracers, and I will ask nothing more of you, I promise."

"Very well." I held out my arms. "Let us get this over with."

As Madigan adjusted the straps, I noticed the generals had assembled in the courtyard and were standing ready. Intimidated by their presence, I stiffened my shoulders.

When Madigan saw them, he secured the final strap and stepped to my side. "Generals of Aarrondirth," he shouted. "Salute your lady."

The men raised their swords. "To the king!" they bellowed. "To our lady!"

Madigan mounted his steed and drew his sword. "Rally the troops!" he commanded.

As I admired the decorations on Madigan's horse, a general rode over. He was older but strong in his demeanor. From under his helmet, his long blond hair extended to his shoulder plates. It held a tinge of grey, as did his beard. "My king." He bowed his head. "What are your orders?"

"Lead your men to the barbican," Madigan replied. "Await me there." He steadied his horse. "If this city is to empty, it will be done in the grandest of scales. To honor and respect our newfound alliances, I will lead the elves and the Miders. At the sounding of the second horn, Arianna will lead our battalions." He paused. "Remind the men of their duty to walk proud. It will give the people hope in our absence."

"Very good, my king." The man bowed again and then turned to me. His cobalt eyes were striking. "Lady Arianna, my name is General Reese." He put his hand to his chest. "I am at your service."

"I am pleased to make your acquaintance, General." I sent

Madigan a brief look. "When I am finished here, I will meet you at the barbican."

"As you wish, my lady." He kicked his horse and rode off.

I turned to Madigan and sighed heavily.

"Do not worry," he winked. "You are doing fine."

"Arianna!" Shallendria called from the stair. "Before you ride out, there is something I want to give you."

In light of my last gift, I pretended not to hear her. Undaunted, she ran over. "Here!" She handed me a sword fitted in its scabbard. "It is a sword. I will teach you of its ways while we travel."

Stunned, I looked at her. "I cannot accept this."

"Of course you can." She took hold of the hilt, releasing the sword from its scabbard. When the forte emerged, it was engraved with elvish markings. The foible shimmered in the light. It was fantastical. "I give you this as well." She handed me a baldric. "With this you can carry the sword on your back." I nodded as I tested the weight of the blade. It was heavy.

"Do you like it?" she asked.

I had never thought to learn such a skill. Grateful, I nodded emphatically. "Yes, it is truly amazing. I will treasure it always." I slid the blade back into the scabbard. "Thank you. I will look forward to your teachings."

She secured the baldric, complete with the sword, around my torso. "I will look forward to our teachings as well. There." She stood back. "How does it feel?"

With all the weight on my body, I could hardly move. "It feels fine," I smiled. "Again, I thank you."

She nodded as she left for her horse, the unmistakable unicorn stallion.

As I searched the crowd for Darwynyen, I saw a stable boy leading out Accolade. To my surprise, his reins and harness were decorated similarly to Madigan's. "Madigan," I grumbled. The formalities were beginning to feel more like a nuisance.

"Arianna." I felt a hand on my shoulder. It was Darwynyen.

Embarrassed by my new attire, I looked down. "Arianna, please. I want to give you something as well."

Dreading more armor, I raised my head slowly. To my relief it was nothing of the sort. "I thought you could use this. It is a quiver for your horse. You may attach it to your saddle straps." He removed my bow, which was secured around his shoulder. "Were you planning on leaving this behind?"

"To be honest, I never thought to bring it." I stepped over to Accolade. "Will you show me how to attach the quiver?" I asked.

"Of course." He unlaced the leather ties.

When the quiver was secured to the strap on Accolade's flank, Darwynyen placed my bow over it. "It is far enough back that it should not hinder you."

Relieved that I did not have to fasten it to my body, I embraced him. "It is a wonderful gift."

"You feel quite stiff," he chuckled, pulling away. "Are you going to be all right with all this weight?"

"We shall see." I mounted my horse. "It is time I made way for the barbican."

He looked Accolade over. "Your horse is nicely decorated," he remarked.

"It is Madigan's doing. I will meet you in the fields when the ceremonial parade is over." I squeezed Accolade with my legs.

He raised his hand as I rode off.

When I arrived at the barbican, the elves and Miders were assembled, awaiting the sounding of the horns. The battle drums were beating from the portcullis.

"Sound the horns!" a soldier on the wall walk shouted. "The king is ready!"

Madigan put his helmet over his head and rode out.

Dregby trotted past me, leading out his men. "Arianna, see you in the fields!" Jeel and Naseyn sat on his shoulders and waved in passing.

As I acknowledged them with a nod, Shallendria and

Morglafenn rode up. "We will see you before long." Morglafenn put his hand to his chest as they urged their horses forward. Darwynyen rode out after them.

I was about to call after him when I felt a tap on my back. "I will await you at the city gates." Archemese lifted his staff. "Be strong, child. Give hope to your people."

I nodded as he rode off.

When the second horn sounded, General Reese rode to my side. "The battalions await you, my lady."

I steadied Accolade as the troops took their place behind me.

"March forward!" General Reese shouted.

Concentrating on the drum beat as a distraction, I nudged Accolade through the barbican.

As I descended the ramp, I raised my hand to the people. Hundreds had gathered to bid us farewell. Many cheered, while others cried. When I looked back at the men, their numbers seemed endless. Even so, each of them had a name and a family whom they would leave behind. I felt proud that their sacrifice was not to go unnoticed and was honored to be leading them, despite the fact that many of them would not be making their return. Unable to cope with my thoughts, I returned my focus to the people as we continued down the royal mile toward the city gates.